Like her heroine, Ann Granger has worked in the diplomatic service in various parts of the world. She met her husband, who was also working for the British Embassy, in Prague and together they received postings to places as far apart as Munich and Lusaka. They have two grown-up sons and are now permanently based in Bicester, near Oxford. Ann Granger is the author of two previous Mitchell and Markby whodunnits.

Cold In
The Earth

Ann Granger

HEADLINE

First published in 1992
by HEADLINE BOOK PUBLISHING

First published in paperback in 1992
by HEADLINE BOOK PUBLISHING

10 9 8 7 6 5 4

ISBN 0 7472 3874 X

Phototypeset by Intype, London

Printed and bound in Great Britain by
Cox & Wyman Ltd, Reading, Berkshire

HEADLINE BOOK PUBLISHING
A division of Hodder Headline PLC
338 Euston Road
London NW1 3BH

Writers make constant demands for encouragement and tolerance from others. I (and Alan Markby and Meredith Mitchell join with me) would like to thank especially John, Judith and Anne for their unstinting support.

'Cold in the earth – and fifteen wild Decembers,
From those brown hills, have melted into spring.'

Emily Brontë

Chapter One

The fly buzzed against the grimy window, trapped. Through the gap at the top warm city air and the drone of Whitehall traffic drifted in but the fly seemed unable to locate its escape route. It kept attacking the same area of glass, increasingly desperate to get out and apparently increasingly unable to find the way.

'Just like me!' said Meredith Mitchell unwarily aloud.

'I beg your pardon, Miss Mitchell?'

The personnel officer stared at her suspiciously. He didn't like dealing with women. It was written all over him. He was small and overweight, rosy-complexioned and pompous. From the moment she'd walked into his office they had failed to reach an *entente*. It had been a case of mutual and instant dislike.

'I meant, I know there are a lot of Foreign Service personnel like me, in my position, working in London but anxious to get an overseas posting.'

'Indeed there are, my dear.'

Patronising nitwit, thought Meredith.

'But well, the number of postings grows fewer. Cut-backs, cutbacks everywhere.'

'Yes, but surely it's in the service's interest to make

1

the best use of me? I'm doing virtually nothing of any real purpose here.'

'I wouldn't say that, Miss Mitchell.' He consulted the file on his desk. 'Your head of department expresses himself satisfied. Of course I realise that previously as British consul abroad you were very much in charge of your own little ship . . .'

Meredith grimaced.

'. . . No doubt a desk job in London is a trifle tedious by comparison.'

You can say that again, chum! she thought, staring morosely at his red-spotted tie. Who had given him that? His wife? His rich Auntie Flo? Had he bought it himself?

She looked up at his face in time to catch a malicious glint in his little eyes. She understood perfectly what it meant. Here she was completely in his power. He was a time-server, a lover of the quiet life. He both envied and resented her desire for independence, uncertainty and challenge. Meredith began to understand for the first time something of the stresses and strains which can lead an otherwise normal person to contemplate murder.

'Now then,' he said placing the tips of his plump fingers together. 'Have you any particular reason for making a posting necessary or particularly desirable at the present time? Are you badly accommodated?'

'No,' she admitted reluctantly. 'A colleague overseas has let me have his flat in Islington. Before that, I leased a cottage in the country but the daily travel was too much.'

'No housing problems, then. You're very fortunate, my dear.'

If he says that again . . .

'Personal problems?' He sounded wary. In his book, all women were liable to such things.

'No!' she snapped.

'Then, Miss Mitchell, I really can't see that you have any case for preferential treatment. But take heart. You received an excellent report on your work in your previous post and though your job here may lack excitement, it is necessary. They also serve, remember, who only stand and wait!'

It was the last straw. Meredith rose to her feet. She was five-ten and towered over his seated form most satisfactorily. He looked distinctly alarmed.

'You may be prepared to kick your heels behind that desk until it's time to draw your pension! I want to get out there and do something before they put me out to grass!'

From pink his face turned puce. 'I hardly think there is anything to be gained from continuing this conversation!' he snarled, slapping the file shut.

With the action he slammed the door on her hopes of a posting and she knew it. Knew, too, she could only blame herself. What the hell. 'No, there isn't!' she snapped and stalked out.

Reviewing this confrontation on her way home, wedged in a crowded, stuffy tube train, Meredith could not feel anything but fury and despair. The fury was not directed now at her adversary, but at herself. She could hardly have managed things worse. And she a person who had handled many a tricky situation with tact and finesse. That's me scuppered! she thought gloomily. A big black mark against me! I'll never get another posting now. I'll spend the rest of my life commuting.

Someone trod on her foot and someone else stuck an elbow painfully into her ribs. Oh, to be out of this daily scrum. Oh, to be somewhere else, anywhere. She regretted now giving up the lease on Rose Cottage, inconvenient though it had proved. If she couldn't be overseas then at least she would like to be back in the English countryside. She began to think of Alan and envy him in Bamford, a nice little country town, surrounded by rural peace and space. Where, moreover, he was doing a worthwhile job which offered variety, the unexpected and occasionally danger. What was more, Easter was coming along. Spring in the country really meant new life rising from the cold clay. 'Oh to be in England, now that April's there . . .'

There was a curious odour about the place despite the fact that – as he'd noticed on his way in – someone had opened the upstairs windows. Probably one of the younger constables, some poor bloke unused to close proximity with outward signs of mortality! thought Alan Markby as he climbed the creaking, uncarpeted stair, taking care not to touch the banister lest fingerprinting should prove necessary. He took care not to brush against the walls either, but that was because they were filthy and grease-encrusted.

He was late arriving on the scene, having been called from the other end of the divisional area. They would already have carried out the first tasks and the ambulance outside waited only for him to come and view the body before taking it away. On the other side of the street a small crowd of the curious and the voyeuristic had gathered. Amongst them would be one true necrophiliac. There was always one, usually stopping police personnel to ask for grisly details. Sometimes the pathetic creeps pretended to be journalists.

Game. That's what the smell resembled most. Well hung grouse or pheasant, here mixed with dust, damp, mildew and general decay. The place was clearly a squat. This whole row of terraced houses was due for demolition to make way for a low-rise block of flats for the elderly. The house next door was still occupied, which was useful because the neighbour might have information. But the one he was in had theoretically been abandoned and the lower windows and door boarded up. Even so, the squatters had got in.

Markby could hear the murmur of voices from behind the door at the top of the stairs. He pushed it open and faces turned to him.

'Oh, there you are, sir!' said Sergeant Pearce in relief. He too wanted to get out of here. The stench intensified in this room. There was a green-faced young constable by the door, sweating. Hot in here, too, and stuffy. The warm weather had hastened the deterioration of the thing on the bed.

'Sorry I'm late!' he said and meant it because they were all clearly suffering.

'Dr Fuller had to leave before you got here, sir. He had an appointment elsewhere.'

'Fair enough. I'll be hearing from him, I don't doubt.'

'They've taken their pictures,' Pearce went on, indicating the two unhappy police photographers. 'Could they—?'

'What? Oh yes, you two can be on your way, by all means.'

They collided in the doorway in their haste, clattering downstairs with their apparatus. The bilious constable watched them go wistfully.

'Let's have a look, then!' Markby said resignedly.

Pearce turned back the sheet which had been decorously draped over the body. He said nothing.

Markby said, 'She must have been pretty – before.'

She wasn't more than twenty-one or two. Her eyes were open, staring, and a cloudy violet in colour. She wore a dirty tee-shirt and jeans cut off raggedly at the knee. The tee-shirt had been pushed up, probably by Dr Fuller making his examination, and the sunken flesh below the rib-cage had a strange greyish aspect. Her left arm was turned palm out and scarred the whole length with red marks and purple bruises, slowly becoming camouflaged by the mottling of decomposing skin.

'Who found her?'

'Bloke next door.' Pearce indicated the partition wall dividing this terraced house from the next. 'He's been keeping an eye on the place, afraid of fire. Thought it was empty and came in to see what damage had been done by the last squatters. Oh, here's the needle, it was lying on the floor by the bed.' Pearce held up a plastic bag in the bottom of which a hypodermic syringe rested.

Foul thing, thought Markby. Aloud he asked, 'How long has she been dead, did Fuller hazard a guess?'

'Two to three days, at first glance.'

'No sign of the stuff she took?'

'No. There were others living here, so the neighbour says, but it's been very quiet the last couple of days and he thought they must all have left. Looks as if her fellow-squatters saw this girl had died, took fright and all did a runner.'

'We'll be lucky to find them,' Markby growled. 'Unless the neighbour knew any of them by name. Unlikely.'

'Funnily enough, he knew her—' Pearce pointed at the corpse. 'First thing he said to me when I got here was that it was Lindsay Hurst. He'd seen Lindsay going in and out of the house over a few weeks and was surprised because her family is local and respectable and he wouldn't have thought she'd end up living here like this. Those are his words, it's all in his statement.'

'Not the first time it's happened! Does our informant know where the Hursts live?'

'Yes, somewhere in Kitchener Close. The number of people living here varied, he says. He also says he complained to the police and the council but nothing was done. You know how it is trying to get squatters out. The council probably was leaving it till the autumn when the demolition chaps move in.'

Markby grunted. 'Someone will have to go over to Kitchener Close and tell her parents. I'll do it, since you've been stuck here waiting for me. My turn for a dirty job. Feeling okay?'

'Got used to it,' said Pearce wryly.

Markby glanced at the constable. 'Want to go outside?'

'Please, sir!'

'Buzz off, then. Tell the ambulance men to come up and collect her.'

He looked round the room again after the constable had fled. The bed was the only proper piece of furniture and that looked as if it had been brought here from some rubbish tip. There was a rusting picnic stove on the floor. The other residents must have left that in their panicked flight from the house. In one corner was piled rubbish of all kinds, bottles, boxes, paper, empty cans, another syringe . . . they'd have to go through it all. The neighbour had certainly been right to fear fire, however.

Thinking of the respectable semi-detached houses of Kitchener Close from which the dead girl had come, he asked aloud wonderingly, 'How did she put up with this squalor? Too proud to go home? Or too far gone?'

'I called in and had a check run before you came, sir, and she was a registered addict being prescribed the substitute stuff. But she was obviously getting the real thing from somewhere. Dr Fuller says it looks as if she had a pretty hefty dose and if those empty wine bottles over there mean they were drinking, then she didn't stand a chance.' Pearce looked thoughtful. 'You'd think, wouldn't you, that if they were into that sort of thing they'd make for some big city where it's easier to get hold of the stuff, not hang around a quiet countrified dump like Bamford.'

'Quiet, yes. A backwater, possibly. A dump, no!' said Markby firmly. He liked Bamford. 'Nor does it surprise me. Nothing in the country surprises me any more.'

Pearce made an effort to take a positive view. 'Nasty business but straightforward enough in its way. I suppose there'll be an open verdict. I thought when the call came in we might have a murder on our hands, but we haven't.' Pearce slapped at the flies which were thickening in the air and hovering ominously above the bed.

'Haven't we?' Markby asked coldly. 'Perhaps not in

the coroner's book. But in my book whoever supplied the drugs, killed her. And we've got to find him before another youngster dies!'

'Eat up, Jess! You haven't got enough on that plate to keep a sparrow alive!'

'I'm not hungry, Ma. I've had enough, honestly.'

'Nonsense. You'll have another potato, here!' Mrs Winthrop plonked another roast potato uncompromisingly on to her daughter's plate. 'One more won't kill you!'

Jessica Winthrop gave a small convulsive jerk. She looked down at the potato, glistening red-gold in its crispy-fat coating, and forced down a bubble of nausea. Beside her, her brother Alwyn was busily polishing off a huge plateful. Alwyn was a big fellow and a working man; little wonder he ate like a horse. Jessica wondered if, by staring at the unwanted vegetable, she could somehow persuade it to dematerialise. Alwyn mopped up the last of his gravy with a hunk of bread, glanced sideways at her and winked. He knew what she was thinking.

'Can you squeeze another cup of tea out of that pot, Elsie?' inquired George Winthrop from the head of the table where he was wedged into an ancient oak carver chair. Nothing could be seen of him but the top of his bald head and the tips of his stubby fingers gripping the cover pages of the open *Farmers Weekly*.

Jessica reflected that her father, unused to handling books of any kind, always grasped his magazine as if he thought it was going to get away from him, by the scruff of its neck as it were – if books had had necks. She was the bookish member of the family, an oddity amongst

9

the Winthrops. It had always pleased them to tolerate her oddness – until, of course, things had gone wrong for her.

Mrs Winthrop had lifted the lid from a large brown earthenware teapot and was deliberating over its contents like a priest over the entrails of a sacrifice. 'It'll take a drop of hot water.' She got up and went to the stove.

Now her back was turned, Alwyn swiftly scooped up the unwanted spud from his sister's plate and ate it before their mother came back. She threw him a small smile of gratitude.

'There now!' said Mrs Winthrop returning with the replenished teapot. She nodded approvingly towards her daughter's empty plate. 'You managed to eat it after all. It wasn't difficult, was it?'

'No, Ma.'

'If you don't eat properly, my girl, you'll get sick again like – well, like you was.'

Jessica said nothing. They didn't understand a mental breakdown and she'd given up trying to explain. To them, a person got sick because he didn't eat or wrap up properly or had the misfortune to pick up one of the more common fevers. Stuffing the invalid with food and rubbing his chest with Vick cured all these ailments. As a puny child she'd announced her presence everywhere by an accompanying pungent odour of Vick. Her brother might have understood but she didn't wish to burden Alwyn who had his own troubles. He hadn't told her about them but she sensed it. They'd always been close like that.

'Too much book-reading!' said her father, laying aside his *Farmers Weekly* and taking off his spectacles

10

(inherited from his father and good enough, he didn't need to pay out good money for new ones). He took up his mug. 'That's your trouble, girl, and always was. Not enough fresh air and your nose always stuck in a book. Don't us get no pudding today, then?'

'Just you wait a minute, George Winthrop! There's apple crumble – and don't you go turning your nose up at that, Jessica!'

'No, Ma. Shall I dish it up?' With luck, put in charge of the proceedings, she could allot herself a minute portion.

'Go on, then. And bring the cream jug. 'Tis over on the dresser.'

Jessica made her way across the familiar farm kitchen. Every nook and cranny, every item it contained from feed bills spiked on a nail by the dresser to the row of copper pans hanging on the wall, formed part of her childhood memories and had contributed to the person she was now. But recollection brought no warm glow. She'd often felt guilty about her lack of affection for the bricks and mortar of her family home. Here she'd always been loved, always been warm and comfortable. Life at the farm ought to have meant happiness and security but it never had. She'd been so pleased to leave and go to college far away. But it had all ended with coming back here. She sometimes felt she was tied to the farm by an elastic rope. She could only run away so far and it jerked her back again.

Even worse, nowadays since her illness the thought of leaving the farm had begun to frighten her so that she was caught between a Scylla and Charybdis of conflicting emotions. Things she knew to be minor problems to be faced in the outside world had begun to

11

appear as terrifying obstacles preventing her from even trying to start again properly, out there. The longer she stayed, the worse it got. Yet she couldn't go.

None of this could she explain to her parents whose lives revolved around Greyladies and who found everything they wanted here. With every action they took dictated by the needs of the farming year, the world outside was hardly relevant. They knew nothing of it and cared less. Only Alwyn could have understood but they never spoke of it together.

Jamie alone had managed to get away for good and make a success of his life outside, away from Greyladies. But Jamie had never minded hurting people. Jessica often wished she'd inherited some of the notorious Winthrop toughness. Jamie must have got her share as well as his own.

She stooped and with hands well protected by oven-mitts, took the great sizzling cartwheel of apple crumble from the oven. As she straightened up, the telephone began to ring in the next room.

'I'll go!' Alwyn said, getting up and pushing past her. He always had trouble getting through the doors which had low lintels constructed in far-off days when folk were shorter. Alwyn had to stoop like a hunchback to get through without cracking his skull.

Jessica put the apple crumble on the marble-topped table by the door and began to spoon out portions on to the waiting blue and white plates. Well, blue and yellowish white plates, glaze crackled all over with age and chipped round the edges. They hardly ever bought anything new at the farm. 'Nothing wrong with them plates!' Mrs Winthrop had opined when Jessica ventured to suggest that perhaps in the cause of hygiene . . . 'If you wash'em up properly a few cracks don't matter!' Truth to tell, of course, there was no spare money for new plates or new anything else.

Closest to the open doorway as she worked, she could hear Alwyn's side of the telephone conversation next door. Evidently the call was for him and she wouldn't have eavesdropped but something about his voice, almost furtive, caught her attention.

'I told you not to ring me!' he was whispering hoarsely. 'Yes, I know . . . Well, I've not had the chance . . . Anyway, 'tisn't for me to say!' On the last phrase Alwyn's voice rose almost to a muffled shout. A long silence followed and then Alwyn's angry, 'I told you before – if I can!' The phone was slammed down and he came back with his face almost as red as his hair.

'Who was that, then?' asked his mother.

'Landlord of The Fox and Hounds, wanting to know if I could turn out for the darts team next Wednesday. I told him a week or more ago I couldn't guarantee to play no more.'

Jessica, carrying apple crumble plates to the table, reflected that Alwyn never had been any good as a liar. Their eyes met as she put his plate before him and he gave her a defiant look.

She respected his right to privacy and wouldn't have asked him about the phone call again if she hadn't come upon him alone later in the afternoon. She'd helped her mother clear away and wash up and been ordered out for 'fresh air, and no taking a book out with you and hiding away with it some place!' So she'd collected saddle and bridle from the barn and set out to catch Nelson in his paddock.

That was where she came unexpectedly on her

brother, sitting on a low ruined wall, part of a collection of such stones in the middle of the paddock. Whisky the sheepdog lay at his feet, panting pink-tongued in the heat as he waited for orders. Alwyn was leaning forward, arms resting on knees, deep in thought. His strong, sun-burned hands were loosely clasped and the brim of his tweed cap shadowed his face.

Jessica put down the tack and perched on the wall beside him. Nelson continued grazing a few feet away but kept an eye on them because he'd seen the saddle.

'That pony is so bloody fat,' said Alwyn, 'you won't be able to get the girth round his belly soon.'

'I take him out every day.'

'Eating his head off. Useless, bone-idle animal, he is.'

'Shut up, Alwyn! You're only saying that to annoy me!' She saw him grin and to get her own back, she went on, 'And why were you whispering away on the phone? Don't tell me it was the landlord of The Fox and Hounds!'

His grin vanished and he scowled. 'No, 'twas Dudley Newman.'

Now it was her turn to frown, puzzled. 'The builder? What did he want?'

'Same thing as he wanted when he came visiting out here at the farm a while back.'

'To buy our land?' She tossed back her long fair hair. 'Dad told him Greyladies wasn't for sale!'

Alwyn grunted.

'So why'd he phone you?' she persisted.

'How should I know?'

'Alwyn! I want to know! Have you been hatching some plot with Newman?'

14

'No!' he snapped. 'How could I? I haven't got the final say-so. But I did say that if Dad were to change his mind, I might be interested in selling – if the price was right.' He paused, as if shocked by his own boldness. 'Come on, Jess, we might as well! You'd get your share of the money and we'd both be able to leave here!' It was the nearest he'd ever come to mentioning the vexed subject openly to her.

'They wouldn't leave!' she said.

'No,' he sighed. 'They wouldn't leave.'

'And if you're dealing with Dudley Newman behind Dad's back, he'll soon be on to it. You're no good at telling fibs, Alwyn. Not like Jamie.'

He turned his head sharply. 'What made you mention him?'

'There was a letter came from him the other day, wasn't there? Addressed to Dad and Ma. It was on the kitchen table but Ma whipped it away quickly in case I saw it.'

'Not quick enough, it seems!' was the dour comment.

'Is he coming home?'

'It wasn't to me, the letter,' said her brother woodenly.

They both sat in silence for a while, the sun shining on their backs. The dog had gone to sleep, nose on paws, and Nelson, satisfied he wasn't going to be caught and made to take some exercise just yet, had moved off to the furthest corner of the paddock.

'Rum old place, this!' said Alwyn suddenly, slapping his hands on the ruined wall on which they sat. 'Could tell a few tales, I bet.'

'I find these ruins creepy,' Jessica said abruptly.

'Thinking a few ghosts are going to pop out of these old stones, are you?' he teased.

'It wouldn't surprise me. This was the scene of a crime once.'

'What do you mean?' He turned his head to peer at her from beneath his cap, his grey eyes sharp.

'The burning of the meeting house. These old ruins.'

'Good Lord, girl, I wondered what you were on about!' he said in disgust. 'That wasn't a crime. An accident, more like it.'

'Arson's a crime.'

'Who ever said 'twas arson? It was over a hundred years ago and no one now can rightly tell. Just a bit of history, these old ruins, for what that's worth.'

'It's an evil place, this spot,' she said quietly. 'I feel it, seeping out of the stones. Unhappiness.'

'Rubbish! Don't you start imagining things.'

'There's a lot of evil about.' Jessica stared across the field as she spoke towards the distant prospect of Bamford church's steeple on the horizon.

'What's that supposed to mean? You do come out with some weird things, Jess. If you start talking like that in front of Ma, she'll march you off to Dr Pringle again.'

'I read about Lindsay in the *Gazette*.'

'Oh, that! I didn't know you knew her.' Alwyn sounded both cross and discomfited. 'If I had, I'd have made sure and hid the *Gazette* away before you found it.'

'I wish you'd all stop protecting me!' she shouted. He didn't reply and after a moment she went on stiffly, 'We were both choirgirls, years ago, Lindsay and I. She was such a cheerful, friendly girl. Now she's dead, and so horribly.'

'Don't go thinking about it!' he advised roughly.

'Silly little bitch did it to herself! No point in you upsetting yourself.' He got up and the dog awoke, wagging its plumed tail. Even Nelson seemed alerted to the fact that the peaceful break was over. He threw up his head and whinnied shrilly.

'I've got work to do,' said Alwyn. 'Don't go trying to jump that pony over any hedges. The fat he's carrying, he'll likely plough right through them and I'll have the job of patching them up again!'

'I've never done that and well you know it!' She shouldered the saddle and set off purposefully across the paddock.

'Ghosts, evil!' muttered Alwyn, kicking at the blackened base of the nearer pile of stone blocks half buried in the turf. 'Just a bit of the farm, these are, like you and me, boy!' The dog looked up, ears cocked, eyes watchful and curious. 'Just like you and bloody me . . .' repeated Alwyn morosely. 'I could tell these old lumps a thing or two about unhappiness! Give me a box of matches and for two pins I'd burn down the whole bloody farm!'

Chapter Two

'Concrete, asphalt and brick, that's all that will be left,' said Alan Markby moodily aloud. 'The whole country, completely built over coast to coast.'

He made these doleful observations to himself as the wind caught at his straight fair hair and blew it wildly around his head. Sticking his hands disconsolately in the pockets of his well-worn olive-green Barbour, he scowled at the scene which met his eyes before sitting on a tree-trunk and taking a bar of chocolate out of his pocket. He wasn't a great eater of sweets but making sandwiches had been too much bother. He'd just put the chocolate in his pocket and set out on his walk.

He had needed to get out of the office, away from the station. An open verdict had been returned on Lindsay Hurst as Pearce had predicted. Nor had Markby expected differently. They had tried and so far failed to locate the dead girl's fellow squatters. With not even a name to guide them, it was a pretty sure thing they never would. Of greater urgency was the need to find out where she had obtained the fatal supply of drugs. Heroin had finished Lindsay's short life and it wasn't a drug they'd had to deal with much in this area till recently. Again Pearce had been right. Cannabis they

19

came across fairly often, but of late the availability of more serious drugs was becoming a real headache to the local police.

Obstinately he'd worked on the matter over the weekend, chasing up every lead and doing his best to make waves, because waves sometimes washed up unexpected finds. But not this time. Inquiries in the pubs and discos the dead girl had frequented had met a brick wall of unhelpfulness. And even if they had picked up the odd pusher, that would have achieved little. They needed to catch the big boys behind the foul business. In fact, what they really needed was a lucky break. Markby felt they were as unlikely to get that as see the proverbial pigs flying.

By Sunday night he'd had to admit they'd done as much as could be done for the moment and they would now have to wait and see if the lines of inquiry thrown out brought in anything useful. He had realised he was tired and bad-tempered and forced himself to recognise that if he didn't take a break to make up for the lost weekend, he'd drive everyone round the bend for the whole coming week. Therefore he'd taken Monday off and set out to walk in the country to blow a few fresh ideas into his weary brain, only to discover that while he hadn't been looking, the countryside he knew and loved had been transformed.

Here had stood a farm called quaintly 'Lonely Farm'. The name had been recorded as far back as Tudor times. The farmhouse had stood on ancient foundations and its chimneys had been tall, narrow square affairs with fancy brickwork. He remembered it well, just as he recalled playing at cowboys, rounding up surprised cows browsing on the sweet grass, and at cops and robbers in the hedgerows.

All of it gone beneath the bulldozer. Fields which generations had lovingly tended and which had been the scenes of his boyhood adventures, vanished. To the right he could just make out the roofs of Greyladies Farm, the next holding, which had not yet fallen victim to land developers, and to the left was a tiny smudge on the horizon which indicated Witchett Farm, also battling to keep back the rolling acres of tarmacadam and brick.

The remembered landscape now seemed but a dream. Before him scarred earth stretched in all directions as far as the eye could see. The great trees had been uprooted by machinery and lay with roots in the air, fallen and pathetic giants, mutilated and shorn of their branches. Those which had cracked but still retained a precarious toehold in the ravaged earth were trying to sprout new spring greenery, sad little tassels of baby leaf attached to trunks which showed great gaping wounds.

What hadn't been destroyed had been horribly perverted. The stream where he'd fished had been cleared, widened, re-routed and encased in a concrete corset to stop it getting any ideas about refinding its natural course. The willows which had shaded it had gone. A strip of new road ran straight ahead for half a mile or so and then came to an abrupt halt against a hillock of mud. There where he and his friends had built treehouses in venerable oaks and dens amongst the bramble bushes, rose a cluster of half-constructed houses, forlorn beneath a sky of scudding clouds. The growl of heavy machinery invaded and affronted his ear. A flight of rooks wheeled above his head, perhaps searching for their vanished rookery, and then set off in a black flurry of wings towards a new home, somewhere the diggers hadn't yet destroyed.

Markby sighed and then brightened. Ahead of him and a little below where he sat on the top of a low rise, a grey hatchback moved slowly and cautiously along the strip of half-finished roadway. It stopped and the driver got out. Also out of the car leapt a small brown and white dog of Jack Russell type which began to race madly up and down the asphalt strip to no obvious purpose and then dived into a ditch and vanished. The driver reached into the car and dragged out a large sheet of paper which he spread out with some difficulty on the bonnet. The wind caught at it and threatened to tear it away. It flapped up into the man's face as he tried to study it and the watcher could imagine, if he couldn't actually hear, him swear.

A smile came to Markby's face. He put away the remains of the chocolate bar and stood up. Even at this distance he had recognised man and dog and in anticipation of some company he began to descend the slope, slithering on damp grass and mud. At the bottom he picked his way across churned earth and when he got within hailing distance, cupped his hands to his mouth and yelled, 'Steve!'

The man with the sheet of plans looked up and rashly raised one hand to wave in welcome. The wind seized its chance. The paper was whipped away and set off on a crazy dance down the strip of road pursued by Steve Wetherall. Patch, the dog, burst into sight out of the ditch and pursued both, racing along on his short legs obviously under the impression that this whole glorious game had been initiated solely for his benefit.

Markby waited by the car until Steve returned, cursing, puffing and red-faced but gripping the sadly creased and muddied chart. He stuffed it into the car and slammed the door on it.

'What are you doing out here?' he inquired hoarsely as he straightened up.

'Walking.' Markby bent to pat Patch who had scampered up recognising a friend and was jumping up grinning, his pink tongue lolling and his paws liberally daubing mud on Markby's trousers. 'Taking a last look at the remains of what was a very nice tract of countryside before you and your ruddy minions dig up the last of it and dump a load of concrete over it.'

'Progress, old son, progress. Folk have to live somewhere.'

'Not here, they don't. In my humble opinion all this is a giant wart. Bamford used to be a nice little market town. You and your developer friends have just about ruined it. Lonely Farm used to be hereabouts. Don't you remember it, Steve? You must! Can't you remember the days when you and I played around the blackberry bushes and caught tiddlers in the stream?'

Wetherall snorted. 'Sentimental claptrap. Yes, I remember. Of course I feel a twinge of sadness at seeing it all go. But times change. Intelligent people change with them! Some of course never grow up and play cops and robbers all their lives!' Steve gave Markby a meaningful look.

'Money speaks, you mean. The price of land, that's it. People tempted to make a quick fortune.'

'No, it isn't, not entirely!' Steve turned and swept a hand across the horizon. 'Farmers are going bust all over the country. A lot of them can't wait to get out of farming and are just praying for someone to come along and offer a good price for the land for development. Don't blame planners, architects and builders. Blame interest rates and reduced subsidies and milk quotas, and Mad Cow disease or scrapie or salmonella or anything else that causes prices to collapse . . . to say nothing of the day-in, day-out grind and sheer loneliness of much modern farming. Do you know how many farmers suffer from depression? Fifty years ago a farm was a thriving community employing umpteen labourers and housing their families. Now most are run by one man, his wife, a dog and a home computer.'

'You can't tell me they're all like that!'

'No, of course not all! Farming's like any other business. One person will fail and another make a go of it. Don't worry, there will still be plenty of farms left working when the planners and the builders have passed by! Look, over there – Witchett Farm. That's Mrs Carmody. She'll never give up. And Greyladies Farm – catch the Winthrops giving up, either. Mind you, I sometimes suspect that Alwyn would, given the chance.'

'I haven't seen Alwyn for ages,' Markby observed. 'Nor his brother Jamie. We were great friends as kids.'

'Jamie pushed off years ago and works abroad somewhere. Alwyn, as the elder, drew the short straw and had to stay. The girl came back home not long ago, too. I don't think they're doing very well. They were into beef cattle at one time but the prices fell so low it wasn't economical for them. They've turned to sheep now but without a lot of success. Bad luck sticks to the Winthrops.'

'Mrs Carmody at Witchett Farm makes out.'

'She leases out a lot of her land for grazing. Anyway she's only got herself. Greyladies Farm has to support all the Winthrops now except Jamie.'

Markby sighed and kicked at a stone.

'Look,' said Steve consolingly, 'by the time we've finished this will be a nice estate. Somewhere you wouldn't mind living yourself. Quality housing. Executive homes each with individual finish and double-garages. Landscaped open areas. We'll have planted trees. There will be a nice little shopping precinct.' He laughed good-humouredly. 'Even you will be forced to eat your words.'

'Don't tell me. I don't want to know.'

'You're a miserable old curmudgeon. By the way, I heard that your girlfriend – the one who works for the Foreign Office – has pushed off and left you. Can't blame her myself.'

'She has not pushed off nor left me, nor is Meredith my girlfriend in the way you mean it.'

Steve sniggered offensively.

'You can cut that out!' Markby said pugnaciously.

'Your – um – lady friend, has she gone off abroad, then?'

'No, she's sitting at a desk in the Foreign Office. She'd like to get abroad again but hasn't been offered a posting. She gave up the cottage here because the travelling was too much for her.'

'See her often?'

'Not often.' No, not nearly often enough. Perhaps he could inveigle her down for a few days. Perhaps for Easter, even if he would be working. What he needed was an excuse . . . Markby glared at a huge mechanical digger which was lurching across open ground. 'What's that fellow doing? Going to churn up a bit more?'

Steve looked in the direction indicated. 'Oh, I told them last week to dig the footings trenches for that plot four feet deep. Luckily I came over this morning and checked. They'd only gone down three feet. To make it worse, I fancy there's a soft spot down there. You get that in clay sometimes, so it's all the more important to take the trench down deep enough. They'll be pouring the concrete in this afternoon so I told Sean to get a move on and dig down another foot. Mind you, if that wretched Hersey did his job—' Steve turned back. 'You fancy a pint in about half an hour?'

'Fair enough. Where?'

'Fox and Hounds up on the main road? Let me finish up here and I'll give you a lift.'

A short distance away the roar of the digger ceased. Sean could be seen clambering down from his seat. Markby watched without much interest. He supposed the driver had come across some obstacle.

'What's he doing?' muttered Steve. 'Oy!' he yelled and gesticulated at the distant figure.

The workman was leaning over something. Suddenly he straightened up and began to run clumsily towards them, both arms held up high in a curious supplicating gesture.

A familiar and unpleasant tingle ran up Markby's spine. He took a step forward, mentally and physically bracing himself. The thought leapt into his head, Oh God, not another one, not so soon!

As the man neared them they could see that the driver's face was ashen and twisted. His mouth was working as if he wanted to shout or scream but could do neither. Markby was reminded of a stone gargoyle in an old church, mouth open in a silent cry of anguish, frozen for all eternity. Sean came up to them, staggering over the last few yards and Steve and Markby both dived forward to support him.

'Mr Wetherall . . .' he gasped, sagging between them.

They hauled him upright. 'All right, Sean!' Steve snapped. 'Pull yourself together, what's happened?'

'It – it's back here, sir – the machine dug it up . . . I saw something – I saw it . . . Holy Mother of God . . .' The speaker wrenched himself free, spun round and doubled over.

'He's being sick!' Markby said briskly. 'Stay here with him and I'll take a look!' Even as he spoke he had begun to run towards the abandoned digger.

He knew what he was going to find. But he didn't know what condition it was going to be in and he was preparing himself, as he ran, for the worst.

If it had been buried a long time, it might be clean, just bones. It might even turn out to be historic, dead a few hundred years. Occasionally diggers turned up important burials together with bronze age jewellery or armour or they found Roman cemeteries. In such cases work had to stop while the archaeologists descended. Such delays cost a fortune and were viewed with dismay by developers. And of course if there were valuables then there was the usual wrangle over ownership, whether it was treasure trove, that sort of thing.

On the other hand, if it hadn't been buried there long, if it had only partly decomposed, turned greeny-brown – Markby wished he hadn't eaten that chocolate. Sean was free to throw up but a policeman isn't supposed to – at least not in front of the public. He found himself glancing at the soil. Bodies decomposed quickly and cleanly in sand or gravel. In wetlands they lingered, sometimes even preserved. This ground was thick sticky clay.

He came panting to a halt and then walked slowly forward to stare down into the partly excavated ditch. At first glance the impression was of some reconstructed Bronze Age fortification. The trench ran round the four sides of an oblong. Sean had barely started to deepen it. Within a few feet the steel jaws of the digger had scooped up the cause of the panic which still lay half in and half out of the metal teeth.

A naked man, mud-smeared, head blood-stained, very dead.

Well, it wasn't an ancient burial or even reasonably old. The body hadn't, Markby noted with great relief, even started to decompose. The colour was good, not even that waxy white which bodies soon take on in water and where this body had been lying the ground held plenty of moisture. It lay in the jaws of the digger face upward and head down. Markby stooped and lifted a mud-stained wrist. It fell limply, rigor had passed off. It wasn't *that* recent then. But in this cold mud the state of rigor might have been delayed. Autopsy would show but it looked very much as if this body had been buried here at least thirty-six hours before.

Markby straightened up, the wind snatching at his hair again and causing his waterproof jacket to flap. He glanced around him. Whoever dug this grave, they had picked their spot believing the digging of the trench to be complete. They had descended into it, scooped a shallow grave in the floor of it and buried their man, expecting that before long the trench would be filled with concrete to the level of surrounding land. Three feet of concrete footings and the buried man beneath the lot. In addition, before long brick walls would rise on the footings and a house stand there. No one would ever have guessed at the grisly secret in its foundations.

But all that had changed with Steve's instruction to take the trench down another foot. Markby frowned as he calculated. Today was Monday. The workers on the site would finish early on a Friday probably and go off to spend the weekend with their families or in the local pubs. Before that they had dug out the original trench. Let's suppose this burial had taken place Friday night or early Saturday morning. The grave-diggers would need a certain amount of light to work by. They? Yes, they. It would have taken more than one person to do it and the body would have to be transported here. That dratted new strip of road wouldn't show a thing, but they might have driven over open ground at some juncture or else carried their grim burden and all this soft mud was criss-crossed with tyre treads and bootprints.

Markby whirled round as Steve came panting up. The architect stopped when he saw the body and gave a strangled gurgle before whispering, 'Cripes . . .'

'All work must stop immediately!' Markby said crisply. 'No one but no one must walk over the ground here. Where's the site foreman? Oh damn, this ruddy machine has probably erased any tyre marks of a car! We'll need prints of your tyres for elimination and any other car used on the site. Have you got any poles and ropes we can put temporarily around this area?'

'Y-yes . . .' Steve made an effort to pull himself together. Patch came bounding up and scurried forward. Steve made a dive and scooped the little dog up in his arms. 'I'll just put Patch in the car. God, Alan – who is īt?'

'No idea. You don't recognise him? Take a look, if you can.'

Steve swallowed and edged forward. He studied the mud-smeared face and shook his head. 'No – never seen the bloke before! Where are his clothes?'

Markby cast an eye over the surroundings. Mud, ditches, brambles, where were the corpse's clothes indeed? Could be anywhere. 'Get hold of the foreman! Did you say his name was Hersey? Have him ask his men if anyone has seen any rags or clothing, doesn't matter how mud-stained or damaged. And get them to direct any visitors to the site away from here!'

We'll have to drag the stream, he was thinking, and search the surrounding coppices and farmland. Miles of it. Aloud he asked, 'Is where the body's lying in the same place you said you thought you saw a soft spot?'

Steve blinked, white-faced, and Patch wriggled in his arms. 'Y-yes, more or less. The clay looked less compacted.'

'In other words, disturbed?'

'Well, yes . . . but I just thought – I didn't think anyone had been down there and dug a – a grave! Soft spots aren't unusual in this kind of earth.'

'Fair enough,' Markby muttered. 'I'm not blaming you for anything! Thank God you insisted on digging down or we shouldn't have found him!'

No indeed we shouldn't! Whoever buried him thought they'd hit on a foolproof way to dispose of the body and nearly got away with it.

'Got a phone in that car?'

Two bodies inside six days, he thought grimly. Certainly misfortunes never come singly but he hoped the other saying about things going in threes wasn't to be proved true. Two was enough for the time being. At least there was no doubt how the coroner would rule on this latest. The results of natural deaths do not get stripped of clothing and buried surreptitiously where they will be entombed in concrete. This time they had a murder case on their hands and no legal hair-splitting would rule otherwise!

Patch, incarcerated in the car with him, jumped up and tried to lick his face. 'Gerroff!' ordered Markby pushing him gently aside as he began to give precise details into the phone and request a murder inquiry back-up team.

Chapter Three

'Hullo, Alan,' said Dr Fuller cheerily. 'We meet again!
You seem to be finding them everywhere! We must
get together on some social occasion, just to keep the
balance right! Why don't you come to the house again
soon? Ellen would be so pleased – we're planning
another of our little soirées. An Evening with Johann
Sebastian Bach.'

Markby muttered and sniffed the air. He hated the
smell of this place, sweet, sickly, formaldehyde or
something. He hated all that scrubbed cleanliness and
all those shiny glass bottles.

'This is an interesting body you found,' said Fuller
who had a nice clinical, positive attitude to his work.
'And in an interesting place. I often find these gumboot
jobs more intriguing.'

Fuller didn't let it get to him. Fuller had a wife and
family. Fuller didn't go home to an empty house.
Markby watched crossly as the pathologist seated himself at his desk and opened up a file, turning over sheets
of paper with precise, oh so cleanly scrubbed fingers.
He began to whistle softly and Markby fancied he
recognised a fragment of Vivaldi. Fuller was an
enthusiastic if amateur violinist. His wife played the

piano. All his gifted, unnervingly self-possessed children played some instrument. They gave musical evenings to friends. Markby, who was as near tone-deaf as made no difference, had sat through one of them and didn't relish being threatened with another.

'In fact,' said Fuller jovially, 'when I was called out there and first saw him, I thought you'd found a sacrifice!'

'You thought what?' Markby exclaimed, startled. Fuller's sense of humour was sometimes a little weird. With a job like his he might be expected to have a penchant for black humour: but this seemed a peculiar notion even for Fuller.

'Making a human sacrifice and burying it in the foundations of a new building was a widespread ancient practice!' said Fuller with unseemly relish. 'In this country in Tudor times it was still common to bury a cat or dog under the threshold of a new house. Out of curiosity, do you know who our chap is yet?'

'No. What can you tell me?' Markby urged impatiently, anxious to get out of here. Sacrifices . . . he could do without those and Fuller's mortuary jokes!

'White male aged between thirty and thirty-five. Hair just starting to thin. Not overweight or showing any signs of bodily overindulgence! Good physical condition. He kept himself fit, I mean.'

'The sort of fitness you'd expect in a professional sportsman? Or just the sort of fellow who plays squash or something like that regularly?'

'Speculation isn't in my line, old chap. He kept fit. Let's see. Old appendix scar. Teeth much repaired – several of 'em capped with gold. Not a manual worker. Nice soft well-manicured hands.'

'Manicured professionally, you mean? He didn't trim the nails himself?'

'I have no idea, Alan. How on earth should I? Do you think I go poncing around beauty salons? You take a look and see what you think.'

'All right, when and how was he killed?'

'He was discovered on Monday morning. I'd say he died some time on Friday night. Rigor varies, may start within a couple of hours and show itself in the jaw muscles and the eyelids, which is why when a person snuffs it those present should close the eyes and mouth at once! If he was in some kind of a barney before he died that would hasten the stiffening process. But it can take up to twelve hours to complete. It lasts about the same length of time and takes another twelve to pass off. Burial in very cold soil might prolong it a bit but it had fully passed off by the time that construction worker dug him up. There are clear dark bruise-like patches on his back formed by the blood draining down to congest the lowest vessels. In this case, as he was buried face upward, they appear on his back. They are not to be confused with bruising caused by violence, by the way. Putrefaction itself however hasn't yet set in. The first sign is usually around the abdominal surface. I'd say he died not later than the early hours of Saturday morning and not earlier than, oh, eight or nine o'clock on Friday night. Sorry I can't be more precise.'

'During Friday night then, most likely.' Markby stared at the window and the view of the carpark beyond. 'They probably buried him in the semi-darkness just before dawn, too risky by daylight. They might have been seen. The site workers wouldn't be around at the weekend but plenty of people still take the last opportunity to walk out that way before it disappears under asphalt. I did, for my sins, and got landed with this.' He sighed.

Fuller sighed in sympathy but he was still humming to himself.

'Find his clothes? Not yet? It's difficult to undress a stiff.'

'I realise that. They killed him, stripped him probably to remove any clues in the event of things going wrong and his being discovered, and transported his body to the place where he was found all before rigor set in completely. Given the general time-table, they could have brought him a long way. So far we haven't a clue where he died. What about cause of death?'

'Let me see . . .' Tum-ti-tum-tum. 'Well, he'd been struck several times very hard on the back of the head with our friend the blunt instrument causing clear depressed fracturing of the skull here and here—' Fuller held an X-ray photo against the window light and pointed with his Biro at the two areas. 'Leading to extensive haemorrhaging in the brain.'

'Battered to death, then.'

'No.' Fuller saw Markby's surprise and repeated, 'No. He would have been rendered unconscious but if he had been taken to hospital quickly he might just have been saved. I say "might", but it would have been an outside chance. Without medical treatment including immediate surgery, he would have died from his injuries certainly. But technically he didn't die from them because something else killed him first.' He returned the X-ray photo tidily to the file and fell silent as he straightened the papers in a pernickety way.

Markby fidgeted. 'Come on, get to it.'

The pathologist said calmly, almost cheerily, 'There were distinct traces of earth in the lungs.'

Silence fell. Markby felt nausea rising and forced it back. He also felt something else, something atavistic and purely instinctive. A thrill of age-old terror, horror at the idea of that most dreadful of fates. 'Oh Lord,' he said weakly. 'Are you quite sure about this?'

'Oh, yes. Earth in the lungs and nasal passages. Definitely breathed in. Forensic tests will tell you for certain but I'm pretty sure you'll find it matches earth around the burial site.' Fuller closed the file. 'Buried alive, I'm afraid. Not a shadow of doubt. He suffocated in his grave.'

'Come on, Alan!' Laura urged. 'Do tuck in! Paul spent hours out in the kitchen concocting this.'

Markby stared down at his plate and tried without luck to identify the sausage-like shapes lurking beneath a dark gravy.

'*Alouettes sans têtes!*' said Paul, who was a professional writer and broadcaster on culinary subjects and never lost the opportunity to practise on family and friends. 'Headless larks it means literally – actually sausagemeat, onion and mushrooms wrapped in paper-thin slices of veal to make those little packets and cooked in a mushroom and wine sauce.'

'It's not that it doesn't smell delicious,' Markby assured his brother-in-law. 'And look, um, interesting. But I had rather a bad experience today.'

'Come on,' ordered his sister. 'Put police work out of your mind.'

Markby glowered at his plate. 'Do you mind very much, Paul, if I have this some other time? Can you stick it in the freezer or something?'

'No problem. Tell you what – have some pud. Trea-cle duff.'

'I have to deal with distressing things too,' said Laura obstinately. 'Solicitors find themselves in very stressful situations sometimes! I've learned to put it aside when I come home.'

'Yes, well, you've got your family – ' Markby began unwisely. He realised how unwisely even as the words left his mouth but it was too late. Laura seized the opening. Her topic was a familiar one.

'If you ask me, Alan, you've been moping round the place since Meredith left here to go and live in London. You miss her. Be honest.'

'Yes, I do. But it hasn't put me off my food, Laura. That really is genuinely due to something else.'

'So it may be, but I've got eyes in my head. For goodness' sake, swallow your pride, ring her up and invite her down for a few days.'

'It's nothing to do with pride!' Markby said crossly.

'Yes, it is. Bruised male ego. If she really liked me, she wouldn't have gone off etc., etc. . . . Don't think I don't understand just what goes through the male mind! Look, she has an important and responsible job and she couldn't keep commuting up to London from here – it was just impossible! She was offered that flat so she took it! It doesn't mean she's given you the elbow.'

'Laura—' Markby began and fell into frustrated silence. Paul was making a great clatter in the kitchen. Something fell down and the cook swore.

'How are the children?' Markby asked, determined to change the subject.

'Okay. Emma's had to have a brace fitted on her

teeth and Vicky fell off her bike. Matthew isn't working hard enough at school, just wants to play football – baby's fine.'

'I don't think,' Markby said seriously, 'I want a family. I never wanted a family. When I was married to Rachel I didn't want one. Well, we didn't have one, so that took care of that.'

'You'd think differently if you had a kid of your own.'

'I'm too old to start with that sort of thing now.'

'Rubbish. How old is Meredith?'

'Laura – for crying out loud, that kind of set-up was never on the cards.'

Paul put his head through the door. 'The pud fell on the floor. I've scraped up most of it. Do say if you'd rather have ice-cream.'

'To tell you the truth, I'd rather have just a cup of coffee!' Markby said firmly.

Laura had propped her elbows on the table and rested her chin on her laced fingers. Her long fair hair tumbled attractively round her face and she had recently abandoned her spectacles for contact lenses. Markby thought how nice she looked and what a pleasant combination of brains and beauty she presented. And he wished she didn't have that bee in her bonnet about marrying him off to Meredith. Not that it wasn't a favourite fantasy of his own but there were problems. Trying to explain that to Laura was a waste of time.

'Sorry dinner is a bit of a fiasco!' Paul's head appeared round the door again. 'I've chucked the pud in the bin. Coffee's on. Cheese?'

'No thanks. Sorry I couldn't do justice to the French cuisine.'

'No matter. But Laura and I had meant to give you a

decent meal to thank you in advance for keeping an eye on the house for the next ten days while we're away.'

Markby looked up and stared at him in undisguised horror.

'Oh Alan!' Laura exclaimed. 'You've forgotten!'

'Cripes, yes, sorry.'

'We made the arrangement ages ago! I explained to you that we could only get a booking at the camping site we wanted if we went before Easter. We'll be back the Tuesday after Easter Monday. Oh, Alan! I'm depending on you!'

'I remember now. But you told me too long ago. I just forgot it. You should have reminded me. But don't fret about it. I'll find time to come over during the ten days and check on the place. But mind you, we're up to our ears in work – two bodies discovered recently and one of 'em definitely murder.'

Laura sighed. 'I was hoping you'd come over more than just once in the whole ten days. But I understand, if you're busy, then you're busy. It's just that empty houses have been broken into along this street so often – well, you should know that down at the nick. Susie Hayman next door would keep an eye on the place but she's a visitor in this country and wouldn't be quite sure what to do in an emergency. Besides she works part-time at the American base. I hardly like to ask her. What I really had hoped was that you'd move in here for the ten days, sleep here.'

'Honestly, Laura, I can't. I'd have to go round giving everyone a new home phone number and half of 'em would lose it or forget it and I just don't want the added responsibility right now! I need to be based in my own home. And there's the new greenhouse in my backyard. It's cost me a fortune to set it up and stock it and I can't just buzz off and leave it. I need to keep a constant check on the temperature. I've put a little oil-heater—' He broke off because neither Laura nor Paul was a gardener and they couldn't be expected to understand.

Laura's gaze had grown absent. 'What we need, then, is a house-sitter, like a baby-sitter. Someone who'd like a ten-day break and would just move in here and make herself at home and comfortable and be around the place.'

'Herself?' asked Paul.

'Well, I was thinking of Meredith, of course,' Laura said simply.

'She's in London, woman!' Markby howled. 'She's working at that highly responsible FO job you were just telling me about!'

'She's been in London almost three months. I bet you she'd jump at the chance to take a few days in the country. She might not have any plans for Easter and could combine this with an Easter break. I could call her up and ask her.'

'No, you will not!' said her brother fiercely.

'Then you call her up and ask her!'

'Absolutely not. I wouldn't dream of doing any such thing! Honestly, Laura, sometimes you do take the ruddy biscuit! Ask Meredith to come down here and house-sit for you? I ask you – why should she even want to?'

'Oh, I don't know . . .' said Laura with an angelic smile. 'Just to help out, you know, and take a little holiday. Change of scene. Or something like that.'

Chapter Four

Markby certainly hadn't intended to phone Meredith when he got out of bed that morning. It wasn't that he'd forgotten his sister's suggestion but it was, he said to himself as he showered, out of the question. She would refuse, he said as he shaved, or worse she might accept because she wanted to oblige Laura with whom Meredith got along like a house afire and not because she wanted to see him again. After this his reasoning became so contorted that he abandoned it. Besides which, on top of the investigation into Lindsay's death which continued, he now had a murder weighing on his mind.

Unlike Lindsay's case in which her body had been promptly and accurately identified, they were no nearer knowing who the dead man was. No one had come forward to identify him. His general description did not tally with any reported missing persons. The soil lodged in the nasal passages and lungs had proved to be from the grave, just as the pathologist had predicted. There was nothing to indicate where the original attack had taken place and the victim struck unconscious. Footprints in the mud around the area had been painstakingly recorded and put on file. They all seemed to be of wellington boots or strong leather work boots. Some of them had already been traced and eliminated. But that left a collection of others, complete and part, which would probably never be accounted for. As Steve Wetherall had pointed out, all kinds of people visit a building site and don wellington boots while they're there. Steve did himself. There were developers' representatives, surveyors and men from the roads department and the electricity, gas and water services, British Telecom, the council and various building business watchdogs. There were the drivers of delivery lorries and all those visitors, prospective buyers and casual strollers taking a look such as Markby himself had done.

'If you want bootprints,' said Steve, 'this is the place for 'em!'

A study of tyre treads had yielded nothing except to clear most of them out of the inquiry. To Markby this meant that the victim had been brought by some vehicle along the strip of new road. Then he had been carried from the car to the burial site. Amongst the many bootprints were those of the men who had carried him. But which? The obvious pointer would be to look for deep imprints, men carrying a heavy load. But on building sites any number of men carry heavy loads. There were prints of any depth from a couple of inches to deep pits in the mud. It had rained hard on Sunday night which hadn't helped. It had washed clean the strip of road, obliterated or smudged much else.

He had talked again with Sean Daley who had unearthed the body and with Jerry Hersey the site foreman. Daley had still been in a state of shock and getting any clear statement out of him a lost cause. He hadn't noticed anything odd about the ditch before he started digging it down deeper. One ditch was like another. He was just doing as he was told. He was shown a photograph of the dead man and promptly started to shake. Markby told him to stay around where he could be contacted and left him to his misery.

The interview with Hersey had been equally unhelpful. Hersey was not by nature a helpful person. Obviously he resented the presence of the police on the site and the necessary hold-up to the work. Asked about general security at times when work was not in progress he had taken the question as a personal affront.

'We can't watch the bloody place all round the clock! We lock the machinery away in that compound over there to stop anyone pinching it. What d'you expect? Electric fence and blooming guard dogs?'

Markby had walked round the compound in question with its high wire fence and gates. 'You put everything away in here? All shovels, picks, that sort of thing?'

Hersey replied sourly that they did. 'All be pinched overnight, otherwise!' That meant whoever had dug the grave had brought his own spade or other implements with him and there was little point in inspecting those on the site. For form's sake, Markby told Sergeant Pearce to take a look at them but he knew that most had been used again since the weekend and if there had been blood on any of them or fingerprints, all traces were gone by now.

Hersey, following behind Pearce, had kept up a continual stream of protest and insistence that everything had been locked away from late Friday afternoon until early Monday morning. 'You won't find what you're looking for there! We've got work to do and we don't need coppers under our feet! It's not my fault that bloke got himself down in that ditch! I didn't ruddy plant him there! How much longer are you goin' to be? What d'you think you're going to find? Because I can tell you now. Sod all, that's what! And how are we supposed to build so much as a brick wall without any tools? So when you've finished messing about with them, Sherlock' – Hersey concluded his torrent with a foray into irony – 'we'd be much obleeged, if you'd push off and let us get on with our work!'

Hersey was going to be a problem. He couldn't prevent their investigations but he wouldn't make them any easier. There were a dozen subtle ways of interfering or obstructing and Hersey knew them all. Markby, at his desk now, studied the photograph which would have to be circulated around other forces and shown to anyone who might be likely to identify it.

That could have been better, too. It was obviously the photograph of a corpse. It had been cleaned and tidied up but that was the head of a dead man, all the same. With emotion, expression, all the flickering changes of life's passions drained out of it, the head was just a papier-mâché mask with the eyes shut. The cheeks had sunken in. It – he – probably looked thinner in the face than he had done alive. Markby had once been called upon to view the remains of a notorious playboy who had met some would have said a not untimely death. What had struck him was how dignified the corpse had looked, how death had smoothed out the puffiness of debauchery, disguised the circles beneath the eyes and closed the lids over pupils in which old acquaintance with vice had left a dull gleam. The red lips had paled and something like peace had erased the satiated world-weariness of the expression.

This face, too, was a dead face. It told nothing. There were cultures in which, at a burial service, the priest addressed his oration to the dead body, candle-lit in its open coffin. The priest's questions could never be anything but rhetorical. If the departed soul had discovered the answer to the riddle of death, it was unlikely to tell anyone still earthbound what it was. All the same, there was something about this face, something Markby couldn't quite put into words. It niggled at the back of his brain. He wished he could pinpoint it.

He sat at his desk and studied the photograph of the victim for some five minutes. At the end of that time Sergeant Pearce put his head round the door and cleared his throat tactfully.

'A Mr Newman here to see you, sir, from the contractors building all those houses.' In a lowered voice, Pearce added, 'He's got the developers on his neck. There's some sort of penalty clause about delay in the contract. He's been out to the site this morning and the situation's put the wind up him. I think they've got a sort of strike or go-slow or something out there. Also Hersey has been griping.'

'Oh yes?' Markby said, turning the photograph face downward in his tray. 'Show Mr Newman in, will you?'

Newman's was a highly successful local firm but Markby had never met the builder himself and looked up curiously as a burly man with thinning hair walked briskly into the room. A wariness in the builder's eyes accorded ill with the air of competence and confidence he exuded as he stuck out his hand across Markby's desk.

'Pleased to meet you, Chief Inspector. I hope we can

get all this sorted out today. Not a stroke of work has been done on that site since Monday and I'm sure I don't have to tell you what that's costing apart from the inconvenience. We keep a tight schedule—'

'We have finished on the site,' Markby said mildly. He had risen to greet the newcomer and now reseated himself and indicated a fat folder on the desk. 'We have our photographs and the results of soil tests and the records of tyre and footprints. You can restart work there.'

'Yes, yes, I appreciate that – but it's the work force.' Newman rubbed his hands together jerkily. He wore a broad gold band, a wedding ring? No, on the wrong hand, decided Markby. 'Of course I appreciate that your people have a job to do but they came out and interviewed every one of the workmen and, well, some of them are very upset about it.'

'Oh? Why was that? They were just routine inquiries.'

Newman looked briefly horrified and hurried to correct the false impression he had unwittingly given. 'Yes, of course they were! Obviously none of them had anything to do – but I mean, oh dammit, some of them just don't like policemen, Chief Inspector! Look, you must realise how it is—'

'I'm not a taxman,' said Markby blandly. 'Nor do I work for the Department of Social Security!'

'We don't have any nonsense of that kind – the kind you're hinting at!' Newman burst out. 'Not on any of our sites! All our men are properly registered for tax and national insurance contributions! You can take my word for it! What I mean is that police inquiries make them nervous. They think they're going to get blamed for something they haven't done. The developer is anxious there shouldn't be any undue delay. You know how it is, he's got the banks breathing down his neck, so he breathes down the contractor's neck—'

'And so you thought you'd breathe down mine?' Markby asked mildly.

'No – all right, yes! Frankly I'm afraid some of the men will quit. The site's gained a bad name because of this wretched business and you'd be surprised how superstitious a lot of men are. Some of the Irish labourers always work together on the same site. They travel round the country from site to site in a gang. If one moves off the site, the others may follow. Daley – Sean Daley the digger operator – he's taken himself off already.'

'He's what?' Markby asked, startled. 'We'll need him for the inquest! He was told to stay around here! Where the devil has he gone? Has he left the area, do you know?'

'He may have done,' said Newman unhappily. 'I'm sorry, no one realised he would be needed. In any case, we couldn't have stopped him. You should have been told, I realise, but it was the last thing on my mind and I didn't know he'd gone until he had . . . He drives an old Ford Capri, if that's any help. I remember seeing it around the caravans. Some of the men live in a sort of small caravan park about a quarter of a mile from where – where the trouble was.'

'Where the body was found, you mean?'

'Yes – one of the others, a man called Riordan, shared a caravan with Daley and told me this morning when I got there that Daley had been having nightmares ever since he dug that – that thing up. It was on his mind all the time and he couldn't even eat. He told Riordan he couldn't stand any more. He went to the site office early and told them he was quitting. That was before I got there. He should have left them a forwarding address because there will be wages outstanding. You'll have to ask the site manager about that.'

Markby scribbled a note on his desk pad to make sure Pearce looked into Sean Daley's departure straight away.

'Incidentally,' he said. 'While we're on the subject of inquiries at the site, it might help if you asked your foreman to be a little more cooperative. Not that he's under any suspicion, you understand, but it doesn't make our job any easier to have someone complaining all the time and refusing to lend even minimum assistance.'

'Oh, Jerry Hersey,' said Newman uneasily. 'He's a difficult sort of chap, is Jerry. I'll see what I can do.'

'Good. Now I wonder if you'd mind looking at a photograph, Mr Newman?' Wariness turned to alarm in the builder's eyes and Markby added soothingly, 'It's all right, it's not gruesome.'

'Yes, well – all right then . . .' Newman said unwillingly.

Markby reached for the photo in his tray and put it face upward before his visitor. Newman studied it and pulled out a handkerchief and touched his lips before shaking his head. Markby reflected that what constituted 'gruesome' depended on how acquainted you were with violent death. Policemen developed a high tolerance level to unpleasant sights. Newman possibly had never seen a dead body of any nature.

'Never set eyes on him!' Newman said huskily.

'I understand from Steve Wetherall that it was because the footings were being redug that the body was turned up.'

'Yes – The concrete was to be poured that afternoon.'

'So then, whoever buried him anticipated that within twenty-four hours or so, the body would be under three or four feet of concrete – and then a house on top of that.'

'Pair of houses, semi-detached the ones on that plot. Four bedrooms, though, and two bathrooms, one *en suite*.'

Newman added the last words automatically and then looked slightly embarrassed, 'Sorry – not trying to sell you one.' His gloom increased. 'It's not the sort of publicity that has buyers queuing up for houses! You can see the developers' point of view. They'll be lucky to interest any new clients now! As for people who've expressed interest but haven't committed themselves, they'll be pulling out, you'll see! And who's going to buy a house built on that plot, on those footings? They'll probably have to tell us to fill them in, grass it over and make an open recreational space there. That's money they can kiss goodbye! They are not happy men, Chief Inspector, and they're behaving as if it were all my fault!'

Markby acknowledged the words with a nod. 'Ever notice any strangers hanging around the site?'

'Chief Inspector, you've been out there, you know the layout of the area! There are people all over the place all the time – some of them are prospective house-buyers looking around, some of them just

51

curious local residents wondering what we're up to and combining a look around with an afternoon stroll. You can't keep people away. No – I didn't notice anyone in particular. You'll have to ask Hersey.'

'We have, and all the workmen. They say much the same kind of thing as you've just said. No one remembers this man.'

'There you are then,' Newman said a little obscurely. 'So I take it you've finished with us, then?'

'For the time being. I can't say we won't be back.' Markby fixed his visitor with a level gaze. 'This is a murder inquiry.'

'Yes, yes, of course. Naturally anything we, I, can do to help! It's just the men getting upset. I don't want anyone else to quit.'

When Newman had taken himself off, Markby called Pearce. 'Get on to the site office and check on the driver, Sean Daley! He quit his job this morning despite what we told him. See if you can find out where he intended going and if he left a forwarding address. He drives an old Ford Capri. Go down to the caravan site where the men live and ask Riordan, he shared with Daley, and anyone else if Daley gave any indication of friends or family he might go to.'

'They won't say,' Pearce said gloomily. 'Even if they know. They'll clam up.' He watched as Markby pulled on his green weatherproof. 'Where are you going, sir?'

'I'm going to call at the two farms, Greyladies Farm and Witchett Farm. They lie either side of the area under development.' He picked up the photograph and brandished it at Pearce. 'This fellow didn't fall out of the sky. There are a dozen building sites or road construction sites in the general area. How did the grave-diggers come to choose this one? It's far from the most handy with regard to the main road. You have to drive down a B road and then turn on to this new road they've built. Strangers to this neck of the woods wouldn't just find it. Whoever buried him knew about the building there. Perhaps they were in the area beforehand, looking around, picking the spot, watching the work in progress, calculating when the concrete would be poured. If they were, someone saw them or saw a car – saw something!'

Pearce looked dubious. 'They could have gone to the site openly and said they were interested in buying one of the houses. No one would think that odd. They could ask about time-tables, work schedules and even the way the houses were built.'

'If I have to interview everyone who ever went anywhere near that site, I will!' Markby said grimly.

Chapter Five

Despite his troubles, it seemed to Markby as he drove through the countryside that this was the best kind of English April day. Crystal sunlight and intermittent showers made the road verges sparkle and diamonds dance on the wet road. The hedgerows were newly decked in green and the birds were everywhere fluttering and twittering in the branches, looking for nesting places. He wished he had time to stop and watch the delightful antics of the new lambs.

Markby slowed and looked over a fence at the sheep in question. These would belong to the Winthrops. It was some time since he'd been to Greyladies Farm and he found himself quite looking forward to the visit. He had reached the turning which was signposted with a mud-splashed wooden board reading 'Farm Only'. To underline this message, the print of heavy-duty tyres and manure freely marked the narrow single-track lane. Markby set off slowly down it. The banks on either side were high and there were not, as far as he could see, any pull-in places. If he met something coming the other way, he would have to back up all the way to the road.

Fortunately he didn't meet any other vehicle, but he

did flush out a surprised squirrel which panicked and ran down the lane ahead of him for some way before scrabbling up one bank and thence to the safety of an ancient oak, leaning perilously out to deck the lane with its gnarled limbs. Markby stopped, stuck out his head and peered up into the branches above but the squirrel had vanished and probably watched him from hiding. It occurred to him that this old tree did not look particularly safe and the branches were quite low. Wisps of hay or straw showed where they had scraped against a load. He wondered why the Winthrops hadn't trimmed it back.

The lane twisted unexpectedly and when he turned the corner he found himself right before the farm gates which stood open. He drove in and parked by a half-constructed barn, open to wind and weather beneath a corrugated iron roof. He could hear sheep maa-ing plaintively to one another and propping his arms on one of the low half-walls, peered in to see an array of ghostly grey-white faces staring back at him.

'Good morning, ladies,' he said politely.

They all stopped chewing and goggled at him.

Markby turned back and saw he was being watched too, by a scruffy collie with a sharp wolfish muzzle, shifty eyes and a distinctly unfriendly air.

'Hullo, boy,' Markby said with a confidence he did not feel. 'I'm not after your girlfriends.'

The dog took a cautious step forward with lowered head, suspicious red-rimmed eyes rolling at him, and then scuttled back. It seemed to be working out how best to round up the intruder and pen him in a corner until help arrived.

Fortunately help did then arrive. A girl's voice called, 'Whisky!'

The sheepdog turned, wagged its plumed tail and performed an obsequious kind of dance, cringing and sidling whilst still signalling friendship with its tail, both wanting and not wanting to go forward and exchange greetings.

The girl asked, 'Can I help you?' Now she was here the dog seemed prepared to relinquish responsibility for the farmyard to a superior. It retreated to a sheltered sunny corner and lay down on a sack spread out there for its use and put its wolf's nose on its paws, red eyes still fixed on Markby.

She was about twenty-four or five, Markby supposed. He did not base this judgement so much on observation as on assuming this to be Jessica Winthrop who, if his memory served him aright, must be about that age now.

She looked younger. A pale, pretty but unhappy looking girl with long, fair hair 'as straight as a yard of pump-water' as he'd heard some old country-people call it. She was slimly built, about five-four in height and wore close-fitting jodhpurs tucked into high riding boots, a sweater and over it a sleeve-less quilted navy-blue bodywarmer. She had just come out of a stable on the other side of the yard and was holding a length of rope. Now she turned and tugged at the rope. There was a clip-clop of hoofs and the rope was revealed to be attached to a leather headstall on a roan pony with a hogged mane which walked out into the sunlight and stood looking over the girl's shoulder towards Markby. The girl turned back too and they both watched and waited.

'It's Jessica, isn't it?' he asked, slightly unnerved by the combined scrutiny of girl, pony and dog. 'I'm Alan Markby – Chief Inspector Markby from the Bamford station. Alwyn and I were at school together once, a good few years ago now! I expect you don't remember me. You were just a little tot then.'

She didn't smile. She just said, 'He's not here, Alwyn, nor Dad. They're both out checking on some sheep. What was it you wanted?'

'Well, I—' He paused, feeling strangely awkward. 'Is your mother here?'

Before she could answer this another female voice, harsher and more assured, called 'Jess?'

'Mrs Winthrop?' Markby called back. 'Alan Markby here! Could I have a word?'

The roan pony threw up its head and snorted, stamping its hoofs and backing into its stable again. Jessica turned away from him to deal with it.

'I'd like to talk to you too, Jessica, if you've time,' Markby said. 'It won't take five minutes.'

'All right,' she mumbled without turning round. 'I'll just put Nelson back in his loose-box.'

Mrs Winthrop had come out of the house as she spoke. She came up to them and her expression, which had been suspicious, mellowed. 'Alan! We weren't expecting you! Do you want to see our Alwyn?'

'All of you. It's a general call. If you've got a few minutes, I'd be grateful.'

'Best come into the kitchen, then. I've got scones in the oven, can't leave them.'

As he followed her into the kitchen Markby wondered which side of the family Jessica took after. Old man Winthrop the senior was built on generous principles, Alwyn topped six foot and Jamie, as he recalled him, had been a useful rugby player. Mrs Winthrop was short but square – as broad as she's high! – he thought,

58

amused. It wasn't quite so bad as that, but that was the
general impression. She had short grey hair, frizzed in
an unattractive perm which was growing out, and wore
a nylon overall. The kitchen smelled deliciously of
home baking.

'Sit down, then, Alan!' she said briskly. 'Jess! Don't
you let that dog slip in! He'll creep in here on the sly if
he can, that animal!' she added to Markby in explanation. 'He knows he's not allowed indoors!'

'Not at all?'

'No – working dog. Belongs outside.'

Markby said, 'I see.' He wasn't surprised that the
collie wasn't allowed in here. It was a scruffy beast
and had looked half-wild to him and the kitchen was
spotlessly clean. Mrs Winthrop stooped before the
oven, her broad nylon-encased beam towards him. She
brought out her tray of scones and tipped them, shining
golden and wonderfully scented, on to the table.

'You'd like a cup of coffee, I dare say, Alan. Want
one of these with it – hot with butter?'

'Yes, please!' he said promptly, as keen as a child.

She looked gratified. 'That's it, then. Jess, don't you
stand about there, girl, doing nothing! You get on and
make the coffee!'

The girl had slipped into the kitchen as quietly and
unobtrusively as, given half a chance, the collie would
have done. Markby found himself watching her curiously as she busied herself taking cups down from the
Welsh dresser. She didn't look at him. She seemed
determined not to. She was either shy or nervous –
what was it Steve had said? Some sort of nervous
breakdown?

Mrs Winthrop put down a pot of homemade jam and

a plate in front of him. 'Pity you didn't come half an hour ago, you'd have caught Alwyn and my husband before they went off. If you fancy a walk over the fields, I can tell you where they are.'

He broke open one of the scones, so hot it burned his fingertips, and spread butter on thickly. It melted immediately and soaked into the crumbly dough making it glisten.

'It's all right, I can call again. Or if either of them is in town and has a minute to call by the station—' Markby mumbled indistinctly through a mouthful of scone.

'Alwyn and George will both be in town Thursday. They're taking those sheep out there in the barn to market. Only they'll likely be too busy to call round to your station. Was it urgent?'

'Yes and no. It's a routine inquiry. You heard about the body discovered where they're building, where Lonely Farm was?'

The girl set a cup of coffee down in front of him with a graceless gesture. It spilled on to the oil-cloth.

'You're all thumbs, you are,' said her mother, wiping it up. 'Not got any on your trousers, have you, Alan?'

'No – it's nothing. Thank you for the coffee, Jessica. This is excellent jam, Mrs W.' He'd fallen unashamedly on a second scone. It was inviting indigestion but this was a time to enjoy yourself now and take your chances later. Oh joy, thick midnight purple blackcurrant jam, so stiff it came out on the spoon a solid chunk and had to be squashed on to the surface of the scone in lumps.

'I'll give you a pot to take with you, we've got plenty. Blackcurrant bushes did well last year. That murder was a nasty business. You got the job of sorting that out, have you?'

'The murder inquiry? Yes, for my sins. You don't recall seeing anything unusual on Friday evening or hearing anything during the night? A car? Voices? Anything like that?'

'Bless you, I sleep like a log!' she said robustly.

'What about you, Jessica?'

'I don't sleep very well,' the girl mumbled. 'But I didn't hear anything. Whisky didn't bark. He'd hear a stranger.'

She stopped speaking abruptly as if she had been caught doing something forbidden or ill-mannered and gave him a haunted look.

'Dratted dog,' said Mrs Winthrop in her brusque way.

'I suppose,' he said humbly, 'I couldn't show you both a photo?' He glanced at the girl and then at her mother. 'I don't want to upset anyone – it's not a particularly upsetting picture, but we're trying to find out who he was.'

'Oh—' Mrs Winthrop glanced at her daughter. 'Let's have a look then!'

Markby brought out his photo and handed it to her. Mrs Winthrop fished in the pocket of her overall and took out a pair of spectacles. She perched them on the end of her nose and stared down the length of it through the lenses. 'No, can't say I know this fellow.' She hesitated and then held the picture out. 'You can take a look, Jess. 'Tis nothing to be frightened of.'

Markby watched the girl take the picture. He felt ashamed of his work as he sometimes did when dealing with nervous witnesses. He must seem like an ogre. This girl was plainly not quite – well, to say she wasn't quite right in the head would be putting it too strongly. But she was obviously not quite as she should be. He wondered if she was receiving any medical treatment for her condition.

She took the photograph with tolerable composure, however, and after a brief glance handed it back to him. 'I don't know who he is.'

'Fair enough, thanks for looking at it.' Markby put it away and concentrated on his coffee. He hadn't expected them to recognise the deceased and he felt more than ever that he troubled them to no advantage and had probably set off some nervous crisis in the girl. Guilt overwhelmed him.

'If you don't need Jess,' Mrs Winthrop said calmly but with a touch of her sergeant-major manner, 'I expect she'd like to be out there grooming that pony.'

'Oh, yes – sorry to take you from your work, Jessica.'

'It's all right—' The girl got up in her awkward way and fairly bolted out of the kitchen.

Mrs Winthrop stirred her coffee, watching the whirl-pools form on the surface. 'She's a lot better now, our Jess, than she was when she come home. A year ago that was.'

'She was at teacher training college – is that right?'

'Yes, but she'd finished all that. Qualified, done her teaching practice and got a job. But she was always nervous, even as a little'un. She took sick and had to give it all up and come back home. But she's a lot better now.'

'That's a pity – I'm glad she's getting over it. Alwyn will be at the livestock market on Thursday, you say?'

He was intruding here. He was a policeman doing a job and he should long have lost any trace of embarrassment at it. But here he was barging in on some private sorrow and the knowledge that he did affronted his own sense of decency.

'Definite.'

'If I don't get back out here before or he doesn't come in to see me – I'll call in there and see him.' The idea of visiting Greyladies Farm no longer filled him with pleasure.

'I'll tell him. You want to see George too? Show them that photo?'

'Yes.'

'I'll tell them.' She got up, sturdy, capable, no nonsense. 'I'll just fetch you that jam.'

Witchett Farm offered quite a different sort of welcome. Mrs Carmody came across the yard to greet him as he got out of his car. She was clad in a pair of man's corduroy trousers, a wonderful hand-knitted sweater of complicated design and wore a red scarf tied round her throat. A gash of scarlet lipstick haphazardly applied marked her mouth and her hair was pinned up on top of her head in a cottage loaf style out of which various strands escaped and hung round her face.

'Hallo, there, Alan!' she boomed at him in a baritone. 'Come about the stiff?'

'Yes, as a matter of fact. I won't take up much of your time.'

'Time? Got plenty of that! Come in!'

This time he was shown not into the kitchen but into an untidy sitting room which already contained a spaniel, two cats and far too much furniture. A fire crackled merrily in the hearth, the flames reflecting in the highly polished old-fashioned fender and on the brass companion set with its collection of utensils, poker, brush, tongs and the little shovel.

'I haven't seen one of those for years!' Markby exclaimed.

'It's older than I am!' said Mrs Carmody. 'That was there when I was a little girl. Used to play with it.' She removed a cat from a sofa, gave the cushions a hearty whack which raised a dust-storm of shed animal hair and invited, 'Sit down!'

'I've been expecting you,' she went on when he'd sat down, patted the spaniel and made apologetic overtures to the ejected cat which it ignored.

'Oh? Why's that?' Markby looked up with a quickening of interest.

'You were bound to come sooner or later, asking questions around, weren't you? I expected one of your young chaps, not you yourself. Glad you think me that important!'

'Considering I've known you all my life,' Markby said with a smile. 'It's nice to have an excuse to come out here and see you, even if it is official. How are you keeping, Dolly?'

'I'm all right. Get a bit chesty in the winter. Getting old, that's it. Heading for the scrap-heap.'

'You? Never!' he denied and she boomed out a great roar of laughter. Markby brought out his photograph and handed it over.

'This the stiff? Can't put a name to him for you, if that's what you want. Sorry.' She sounded regretful and studied the picture carefully, frowning. 'No!' she repeated with a shake of her head. Another strand of hair fell out of the cottage loaf. 'Don't know him.'

'Never seen anyone even faintly resembling him around? In life you see, he'd have looked a bit different.'

Mrs Carmody had returned the photo and was fixing him with a thoughtful gaze. 'No, but someone was snooping round the place one night last week.'

'Yes?' He leaned forward eagerly. At last!

'But I didn't see him! That is, I did and I didn't. It was, let's see, last Thursday night. I'd stayed up watching television and I went on to bed a bit later than usual. I'd only just got off to sleep and I woke up suddenly. I heard the horses give a whinny and start stamping about in their stalls. They don't belong to me, you understand. I don't own any livestock nowadays. But I rent out the fields as grazing to other people and two or three horse-owners stable their beasts here. I keep them mucked out and fed and Jessica Winthrop comes over and helps out most days. Poor kid, she has no life, you know.'

'Yes, I've just been to Greyladies . . .' He didn't want to interrupt the story or divert it but it seemed in danger of going off at a tangent anyway. 'And you suspected an intruder?'

'I got out of bed and pulled on my old dressing-gown. Course, that dog there, she's as deaf as a post, nearly fourteen years old she is, so there's no use relying on her to hear anything! I popped my head out of the window. It was a fairly clear night last Thursday if you recall. It could have been better, mind, for seeing purposes. I saw a shadow move, just by the entry to the yard. I gave a shout, asked him what he was doing down there and he slipped away. I got up, dressed, found a torch and went down to check the horses were all right.'

'That might have been rash, Dolly,' Markby said in some concern. She must be over sixty.

'If I was scared of living here on my own I shouldn't do it, Alan! I've lived here all my life. I was the only child my parents had and when I got married my husband came here and we took the farm on from the old folks. When I leave here, I'll do it feet first in a wooden box! Anyhow, the stable doors were still fast and there wasn't any other sign of anyone trying to get in. I checked the windows in the house. So I reckoned it was a tramp looking for a barn to sleep in or maybe after a chicken. I've only got a couple of hens and the old cockerel since the new testing regulations came in for salmonella. It's no use keeping a small flock of birds for commercial production now. More trouble than it's worth. But I keep a couple for myself, I like a nice new-laid egg. But they hadn't set up a squawk. If it had been a fox, now, the old cockerel would have played merry hell. No, it was a fellow all right but all I saw of him was a shape.'

'And no one's been back?'

She shook her head.

Markby put away his photo. Two steps forward, one step back. It was a lead, though, however tenuous. 'Thank you,' he said. 'That's very helpful.'

Mrs Carmody got to her feet and made for a very nice early Victorian sideboard. She opened a little door in it and bent down. 'You could do with a drop of scotch by the look of it. Don't tell me about being on duty. There's no one here but the two of us and I'm certainly going to have one.'

'Oh, all right, then.' He watched as the amber liquid filled the glass with a satisfying glug-glug out of the bottle.

'Here's to the stiff whoever the poor blighter was,' said Mrs Carmody. 'Bottoms up!'

'The old man,' said Sgt Pearce to Wpc Jones, 'has taken the farmers and I've got the builders.'

'Going back to that site, are you?' asked Jones. 'Take your gumboots.'

'I hope he's taken his!' retorted Pearce with a grin.

When he reached the building site it appeared at first glance to have returned to some normality. But Pearce soon discovered this to be an illusion. The area surrounding the trench in which the body had been found was still roped off and deserted. No one went anywhere near it and it was clear this was not because they all respected police inquiries. It was because the spot had become taboo in the most ancient sense. To the tribe constituted by the men who built these houses, to venture on this place was death. Two thousand years ago it would have been marked with skulls on posts and the tattered scraps of votive offerings. Today it was marked with an empty canned drink tin and oddly, a small bunch of primroses. Pearce frowned. He couldn't have imagined the navvies placing the flowers and wondered who on earth had. Someone who had known the dead man yet who had failed to come forward and identify him? He made a note to tell Markby about it.

'I don't know what we're going to do about that plot!' said the site manager when Pearce ran him to earth. 'I've told Newman we'll have to hire another gang of navvies. This lot won't go near it. No, Daley didn't leave an address. He said he'd be in touch. Scared out of his wits, poor devil, and couldn't leave here fast enough! Ask Joe Riordan by all means. I think he's down at the caravans.' The manager hesitated. 'You'll find him tricky, I don't mean bolshie like Hersey, just . . . well, you'll find out for yourself. You'll have to pin him down.'

Pearce acknowledged the warning and set off across the site, clumping along self-consciously in the boots he had brought for the purpose. There had been a downpour during the night and the thick sticky clay clung to the soles and heels of his wellingtons, gradually building up until he proceeded with awkward, stiff-legged gait on feet encased in two clay-balls. He must look, and he knew he felt, ridiculous.

The caravan site was not attractive. The trailers themselves were dilapidated and rusting. Washing hung on an improvised clothes line and cars were parked here and there between the units. Other things: Calor-gas bottles, discarded plastic mineral water bottles, empty cardboard boxes and black plastic rubbish sacks which had split, spilling their contents, littered the ground. There was an odoriferous toilet block. Pearce wrinkled his nose in disgust and muttered, 'Faugh!'

Someone else also found it unacceptable. As Pearce approached he heard voices raised in vehement altercation.

'—get the bloody place cleaned up!' roared one which Pearce identified as belonging to Jerry Hersey. His heart sank. He had wanted to see Riordan before Hersey discovered the police were back.

'Not my bleeding responsibility!' bawled another voice in reply.

Hersey's answer to that was such that even Pearce, who had heard some colourful language in his time, blinked and muttered 'Blimey!' He turned the corner of a trailer and came across the foreman standing arms akimbo, eyes glaring through his horn-rimmed spectacles, facing Joe Riordan who stood in the open doorway of the trailer provided for his use and Daley's – until Daley had done a bunk. The labourer was a large, red-faced man with powerful shoulders, a beergut and tattooed forearms. He was wearing worn corduroy trousers and a grimy singlet out of which burst a veritable jungle of chest hair.

Both men looked up as Pearce appeared. Hersey spat to one side. 'Is it me you're wanting or him?' Riordan asked. He jerked his head disdainfully towards Hersey.

'You, Mr Riordan, if you can spare a moment,' said Pearce politely.

'Always at the service of the polis!' said Riordan genially and, Pearce suspected, inaccurately. He gestured towards the interior of his trailer. 'Won't you come inside now?'

Hersey growled and stomped away.

'That man,' said Riordan, 'is a bastard, pure and simple. Calls himself a foreman! I could do that job better than he does, and with one hand tied behind my back! Take them boots off before you come inside!'

Pearce divested himself thankfully of his weighty footwear and entered the caravan. Inside it was warm, fairly clean and reasonably tidy.

'I'll make us a cup of tea,' Riordan said. 'Will you have a drop of something in yours?'

'No thanks!' said Pearce quickly. 'Just the tea. I came about Sean Daley.'

'He's gone, didn't they tell you?'

'We've just learned. Would you happen to know where he's gone?'

'No,' said Riordan simply. He picked up a hissing kettle from his little Calor-gas stove and poured boiling water into an enamelled teapot. He then stirred the brew briskly with a handleless table-knife and poured the resultant infusion into two large mugs.

'Didn't he give any warning he was about to take off?' Pearce accepted the mug. 'Only he should have stayed. He'll be needed at the inquest. He found the body.'

'It gave him the habdabs,' said Riordan, producing a hipflask and pouring lavishly of it into his mug. A strong smell of whisky filled the air. 'He kept waking up screaming. Kept me awake. I'm a light sleeper myself.'

'Had he any family he might have gone to?'

'He came from County Cork,' said Riordan placidly.

'You mean, he's gone back to Ireland?'

'I don't mean anything. He might or he might not, as the case may be. I couldn't say what was in his mind.'

'No one in this country he might have turned to?'

'I told you, he's a Cork man.'

'Damn!' said Pearce moodily and took an unwary sip of the tea. 'Damn!' he repeated more forcefully as he scalded his tongue.

'Burn yourself?' Riordan paused, his mug half raised, the veins standing out along his tattoos. He took a long swig of his own tea, apparently impervious.

Must have a cast-iron throat! thought Pearce. And a cast-iron system of dealing with police questions, too! 'How about friends on the site? Was he friendly with anyone in particular?'

'No,' said Riordan. 'A quiet feller. We'd play a game of cards of a wet evening, him and me, sometimes.'

'Did he leave anything behind?' Pearce looked round the trailer. 'Personal belongings, clothes, letters or other correspondence of any kind?'

'No,' said Riordan.

'So there's nothing you can tell me?'

'I can tell you,' said Riordan, 'that one of these days someone will break Jerry Hersey's ugly neck for him. I can't stand the sight of the feller and neither can anyone else. It's not surprising.'

'No,' said Pearce unwarily, adding hastily, 'I'm not asking about Hersey, but about Sean Daley.'

'No, can't say I can tell you anything about him.'

Pearce put down his mug and tried to say 'thank you' without sounding too sarcastic.

'You're surely welcome,' said Riordan.

'Oh,' Pearce paused in the doorway about to redon his mud-caked boots. 'Did you say you were a light sleeper? During last Friday night, did you happen to hear a car engine or any noise indicating activity at the site?'

'Now there's a strange thing . . .' said Riordan, thoughtfully scratching the tangled undergrowth on his chest. He fell aggravatingly silent.

'Yes?' urged Pearce.

'I did not,' said Riordan.

'I'm not surprised,' muttered Pearce as he clumped away on clay-encumbered feet, 'that the old man chose the farmers!'

Somehow, when Markby went back home that evening, picking up the phone and calling Meredith didn't seem such an outlandish idea after all. He wasn't sure quite what had changed his mind but Jessica Winthrop's pale face haunted him, so lonely and withdrawn. The feeling that he'd intruded there still lingered. This case was in danger of getting to him. And there was Laura and the house, of course. It was only fair to try and help Laura. Meredith could always turn the proposition down. She probably would.

But she didn't. Instead she fairly jumped at it.

'As a matter of fact, Alan, I'd like to come down for a few days and, as it happens, I've got next week off plus the Easter break. It's a long story – I'll tell you when I see you. When's Laura going on holiday?'

'Very early Saturday morning, hoping to leave about five-thirty. Rather her than me. Can you imagine, four kids and all their gear crammed into the car at that ungodly hour, driving like mad to the coast for the ten a.m. ferry?'

'Then I'll come down on Saturday morning later, about eleven.'

'I'll be in my office most likely. We're very busy at the moment. That means I won't have much free time I'm afraid.' He thought that bit, all perfectly true, was none the less rather cunning. He knew quite well she was more likely to come if she thought he was too tied up elsewhere to make a nuisance of himself. 'If you call at the station when you get here, I'll have the keys to the house.'

'Fine. See you Saturday morning then.'

He put the phone down hardly able to believe his luck.

Chapter Six

'Mind yerself! Muck lorry's coming through!'

Alerted in the nick of time, Markby jumped nimbly aside as the euphemistically labelled Liquid Refuse Removal tanker surged past him in the narrow entry to Bamford livestock market. Thursday mornings were always busy in the town. From early morning the cattle transporters had been arriving, some towering double-deckers, others relatively modest animal Black Marias. The whole market area was subdivided into squares made by metal gates, each containing some kind of animal. In the middle was the covered area which marked the auction ring. It was just like a toy farm he'd had as a boy except that this assaulted his ears with the cacophony of bleating, lowing, squealing and clanging of metal gates. With a deafening rattle of hooves a new transporter discharged its odoriferous cargo, the animals scampering down the lowered tailgate in a miniature stampede while the attendant stockmen whistled shrilly and shouted. Elsewhere beasts which had already passed through the auction ring were being loaded unwillingly into other transporters. Some, perhaps alerted by instinct, made futile efforts to escape but were rounded up swiftly and efficiently and removed to whatever fate awaited them. Above it all a plaintive call on the loudspeaker system requested that whoever had parked a Land-Rover in the entry would he please go and remove it immediately.

Markby pressed against a hoarding advertising a variety of agricultural commodities as a large young man in a soiled white overall and vast gumboots urged a recalcitrant and mud-smeared bullock past. But he sought sheep. Where there were sheep, there would be the Winthrops, father and son. Just then a tumbril with chain-link sides in which two black-faced ewes stood and one lay on straw was towed slowly past. Markby set off in the direction from which it had come.

He pushed his way through a throng of bucolic faces. Large stout men in greenish trilby hats and Aran knitwear worn under stretched Harris tweed jackets; thin-faced, leathern-cheeked men in waxed coats and green wellies; healthy-looking pink-faced women with sensible shoes and county-style haircuts; men who looked like retired Guards officers and probably were and other men who looked as if they'd somehow grown out of the soil their families had tended for generations. Many greeted him. They knew him here not only because he was part of the local police force but because his was a local family and had once owned land around here. Not for a generation now, but in the countryside memories are long. He reflected guiltily that perhaps his family had been among the first to commit the cardinal sin of selling out to builders and developers. It made his high-flown grumbling to Steve ring a bit false now he recalled it.

The sheep were in the far corner but before he got to them he'd already spotted Alwyn Winthrop, not a man to be missed in a crowd at well over six foot in height, his flame-red hair confined under a flat cap. Beside him could be glimpsed the bulky form of his father, shorter but broad and bulging, heavy-shouldered, seemingly without a neck and planted foursquare and immovable like a Sumo wrestler.

'Alwyn!' yelled Markby above the general clamour.

Alwyn turned, gesturing in acknowledgement and welcome. 'Thought we'd see you,' he said amiably as Markby came up. 'Ma told us you might come round here. Here's Alan come about the dead feller, Dad!'

'Oh, him!' boomed Winthrop senior. 'Got you running round in circles, has that, then?'

'Pretty well,' admitted Markby frankly. He dug in his pocket and produced the now fairly dog-eared photograph. He passed it to the elder man first by way of courtesy.

Winthrop senior pushed his extraordinarily ancient hat to the back of his head and hooked one stubby thumb in the armhole of his waistcoat as he prepared to give judgement. A massive gold and probably antique watch-chain spanned his ample stomach and disappeared into a watch pocket on the waistcoat. In honour of market day he'd donned a tie, a creased strip of material of uncertain age which encircled the rolling folds marking the join between his head and his shoulders, that being the nearest it could get to being round a neck. He held out the photograph at arm's length and in his massive paw it looked like a postage stamp. 'Ah, that'll be him, then!' he pronounced in sage if enigmatic tones, adding, 'Can't say I recognise the poor bugger!'

He passed the photo to his son and hooked his other

thumb into his other armhole. Beside his father Alwyn looked smarter, positively well-dressed in a relatively new tweed jacket probably kept for best. He studied the picture for a moment in silence then said soberly, 'Seems a funny sort of thing to be taking a photo of a dead man. This is a photo of a dead 'un, isn't it?'

'Fraid so. We've no idea yet who he is.'

Alwyn shook his head and passed the photo back. 'Sorry we can't help you.'

'Oh well, thanks anyway,' said Markby gloomily, returning the picture to his pocket. 'How are sheep prices?'

'Down!' chorused the Winthrops, father and son, immediately.

'Oh, sorry to hear that. Will you try something else next year?'

'Tried potaters,' said Winthrop senior. 'Prices went down. Tried beef cattle. Prices went down. Reckon we'll stick with the sheep.' He removed the gold half-hunter attached to the watch-chain from his pocket and consulted it before tucking it back.

Alwyn looked restive, opened his mouth but then closed it as if he'd thought better of what he'd wanted to say. He turned aside and leaned on the nearest metal gate. The sheep clustered in front of him and stared up at him as if they expected him to make some sort of speech. Winthrop senior was hailed by an acquaintance and moved away. Markby joined Alwyn, leaning on the metal gate.

'Farming a bit of a struggle these days,' he observed conversationally.

'You can say that again. Not the bloody half of it!' Alwyn paused to resettle his cap on his red hair and added, 'Don't mean to sound brusque. Trouble is that Dad, he doesn't – well, he's getting along in years and he can't change his ideas now. His father farmed at Greyladies before him and his father before that . . . He can't imagine us not being on the farm. Even if we go bankrupt – which, I may say, we might end up doing!'

Thinking of Steve Wetherall's remarks, Markby asked tentatively, 'You'd consider giving up altogether, would you?'

'Not while the old man's alive. It'd kill him if I said I was packing it in. He couldn't go on by himself. Mother's getting older too. But he'd try, you see, if I left. He'd try to go on. I can't abandon them.' There was an echo of real despair in his voice.

Markby felt awkward again. Around the Winthrops, any of them, he seemed to end up this way, feeling he was poking about in their business without due cause, aggravating already open wounds.

But Alwyn had started speaking again. Perhaps he had few people he could confide in and once started, the words were now hard to stop. 'I don't blame Jamie for going off like he did. He took his chance. Good luck to him. But it means, you see, I can't leave. And there's Jess. It's no life for her. She goes over to Witchett Farm and spends quite a bit of time over there with old Dolly Carmody but she ought to have young friends.'

'You've never thought of getting married, Alwyn?' Markby heard himself ask, much to his own surprise.

'Got nothing to offer a woman. I tell you, Alan, if I got a halfway decent offer for the land and it was up to me—' He broke off and chewed furiously at his lip, tugged his cap down over his eyes and glowered at the harmless sheep in front of them. 'But it's not up to me, is it? Anyway, I've yet to meet the right woman – as will take me on!'

'Oh well,' Markby said again because there was not, after all, much else he could say. 'Meet you for a drink one evening, Alwyn?'

'Fine by me. I usually drink up at The Fox and Hounds and you can pretty well find me there most evenings. That makes me sound like a regular old soak – but I'm the feller you'll find nursing a single pint for an hour. Even bloody beer costs money.'

'See you there then!' Markby said and took himself off with what he felt was indecent speed.

The following Saturday Meredith saw the roadsign which read 'Bamford 3' and felt a warm glow of pleasure. And why not? It was a beautiful spring morning, even if the wind was fresh. She could have driven all the way here on the motorway and main roads but she'd chosen to turn off and approach the town by the old road, lined on either side by fields. The newly burgeoning trees balanced their branches in the breeze and the birds, caught by gusts of air, wheeled away in midflight and soared off in unexpected directions. In the distance the lorries thundered down the dual carriageway but she had only passed two cars, one tractor and a keep-fit enthusiast on a bicycle since she'd turned off.

Now though, up ahead, was a girl on a plump roan pony. Meredith slowed down as she passed the rider and the girl raised a hand in acknowledgement of the courtesy. Meredith returned a brief wave and glanced back. The rider wasn't a child as she'd imagined from the long fair hair showing beneath the hard hat and slight build, and the mount being the sturdy pony not a horse, but a girl probably in her late twenties. She drove on and the horsewoman was lost from sight. Meredith forgot her in anticipation of seeing Alan.

It was ridiculous to feel so cheerful about it, she reproved herself. Every time they met up it ended with distinct signs of Alan getting 'serious' and a reciprocating panic in Meredith herself which led her to flee the scene. But to be out of London, out of the office and out of that depressing flat of Toby's in Islington for a whole nine days, that had to be a prospect of bliss!

The flat Toby had kindly lent her was grotty, there was no denying. Not that its absent owner cared twopence about the state of the paintwork. When Meredith had moved in, the kitchen had had brown walls, bottle-green paint and a tomato-coloured stain on the ceiling which could have resulted from anything from an accident with a ketchup bottle to a ritual slaughter. Meredith, in desperation, had painted the kitchen cream and blue and put up some cheap and cheerful curtains. However, she wasn't going to spend any more on someone else's property so the rest of the place remained depressingly mustard-walled with scratched mud-coloured wood.

The road now curved to the left and the view was obstructed by overgrown hedgerows and an ancient, vast horse-chestnut tree. Meredith almost paid dearly for her day-dreaming. She rounded the bend to find the narrow road immediately ahead blocked with sheep. Hundreds of them, so it seemed to her horrified eye, stretched in a woolly mass in all directions and allowed no way round or through.

Meredith slammed on the brakes and twisted the wheel desperately to avoid the leaders of the flock. The car leapt on to the grass verge, bumped full pelt up the bank, scraped the hedgerow, gathering a garland of thistle and couch grass and, as she fought for control, headed remorselessly for the solid trunk of the horse-chestnut directly in front. Meredith released the wheel and threw up her hands to protect her face in what seemed inevitable and imminent collision.

The car jerked, the engine coughed and died. They stopped. She lowered her arms and stared bemusedly through the windscreen. By some miracle she hadn't crashed but come to rest, the car's radiator against the bark of the tree and the whole vehicle tilted upward at a perilous angle.

Automatically she reached for the handbrake. It seemed very quiet all around, even the noise of the sheep had receded. Suddenly the door on her side was wrenched open, the dark outline of a man's head and shoulders filled the gap, blotting out daylight, and his voice rasped, 'Are you all right?'

Meredith turned her head and gave a startled squawk, finding her face only inches from that of the questioner. Grey eyes in an uncompromising weather-tanned face glared at her but her attention was chiefly taken by an amazing shock of red hair.

'Yes, thanks!' she faltered. Pulling herself together, she added more steadily but with a note of anxiety, 'I hope I didn't hit any sheep!'

'No. But I thought you were going to smash yourself on that old tree.' He backed his shoulders out of the car as he spoke and straightened up.

Meredith leaned out to ascertain her situation and

found herself staring down at his gumbooted feet. She looked up and met the grey eyes again. 'I think,' she began shrilly and then, overcompensating, went on in a contralto, 'I can back down on to the road once the sheep are out of the way.'

'Hold on,' he advised, 'I'll get the dog to send the first lot back.'

He jumped down the bank, a hulking figure in an old sweater, red hair glowing in the sun. She heard him whistle shrill commands and the sheep began to bleat more furiously and to scurry to and fro. From time to time between their woolly bodies she glimpsed a flash of black and white.

The shepherd was now shouting to her and beckoning. ''Tis all right. Let the brake out and you'll just slip backwards. Road is clear! Gently, now!'

Meredith released the handbrake but nothing happened. She switched on the engine, put the car into reverse and cautiously tried again. Nothing. 'Damn it, I'm stuck!' she exploded. 'Ruddy sheep!'

Her words floated through the open window. He came back, stooping by the door to speak to her. 'I'll push you free.'

'No, I'll think of something!' she snapped.

'You'll stay there all bloody day just thinking about it!' he retorted. 'I'll either give the car a shove now or leave you here, just as you please.'

To add to her annoyance he didn't give her a chance to express her pleasure in the matter, but taking his argument as won, walked round to the front of the car and put his brawny shoulder to the task. His jaw set grimly and the veins on his neck swelled like cords in the effort.

'Don't blame me if you rupture something!' she muttered.

He must have had sharp ears, because he glanced up and gave her a distinctly old-fashioned look through the windscreen.

The car rocked and suddenly began to roll backwards. In the nick of time she managed to control her rearward descent and arrived back on the road facing the right way and intact.

The sheep, sensing all was well again, flowed back, pressing against the car and setting up a chorus of plaintive and aggrieved bleats. She turned off the engine and got out with some difficulty to stand among them. They surrounded her, fixing her with glassy-eyed curiosity. Sheep, she reflected, were not nearly so daft as they were supposed to be. There was something crafty and feral in those china eyes and they were showing themselves to be surprisingly athletic. One had just jumped nimbly on to and then over a low stone wall on the other side of the road.

He was back and accompanied now by the evilest-looking sheepdog she'd ever seen. It ran up to her giving her a wicked look, cringing as it did in an attitude of false servitude, a Uriah Heep of a dog. He ordered it away and it sidled off looking malicious.

'Thank you for your help,' Meredith said, determined to put the matter in its right perspective. 'And I'm glad I didn't run over any sheep, but it wasn't my fault. It's very dangerous to block the road like that.'

'No one said as 'twas down to you. But this is farming country and no one uses this old road much nowadays. You want to drive a bit more careful and slow.'

'I wasn't going fast!'

'You headed for Bamford?' He scowled at her, large and pugnacious. 'New motorway is quicker.'

Meredith bristled and glowered back. 'Look, you might farm around here but you don't own the public highway and I had a fancy to drive in the country. I've driven down from London and I've had enough of motorways.'

'London, eh?' The red-haired giant's aggression faded and for a moment he sounded almost wistful. He began to stare at her again, openly appraising her and making her feel more than a little uncomfortable. When he had made a careful note of her whole appearance from head to toe, he said, 'You'll be some sort of high-powered businesswoman then, would you?'

Startled, she exclaimed, 'No, I'm a civil servant!'

'Oh?' Suspicion entered the grey eyes.

'I'm nothing to do with the Min. of Ag. and Fish!' she expostulated, nettled by the scrutiny and quizzing. 'I haven't come to check whether you're exceeding your EEC quotas! I've come for a short holiday. Okay by you?'

She thought she might receive an ear-tingling reply, but instead he smiled quite pleasantly. 'Do as you please, 'tis no business of mine. I wouldn't mind if it was!' he added disconcertingly.

This unexpected expression of rustic gallantry silenced Meredith rather more effectively than a robust retort would have done.

'You'll find Bamford a bit quiet after London, won't you?' he was asking.

'I doubt it!' she said starchily, recovering.

'Oh, centre of the universe, is Bamford.' He too could be sarcastic.

He was also unsettling with his abrupt changes of tone and the amused challenge held by his grey eyes.

'I know Bamford already. I've lived in the area before, very briefly.'

'Oh yes? Couldn't wait to get away, I dare say?'

She didn't know whether he was joking or jeering. 'I liked it very much. It just was difficult for me, getting up to London and back every day.'

'I see. Well, enjoy your visit, then!'

He whistled to the evil-looking dog and walked away. His woolly charges had taken advantage of the lull to spread out and start grazing on the verges but the dog soon put paid to that and it slithered over the wall and brought back the wanderer too. Meredith felt sorry for the sheep with that wolfish-looking dog running round them. She supposed it must be well trained and reliable though. She started up the engine. As she did, she glanced in the mirror and saw behind her, the girl on the roan pony had caught up and had stopped to exchange a word with the red-haired shepherd. As she watched, he reached up a huge paw to pat the pony's neck. The scene: sheep, pony, girl, budding hedgerows and handsome shepherd looked a perfect rural idyll. Even the shifty dog looked right. Perhaps she'd been wrong to imagine that wistful note in the shepherd's voice at the mention of London. He was better off leading the life he had, anyway. Meredith drove on.

'I've never tracked you to your lair before!'

She'd asked for Chief Inspector Markby at the desk downstairs and halfway up the stairs, escorted by a young constable, had met Alan running down to meet her. They grinned at one another. Alan, she thought, looked well if a little tired. He also looked delighted to see her and she knew the delight was unforced. That was both flattering and unnerving.

'You don't generally find me in it on a Saturday and I'm not going to spend the whole weekend here, never fear!' he said firmly. 'Good drive down?'

'Yes, thanks.'

They smiled again at one another in pleasure and then both looked away furtively as if each were afraid the other might misinterpret the pleasure as being more than friendly.

'I thought I'd come in this morning and try to shift the paperwork,' Markby said. 'So as to have a bit more free time during the week. But then someone rang me and asked if she could come and have a word. She's here now, but she's just going and then I'll hunt out Laura's key for you and come with you to the house. Perhaps you'd like to meet her, my visitor? I think you'd like her.'

He ushered her the rest of the way upstairs and into his office. An untidy elderly lady with a cottage-loaf hairstyle and a vast tent-like tweed skirt was just gathering herself up ready to depart.

'Didn't mean to take up your time, Alan!' she boomed.

'You haven't – that is, you were right to come in and tell me about it. I'd like you to meet a friend of mine – and of Laura's – Meredith Mitchell. She's come down to take care of Laura's house while the family's on holiday. This is Mrs Carmody, Meredith, from Witchett Farm.'

'Nice to meet you, my dear!' said Mrs Carmody,

giving Meredith a smile and a shrewd look. 'You must come out to Witchett while you're here if you've nothing better to do and Alan's working. Come to tea.'

'Thank you,' Meredith said.

'I'll be out there this afternoon sometime,' Alan said to Mrs Carmody. 'And take a look. Don't move anything, will you?'

'Haven't touched a thing. It's just as I found it this morning.' She paused. 'I don't want to interfere but so long as you're going to come to the farm this afternoon, why don't you bring Miss Mitchell along with you? You can take a look and then we'll have a spot of tea.'

'Well—' he glanced at Meredith in a way which seemed to be meaningful.

'It's very kind,' said Meredith a little at a loss and not sure what he wanted her to reply. 'It – um – depends on Alan, if Alan is making an official visit . . .'

Markby suddenly said, 'How about if you went out to the farm ahead of me, Meredith? After lunch. I'll come along later when I've finished here and Mrs Carmody can revive us both with tea and her very good cake?'

So it was arranged. Mrs Carmody gave instructions for reaching Witchett Farm and left. Markby hunted out Laura's keys and they went downstairs. 'I'll be back after lunch!' he told the desk.

'What's going on at Witchett Farm?' she asked bluntly as they drove to Laura's in Meredith's car.

'I'll explain over lunch. Paul says he's left the freezer stocked and all we've – you've – got to do is stick things in the microwave.'

'Paul obviously remembers what a duffer I am in the kitchen!'

'They're very grateful, Laura and Paul, that you've come down. And so am I – I mean, I'd have to trail over here and check out the place. I've got a new greenhouse now and what little spare time I've got – I hope you'll come and see it, my greenhouse.'

'Love to. What will you grow?'

'I hope, tomatoes. I thought next year I'd try cucumbers and perhaps eventually a grapevine. A few flowers too, of course.'

A far-away look had entered his eyes and Meredith repressed a smile.

She remembered the Danbys' house well and felt a glow of pleasure at seeing it again. It was a detached, red-brick Thirties-built family home. The front garden was tidy but not immaculate and contained old-fashioned plants such as hydrangea behind a hedge of laurel. The back garden, viewed from the kitchen windows, revealed a child's swing and a sandpit prudently covered over with a wooden lid to keep cats away. A more recently constructed patio area had bright modern garden furniture and a brick-built barbecue stand.

A home, not just a house, thought Meredith. She had been very slightly apprehensive at the thought of being responsible for it for the whole next ten days, but now that she was here, she knew this mellow building was set to welcome her in its amiable way. A glance into the drawing room as they passed allowed a glimpse of cretonne-covered chairs. The watercolour sea-scapes Paul Danby collected hung haphazardly on the walls at eye-level, here in groups, here singly, as Paul fancied. Photographs of the children at all stages littered the shelves and tables and Laura's tapestry frame stood in one corner with a half-worked scene on it. Meredith saw that in the four months since the previous Christmas it had progressed about a square inch.

The kitchen held its own welcome and a delightful surprise in a huge vase of spring flowers on the table with a letter from Laura propped against it. As Meredith admired purple iris and golden daffodils, mauve and rose-pink freesia and scarlet tulips, Markby was pulling out drawers and opening cupboards as he set a table for lunch. Meredith wrenched herself from the flowers and turned her mind resolutely to food.

Paul had stocked the freezer all right, to the brim. Layer upon layer of neat silver bricks lay before them. 'Crumbs!' said Meredith in awe. 'Or rather, not crumbs but *cordon-bleu* delights! I'll put pounds on! What do you want for lunch?'

'Don't mind. What's that packet there?'

'I don't know. The label's come off . . .' Meredith picked up another foil-wrapped block. 'The label's come off this one, too.'

For a minute or two they hunted silently through the freezer.

'I've a strong suspicion,' said Markby, 'that Paul let one of the kids help him with the labelling. This, I fancy, is my niece's handwriting. That's probably why so many labels have come off.'

'Fair enough. Saves the hassle of decision. We'll have this.'

It turned out to be steak and kidney casserole.

'So tell me about Mrs Carmody and the Mystery of Witchett Farm,' she invited when the meal had got underway.

'Oh that, sorry to mention it at table, but it starts with a body.' He explained about the discovery of the dead man, the failure to identify him and his visits to Greyladies and to Witchett Farms.

'The only lead I've got – if lead it be – is that the Thursday before the discovery of the body, which if our deduction of the time of the murder is right means the night before the murder took place, Mrs Carmody disturbed an intruder. She didn't see him properly and she thought he hadn't had time actually to get into any of the buildings. She doesn't farm any more as such, you understand. She leases out the land for grazing and she lets a few horse-owners stable their animals there. Most of the buildings in the farmyard are unused now. She doesn't go into some of them for weeks on end. But yesterday she went up into an old hayloft and saw signs of someone having been up there. She thought perhaps it was the man she'd disturbed so she came to tell me. I said, I'd call out there this afternoon.'

'Why were you so keen for me to go out there first, ahead of you?'

Markby put down his wine glass. 'I could see you were thinking that one out. The fact is – and I don't quite know how to put this – but I find it difficult to make inquiries at the farms, especially Greyladies and even Witchett. I could send Pearce of course or a wpc, but I've known these people all my life and I owe them the courtesy of going myself. But at Greyladies they already have enough troubles without me barging in and even Dolly Carmody is rather a lonely sad figure, even though she doesn't look it. I thought you – I mean you're good at dealing with people and I thought you might chat to Mrs Carmody and if I could get you over to Greyladies somehow, talk to them. I can't get any trace on this dead chap, you see. Not even after a week. It's worrying and it's dashed odd.'

'He didn't have any scars or anything?'

'Old appendix.'

'Teeth?'

'You have to be able to make a guess at identity first to turn up the records, then you can confirm or not. This fellow has a mouthful of gold teeth but I wouldn't have a clue who his dentist was.'

'Gold teeth?' Meredith said in surprise. 'You mean, he's – he was – a foreigner?'

He stared at her. 'Why do you say that?'

'Oh, come on, how many English people have gold teeth? Not many. But on the continent they're quite common, especially in some countries. Wherever there's a strong peasant culture you get gold teeth. One way of carrying your life savings around on you.'

'Foreign . . .' Markby muttered. 'You know, something about the bloke has been worrying me. That could be it. He looked foreign. Trouble with a dead man is, looks can mislead you. But yes, why not? If he were a foreigner, a visitor . . . no wonder no one has reported him missing!'

'What about his passport, clothes, perhaps a car?'

'Haven't turned up. That's another thing. Naked as a jaybird but if someone really wanted all his valuables, if it was that sort of motive, they could have knocked his teeth out if they'd been minded to! As you say, a set of gold teeth represents a fair amount of cash, if you extract them and melt the gold down.'

'It really is grim,' she said after a pause.

'Yes, it is.' He hadn't told her yet that the victim

had been buried alive. It wasn't much of a lunchtime conversation as it was and considering he hadn't seen her since the end of January . . .

'I don't want,' he said earnestly, 'to spend all your time here talking about bodies.'

'Neither do I, really.' They smiled at one another again in a way which, Meredith thought, was getting to be a habit, one that needed watching!

'Look,' he said, consulting his wristwatch. 'I must go back. I've a couple of things to do. I'll see you around four o'clock at Witchett Farm. Sure you understand how to get there?'

Chapter Seven

'Ah, there you are, my dear!' greeted Mrs Carmody as Meredith parked and got out of her car. 'Nice and early, good girl! Didn't have any trouble finding me, then?'

'No – you'd given excellent instructions and Alan repeated them half a dozen times over lunch.'

She had also managed this trip without ending up stuck on a bank, she reflected. She hadn't told Alan of her earlier mishap. She didn't think he was the sort who made stupid cracks about women driving, but it wasn't the sort of episode which showed her at her calmest and most competent. The memory of her red-haired rescuer's off-hand gallantry niggled. She wished now she'd made more of a fuss about his wretched sheep causing a hazard to motorists. Yet somehow, in a strange way she couldn't quite fathom, there had been something oddly vulnerable about him for all his truculence. 'London . . .' he'd said, so wistfully. Aloud to Mrs Carmody she said, 'It's very kind of you to invite me.'

'Nonsense!' said the old lady robustly. 'Come along, I'll show you round the place.'

It was certainly the tidiest farmyard Meredith had

ever seen. Only the stable to the right showed a scattering of straw and hoofprints in the dust, and a faint warm acrid odour indicated it had recently been used, though it was empty of occupants just now.

'Not my horses,' said Mrs Carmody. 'Other people keep them here, three of them and being a Saturday, all of them are out. Surprising how many town folk want to keep a horse. If the word gets round you've got spare stabling or grazing, you get inundated with inquiries. I can't manage more than three or four because during the day I look after them together with Jess Winthrop from Greyladies Farm. She rides over and helps out. Nice girl, Jess.' Mrs Carmody paused perhaps for breath, perhaps to decide whether or not to confide in her visitor. 'The truth is that the reason I let folk keep their beasts here is because it makes the place still seem a bit alive. Looking at it now, you can't imagine what it was like when it was a working farm.' She sighed. 'We never had children, my husband and I, and who'd have thought he'd have gone early to his grave. Big healthy fellow he was and neither of us expected – he was only fifty-seven. Heart, you know. I carried on for a couple of years but it was too much for me. Anyhow, so long as there's a few animals around the place and a few people, it's not so bad.'

She finished her speech on a robust note. But Meredith understood what Alan had meant. An indomitable and realistic old lady, but a lonely and sad one too. It must break her heart to see the farm more or less idle, but to sell up and leave would be worse. All the buildings were immaculately maintained. Under the eaves of an open hangar old farm machinery was parked in neat rows, some of it under tarpaulins. A couple of chickens scratched about under the eye of a vainglorious cockerel. It was very quiet everywhere. She didn't quite know how to raise the matter of Mrs Carmody's intruder but in the event, Mrs Carmody got round to it herself.

'The reason I went in to see Alan this morning was about the hayloft.' She pointed up to an opening high under the eaves of the stable block. 'We don't use it now, not for hay. What little bit of hay we need for the horses is over there in that barn. I've got a few old bits and pieces stored up in that loft there and I don't suppose I go up there once in three or four months. I don't know if Alan told you, but I had a fellow hanging round the place one night recently. I scared him off. I thought at the time he hadn't got in anywhere. But this morning I went up in the loft, first time for, oh, ages as I said. I thought I might clear some of the stuff out. It might as well go as sit up there. I had a chap come round about six months ago asking about old farm implements, harness, anything. Dealer he was, liked antiques, only more practical things, and it seems people will buy almost any old thing nowadays. I told him I didn't want to be bothered at the time but then I thought, well, might as well.' Mrs Carmody paused for breath. 'But I'm getting off the point.'

Meredith started guiltily. She must have let her impatience show.

'I'll show you what I mean,' said Mrs Carmody, setting off towards the stable.

'Oughtn't we to wait for Alan?'

'We won't touch anything. I'll just show you. See what you think.'

The hayloft was reached by a wooden ladder which

Meredith hoped was secure because Mrs Carmody was
no lightweight. She climbed up cautiously behind her
hostess and they emerged, Mrs Carmody puffing, at the
top into the loft itself. It ran the length of the building
and was dimly lit by openings in the front wall out of
which hay had once been forked down to the yard
below. The old harness and farm implements which
had taken the dealer's eye were arrayed on pegs on the
facing, blind wall and at the far end was a stack of tea-
chests.

'Now then, you see what I mean,' said Mrs Carmody.
'That lot there, those are my footprints as I walked
down to see what had gone on. That lot there – ' she
pointed to another set of footprints on the dusty floor,
'the bigger set, those are his. Whoever he was. I was
careful not to step on top of them.'

Meredith moved carefully forward. Beneath her feet
the wooden planks creaked ominously. Several had
warped with age and one or two bounced beneath her
weight, opening up cracks in the floor which let her see
straight down into the loose-boxes beneath. Someone
had been up here all right, recently. He'd searched. For
what? The tea-chests had all been pulled out, leaving
scraped trails in the dust. The tops had been prised off
and inefficiently, probably hastily, replaced.

'I reckon,' said Mrs Carmody behind her, 'it was
him, the fellow I chased off that night. But if he was
just looking for a place to sleep, why go ferreting
around in those old boxes? What did he think he was
going to find?'

'This dealer.' Meredith turned back. 'You don't
think he – or an associate of his – came back to take a
look while you were, as he thought, asleep. It does

happen. He came once openly, saw one or two things which interested him and thought there might be more, more valuable things. What's in the tea-chests? Sorry, don't mean to be nosy!' she added hastily.

'Bless you, dear. It's mostly old pots and pans and stuff, bits of china – but not valuable. Old, certainly, some of it. It was my mother's. She used to make jams and cheeses and her own sausages as folk did then. There's the old kitchen cream-maker in there, you ever seen one of those? Got a big handle you pump up and down. You put fresh unsalted butter in the top and the thick Jersey milk and away you go, cream comes out the bottom. They didn't worry about germs in those days. Didn't worry about calories, either! All kinds of bits and pieces like that you'll find in those tea-chests. The old flat irons that you heated on the stove. Got wooden handles that slip on and off. Some of the irons are hollow and you put the hot coals inside. Weight of them near broke your wrist. You had to be strong in those days. Most modern women wouldn't be able to work with any of those gadgets for five minutes. But in those days, you see, they were the height of sophistication!' Mrs Carmody's hearty laugh boomed out. 'The housewife's friend!'

'I'm sure a dealer would be interested.'

'Well, one was, my dear. I told you.'

'Yes – but not all of them are, well, completely straightforward. You see, he may have thought the china was really valuable, just as an example. But if you didn't know that, he might not want to tell you. That way he could offer you a price for the lot, take it away and resell at a vast profit. But he'd like to see what there was first. Did he, this dealer, try to get into the house? I don't mean the other night when you disturbed the prowler. I mean, when he came openly about the farm implements.'

'Oh yes, he did that,' said Mrs Carmody. 'But I wasn't having any. He kept sidling off towards the windows thinking to take a peek in, I dare say.'

I bet, thought Meredith, he's been out here and done that one day when she's been away from the farm, in town.

'Well, anyway,' said Mrs Carmody placidly. 'I thought I'd tell Alan. Seeing as he was so keen to know anything unusual that had happened.'

They climbed cautiously back down the wooden ladder. As they reached the bottom hoofbeats were heard outside.

'Sounds like one of your lodgers coming back!' said Meredith with a smile.

Mrs Carmody went outside and Meredith heard her say, 'Oh, Jess – it's you!'

There was a murmur of voices and Meredith, tired of lurking in the stable, walked outside. It was the girl on the roan pony she'd seen on the road that morning. She was sure of it. She was pretty sure, too, that the girl recognised her or had recognised the car parked in the yard.

'Oh, hullo!' Meredith called. 'We meet again!'

The girl blinked and the roan pony snorted as the rider jerked at the reins. 'I've got to be off!' She didn't return Meredith's greeting and looked panic-stricken. 'I'll come tomorrow, Dolly!'

She turned the pony and rode away at a fast clip.

'Sorry!' said Meredith ruefully but puzzled. 'I seem to have frightened her off!'

'Now you mustn't worry about that!' Mrs Carmody reassured her. 'That's only Jessica's way. Once she gets used to seeing you around, she'll be fine. Why don't you come indoors now?'

The fire leapt up merrily in the grate surrounded by snoozing animals as it had been when Markby had been here. Meredith greeted the spaniel and made polite overtures to the cats and sat on the edge of a chintz-covered sofa.

'I like to see a fire. I light it most days,' said Mrs Carmody. 'Excepting when it turns very warm outside, mid-summer. I'll make us a cup of tea while we wait for Alan.'

Alone, Meredith got up and made a hasty but unashamed examination of the room. The brass fender and fire-irons, and that wonderful long Victorian brass toasting-fork hanging by the grate, the copper kettle, that looked very old, perhaps Georgian, yes a dealer would be interested. But would he come back at night when he couldn't see anything through the windows? He wouldn't risk breaking into the house even if he might prowl round the barns and hayloft. It certainly looked as if the nocturnal visitor and the searcher in the hayloft were the same man and tempting to assume that it was the dealer returned. But it would be dangerous to make such an assumption.

Meredith sat down again and one of the cats, a tabby, after studying her thoughtfully, sprang up on to her lap and curled up. She lay back on the cushions and scratched at its ears gently. She didn't like to think of Mrs Carmody out here all alone. Especially not with a murderer on the loose.

The old lady had returned with the tea-tray. The

teapot wasn't silver, it was early Sheffield plate and that too was highly collectable nowadays. Meredith suspected that Mrs Carmody really had no idea how much all these family knick-knacks were worth. After all, she'd lived with them all her life. She'd used them every day and her mother before her. She probably couldn't imagine they had any value. They were just 'old stuff'. She struck Meredith as someone who would appreciate plain speaking. Sometimes the direct approach was best.

'Mrs Carmody!' Meredith said firmly. 'You can tell me to mind my own business if you like and you probably will—'

Mrs Carmody twinkled at her approvingly over the rim of her tea-cup. 'Go on, then, let's see if I do!'

'But I think you ought to get a reputable expert out here, go through the house with him, and get the lot valued properly. You might find a few surprises.'

'I doubt I'd want to sell any of it, if I did.'

'No, but there's the insurance. Your insurers would like to know and, anyway, you should know. In case any more dealers come snooping round.'

'We'll see,' said Mrs Carmody evasively. She wasn't going to discuss this any more.

Meredith recognised the blocking off of that line of conversation and turned to another. 'Jessica, isn't that what you called the girl on the pony? I saw her earlier today. I passed her in my car and a little later I saw her again. I was stopped by a flock of sheep and she caught up. She was talking to the shepherd, he was a big chap with red hair.'

'That's Alwyn Winthrop, her brother,' said Mrs Carmody, nodding.

'Oh, I'm afraid I was imagining a rustic romance! Serves me right!'

Mrs Carmody sighed. 'Be nice if Jess could find herself a follower. There's a big age difference between her and her brothers. Alwyn is the elder and James – you won't meet him because he's left and gone overseas to work somewhere – he's about three years younger than Alwyn. Then when the boys were around twenty or so, Elsie Winthrop surprised us all with another baby. Change of life baby, as they call it. That's young Jess. She was a pretty little thing as a tot but always a bit sickly and nervous. Child of elderly parents, I dare say.'

So was I, thought Meredith. Perhaps we all turn out a bit different.

'Mind you, she was bright enough. Very good at her schoolwork and wanted to be a teacher. She went off to training college and she got a job teaching, too. But she didn't have the toughness for it. You need a strong nerve to teach, especially nowadays! She had a very bad experience . . .'

'Yes . . .' prompted Meredith.

'She was attacked by a pupil. Big lad, not quite twelve years old but built like a much older boy! Some are, you know. He came from a bit of a rough family, lot of violence in the home I dare say. Anyhow, one day he went for poor Jess with a pair of those scissors they have for cutting out paper shapes and so on in school. Only blunt but all the same, depends where you get jabbed with them! She had to fight him off, quite literally! She pushed him away in the end and he lost his balance and hit his head on a chair. Of course then, as you can imagine, there was an inquiry! The boy's family smelled money! They came claiming Jess had attacked him, not the other way around, and that he was worse hurt than he was. It was a very nasty business and got into court. Jess was cleared. Everyone knew the boy's background! But all the same, a kind of slur sticks after a thing like that. You never leave court quite unpunished, you know, even if you're innocent. Jess knew if she had the misfortune to have it happen again, even after years, there would be some who'd say, twice was too often to be only bad luck. The boy's friends knew that too. They would taunt her, dare her to do anything about it, try to make her lose her temper or push them away just out of fear. It broke her nerve and finished her in teaching. She was ill over it. It was even in the national press and one of the teaching unions got involved. Poor Jessica.'

'I do see. Yes, rotten.'

'So she packed in the teaching and came home to the farm. She's better now. But she's nervous around strangers. I'm fond of Jess. I—' Mrs Carmody fell abruptly silent. Meredith saw her glance round the room. Then the old lady began to drink her tea, her eyes fixed obstinately on her lap.

What's the chance Jessica is Mrs Carmody's heiress? Meredith asked herself. If Mrs Carmody hasn't anyone else yet she doesn't want to sell off any valuables, it could be because they're all left to someone in her will. Jessica comes over most days and helps out. Mrs Carmody's obviously fond of her. I wonder if she imagines Jess might get married one day and come here and restart the farm? Or is my imagination running riot?

'The Winthrops' farm, Greyladies – that's a strange name. Greyfriars I've heard of, but not Greyladies. I suppose it means nuns, an old convent.'

'Oh no, dear. Religious yes, but not that sort.' Mrs Carmody put down her cup. 'It was a sect, very strict, in the eighteenth century. It took hold in the town, in Bamford. But the local vicar and magistrate, the local authorities if you like, they managed to stop them building their own meeting house in the town. So in the end, they built it outside of town on land which is part of Greyladies Farm now. Of a Sunday, people would see them walking to their meeting house across the fields, men first together and the women coming behind, two by two, in their long grey dresses. They didn't hold with bright colours. Course, in that kind of sect there's generally more women than men. Must have looked strange to see them walking over the open fields with their prayerbooks, like a school crocodile! Numbers fell off as the years went by and then the meeting house burned down, must be over a hundred and fifty years ago. It was never rebuilt and there's none left now belonging to the sect. Only the name remains. If you're interested to see the foundations of the meeting house, they're in a field near the farm buildings. Winthrops will be happy to show you if you like. It's just humps and bumps in the ground. But about ten years ago, some fellows came out from Oxford and dug around there. That's how I know so much about the history of the meeting house. But they didn't find anything and haven't been back.' Mrs Carmody reached out for the brass poker and rattled it energetically in the fire. A shower of sparks flew out and the old spaniel moved prudently back. 'They had a burial ground too, those Grey Folk, of their own. But the exact spot would be hard to pin-point now.'

'Oh?'

'There's just the one old map in the library that has it marked on land that belonged to Lonely Farm. But it had gone, oh, even by my grandmother's day. She used to tell tales of how when she was a little girl men ploughing on Lonely Farm would turn up a few bones from time to time. But no one paid much attention. Perhaps that was just a scary tale put out to frighten the children. They liked to frighten the children in those days. Thought it did them good somehow! There was never anything to mark the exact site because the Grey Folk didn't believe in putting up headstones, you see. They had some idea of returning to the earth completely, dust to dust, not leaving a trace where they'd been. Of course, Lonely Farm itself is gone now. That's where they're building the houses and found the poor murdered fellow.'

'Oh, yes, Alan said . . .'

'Nasty,' said Mrs Carmody with sudden vehemence. 'Burying a fellow alive.'

'Alive!' Meredith's cup rattled in her saucer. 'Alan didn't tell me that bit!'

'Didn't want to upset you, very likely.' Mrs Carmody looked apologetic. 'Sorry I let the cat out of the bag!'

'Well, we were having lunch so I dare say he thought it best to keep that bit quiet.'

'Mind you, he'd been knocked about the head, so I read in the local paper. Inquest reckoned he'd been buried unconscious, he wouldn't have known about it.' Mrs Carmody spoke earnestly, obviously hoping to put Meredith's mind at rest. 'Then the inquest was adjourned for police inquiries. They have to do that these days when there's foul play. Unlawful killing, they call it.'

'So whoever buried him might not have known that he was alive.'

'Might not.' The fire rustled as it fell in on itself. 'Just by your feet here, in that coal-scuttle,' said Mrs Carmody. 'Got a bit of wood in it, chopped up ready. Just put a bit on the fire, dear, if you don't mind.'

Meredith obliged. 'It must take you hours to clean all this brass and copper, Mrs Carmody. The fender and fire-irons, the toasting-fork and coal-scuttle, the kettle . . . all those horse brasses on the wall there.'

'My dear, time is what I've got plenty of!' Mrs Carmody indicated the horse brasses. 'I remember when those were on the harness on the horses! When I was a little girl. We employed a carter then. He'd lift me up on one of the big Shire horses and lead it round the yard. Fine animals, the Shires. Very good-natured. They always had the same names, traditional. Rose and Violet – they were the plough team. Blossom was another. And old Major, I remember him. Only had the one eye and you had to be careful not to come up on his blind side or he might swing round – not nasty, just startled. Big beast to go bumping into you, a big Shire gelding like that. In the winter when it was frosty we'd tie sacking over their hooves, like boots, to stop them slipping about. I'm talking now of way back. The heavy horses, they went after the last war. Got tractors in. Not the same but made money sense then. Now I believe they're starting to bring the horses back, but not so much the old English breeds, more these French ones, Percheron and Ardennes.' She paused and added in response to the question she sensed on Meredith's mind, 'I'm seventy-two.'

'It hardly seems possible!' Meredith exclaimed in genuine surprise.

Mrs Carmody smiled. 'Time flies, faster and faster too, as you get older. You've never been married, my dear?'

'No, never.' These old ladies inevitably came to this question sooner or later and Mrs Carmody, not being one to beat about the bush, had come to it straight away. Meredith waited, anticipating the follow-up.

'You and Alan are old friends, I gather?'

She meant, of course, 'close' not 'old'. Meredith said firmly, 'Only friends, nothing more.'

Mrs Carmody ineffectually tucked a few stray strands of hair back into the cottage loaf whence they promptly escaped again. 'Growing old alone is no joke!'

'No one can guarantee they won't find themselves alone!' Meredith pointed out before she could stop herself. Too late realising how tactless she had been, she made a belated attempt to minimise the damage. 'One ought not to marry only for that reason – as a sort of insurance.'

The old lady waved a hand to dismiss Meredith's embarrassment. 'Of course not. My husband didn't think he'd leave me alone here all these years. But all the more reason not to dilly-dally if there is something your heart wants. Seize it now. Tomorrow may be too late.' The noise of a car was heard. 'Here's Alan now,' said Mrs Carmody placidly, rising in a waterfall of tweed and displacing a disgruntled cat. 'Just unhook that old brass toasting-fork and I'll cut some bread and we'll do the old-fashioned toast in front of the fire. It's not the same when you try and toast bread under electric or gas grills. No flavour and it goes hard.'

Meredith watched her go out with some relief.

She must have taken Markby to view the disturbed hayloft because it was some time before voices were heard approaching. Markby came in on his own and threw himself down in an armchair facing Meredith who was now seated holding the toasting-fork like a trident. He grinned.

'Hullo, Britannia! Been chatting to Dolly?'

'Yes, she's very interesting – most of the time!' Meredith heard the starchy note in her voice.

'Ruffled your feathers, did she? She's a plain-speaker. I won't ask what she said. She's making us tea and cutting huge doorsteps of fruit cake.'

'I'll go and give her a hand!' Meredith got hastily to her feet. 'I expect she'd like me to start the toast. Here, hold this—'

He took the trident but reached out with his other hand to halt her. Lowering his voice and glancing at the door he went on, 'We may know soon if there's anything in your idea.'

'My idea? Which one?' she asked surprised.

'About the gold teeth. I've requested that the dead man's description and fingerprints be circulated internationally. If he is a foreigner and if he's on file in any country, we'll soon learn of it.'

'Oh, I see.' Meredith hesitated. 'I've got a couple of other ideas for what they're worth. Not trying to do your job, of course.'

'That'll be a change.'

'Okay, I'll keep them to myself!'

'I'm sure I'd rather know what they were.'

'Right, ask Mrs Carmody to tell you about a dealer in farmyard antiques, agricultural Victoriana, who came here about six months ago.'

'Fine, and the other idea?' he asked sharply.

'I'm not sure what you'll think of this one . . .' He groaned. 'Mrs Carmody has been telling me about the "Grey Folk" as she calls them, that weird religious sect which set up round here in the eighteenth century. Their meeting house was on Greyladies Farm and gave the farm its name.'

'I didn't know that! I thought it might be to do with sheep. Go on.'

'Feelings ran high against them in the 1750s whipped up by the then vicar of Bamford and a local magistrate. Then in the 1840s the meeting house burned down but there are ruins. It would be interesting, don't you think, to write a pamphlet about them? It would mean doing research, asking lots of questions round the farms. For instance, I could try and find the location of their lost burial ground which incidentally appears to have been slap bang in the middle of the new housing estate.'

'Where the body was found?'

'Aptly, yes. A hundred years ago ploughmen were still turning up the odd bone. Perhaps the modern contractors found things too, nothing they would think to mention to the police. Things they dismissed as curiosities, no value or significance. If you're intent on digging a hole and you unearth some piece of junk which doesn't appear worth anything, you chuck it aside and go on digging. The police may,' said Meredith the serpent, 'have lost valuable bits of evidence like that.'

'I do realise it. And you realise, do you,' Markby

110

said slowly, pointing the brass toasting trident at her, 'that the words "historical site" give builders heart attacks?'

'I know that! But I'm not an official of any kind. I'm an amateur. They might tell me things they wouldn't tell you or report to the local museum. Good Lord, I'm trying to trace a two-hundred-year-old cemetery used by Bible-bashing tradesmen, not another Sutton Hoo!'

'They don't know that! Why should they believe you? They wouldn't see it as a reason to go spending all day routing about in mud and asking a lot of tomfool questions.'

'What's to lose?'

He fidgeted and the cat which had been eyeing him as a possible lap to climb on, stalked off in disgust towards the kitchen. The spaniel bitch lay flat before the fire, so close it was a wonder her fur didn't singe, and was uttering small snores.

'I'm against it!' Markby said suddenly in a firm voice and brandishing the trident Neptune-like in judgement. 'Apart from any other consideration, that area is part of a police investigation—'

'That's why I'm clearing it with you first.'

'And what's more, you risk an earful of colourful brickie's abuse! Jerry Hersey, the site foreman, is no respecter of persons, male or female, and not the helpful kind as we've found out. I don't think your being in mufti will make any difference. He'll chuck you off his site.'

'I've dealt with tough characters before and my ears are proof against most bad language.'

He was still shaking his head vehemently. 'They'll claim a problem with their insurance cover and refuse to let you wander round. Hersey himself has an unpleasant disposition, as distinct from being simply rude. If you persisted he wouldn't be above trying to frighten you off. You know the sort of thing, the falling brick which just misses your head or the wheelbarrow which almost crushes your foot.'

'It wouldn't be worse than travelling on the underground in rush hour!' she interrupted with the bitterness of recent memory.

Markby was not deflected from his argument. 'Moreover if you managed to get round all that and, knowing you, I dare say you would manage it somehow, and started chatting up the labourers, then Hersey would smell a rat.'

'Oh blow Hersey! Let me see if I can handle him first, all right?' she argued, annoyed at his assumption that she would lose the confrontation.

'I don't want police investigations screwed up.'

'I'm not going to screw them up. Give me credit for some tact and diplomacy and for not being a complete leaden-footed numbskull!'

He sighed wearily. 'I appreciate you want to help, Meredith, and I know I let myself in for this by asking you to chat to Dolly—'

'And to the Winthrops. Dolly says the Winthrops will be happy to let me inspect the ruins of the meeting house. They lie near the farmhouse.' She paused. 'How can I go wrong? Look, I shan't be asking about the murder. I shall be asking about a set of cranks who'd died out after the 1840s.'

'You'll be asking questions in a sensitive area!'

'Not about the dead man!'

Mrs Carmody's voice could be heard ordering, 'Get

out from under my feet you daft cat, you can have yours later!'

'She's coming!' He leaned forward. 'Now you listen to me, Meredith, I suppose I can't stop you. You'll do it anyway no matter what I say now. But if you come across anything at all which might interest me, you'll tell me straight away and if there's any following up to do, I'll do it, agreed?'

'Yes, of course!' she said virtuously.

Markby growled. 'And if you do start fancying yourself as Supersleuth, just remember this: the Grey Folk are dead and gone. Our gold-toothed corpse is dead if not gone. But they are very much alive and possibly out there!'

'Who?' she asked unthinkingly as Mrs Carmody appeared pushing an aged oak trolley groaning under cake and china.

Markby gave an extra-vigorous jab of the toasting-fork. 'Those who buried our man alive, his murderers!'

Chapter Eight

'Well, there it is,' said Markby, pointing.

Meredith raised her hand to shield her eyes and squinted in the direction he indicated. She saw an irregular jumble of new brick staining the countryside in a wide splash of orange-red.

'Scene of the crime!' she commented.

'You can say that again!' he growled. 'Tearing up good farmland and replacing it with bricks and mortar!' He noticed she was about to protest and went on fiercely, 'And don't tell me the one about people having to live somewhere! I've heard it!'

'I was actually going to quote the one about "not in my back yard!" ' said Meredith mildly.

'I've heard that too. All right, I don't like it happening here because this is my patch that's being ripped out. But I deny I'm being selfish. I don't like it anywhere. Where are today's children going to roam freely and learn how to tell which wild berries are safe to eat and how to make clay cups and saucers from the river bank mud?'

Meredith shrugged, smiling at his bucolic nostalgia.

'I don't know. But I expect in these less than innocent times parents aren't inclined to let their kids roam far from home all day as our parents were happy to do. I have those memories too. My mother used to cut us a packet of Spam sandwiches. I'd set off with a friend and our bikes, stopping at the corner shop to buy a bottle of pop . . .'

'Dragon's Blood!' said Markby sadly. 'Dandelion and Burdock!'

'You're older than me! I can't remember those! But we'd be gone all day and our parents didn't worry about us. But today's parents couldn't allow it. Nor do today's kids want Spam sandwiches. They want hamburgers and fries and all kinds of snacks in lurid packets.'

There was a silence. 'Not the same!' said Markby firmly.

'No, nor should it be. Times change and people change with them!'

He stared at her. 'Steve said that to me. The selfsame words. But why the heck should I change my ideas just to appease other people?'

Meredith said exasperated, 'Of course you shouldn't! But although it's nice that you and I both have happy memories of childhood, we can't wish our experiences on others. Today's kids will have their own memories, different but just as good.'

They fell to contemplating the scene in front of them again.

'It's the scene of the crime in another sense, isn't it?' Meredith asked. 'Isn't this where that poor unfortunate digger operator dug up the body?'

'Yes, it's the scene of the burial part of it. We don't yet know where the actual attack took place,' he replied pedantically. 'But it's where he died, if you care to put it that way.'

They both fell silent at the grisly recollection, probably both comforting themselves with the thought that he was unconscious, probably knew nothing about it.

It was Sunday morning, fine and sunny even if the wind was chilly and necessitated warm clothing. Meredith had tied a scarf, red and blue and patterned with yellow horseshoes, over her hair to keep it from flying about and she was wearing the wellingtons she had thoughtfully put in the boot of her car before leaving London. Alan Markby, likewise gumbooted, started forward again, leading the way along a rough footpath across open meadow towards the distant building site.

She trudged along behind, hands shoved in pockets to keep them warm, and reflected that even if the surroundings were sinister by association with an evil deed, they were still preferable to the daily scrummage to and from work in London. On the other hand, if she remained in the countryside for any length of time, she soon found herself itching for a bit more noise and bustle. She supposed it was human nature never to be satisfied. One thing to be admitted about the country, you couldn't say nothing ever happened there. Things happened all the time, some of them definitely weird. She tried to imagine Dolly Carmody's Grey Folk making their sombre and pious way, two by two, across these same fields towards their meeting house. According to Dolly, the sect had buried its dead around here somewhere. Here they stood in all weathers conducting their graveside ceremonies. Finding out more about them was already more than just an excuse for snooping around. Meredith had begun to be really interested in these strange vanished zealots.

As they neared the site she asked, 'The builders have started work again already, have they?'

'Yes, some days ago. But not at the actual scene of the discovery. That's not because we're stopping them. It's because the developers can't make up their minds what to do about the spot and the navvies won't go near it. If they carry on and build a pair of houses there as planned originally, they may have trouble finding buyers for them. A body in the basement isn't much of a recommendation.'

'People have short memories.'

'Not for gruesome murders, they don't! They remember those for years. The British public loves a nice sensational murder, although not if it means literally living on the site of it. The last I heard there was talk of some sort of mini park being created there. You know, grass it over and stick in a few trees and shrubs, a place for people to walk their dogs.'

'That sounds nicer. More respectful to the dead, anyway. Probably add to the attraction of the estate.'

They had reached the first stack of bricks and here Markby stopped. 'Those are the estate offices over there. That wire compound is where they lock away valuable equipment overnight and at weekends. That's the sales office, those prefabs are the contractor's and site manager's offices and over there somewhere is the show house. That's open all weekend during daylight and someone is on duty in the sales office to show people round it.'

'So the murderers couldn't have buried him during daylight. Someone might have seen them.'

'The sales office is manned, or rather womanned, from ten in the morning until about five-thirty. If the weather's bad the sales rep goes home earlier, about four. People don't come out here to tramp round in the rain and mud. It did rain over that weekend but not continually. She was here on Saturday until after five and on Sunday until about four-fifteen. And of course there are casual wanderers like us. But they certainly buried him either early in the morning or late in the evening. I'm inclined to think early morning. It's the time I'd choose, not least because rigor wouldn't have set in.'

'Wouldn't it still be difficult in poor light? I would have thought climbing down into a trench and digging out a hole, moving the body and covering it over so that no one would notice, you'd need to see what you were doing and it would take time.'

'It would take more than one grave-digger. But if they knew what they were doing and were fairly handy, I don't think it would be that difficult. Exhumations have to be completed in the early hours. I've stood shivering at dawn by a few opened graves in my time.'

'Thanks for the grisly detail, Dr Frankenstein. "Knew what they were doing" you said. You mean, they'd done it before? Is this a gangland killing? Out here?'

'The body could have been brought a long way and thanks to our modern motorways, in a reasonably short time. If he was a local man he'd have been identified by now. I'm not ruling anything out.'

They were standing by the spot itself now. It was still surrounded by police tape and notices, flapping disconsolately and abandoned in the wind. A withered bunch of primroses lay amid the other débris highlighting for Meredith the sadness of the scene. The surrounding mud was heavily churned up and down in the bottom of the trench the fresh excavation begun by Sean Daley came to a sinister and sudden halt. She shivered. 'Creepy.'

Markby was staring down at the excavation, scowling. 'I find it ruddy annoying. He might as well have dropped from the sky. We still don't know a thing about him and haven't even found his clothes. We've appealed to the public, dog walkers and ramblers especially, to keep their eyes open. Not a thing.'

They walked a little further and sat down on a low wall. They had been joined on the site by two other people, a very young couple who smiled nervously at Markby and Meredith as they exchanged greetings. The girl wore unsuitable high heels and tottered uncertainly over the rough ground, clinging to the young man's hand.

'Prospective buyers looking the place over,' said Markby when the young couple had moved on. 'Newlyweds, I bet.'

'Yes,' said Meredith suddenly. 'I can understand not wanting to buy a house with a ghost in the foundations as your first home!'

'First home . . .' murmured her companion and fell silent.

She glanced at him curiously. 'When you were married to Rachel, did you and she live here in Bamford?'

This, she knew, was sticking out her neck, really pushing her luck. He hardly ever mentioned his marriage. She'd often been curious about it.

He was shaking his head. 'No, Rachel and I bought a

great white elephant of a place in the West Country. Her idea, of course! What did we want with five bedrooms and three reception? All of it falling to bits, I may add, which meant it didn't cost that much to buy, relatively speaking. But it did cost a fortune to renovate, to say nothing of heat and decoration generally, and furniture! The roof had a leaky gable at one end and we spent our entire married life trying to get it fixed. We never did. All the electrical wiring had to be redone to avoid the whole place going up in flames as soon as anyone plugged in a toaster. And it had bats!' A moment's moody silence, then he added in regained enthusiasm, 'But it had a wonderful big old garden including a proper brick-walled kitchen garden with espalier fruit trees!'

'Aha!' said Meredith. 'So deciding on that house was not all Rachel's idea!'

'I admit I did fancy the garden, only I never got the time to do it because I spent all my time crawling round the attics with buckets and bats in my hair! Well, after we split up I came back here. Laura and Paul had just got married and settled here and I was offered the chance of a job with the Bamford force. So I thought, why not go back to where I grew up? Only look what they've done to it!' he added bitterly, sweeping his arm out in a large gesture. 'Incidentally you'll probably meet Steve Wetherall, the architect. He's a pretty unhappy man at the moment. He was there when the body was unearthed and now the building is held up. Poor old Steve.'

Markby kicked at a lump of broken brick by his foot, sending it rolling away. He hunched his shoulders. 'Enough of me and the past. What about you and the future? No hopes of a posting abroad, then? Or so I gather.'

'Not a chance, not for the foreseeable future.' She hesitated and added with unconvincing nonchalance, 'I might give it eighteen months or so and then if there's still no prospect of going abroad, well, maybe I'll look for something else.'

He was staring at her in disbelief. 'Give up the FO? I never thought I'd hear the words from you, Miss Mitchell!'

'I never thought you'd hear them either,' she admitted ruefully. 'But you know how it is. All good things come to an end and I've had a good run with them. Perhaps the time has come for me to look elsewhere, outside the FO. Don't ask me what or where. I don't know.'

He was silent for so long that she asked, 'Do say what's on your mind. You know I'd much rather you did.'

The young couple were coming out of the sales office, still linked like Siamese twins, and clasping a sheaf of papers apiece. They were accompanied by a trim young woman in a blue suit. All three disappeared into one of the completed houses above which a flag fluttered bearing the name and logo of the development company.

'Visiting the show house,' said Markby gloomily. 'Look, if you want me to be absolutely honest and selfish, then I've got to say, of course I'd like you to give up travelling abroad and stay in this country. But I also know that if you did make such a decision and it turned out you were absolutely miserable and longing to let your wandering feet take you far away to some exotic spot, that wouldn't be any good.'

Meredith shook her head. The knot of her scarf had slipped so she took it off. The wind seized her hair and sent it flying across her face. She scraped it back from her eyes. 'Perhaps I've gipsy blood,' she said with a sigh. 'Whether I was miserable would depend on what I found to do as an alternative.'

This time when he didn't answer she didn't ask him to speak his mind. At last he broke the awkward silence by getting up and holding out his hand to help her to her feet. 'Come on, you'll get a numb backside sitting on that wall. Let's go and find some lunch.'

By Monday morning Meredith was getting used to living in Laura's house. She no longer felt the impulse to tiptoe about everywhere and the need to straighten up every cushion after she'd sat in a chair for five minutes. The house was beginning to look more as if it, too, was used to having her around. The kitchen was still a daunting place because it was equipped for Paul's benefit with every kind of culinary device. Meredith hadn't a clue what half the gadgets were for. She was strictly a grill and tin-opener cook and was cracking eggs to scramble for breakfast, about the limit of her skills, when there came a knock at the back door.

'Anyone home?' called a woman's voice.

'Hang on!' Meredith replied, hastily putting the eggs in a bowl. She wiped her hands and opened the door. A young woman wearing a pink jogging suit stood there holding a box. Her white-blonde hair was secured in two bunches by coloured plastic slides and stuck out one bunch on either side of her head like two hanks of flax.

'Hi!' she said brightly, 'I'm Susie Hayman, next door neighbour.'

Hayman . . . Meredith rooted about in her memory. Laura's letter of general information left for her to read had mentioned the Haymans. They were Americans; Ken Hayman was posted to the USAF base about ten miles away. 'Come in,' she invited. 'I'm just about to make coffee.'

Susie bustled in and put the box on the table. 'Cupcakes. I thought, well, you might not have time to make anything like that.'

'Not only no time, no talent!' said Meredith promptly. 'Thanks. That's very kind.'

'Well, I feel sort of guilty because we were away at the weekend and not here to welcome you. We went,' she announced breathlessly, 'to Stratford upon Avon! But I did promise Laura I'd keep an eye open for you. You're all settled in?'

'Yes, fine.' Meredith switched on the coffee-maker. 'Now, your husband's here with the airforce, am I right? At the American base?'

'Right, but he's a dentist, not air or ground crew. People always seem kind of surprised when I tell them that. I work up there three mornings a week helping out, mostly clerical, keeping Ken's records up to date, though I was a dental nurse before Ken and I married. Mondays I don't work so here I am.' Susie was balanced on a bar stool with her pink knees together. She looked about sixteen but Meredith supposed she must be at least ten years older than that. She had a round cheerful face and snub nose and no make-up. 'We hope you'll come over and eat dinner with us one day.'

The coffee-machine hissed and Meredith went to

pour out. 'Did Laura tell you I used to live in a cottage near Bamford? Just for a little while. I work in London and the travelling was too much.'

'She told me all about it. She was really pleased you could come down and stay in the house. I'd have kept watch on it but I'm not here all the time. We had burglaries in the neighbourhood recently, quite a few of them. Nothing big, just little break-ins. Ken thought it was probably kids.'

'Did they break into your house?'

'Oh no, and it's not our house, we only rent. We made the agents fix security locks before we moved in. The thieves broke in two doors down, though, and took a radio and a video recorder, and across the street, right opposite. That time they took the television set. Ken says they sell those things in pubs and bars.'

Meredith leaned her elbows on the table interestedly. 'Did you hear of any antiques being stolen at that time?'

'Antiques, no!' Susie blinked her round blue eyes. 'Why?'

'An old lady I was talking to on Saturday had a dealer visit her about six months ago, asking about antiques. He may have been absolutely honest, of course. But sometimes, you know, these people who call at the house, well, you need to be careful.'

Susie was looking thoughtful. 'Laura didn't mention anyone losing antiques. But now you mention it, I remember a guy calling oh, may be four months ago, not quite so long ago as your old lady's visitor. When he realised I was an American, he stopped asking me if I wanted to sell anything and started asking if I wanted to buy. He said if I had any particular interest, he could probably find what I wanted for me. But I'm not really into antiques. I mean, Stratford was really interesting but buying things, that's something else. I don't know anything about them and Ken says if you don't know what you're buying you can get really cheated. They make wonderful fakes nowadays and you'd hardly notice the difference. So I told the guy no. Although Ken is interested in old maps and books. There's a shop in Oxford where he likes to go and I guess before we go home, he'll buy something there. But that's different. It's a regular shop where they have all kinds of things and the man knows all about it and explains to you. And you can tell by the other people there, other customers I mean, that it's really reputable. Someone who comes to your front door, that's not the same, is it?'

'No,' Meredith said. 'Nobody's been recently? You haven't heard about anyone?'

Susie shook her bunches of hair. 'No, why? Has someone complained?'

'No, I just wondered. The old lady I was telling you about, she thought someone may have come back. You know, a prowler, and perhaps he was the same man.'

'A prowler?' Her visitor looked concerned. 'I don't like that. I'll tell Ken. But we have a Neighbourhood Watch Committee, you know, for crime prevention! We're meeting on Thursday night at the house right over the way if you'd like to come along.'

'Thanks, I might.'

Susie slipped off her stool. 'I have to go now. But I meant what I said about coming over for dinner one night. Thanks for the coffee. We'll be seeing you!'

She took herself off, hairbunches bouncing.

Meredith frowned and drummed her fingertips on the table. It really looked as if the antiques dealer had nothing to do with Dolly's nocturnal visitor. Well, she had her own plans for today and sitting here wasn't going to get anything done. She abandoned the eggs. She could have those for lunch. Meredith put them away in the fridge, washed up the cups and, having provided herself with a notebook and pen, set off.

First call was at the library. It took a little while to hunt out the old map which showed the burial ground but the librarian was interested and checked to see if any other material was available. Local histories had little to say on the subject, however, other than that the meeting house burned down in mysterious circumstances in 1842. One book contained a blurred photograph showing some excavations in a field.

'Some archaeologists did excavate a few years back,' the librarian said. 'But they didn't find anything. Perhaps you should try county records or the local museums.'

Meredith made a photocopy of the map and set off again. First stop was at the stationers where she bought an Ordnance Survey map of the area against which to check her map from the library. As she came out she was surprised to observe a familiar figure. It was Jessica Winthrop. She was standing before the window of a dress shop and staring in.

From the part-shelter of the stationers' doorway Meredith studied her. Jessica was still wearing riding breeches, boots and a pullover. But the dress she was studying in the window was a party one, very chic in black with a diamanté spray on the left side of the bodice. Jessica looked wistful and was chewing at her bottom lip.

'Hullo,' said Meredith, hoping she wouldn't startle the girl.

Jessica spun round and her pale face flushed a deep crimson. Alarm leapt into her eyes and she backed away.

'I'm Meredith Mitchell!' Meredith said quickly, wishing this girl wouldn't always react like a startled fawn. 'I was visiting Dolly Carmody the other day when you rode over. It's Jessica, isn't it? Jessica Winthrop.'

'Yes, I remember you,' Jessica mumbled, shuffling her feet. She looked as if she would like to bolt again.

She was quite a pretty girl, viewed closer to hand, but a fixed look of unhappiness had made her appear plain. What she needed, Meredith decided, was some decent clothes and a decent haircut, to say nothing of a sizeable transfusion of self-confidence. She glanced into the window. Perhaps Jessica also realised she could be more attractively dressed.

'That's a very smart dress. It looks like a nice shop. My trouble is I'm so tall, I always have to be very careful what I buy or I look like a maypole!' Meredith volunteered encouragingly.

Jessica gave a fleeting haunted smile and then looked guilty as if smiling was forbidden.

'I believe you help Dolly with the horses?' Meredith pursued with determination. This conversation was all uphill work.

'Yes.'

Obviously the girl was desperate to get away. She was edging her way round Meredith as she spoke and any second now, she'd bolt completely and Meredith couldn't think of any way to stop her. But suddenly a new voice broke in. 'Jess!' it exclaimed.

A sweatered and jeaned young man had stopped beside them. He was staring at Jessica incredulously. 'Yes, it is you! I couldn't believe my eyes! What are you doing here?'

'Michael?' Jessica blinked and before Meredith's eyes became transformed. Her cheeks became pink and her whole face glowed. 'I – I live near here. What are you doing here?'

'Got a teaching job, local primary. I've only been here since the beginning of Spring Term. But this is marvellous!' He turned to Meredith and said belatedly, 'Sorry to interrupt, but Jess and I were at training college together and I really hadn't any idea she lived here. I thought I didn't know anyone in this town.' He was a pleasant-looking young man, not particularly handsome but agreeable and good-natured in appearance. He really did look surprised and delighted.

'I'm just off,' said Meredith quickly. 'Nice to see you, Jessica. I expect I'll see you again at Witchett.' She hurried off down the street but could not resist glancing back. Jessica and the young man were in animated conversation. As Meredith watched, they moved off together, the young man talking nineteen to the dozen and Jessica nodding and looking like a different girl altogether. It seemed as if Jessica's fortunes were about to take a turn for the better. Meredith mentally scratched out her list of things Jessica needed, i.e. clothes and haircut, and substituted 'boyfriend'. Supply the last and the self-confidence would supply itself.

Much cheered by this unexpected turn of events,

Meredith sought out the vicarage and Father Holland. She was hoping the church might have some records relating to the Grey Folk. According to Dolly, the eighteenth-century vicar of Bamford had joined forces with the magistrate and other local bigwigs to turn the town against the sect. There must be some reference to it all somewhere in church papers.

The vicarage was a large Victorian house with an overgrown garden. A youth with close-cropped hair and a spotty face was pushing a motor mower up and down the lawn in an inefficient and bored way. He wore a denim jacket emblazoned with a hand-painted picture of a skull and lightning bolts and the stark legend 'Death Rock!' and a belt made up of spent cartridges. Grass flew this way and that as he ambled along to be trodden down by his Doc Martens' boots. Where he'd been looked if anything more untidy than the area he hadn't yet reached. A large black motorcycle was propped up near the front door of the vicarage itself and every time he drew near to it, the gardener, if that was what he was, cast it a wistful glance. Seeing Meredith, he stopped work in a way which suggested he did so at any opportunity, leaned on the handle of his machine and hailed her.

''Ullo,' he said amiably. 'You lookin' fer the vic?'

'Yes, Father Holland. Is he at home?'

The youth rubbed his nose with a grimy hand. 'Yes. Door's open. You just go in and shout.'

Meredith wasn't quite sure if this was the right way to announce herself, but the door was ajar. She pressed the bell, pushed the door open a little further and cleared her throat noisily.

'In here!' roared a voice from within.

She followed the sound and found herself in an

untidy study. A large man with a black beard and a cassock rose to his feet.

'Ah, good morning! I thought it was just Barry wanting something. I didn't realise it was a proper visitor!'

'Barry? Oh, is that the gardener?'

Father Holland snorted. 'Gardener! Barry? He's doing his community service.' He lowered his voice. 'Barry has a tendency to get into trouble. But he's not a bad lad. Easily led.'

'Oh, I see. My name is Meredith Mitchell. I hope I'm not disturbing you—'

'No, no . . .' He ushered her towards a chair. 'Make yourself comfortable. What can I do for you?'

Meredith explained. Father Holland listened attentively, looked mildly surprised and then interested.

'The Grey Folk, eh? Well, I don't know much about them myself and I don't know where you can find out. Most of the old records were sent off for safe-keeping years ago. I remember reading about the sect, though. They were distinctly odd. They used to go into trances at their meetings and when they came out of them, they were supposed to have had visions and recounted them. Pretty lurid visions, too, if rumour was true. No wonder the church and forces of law and order got rather worried. Sublimated sexual fantasies we'd call them nowadays, I dare say. As a matter of fact,' he paused and got up to scrutinise his bookshelves, 'there is something about them in one of these old histories. Here we are, I fancy it's in this one.' He pulled a venerable leather-bound tome from the shelf and blew dust off it.

'Local history books in the library don't have much to say.'

'The library won't have this one. It was printed in

1880.' The priest was thumbing through the tightly packed pages. 'Ah, here we are, oh, and here's an engraving of the meeting house as it was just before the fire. And oh my, now that is interesting!'

'Yes?' Meredith asked impatiently because he'd started to read the book to himself and showed signs of forgetting her.

Father Holland was recalled to his visitor's presence. 'Some claim was made at the time that the trances were opium-induced.'

'Opium!' exclaimed Meredith.

'Oh well, drug taking of one kind or another isn't all that new.' Father Holland sat down and rested the book on his knees. 'It wasn't on the scale it is now, however.' He sighed. 'Parishioners of mine lost their daughter only recently. Very sad case. She'd run off from home and was living in a squat with others. She died from a heroin overdose. She was a registered addict being prescribed a substitute, but she was obviously getting the real stuff from somewhere. When she was younger she was a choirgirl. She wasn't a tearaway. I think we all feel responsible when a youngster like that goes wrong. We ask ourselves why? What could we have done to prevent it? What did we do that was wrong or inadequate? Why didn't we notice earlier? Now young Barry out there has been in children's homes and council care all his life. You expect problems. But Lindsay had a nice home, loving parents, was bright at school . . .' He sighed. 'A bright young promising life, snuffed out.'

Meredith nodded sympathetically but her eyes were on the book. 'I suppose,' she said tentatively, 'I couldn't borrow that? I would bring it back and take great care of it. I'll give you my address and if you want a reference, Chief Inspector Markby will give you one for me.' Father Holland looked mildly startled and interrogative. 'I mean,' said Meredith hastily, 'he's a friend of mine.'

'Oh, I see.' He glanced at the book. 'Well I don't see why not. I would be glad to have it back. I don't suppose it's been off that shelf for the past year, but there, you never know. Here are you today asking about the Grey Folk and it's come in useful. Someone else might be interested another time. You're hoping to write a pamphlet about them, are you? I'd be interested to see it.'

'If I get enough information.' She took the book gratefully and Father Holland escorted her to the door. The motor mower had fallen silent during their conversation but as the front door was opened to let her out, it sprang into energetic life and Barry was seen steaming determinedly up and down the lawn as if his very life depended on it.

'Seizing the chance of a quick smoke behind the tree there, I bet,' said Father Holland cheerfully. 'Barry has to be supervised.'

'Is that his motorbike?' Meredith glanced at the black monster.

'Oh, no,' said Father Holland. 'That's mine.'

Chapter Nine

Meredith might feel with justification that she had made a good start. Markby felt he was getting nowhere with any of his investigations.

'We've had someone trying out all the usual places,' Pearce said, 'but no luck. Once the word got round that the Hurst girl had died, all the local pushers disappeared. They're lying low and if anyone knows a name, well, no one is going to give it to us! You know how it is, they're scared or they're addicts themselves and need the contact to get a fix.'

'We don't need a couple of miserable small fry,' Markby muttered. 'We need the big boys, the dealers and smugglers of the stuff!'

Pearce hunched his shoulders. His chief sighed and went on to the next subject of inquiry. He held up a folder. 'One file of blank paper on the body in the trench. We know little more about him than when he was dug up by the wretched Daley – another disappearing act!'

'Nobody knows him,' said Pearce philosophically.

It wasn't received well. Markby hissed, 'Of course somebody does or did! He didn't drop out of the sky. We just haven't yet traced a person who can identify him. Legwork! That's what'll do it!'

Pearce opened his mouth to point out that he had already done plenty of that and so had others. But he thought better of it and just picked up the photo of the dead man and gazed at it morosely.

'Right!' said Markby briskly, slapping his palms on the top of his desk. 'Let's start again, from the beginning. That's the way police work is done, going over it again and again. Boring and routine but it gets results in the end so put your mind to it! Either he was killed elsewhere and brought to this area dead to be buried or he came here under his own steam and was killed here. Agreed?'

Pearce agreed.

'Well, go on, then!' Markby urged him irritably. 'Pick holes in it! Take the first scenario. Have we got anything to support it? Is anything against it?'

'Well,' said Pearce cautiously. 'The fact that no one's identified him locally or admits to having seen him, suggests he may have been killed elsewhere and brought here.'

'Why here? Why to that building site? Why that trench?'

Pearce said he didn't know.

'No, neither do I. But it does suggest local knowledge and don't forget your flowers, the bunch of primroses you saw at the spot when you returned to the site to talk to Riordan! I can't see any of those men working down there placing flowers. It suggests to me someone else, someone who knew the man or at least something about him. Both things suggest to me that he came here of his own volition, possibly to see someone, and was killed here in this area by someone local. We don't know why he came or why he was killed. But something brought him. So we dismiss scenario one in favour of scenario two.'

'If he came here looking for something or someone,' said Pearce, 'he could be the fellow Mrs Carmody disturbed on Thursday night.'

'Yes, I wish we could establish that definitely. The intruder still could have been that chap who was interested in buying the old harness and other stuff. If we can't trace our corpse, then perhaps we can trace the antiques dealer! Yes, get on to it from that angle, Pearce! Try Yellow Pages, all the local dealers in antiques or bric-à-brac, particularly the smaller businesses because they are more likely to be the ones out looking for things they can pick up cheaply.'

Pearce reached for the telephone business directory as bid and riffled through its ochre sheets. 'Dozens of 'em!' he groaned.

He got no sympathy. 'So you'd better get started.'

'Yellow,' said Pearce, tapping the open page of the directory. 'I was thinking, sir. Those primroses I saw at the site, you were saying none of the workmen would have put the posy there. But to my mind it's not a man's action at all, it's a woman's.'

Markby rubbed his chin. 'You could be right but that suggests he was more than just visiting the district on speculation, that he had a woman friend here. Confound it! As soon as we come up with one theory, then we think of another one which contradicts it! No, you stick to your job of checking antique dealers, especially the ones who deal more in memorabilia than in high class fine art collectors' items. I'm going down to the railway station.'

Pearce raised his eyebrows questioningly.

'If he came here of his own free will,' said Markby patiently, 'he had transport. No one has yet reported an abandoned car or one which has out-stayed its time in a local carpark by several days. But check that again to make sure. However, I'm betting he didn't have a car. He came by bus or train and of the two, the train is more likely. I'll take our photograph along to Bamford station.'

Bamford railway station had changed little since the 1930s. It was on a mainline but not on that account particularly busy throughout the day. There was a flurry of activity in early morning when the London-bound commuters set off and at mid-morning when the shoppers or sightseers bound for the capital did. A similar buzz of activity occurred in late afternoon and early evening when they all returned. In early afternoon the principal platform had the drowsy, abandoned air of an old-fashioned Western film set. One almost expected to see tumbleweed rolling down the tracks as the hero rode slowly out of the desert sun into town.

Markby was at first alarmed to see that a new intruder on the platform was an automatic ticket-dispenser and he wondered whether the station had become unmanned or, as he privately thought of it, dehumanised. Certainly there was no one in the booking office and no one in the parcels office. The taxi office was occupied by a middle-aged woman reading a magazine. She said Harry would be around somewhere. Markby was relieved to hear it. Harry had been a feature of Bamford station for as long as he could remember and he didn't relish the thought that Harry had been replaced by a metal box.

Sure enough, when he emerged from the taxi office, he saw a uniformed figure ambling down the platform towards him carrying a watering can. He hailed the fellow gardener and explained his purpose. Then he produced his photograph.

Harry put down his watering can and took the little oblong card carefully. 'Hullo there, Mr Markby. I put wallflower seedlings down there last autumn, you can't see them from here. There's a little strip of earth between the platform and the carpark, by the railings. They all come on and are starting to come out. You go down and have a look, wonderful smell, them wallflowers has. Yellow 'uns and rusty-red 'uns. I put 'em there so's folk can see 'em from the train. Pity they can't smell 'em!' Harry screwed up his face as he studied the photo.

'He may,' said Markby, 'have come off the London train.'

'Ah,' said Harry. 'He may at that.'

'You mean, you recognise him?' Could he at last have struck oil?

Harry scratched his head. 'Let's see now. I was taking the tickets at the gate down there, let's see, Tuesday or Wednesday before last. No, Wednesday before last, mid-morning. It's coming back to me. I remember because not too many folk get off the London train mid-morning and even fewer on a Wednesday. Quite a few get on the one going in the other direction from here up to London, but not the one down, if you follow. I know all the regulars. This fellow, he asked me which way to go into town.

139

Must've been a stranger because you can only go across the carpark and turn up left. If you turn right, you ends up in Newman the builder's yard. Yes, I'm pretty sure this was the fellow.'

'Can you remember anything about him at all? Had he a suitcase?'

'No, don't think he did. He had a plastic carrier bag, that's what he had!'

'You can't remember if it had anything written on it?'

Harry grinned broadly. 'Yes, and I'll tell you for why. I got one the same at home. Got it last summer coming back from my holiday. Got my duty-free in it on the boat.'

Markby's heart gave a hop of delight. 'You mean a duty-free bag from a shop on a cross-Channel ferryboat?'

'Ah . . . the missus kept 'un for a souvenir. So's she could show off around town.'

'How about his clothes?'

'Ordinary,' said Harry vaguely. 'Not so's you'd notice 'em. Casual. Clean and tidy.' He paused. 'He had a funny sort of voice.'

'In what way?'

'Spoke funny. He only asked me the one question, how to get into town and I told him and said he couldn't miss it, and then he said thank you, very polite. He spoke sort of careful and through his nose. All the words was separated out, if you know what I mean. Seems to me, he could have been a foreigner. They allus speaks English better than what we do, don't they?'

Bless you, Harry, thought Markby as he left the

station. No automatic ticket dispenser could ever replace you!

Father Holland's old local history book really was a find. Meredith debated whether to go home and read it before she carried her investigations any further. But it numbered two hundred tightly packed pages in small type and started its chronicle in Anglo-Saxon times. Such a formidable work of scholarship deserved time and respectful perusal. Still, she fancied a cup of coffee, so Meredith found a tea-room and whilst she took her elevenses, read rapidly through the chapter on the Grey Folk.

The engraving of the meeting house showed a plain, almost severe, building with sheep grazing outside the door. The writer spent some time speculating on the cause of the final fatal fire. Arson had not been ruled out but there were dire hints at important local names behind it. No investigation had been held.

A mystery then and a mystery now, she thought. Her anorak had sensible square pockets with press-studded flaps and she just managed to squeeze the book in. Nearly lunch-time and possibly a good time to visit the building site.

It took her half an hour walking to reach it from the middle of the town. It was still busy with men working at various points about it. Meredith made her way to the site manager's office and knocked on the door.

She could hear voices on the other side and it was jerked open by a young man in his shirtsleeves. 'Yes?' he asked crossly.

'Sorry,' said Meredith meekly. 'I was looking for the person in charge.'

He stared at her for a moment and then held the door open wider. 'You'd better come in. Can you just hold on a minute?'

Meredith hopped up briskly into the prefabricated building. There were two other people inside. One was a young woman in a blue suit, either the same one she had seen on Sunday in the distance or another similarly employed to demonstrate the amenities of the show house. The other was a tall, gangly, sinewy man in dirty work clothes and a flat cap. He was unshaven and his eyes glared morosely through horn-rimmed spectacles. He had the look of a world-hater.

'It's all right, Jerry,' the young woman was saying in placating tones.

She didn't have much success. 'It's not bloody all right!' growled the man in work clothes. 'It's the worst bloody site I've ever worked on! Not a sodding thing's gone right since I—'

'All right, all right, Jerry!' interrupted the young man with a hunted look at Meredith. 'We'll sort it out later.'

'It's always bloody later!' Jerry Hersey, presumably it was he, turned his paranoid glare on Meredith. 'Who's she?'

'My name is Mitchell!' said Meredith brightly. 'I'm engaged in some historical research.'

Now all three of them stared at her. The girl looked blank, the young man taken aback. Hersey looked furious.

'Snooping! Another one snooping! I've had enough of these buggers! First one, then another! Police—'

'Yes, yes, Jerry!' The young man raised his voice and

142

temporarily succeeded in talking down the truculent foreman. 'I'm not quite sure I understand, Miss Mitchell . . .'

As briefly as possible she explained. 'I've got a photocopy of an old map here, look!' She opened out her folder and hastily spread the copy taken at the library out on the table. 'Here is the burial site, clearly marked. And here . . .' She fumbled at the Ordnance Survey map. 'Look, it does seem to correspond to this area and that is more or less here.'

'More sodding bodies!' yelled Hersey. The walls of the flimsy office seemed to shudder at the force. 'As if it isn't enough to dig up one dead bugger, now this ruddy woman wants us to dig up half a dozen more of them!'

'No, I don't!' said Meredith loudly. 'There won't be any. Well, maybe the odd bone or two. They'll clearly be very old. There might be some remnants of leather shoes or belts, metal buckles, bone or metal buttons . . . that sort of thing. Have any of your men found any items like that?'

'I don't know . . .' began the young man uneasily. 'Of course they have orders to report any unusual finds. I mean, if we found anything of archaeological interest of course we'd stop work at once—'

'Ha!' roared Hersey, literally shaking his fist under Meredith's nose. 'Lot of rubbish! We dig up junk all the time! Worthless! Do you think we can stop work, down tools just like that, every time a navvy digs up a bloody belt buckle?'

'Now, Jerry,' began the young man but was mown down by Hersey's fury.

'You,' said the foreman, jabbing a grimy finger at

Meredith, 'can just clear off! If I catch you hanging round here, your feet won't touch the ground! You got my word on it!'

'Now, Jerry, there's no need . . .'

'You keep quiet and all!' snarled Hersey. 'I'm in charge of the men. I don't want her out there spreading ghost stories, tales of buried bodies . . . By five o'clock tonight there wouldn't be a man left working out there! They'd all have buggered off like that other one!'

There was an uneasy silence.

'Jerry has a point,' said the young man apologetically. 'And there is the question of insurance. A building site is quite a dangerous place. If you fell over something, or down a hole, twisted an ankle for example . . . I think it would be better if you didn't conduct your research here.'

'I'd be very careful!' said Meredith. 'Couldn't I just ask if anyone found anything? I wouldn't mention bodies.'

'Wouldn't need to!' muttered Hersey. 'And who wants to know about cemeteries? Lot of rubbish. She's snooping. She's a journalist, that's what she is . . . off the local rag, most likely.'

'No, I'm not!' said Meredith indignantly. 'I'm a member of HM Diplomatic Service working in London at the Foreign Office, if you must know. And my hobby is – is eighteenth-century religious minorities. I'm writing a pamphlet!'

'If you're writing anything, you're a journalist!' countered Hersey obstinately. 'So you needn't try and spin some other yarn!'

'I think, Miss Mitchell,' said the young man nervously to her in a low voice, 'that we already have trouble enough on this site.' He glanced meaningfully at Hersey, simmering in the background. 'You have probably heard about our murder, I mean, a murder victim being found here. Some of the men are still very upset and they've had to answer police questions. We all have. I'm sorry we can't help you. I doubt anyone found anything such as you described anyway. Attention would have been drawn to it.'

Meredith had no choice but to accept defeat, apologise for having intruded and retreat. Outside the office she stood in the mud, listening to the rumble of voices which had recommenced their three-sided argument within. Then she pressed her lips together, shook back her hair and reflected that as the unpleasant Hersey was occupied in the office for the moment, if she meant to ask any questions, now was the time to do it. She set off purposefully.

To get out of sight of the office would be wise. Meredith turned the corner round a pair of half-finished houses. There she found two men sitting on a plank balanced between two stacks of bricks and eating Cornish pasties washed down with cans of lager.

'Good – good afternoon!' she said brightly, with a quick glance at her watch.

'Hullo, sweetheart!' they responded amiably.

'Nice day.' She debated how to get round to the matter which brought her in the shortest time. 'I'm an amateur historian, local history society.' Meredith was mildly surprised to hear herself speak these words with glib assurance. 'It seems such a shame that all this building takes place so quickly that there's no time to see if there's anything of interest to local historians here. These houses seem to go up overnight.'

'Not on this site,' they said. 'Keep getting stoppages. Unlucky site, this one.' They exchanged meaningful glances and fell silent.

'What I – what we in the local history society are interested in are things you probably wouldn't notice. Just any odd item, the sort of thing you might just toss aside. No one has dug up or come across anything of that nature, I suppose?'

They were eyeing her suspiciously. They exchanged glances again. 'No,' they chorused.

'I'd pay a fiver,' said Meredith firmly, 'for a belt buckle, piece of cloth or a leather shoe. These things are often preserved.'

They looked interested now but regretful. 'Not found anything like that, ducks. But we'll put the word round. If anyone finds anything, he'll stick it to one side and if you come round again in a day or two . . .'

There was a sudden ferocious and familiar roar. 'Oy! You!'

The foreman's gangling form hove into view, arms waving fiercely, face contorted with rage.

There were times when the old adage 'He who fights and runs away, lives to fight another day' was a very sound one.

Meredith fled.

As it seemed prudent to remove herself from the actual site as quickly as possible, she made for the open farmland behind it. Hersey's oaths and imprecations followed her on the breeze, growing fainter as she walked on. Alan had been right to warn her that the foreman was unpleasant. Hersey was also, thought Meredith, almost certainly handy with a shovel and he would know exactly when the footings concrete was to be poured in any of the trenches. It would be very satisfying indeed to tie Hersey into the burial of the unknown man.

She climbed over a stile and made her way across a field in which sheep were grazing. She was no longer quite sure where she was. Bamford lay behind her, Witchett Farm somewhere to the left and so Greyladies was presumably to her right. She must be on land belonging to one of them and the sheep suggested Greyladies. But Mrs Carmody leased land for grazing and it was not unlikely she leased some of it to the Winthrops. Meredith stopped to spread out her Ordnance Survey map and work out her position. The stream which skirted the building site joined a river further over, no more than a mile from where she was at the moment, even less. She folded the map away and walked on.

The ground had become uneven. There were no more animals to be seen and clumps of trees had begun to appear. It was more like heathland than farmland now. She opened a rickety five-barred gate, remembering to shut it before she crossed an overgrown abandoned-looking track and then over another fence. A line of trees, regular as soldiers on parade, indicated a river bank and a little further on, she reached it.

It was a silent, lonely spot. The river ran fairly fast. Green weeds streamed out on the current like drowned Ophelia's hair. Deep pits in the mud at the edge indicated cattle had been down here to drink at some time but it looked like fairly long ago. The imprints had dried. The wind whispered in the treetops and with a sudden flicker of electric blue a kingfisher shot out from the bank and darted across the river and back into bushes which screened the further bank. Meredith turned and looked behind her. The building site was far away, invisible. If Alan walked out this far he would have no cause to complain. Here the countryside looked as if it hadn't been touched for fifty years.

She began to walk alongside the gurgling river. But first appearances were deceptive after all and even here, man had been recently. And as always, where man passed by he left some kind of rubbish behind him. Animals marked with their scent but humans with old supermarket trolleys and abandoned baby-walkers. There was quite a little pile of such delights here but it was largely overgrown with nettle beds and bramble bushes. But by it, much more recently, someone had lit a fire and at least tried to burn the refuse they had taken the trouble to bring all the way out here. Meredith stopped and clicked her tongue disapprovingly. It might, of course, have been gipsies. But the fire had been a fairly large one. A few partly consumed branches lay around the perimeter of the area of grey-black ash and in the centre was a burned out amorphous lump, all that was left of whatever had been destroyed. Meredith picked up one of the branches, longer than the others, reached over the ash and poked curiously at the heap.

It disintegrated in a puff of white dust. She scratched about in the ash and burned topsoil and pulling out the stick studied something caught on the end of it. Grey, wispy, frail . . . it was, or had been, a fragment of cloth.

Meredith felt a prickle run up her spine. Treading carefully she stepped into the ash and began to scrape about slowly and methodically in the very centre of the pile. Suddenly something gleamed, half-hidden in the dirt. She stooped and carefully brushed away ash and soil to reveal a long, thin metallic snake of an object which had survived the flames intact. It was a zip-fastener.

Meredith retreated from the fire, placing her feet in the same prints as she had made already and spread her Ordnance Survey map out on the ground. After a few minutes she was sure of her position and ringed it with a pencil. She had to be able to bring Alan straight here. She had a funny feeling she had stumbled on all that remained of the dead man's clothes.

She stood up, folded her map and glanced to either side. What her map couldn't tell her was which farm-land she stood on. 'Witchett?' she murmured aloud. 'Or Greyladies?'

She had expected congratulations of the highest order on reporting her find to Markby. To her chagrin and considerable annoyance, her news was received with polite thanks and a promise that the police would look into it.

'Well, don't you think it could be all that's left of the clothes you were looking for, the dead man's things?' she demanded impatiently.

'Yes, it might be,' Markby replied with irritating calm.

'Then you might have the decency to look pleased!'

'All right, I, we are pleased.'

'But . . . There is a but, isn't there? Something's put your back up. You have that "we are not amused" look which got Queen Victoria such a dull name.'

'But it has to be checked out carefully. We don't assume things, we prove them, or do our best.' He paused and then burst out, 'And I've had men scouring the countryside for something like this and they should have found it, not you!'

'Aha!' said Meredith smugly and left him muttering to the long-suffering Pearce.

Chapter Ten

The following morning was everything spring ought to be. The sun shone. Nodding yellow trumpets of daffodils splashed vibrant colour on roadside banks. Bushes and trees appeared to have greened up considerably even in the course of the last few days. Thin pale yellow-green catkin tails dangled from hazel boughs and the silver-grey silky cat's paw buds sprouted on pussy willow. Meredith, driving along the narrow road in the direction of Greyladies Farm, felt light-hearted and optimistic.

All this despite a certain misgiving hovering somewhere at the back of her mind about seeing Alwyn Winthrop again. Of course, last time they'd met she hadn't known who he was. Knowing now meant going to Greyladies was on the one hand easier and on the other hand slightly trickier. Alwyn might not be there which would obviate any embarrassment. He might be out with his sheep. Whatever happened to Bo-Peep? she wondered, picturing his massive figure. Were there ever real milkmaids and shepherdesses such as those depicted in nursery-rhyme books? Probably not. Those were the creation of Marie-Antoinette and her bored ladies. Reality had always been far more workaday.

But despite any reservations, she found she was still quite looking forward to seeing Alwyn again and hoped he would be there, if only to enjoy the surprise on his face when she appeared on his doorstep.

The sight of Greyladies farmyard put a minor blight on her blithe mood. It seemed to be deserted. There were not even any sheep in the barn as described by Alan. Presumably those had all been sent to market. Meredith left the car and after a brief glance into out-buildings advanced to knock at the door of the house. The sound echoed hollowly within as always in an empty building. The place was like the *Marie Celeste*. No Alwyn. No anyone. Where were they all?

She took one last frustrated glance at the façade. The house was old and up there, between the central windows on the first floor was a weathered plaque with crudely intertwined lettering she at first read as MW 1692, assuming the W to stand for Winthrop. But then she realised that they must be WM, for William and Mary, in whose reign the building had been completed. This made the building something more than just a farmhouse. Built a mere four years after the 'Glorious Revolution' of 1688 when William of Orange had landed in the West Country and driven out Catholic James, this solid old building had been marked not only with its date but with its owner's declaration for the Protestant cause. In those troubled times it had been wise to show you were on the right, i.e., the winning side.

Meredith turned to go back to her car. As she reached it she heard a whistle and a shout and saw Alwyn striding towards her across a paddock, the shifty-looking dog at his heels.

'Good morning!' he hailed her as he came up. 'Can I help?'

He was wearing muddy cords and gumboots and a Fair-Isle sweater which had seen better days, similar to the one he'd worn on the first occasion. The sun shone on his red hair to fiery effect. His eyes showed surprise, all right, but hardly any pleasure and somehow she was disappointed, having expected for no real reason that he would be pleased to see her. He was, one couldn't deny, a big strong handsome fellow and she found herself wondering briefly how the isolated nature of his work suited him or if he even liked women.

Rather cast down, she asked, 'Do you remember me?'

Now she fancied she saw the faintest glimmering of a smile in the grey eyes. 'Oh, I remember you. Got yourself stuck again somewhere and want me to come and push you out of it?'

'No!' She heard herself rise to the bait.

'So what are you after, then?'

Somehow his voice wasn't friendly at all. Had she really managed to upset him that much at their last meeting? Or had something happened to upset him since, unconnected with her? She hastened to explain her presence.

'Mrs Carmody at Witchett tells me the remains of the eighteenth-century meeting house are on your land and I wondered if I could take a look.' Meredith pulled Father Holland's local history book from her pocket and opened it up at the engraving of the meeting house.

Alwyn glanced at it, plainly unimpressed. 'There's nothing like that to be seen now. Just some stones and a few feet of wall. Some chaps came out from Oxford a few years back and messed around, measuring and digging a trench or two. They didn't find anything.'

'But could I look? I wouldn't damage anything, dig holes, break fences down. I'm a friend of Alan Markby's. He said to mention his name to you.'

There was a flicker in the depths of the cool grey eyes watching her. Alwyn hesitated then seemed to relax. 'Fair enough. I'll show you where it is. Over here, in the old paddock.' He indicated the pasture land behind him.

The dog meantime had been skirting Meredith as if she'd been a recalcitrant ewe. Now it sidled up, head flattened, red-rimmed eyes suspicious.

'Hullo, old chap!' she said encouragingly.

The dog wagged its plumed tail but scuttled back at the sound of her voice.

'He doesn't seem very friendly,' she observed.

'Working dog!' said Alwyn, looking mildly surprised. Obviously her remark plumbed the depths of irrelevance.

And he rightly scorned it, she thought. Farmers don't keep pets; they keep working animals. The countryside isn't sentimental. It's a place of grinding hard work, harsh decisions, life and death. The dog was a good sheepdog and earned its keep. That was all that mattered.

Alwyn was walking briskly back the way he'd come, the dog trotting along before. Meredith had almost to run to keep up with his long strides. He led her across a small paddock, past a shimmering green, stagnant pond, into a larger field ringed about with ancient trees and bordered on one side by the track down which she'd driven to the farmyard. In the middle some humps and bumps in the turf were visible together with some rough masonry remains.

'There it is, then!' he pointed.

There was a roan pony grazing in the paddock and seeing them arrive it threw up its head and snickered hopefully.

'Isn't that your sister's pony?' Meredith asked.

'How come you know Jess?' Alwyn returned quickly, suspicion again leaping into the grey eyes.

'We met at Witchett.'

'Oh, yes, she helps out old Dolly.' He shrugged his massive shoulders.

It struck Meredith that Alwyn and the dog, which lay by his feet waiting for him to move on, resembled one another in some ways. They shared that mixture of caution towards strangers and spasmodic signs of friendship. The difference between them was that the dog was servile in its movements. Alwyn was sturdily independent, an awkward customer some might say. She wondered uneasily if, had she not mentioned Alan Markby's name, Alwyn would have ordered her off the farm. But perhaps he just had something worrying him and was not his usual self.

'Jessica isn't about today?' Meredith probed.

'Gone into town with Ma.' Alwyn shifted his feet and the dog looked up expectantly. 'Ma keeps an eye on her. She's, she's been ill, my sister, in case you didn't know.'

'Yes, I did actually. Dolly told me.'

'Oh, it's common knowledge!' he muttered.

It's to do with Jessica! Meredith decided. Whatever he's brooding over, it's to do with his sister. Has Jessica told them about that nice young man who greeted us outside the dress shop yesterday? Don't the Winthrops approve? But she wasn't here to ask about Jessica.

'The building of all those houses must have made quite a difference to you,' she said conversationally.

His grey eyes rested on her, hostile. 'To us? No, how should it?'

'I meant, losing the farm alongside yours.' Meredith felt oddly flustered. She was beginning to understand Alan's problem with the Winthrops. Whenever you talked to them about anything at all, you always ended up feeling you were prying in an ill-mannered and hurtful way, picking at an open wound.

'Makes no difference to us!' said Alwyn sourly. 'We just go on as we always have. Dad won't have it any other way.' The bitterness she had noticed before was back behind the words.

'I see. Is all that land behind the building site yours? Or is that Witchett? I saw sheep there.'

'River marks the boundary between Witchett and Greyladies. But we lease some of Dolly's land for extra grazing.'

'So you won't be selling off any Greyladies' land for development?'

He snorted. 'Chance would be a fine thing! Dad would throw a fit at the idea!' Alwyn turned abruptly and whistled to the dog which leapt up. 'I hope you've got what you wanted!' He nodded towards the remains of the meeting house but his voice was mocking. 'I've got work and so I'll leave you to it. Come on, Whisky!'

He strode off, dog at his heels, leaving her wondering whether his remark 'what you wanted' was a simple comment or a sarcastic dig at her. Alwyn was certainly no fool. He didn't like answering questions and she had asked too many. He would probably look back to see if she was really showing any interest in the ruins. Meredith walked over to them and began to scout round.

The foundations of all four outer walls could be discerned but only the rear wall rose to any real height. The stones were ominously blackened. The fire which had destroyed the building had been fierce and total. Whoever lit it, if arson it had been, had made a good job of it. Yet here was a curious thing, thought Meredith glancing towards the farm buildings. She hadn't realised from Dolly's description just how close to the farm the meeting house had been. When the fire took hold that night in 1842, it must have been clearly visible at its outset to anyone at the house. Water would have been nearby in the farmyard and that old duckpond in the next meadow almost certainly had been there at the time. Farewell to the heavy horse had spelled farewell to carter, ploughman, his boy and their families and today the Winthrops worked the land in lonely isolation. But in 1842, days of labour-intensive farming, many pairs of able hands could have been summoned to help. Yet the meeting house had burned down completely. Had word been passed beforehand to let it burn? Or had the hand which set it alight dwelt there, at Greyladies?

Meredith sat down on the remains of the wall and carefully sketched out a ground plan of the ruins in her notebook, indicating by arrows the directions of pond and farmyard and approximate distances. As she drew she became aware that a breeze had sprung up. It flicked her hair over her eyes and rustled the leaves of her notebook as if it would have drawn her attention to something. She felt she was being watched although

Alwyn had long disappeared. She tried to tell herself that it was his morose air and that curious brooding unhappiness which seemed to hang over Greyladies which made her feel this way. But the silence here was – unearthly. Yes, that was the word which sprang to mind. The grass was green, the trees and hedgerows in leaf, the sky blue and dotted with scudding puffballs of cloud. Yet here spring was somehow absent. It was as if here things did not begin, they ended. They ended in violence, flame and destruction, all born of bigotry.

She folded her notebook and put it away in her pocket, wishing now that Alwyn had stayed. Even that uncertain-tempered dog of his would have been a welcome companion. At that moment she felt a warm breath on her neck and something soft and alive touched her ear.

Meredith shrieked and leapt up. Jessica's pony which had plodded over unheard on the soft turf, snorted and shied away. 'Good grief, it's you! I'd forgotten you!' Meredith said in relief.

The pony pricked its ears, whinnied reproachfully, and came forward again. It pushed its soft muzzle against her pocket.

'I haven't got anything for you.' She patted its nose. 'But at least you're friendly.' She began to walk back across the paddock towards the farmyard. The pony followed her to the gate.

Back in the yard she couldn't see Alwyn but she heard a clang of metal from the barn. Alwyn emerged carrying a pair of strong heavy metal hurdles as casually as if they had been almost weightless. He dropped them on the ground with another resounding crash.

Sighting her, he asked, 'All in order, then?' He

seemed to have got over his bad mood and sounded quite affable, much as when they'd originally met on the road. Perhaps he'd worked it off as some people do, sweating out ill humour like a fever.

'Yes, thanks, though it's a bit of a creepy spot. Jessica's pony came up behind me and gave me a fright.'

Alwyn chuckled unexpectedly. He had an attractive grin. 'What's your interest in the old Grey Folk, then?'

'It seemed a romantic story as Dolly told it, and a mystery. Who farmed here in the 1840s? Your family?'

He nodded. 'Been here since the 1700s. The place was called Manor Farm first, the name got changed later on account of the Grey Folk.'

'Gosh, that is a long time.' Her interest quickened. 'You haven't any old family records, letters or diaries, I suppose?'

Alwyn gave her an old-fashioned look. 'Working men don't have time to sit writing diaries like a lot of schoolgirls!'

He said this in much the same way as he'd said 'working dog' in reply to her earlier comment. She didn't understand country life, he was really saying.

'They used to write things in family Bibles.' She spoke the words to justify herself but saw a momentary flicker of recognition in Alwyn's face. 'You've got such a Bible!' she exclaimed. 'You have, haven't you?'

He sighed. 'Up in the house. You want to see it, I suppose?'

'Oh, please!'

Her unforced enthusiasm appeared to disarm Alwyn completely and wiped away the last traces of his reserve. 'Oh well,' he said, rubbing his dirty hands on the Fair-Isle sweater. 'Anything to keep you happy and

I could do with a break. Come on, then. And mind you tell Alan you pestered the life out of me!'

He led the way into the house, taking off his boots at the door by means of an ancient wooden bootjack, and washed his hands at the kitchen sink while she watched. Drying them, he turned and suggested with a kind of chivvying patience, as one urging an idler to turn to and make herself useful, 'Put the kettle on, why don't you? I'll look out the old Bible. That brown mug there, that's mine.'

She had the tea made by the time he came back. He must have gone up into the attic because she heard his feet coming down more than one flight of stairs. He had to stoop right down to get under the low lintel of the doorway. He was carrying a worn wooden box with a metal hasp and a date burned on the lid in pokerwork, 1768.

'That,' said Meredith faintly, 'is a Bible box. They're quite valuable.'

'I dare say.' He didn't seem impressed. He opened it up and took out a venerable tome. 'Here you are, mind now, 'tis fragile.' Inside the front cover of the Bible a piece of yellowish parchment had been carefully pasted. In tiny beautiful copperplate script she saw recorded births, marriages and deaths as Winthrop succeeded Winthrop. Interspersed were one or two other events of note. In 1820 it was recorded that 'the old king' had died. In 1833 a gale tore away half of the roof. And here, on 21 January 1842, fire had destroyed the dissenters' meeting house. 'Act of God' opined the writer piously and possibly with a touch of defiance.

'Don't you think it strange that the meeting house burned so well in damp, drizzly January weather?' she asked Alwyn.

Alwyn shrugged and replaced the Bible in its box. 'Winter time was when they lit big fires to keep places dry and warm. It wouldn't be any surprise if perhaps embers left smouldering in a brazier fell out and caught hold.' He paused to look down at the Bible before closing the box. 'Ma wrote our births in there. Mine, Jamie's, Jess last of all. 'Tisn't likely there'll be any more written in.' He was speaking to himself, not to her and she felt a return of that awkwardness which Alan too felt here.

Meredith touched the metal hasp of the Bible box with the tip of her finger. 'Alwyn, have you ever had antique or other dealers call at the farm? Or strangers of any kind hanging around the place? Mrs Carmody has.'

Over the rim of the mug from which he drank his tea, Alwyn's cool grey eyes surveyed her. Then he nodded. 'She told me about that. I told her she should get a guard dog. That deaf old spaniel's no use. I said if she had another fellow come round to get straight on to the phone to us and either Dad or I would drive over and sort him out.'

'But no one has called here?' she persisted.

He smiled slightly. 'We don't encourage odd callers at Greyladies.' The shock of red hair bent over the mug and she couldn't see his face. 'Present company excepted,' added Alwyn politely.

She wasn't deceived. She'd seen the ruins and been shown the Bible. She had neither need nor reason to call here again. He was making that clear.

Susie Hayman was spending time that fine spring morning putting up new curtains. There had been curtains in the house already when they'd taken it on, but they weren't exactly to her taste and the ones in their bedroom were by far the worst. As she'd explained to Ken, she really couldn't stick them any longer. Just waking up every morning, opening her eyes and seeing the bright sun shining through that hideous pattern and those colours . . . And then in Oxford she'd seen curtain material on sale and just the right thing. It really cost very little and she'd run them up on her electric sewing-machine in no time. She was really proud of them. Susie teetered on the chair she stood on and, tongue protruding slightly between clenched lips in concentration, hooked up the last one. She gave it a little tug to straighten it and thought that she must go outside in the front garden and look up to see how they looked from the street.

Thought of the street led her to glance from behind the fold of material to the sunshine outside. From high up here she could see across the road and right across the hedge which formed a border between the road and the front garden of the large old house opposite. There was a man, standing by the windows of that house. A man who shouldn't be there because the couple who lived there ran a business in the town where both worked full time. They were never home before six-thirty. What's more, he was behaving in a strange manner.

Susie felt a thrill of excitement and alarm. She pulled the curtain across slightly and peered furtively from behind it. What was he doing? He'd rung at the front door and waited a little to make sure no one was coming to answer it. Now he had gone to the window of the lounge and was peering in. If she hadn't been up here she wouldn't have been able to see him because of that hedge and he almost certainly thought he was unobserved. He was fiddling about at the window sill. 'Oh my goodness!' she breathed. 'He's trying to open the window!'

Now she remembered what Meredith had told her about a prowler. He'd come back! Yes, it must be the very same one! And thanks to Neighbourhood Watch committee meetings, Susie knew exactly what to do. She jumped down from her chair, scurried to the telephone and with agitated fingers dialled 999.

Chapter Eleven

When Markby returned to the station just before lunch-time that morning, a scene out of Hogarth's Bedlam met his eyes and ears. Voices howled and ranted and bodies surged to and fro.

He stopped in the doorway and blinked. Too early in the day for drunks. A domestic, as it was generally termed? Husband and wife using the police station to fight out their differences instead of the divorce court? But no female voice could be heard except an occasional muffled and vain call for silence from Wpc Jones. Everyone, including the traffic warden, seemed to be milling about in the reception area by the desk. Markby became aware that the ranting was all being done by one voice and the other shouting by the desk officer trying to get a clear account of what had happened from a police car patrolman who was pointing fiercely at someone and bellowing his report while his partner ineffectually tried to get in a word edgeways in corroboration. Against all this, a rather pretty girl with blonde hairbunches, wearing a lemon yellow track suit and trainer shoes, was attempting fruitlessly to whisper her tale into Wpc Jones's willing but deafened ear. The girl looked faintly familiar but he couldn't place her just at the moment.

Markby distinguished at last that the commotion centred on a small man whom he couldn't see very well for the press of bodies. But, owing to the desk officer and the two patrolmen falling silent either in frustration or to get fresh breath, he could hear the small man at the moment excellently.

'Legitimate businessman!' the small man was shouting hoarsely. 'I'm going to get on to my solicitor! You'll hear more about this! Harassment! Dragged here in a Panda car for everyone to see! What do you think that will have done to my reputation!'

Markby didn't know what it was all about, nor did he wish to. It wasn't any business of his. Someone else could and was dealing with it. It didn't sound like a CID matter. However something familiar about the voice made him pause and peer into the group in an attempt to see the face of the aggrieved gentleman. At that moment the traffic warden, who did not seem to be involved but only to be an interested spectator, moved aside.

'Well, well,' Markby murmured. 'Ferdy Lee! We haven't seen him for a while. What's he up to these days, I wonder?'

But he didn't wonder it enough to want to find out and before Mr Lee, the legitimate businessman, spotted him and drew him into whatever item of bother this was, Markby ducked through the door and hastened upstairs to his office.

A few minutes later Pearce came in, a funny sort of expression on his face. 'They've got Ferdy Lee downstairs, sir.'

'So I saw. Keep him away from me.'

'As a matter of fact,' Pearce hesitated. 'I thought you might like to have a word with him. Only they're just about to let him go with a warning, so if you did—'

Markby raised his eyebrows. 'What's his racket nowadays?'

'It's not, according to Ferdy. Not a racket, that is. He says he's a—'

'Legitimate businessman, I heard.'

'Antiques,' said Pearce, wooden-faced. 'He's gone into the antiques business.'

Markby stared at him incredulously. 'Ferdy? What on earth does Ferdy know about antiques? He wouldn't know Regency from Woolworths!'

'I don't know about that.' Pearce shuffled his feet. 'But it seems he's in partnership with another chap and he, the other fellow, knows his stuff. He can tell what's good and fixes the prices, I mean, makes the valuations. What Ferdy does is to go round the countryside in his car or walk round the streets in likely areas, peering in folk's windows, looking out for unsuspected antiques. You know, things people don't know they've got, especially elderly people. The other chap has told him what to look for and he does have a copy of an antiques' guide in his car. If he sees something interesting, well, he lets his partner know. Later on the partner calls on the householder and tries to strike a bargain.'

'Get him in here!' Markby exclaimed. 'Go on, quick! Before he leaves the station!'

Pearce dashed out of the door.

Mr Lee was small and wiry with waved, rusty-black hair. His complexion suggested he was prone to get through the day with the help of a dram or two of the amber liquid. He was smartly dressed in a pale grey suit and wore what looked like a silk shirt.

'Business looking up these days, Ferdy?' inquired Markby.

'You're just the fellow I want to see!' said Mr Lee hoarsely, jabbing a finger at him. 'You're a sensible man, you are. Load of loonies you got downstairs! Harassment, that's what it is! Stopping me going about my lawful business. I'm going to take legal advice, I am!'

'Sit down, Ferdy,' invited Markby soothingly. 'And tell me all about it.'

Mr Lee was only too pleased to do so. He had, it seemed, been in the antiques trade for about a year, together with a partner by the name of Smith.

'Smith?' asked Markby resignedly. 'Christian name?'

'Jack, Jackie Smith.'

'John Smith,' murmured Markby. 'Hardly original, but go on.'

'Jackie,' said Ferdy sternly, 'has been in the trade for twenty-five years, man and boy.'

Mr Smith, Markby learned, owned no fewer than three shops strategically located where the passing tourist trade made them profitable. But antiques, it appeared, were not so easy to pick up these days as they once were, not from the point of view of an honest dealer. The fault lay with various television programmes which had educated the public with regard to the possible value of their family bric-à-brac. It was, indicated Ferdy morosely, highly irresponsible of television to interfere in this way. People now expected you to pay them the earth for any old junk. Even if you told them it was almost worthless they didn't believe you. It threatened the dealer's profit and without profit, who'd stay in any business? Just take into consideration the overheads . . .

Markby dragged him back to the core of the matter. Ah, well, the way Ferdy and Mr Smith got round the problem was simple. Ferdy scouted round and tried to find items of interest lurking unsuspected in people's homes. Many people were both surprised and delighted when they found out that they had something worth selling and more than willing to dispose of it.

'We do them a favour,' said Ferdy virtuously. 'A lot of people are strapped for a bit of extra cash and then we come along and pay them a fair price, fair mind you! Very pleased they are. They're glad to get rid of the old sideboard or tea-set, and the bit of money means they can go on holiday, lie in the sun, buy themselves a few luxuries.'

'You're quite a pair of social workers, you and Mr Smith,' said Markby.

'Yes,' agreed Ferdy cheerfully. 'I knew you were a sensible bloke and would see how it was. Downstairs, I don't like to say it, but they're ignorant, pig ignorant. I tried to explain and I might just as well have been speaking Russian. Falling standards in the police force, that's what it is and I'm very sorry to see it.'

'So what are you doing here today?' Markby demanded a little sharply.

Ferdy leaned forward. 'Doing here? You may well ask!'

It turned out that Ferdy had been lawfully engaged on one of his scouting expeditions in a prosperous area of town where there were plenty of large likely houses. Unfortunately the same area had recently seen a spate of petty thefts and break-ins. Ferdy clicked his tongue disapprovingly and gave it as his opinion that the schools were at fault, teaching no discipline. Anyhow, as a result of the mini crime wave, the residents had formed a Neighbourhood Watch group and one of these old busybodies (Ferdy meant, of course, responsible citizens, slip of the tongue!), had looked out of her window and seen Ferdy apparently trying to break in to the ground floor of the house opposite. Knowing the house empty, she had picked up the phone and dialled the police. If she'd walked over and asked him, Ferdy could have explained to her.

The police, who in Ferdy's experience were never around when you wanted them, this time arrived with unseemly speed.

'I turned round and there they was, the Lone Ranger and Tonto. They asked me what I was doing, and not very politely I may say! I explained. I told them of course I wasn't trying to open the window! I ask you, in broad daylight? Commonsense should have told them I wasn't! I was trying to see through it and that, as far as I know, isn't against the law. If the householder is out, what am I supposed to do? And if my dabs are on that window ledge, it's only natural. I'm not a tall bloke, as you can see for yourself, and I hoisted myself up, holding on to the ledge to have a look!'

'And was there anything of interest in the room?'

'Set of late Victorian dining chairs, very nice. That's another thing should have told your boys I wasn't breaking in! How was I supposed to carry away six chairs, stacked on my head? What I intended was to report back to Jackie and this evening or tomorrow he'd come round and make the owners a fair offer. But could I tell your boys that? They marched me off down here. This has been,' said Mr Lee emotionally, 'a very upsetting thing and I'm all of a shake. My old ticker isn't a hundred per cent these days and this hasn't done it any good!'

'You do have form, Ferdy, you can't blame them,' Markby pointed out.

'Nothing for years! I told you, the old ticker doesn't stand the strain! You can talk to my doctor. And you can look me up on that computer of yours and you'll see I've been legit for ages! And Jackie hasn't got no form at all! Look us both up, go on!'

'I dare say someone will. Actually, Ferdy, I'd like to talk to you about something else, not today's hoohah. Hold on!' Mr Lee had opened his mouth to begin an outraged protest. 'I just want to clear up a point which is bothering me in another case. If you could just answer a couple of questions, Ferdy, I'll be quite happy and you can go home. I'd appreciate your help.'

Mr Lee sucked his teeth and contemplated Markby thoughtfully. 'On the level? Go on, then.'

'Right. Were you searching for antiques in this area six months ago?'

'May have been.'

'Try harder, Ferdy.'

'What's it about?' he countered suspiciously.

'Did you call at Witchett Farm and see Mrs Carmody and ask her about old agricultural implements?'

'Oh, yes, that.' Ferdy sounded relieved. 'Old dear who wears her hair pinned up in a sort of bun on top of her head? Yes, I did call there. But she didn't want to sell. Pity. I mean, no use to her any of it. But sometimes they get a bit funny about parting with things.'

'Did you go back? Call again?'

He shook his head. 'No, I told you. She didn't want to sell and she meant it. You can always tell if they mean it. It would just have been wasting my time.'

'So you wouldn't have been out there the week before last? A Thursday night after dark, say?'

'At night? Do me a favour,' exclaimed Mr Lee, 'in my state of health? Of course I wasn't!'

Markby suppressed a laugh. Ferdy's genuine dismay left no doubt as to the truth of his denial. 'Okay, Ferdy, but watch out! No more prowling round empty houses! And I trust you and Smith don't call on elderly house-holders together? Two strange men might be intimidating to an old person. I'm sure you understand.'

'You'd think,' said Ferdy bitterly, 'that no one wanted me to earn an honest living!'

'So much for the theory that Mrs Carmody's night prowler was the dealer returned!' said Markby to Pearce. 'I never held much to it anyway. I'm glad it's out of the way, because that means whoever was in Dolly's hayloft, he was not looking for antiques!'

'What else could she have out there on that farm to interest anyone?' Pearce asked. 'It's a sort of museum, all closed down and nothing working. There's just a few nags in the stables and they are just ordinary dobbins, not racing certs! He wasn't trying to nobble them!'

'What indeed?' Markby tapped on the desk with the end of his Biro. 'What could he have been looking for on Witchett Farm of all places and who was he?'

'And is he the same fellow as our corpse, or does he have anything to do with our corpse?'

'Exactly.' Markby rubbed his hand over his mouth

and swivelled his chair to that he could see through the window. A lovely day. All the trees outside bursting into leaf and he was stuck in here. Meredith had gone to Greyladies, lucky her, out in the country. 'If the prowler and our corpse are one and the same, then more than one person was looking for whatever it was.'

'Do you think he found it?' asked Pearce after a moment.

'You mean, was he killed to prevent his finding it, or because he found it?'

'Whatever it was,' repeated Pearce.

Markby got up. 'I'm going to lunch!'

'Is the lady still staying in Bamford?' asked Pearce artlessly.

'Yes.' Markby paused. 'But she's gone out to Greyladies to do some historical research.'

Pearce looked suitably impressed.

As far as her efforts at such research went, Meredith herself was not particularly satisfied. So far her success rating hovered around nil and it niggled. She was going to have to do better than this! Confrontation with Alwyn has also served to reinforce her originally vague intention of solving the riddle of the meeting house fire.

She had, before leaving Greyladies, won a last concession from Alwyn. He was an odd chap, she thought. He veered disconcertingly between extreme unhelpfulness and bursts of confidence. As she had been about to leave he had remarked quite unexpectedly and casually:

'Those fellows who came out from Oxford about ten years ago, they'd be the ones you should ask.'

'Yes!' she'd replied, stopping in the kitchen doorway

and knowing she sounded cross. Bad enough to be given the brush-off and politely turfed out, without the obvious and impractical being offered as a parting shot to speed her on her way. 'But I can't ask them, can I?'

Alwyn had wrinkled his nose and scratched his mop of red hair. 'I can give you the address of the fellow who was in charge of them.' If he noted her amazement he showed no sign but continued placidly, 'He wrote to Dad before they came, asking permission. Any correspondence to do with the farm Dad keeps. It was ten years ago, mind! He might have moved or something.'

'Thank you,' she'd mumbled.

'Ah,' said Alwyn, grinning. 'So it wasn't such a damfool suggestion as you thought, eh?'

Meredith sat in her car in a lay-by studying the scrap of paper with the address, given her by Alwyn. She wondered whether he had offered it in one of his bursts of good nature or was simply directing her efforts away fro Greyladies. Perhaps it amused him to catch her una ares. Now, if she failed to follow up his lead, he would be rightly very suspicious. Nor could she safely assume he wouldn't know. With Alwyn, she was beginning to learn, it was wise to make no assumptions. Like it o ot, at least she ought to attempt a call at this addi . In any case, it was a lovely day and Oxford a city she liked and hadn't visited in a while.

She w s not, however, familiar with its residential areas or its backstreet traffic problems. It was a while before she located the house, a red-brick late Victorian villa in Park Town. She squeezed her car into a space by the kerb and got out to survey the building. It looked formidably respectable behind its clipped laurel hedge and oozed academic distinction. It had the sort of front door one instinctively expected to be opened by a parlourmaid in a frilled cap. There was even a polished brass 'dog' by the entry to enable visitors to scrape street mire from their boots before entering.

As it was, the door was opened by an eleven-year-old girl in blue jeans and a pink sweatshirt who was masticating an apple. She stared at Meredith in the baleful way of children.

'Ah,' said Meredith, disconcerted. 'I wonder, are—'

But here she ran into a problem. To ask 'are your mother or father at home?' would risk the door being shut in her face. The letter sent to Greyladies had been signed 'Matthew Gretton'. The problem was that almost certainly there ought to be some distinguished handle to the name and she didn't know what it was. She had to plump for 'Does Mr Matthew Gretton live here?'

'Yes,' said the child, crunching. 'But he's in Switzerland.' The last word came out as 'Shwizzerlan' through a mouthful of apple.

Drat! thought Meredith and must have looked her disappointment because the child volunteered, 'Dr Gretton's at home.' She swallowed an alarmingly large half-chewed lump but miraculously didn't choke.

'Oh.' Further complications. Perhaps it was Dr Gretton she ought to be asking after? Dr Gretton sounded like a person who would dig in a field for obscure artifacts. 'Could I have a word with Dr Gretton? My name is Mitchell.'

'Hang on!' said the child and disappeared. Her treble screech duly wafted back from the bowels of the house. 'Auntie Ursie!'

Meredith waited awkwardly, preparing to be led into

a sanctum inhabited by a professorial figure with snuff on his waistcoat. He would probably be testy at being disturbed by a stranger. She hoped the car was all right, not blocking anyone or illegally parked.

Footsteps approached and a young woman of her own age appeared. She had abundant dark hair tied back with a ribbon and startling cornflower blue eyes. She was wearing a paint-smeared smock apron and carried in one hand a tin of Dulux and in the other a paintbrush stained green.

'Hullo,' she said breathlessly. 'You want me?'

'Dr Gretton?' Meredith asked, taken aback.

'Yes. I'm just doing a spot of painting. The garden shed actually. If you'd come in and wait just a tick, I'll put the brush in some turps and the lid on the tin.'

'I'm sorry to have called at such an awkward moment . . .' Meredith began in some dismay as she followed Dr Gretton down the hall.

'Doesn't matter!' floated back. 'Listen, Enid, you are absolutely not to touch the shed, right? It's wet!'

They had emerged into the back garden. Surrounded by high brick walls it was a natural suntrap. There was an espalier peach on one wall and the child Enid was perched on a swing under a large chestnut tree, swaying back and forth and keeping her baleful eye on them.

'My niece!' explained Dr Gretton between blows as she efficiently hammered the lid on the paint tin. She put the brush in a jam jar which smelled strongly of spirit. 'Okay, we can talk. Would you like to sit out here?' She indicated a pair of garden chairs and as she spoke she took off the paint smock. She was wearing a bright royal blue blouse and she had a very good figure.

'Look, Dr Gretton,' said Meredith, embarrassed.

'I'm intruding. I should have written first—' She explained as best she could about her so far abortive research and how she had obtained the Gretton home address from Alwyn.

'It's my father you want, of course,' said Dr Gretton. 'My name is Ursula, by the way. He conducted that dig. I remember it. It was a complete waste of effort but he felt it was worth a try. What a pity he's away because he'd love to meet you. The Grey Folk aren't my subject so I can't really contribute much. I'm a palaeontologist myself, no use to you at all.'

Meredith sighed.

'I tell you what!' said Ursula suddenly. 'He's got a copy of Elias Linton's diary!' She saw Meredith's bewilderment. 'Don't you know him?' Ursula's tone indicated Elias was still to be seen around socially. 'He died in the 1850s. He was schoolmaster in Bamford and kept a diary over a period of something like thirty years. It's never been published and the original is in the Bodleian. But my father has a photostat copy of most of it. There is something in there about the burning of the meeting house. I remember his reading it out to me because it was quite exciting, you know. Come into his study and I'll dig it out.'

Matthew Gretton's study was suitably impressive, furnished with leather armchairs and a huge Victorian desk. The walls were covered with bookshelves. Ursula rummaged in a cupboard and emerged with a pile of loose sheets tied up with ribbon. 'Here we are!'

'This really is most awfully kind of you,' said Meredith. 'I hope your father won't mind.'

'My father would want to help. Wish I could.' She began to turn the sheets over carefully. 'Hope that dratted kid isn't meddling with the paint. Here you are. Can I leave you to read it while I just pop outside and check on Enid?'

She disappeared through the door and Meredith took the sheets of paper she had been given to a chair in a bay window and sat down in a shaft of sunlight to read Elias Linton's account of the destruction of the meeting house. It was written in a crabbed regular hand and she knew as soon as she set eyes on it she had to see the original. But even this copy achieved by modern technology could rub away the years.

'This morning I learned that during the night the meeting house of the congregation called by the town's people the Grey Folk, has burned to the ground and is quite destroyed. It appears the fire took hold at ten at night. Mary Anne Winthrop – ' (Meredith started) ' – seeing the blaze from her window but unable to leave her room, the door being locked, climbed from the same window by means of a sycamore tree growing close to the house. She ran clad only in her petticoat and a blanket taken from her bed, across the fields (which are under some snow at the present time) to the house of Mr Phillips and roused his household to give the alarm. My informant tells me that Mary Anne was in great distress and spent the remainder of the night beneath Mr Phillips' roof, his wife taking care of her. This morning early, however, two of her brothers arrived at the house and fetched Mary Anne away before even it was light, she crying and still in great distress. Of the meeting house I am told nothing remains but a few blackened stones and timbers which smoulder yet. This afternoon I shall take my faithful dog and walk there to view the sight, provided it does not snow again and become inconvenient underfoot.'

Sadly it must have snowed or something else had prevented Elias because there was no following eye-witness description of the scene.

So fascinated was Meredith by this sparse account which surely raised more questions than it answered, that she failed to see Ursula had returned and was standing nearby and watching her with a smile.

'Wonderful, isn't it?' she said.

'I'll say!' agreed Meredith with feeling. 'May I take a copy?'

She didn't want to let this fascinating old tale distract her from present-day inquiries or colour her judge-ment, but if one believed at all in heredity, it cast an interesting light on the Winthrops.

'Why do you think,' she asked impulsively, 'that Mary Anne Winthrop was locked in her room and had to escape, risking her neck, and run half-dressed over snow-covered fields to raise the alarm at the house of this Mr Phillips? What about the rest of the Winthrop household and the farm workers?'

'No idea,' said Ursula frankly. 'But it makes you wonder what was going on at that farm, doesn't it?'

Evening was setting in. The carpark was already dark and deserted. The old Ford Capri parked in one corner was alike in condition and age to nearly every other vehicle there and unlikely to attract attention even though it was a stranger. In a top-floor flat of the grey council block Sean Daley was sitting down to table before a heaped plate of fried food.

'It's good of you, Auntie Bridie. Do you know, this is the first food I've been able to look at since – since it happened?'

'A terrible thing,' said Auntie Bridie. 'God rest his soul, whoever he was. But a man needs to keep his strength up, Sean. Will you need the tomato ketchup?'

'And then the police came asking us all questions.'

'Ah, the polis—' murmured Auntie Bridie enigmatically. 'You don't want to get on the wrong side of them fellows, Sean!'

'It wasn't my fault I dug him up!'

'Of course it wasn't – I'll just make a pot of tea. We've always been a respectable family. I've nothing against the polis though the vandalism's terrible on this estate and they do nothing about it! I made a fruit cake yesterday as it happens. I must have known you'd turn up.'

'I don't want to put you out, Auntie Bridie. I'll just stay the night. I've been sleeping in the car. But I needed to talk to someone about it.'

'It's no trouble. Aren't you my sister's boy? Sleeping in that car, indeed! You'll sleep here in a bed like a Christian! I've a letter from your ma, by the way, over there on the dresser.' She made for a piece of furniture half buried beneath plaster statuettes from Lourdes, shell grottoes, mementoes of Knock and a framed picture of His Holiness. 'This is it. Her writing's very good. You'd never think she took a drop now and again.'

'Auntie Bridie, look, there's something on my mind and I've got to tell someone.'

His aunt paused, the letter in her hand pressed flat against her chest. 'It's not a girl, is it, Sean? You've not got some girl into trouble? It was bad enough when your sister Cathy—'

'No – it's about that fellow, the one I dug up.'

'Oh yes?' She sat down and fixed him with a steely eye. 'Now speak up, Sean! I won't have any nonsense!'

'It's not nonsense – it's just that the police came around with a photo of the feller – after I'd dug him up and they took him away. I said, I never saw him before the digger scraped him out of the bottom of that trench! They didn't bother me too much. They were quite sympathetic.'

'And shouldn't they be? You having a terrible shock. Enough to turn the brain.'

'But you see, Auntie, I'm almost sure I had seen him. I didn't think it when I dug him up – I mean, I didn't really look at the fellow then. I just ran! But when they showed the picture of him, he had a familiar look about him. I sat puzzling about it. Then I remembered where I'd spotted him before. Auntie Bridie, I don't want any trouble. I don't want to go back to that place any more. And I don't want to put the finger on anyone. After all, there's a murderer out there on the loose and I don't want him looking for me! But then the police, you see, they said I was to remain available, that's their way of putting it. They talked about an inquest and it would mean I'd have to stand up and tell how I'd found him. I'd have to answer questions! I can't answer them, it'll make trouble for me! But now I'm in trouble anyway with the police because I ran away and didn't stay there. They might even be out looking for me. What do you think I should do?'

'You didn't do anything wrong, Sean! No one is going to blame you for taking fright! Now then, let's see, perhaps we should have a word with Father Brady at St Dominic's.'

'I don't want anyone knowing, Auntie!'

She got up and reached for the teapot. 'You'll finish your tea and have a piece of my cake and read your ma's letter.' She paused. 'And we'll think about it tomorrow.'

Chapter Twelve

'How did you get on at the farm?' Markby asked as Meredith opened Laura's front door to him that evening.

Sight of her cheered him considerably. She wore a red shirt dress he particularly liked and he guessed she had just washed and dried her hair because it bounced around her head in flyaway fashion and glistened in the glow of the hall light. He indulged in a brief fantasy in which she was always there, like this, at the end of the day.

'There were certainly a few things to puzzle over with regard to the Grey Folk, but as far as the Winthrops are concerned, I didn't make much progress. Alwyn showed me the family Bible which was interesting. But he doesn't exactly chatter, does he? He won't talk about the building site and he doesn't like strangers. He says they don't encourage visitors at the farm and I believe him! What a curious place it is. Did you know the farmhouse dates from 1692?'

'No, no more than I knew the Winthrops had a family Bible! You obviously made more progress than I did!'

'Well, perhaps I've just stirred up another mystery.'

She told him about Dr Gretton and Elias Linton's account of the burning of the meeting house.

'Alwyn did come across with the Grettons' address but I suspect it was to get rid of me. The Winthrops just don't like questions. What is it about Greyladies? The whole place has a strange atmosphere. As for those stones, I'm not being fanciful but I really felt a sort of presence, not a very happy one, either. If you ask me, that family has a distinctly odd history. Do you think the 1840s Winthrops set the fire themselves?'

'Why on earth should they?'

'As yet I don't know, but I'm working on it. Ursula thinks they must have been a rum bunch back in 1842. If you consider that today's Winthrops are the Victorian lot's genetic descendants, it really begins to make you think.'

'We've all got a weird ancestor or two in our family trees,' he protested. 'In the day when the Markbys had money for expensive eccentricities one of my great-uncles kept a pet cheetah which he said was the temporal habitation of his late wife's spirit.'

'He was just nuts, no disrespect. The Winthrops are definitely sane but different. Anyhow, Ursula's father, the Matthew Gretton who conducted the dig, is not really interested in the fire so much as how the Grey Folk conducted their services and laid out the interior of the meeting house. But he's certainly got ideas about it and what's more, knows a lot about the general harassment to which the sect was subjected. That's why I've got to meet him. Ursula says she'll fix it up and she'll give me a letter for the Bodleian, confirming I've a legitimate interest in the subject so that I can get a reader's ticket. Then I shall be able to read Elias Linton's diary in the original!'

'Seems to me you've done pretty well in the course of your day!' he said.

'Um, in a two steps forward, one step back sort of way. Although I'm not sure how relevant it all is to your poor dead body. Talking of progress and working on things,' Meredith probed, 'have you learned anything from the burned clothing I found? Any identification?'

'It's forming part of our inquiries.'

He didn't really expect to get away with that. She rebelled immediately. 'Oh come on, don't be so stuffy! I found it!'

'That doesn't make you a party to privileged information.'

'You're not playing fair! I told you about my progress!'

'Yours isn't police business.' Markby observed the light of battle in her hazel eyes and relented, possibly because of the eyes themselves. Although he knew she'd pester until he told her something. 'We don't know if it was the dead man's but it's possible. The zip, which was the only piece intact, is of foreign manufacture and it's the sort used in heavy denim jackets or the leather blouson type.'

'I told you he would be foreign, all those gold teeth!' She gave a nod of triumph and the fly-away hair bounced around again.

'Oh God,' he said helplessly.

'What?' She was peering up at him, puzzled.

Markby pulled himself together, relegating the

185

wilder images thrown up by his imagination back to his subconscious. 'Don't give yourself airs!' he said severely. 'Someone else has also suggested he may have been a foreigner, as it happens. A question of speech.'

'Ah, you've found someone who spoke to him!'

He heaved a sigh. 'I suppose there's no reason why I shouldn't tell you this, since I've had them stick up a poster at Bamford railway station carrying the information. The ticket collector there thought he recognised the photo. It's likely he arrived in Bamford by train on the Wednesday morning before he was killed. Harry, the ticket collector, said the man had a foreign way of talking and was carrying a plastic bag of the sort you get if you buy something in a cross-Channel ferry's duty-free shop. Harry's reliable. So I had them make up a poster with a photo of the dead man on it, asking if any travellers on the London to Bamford train which arrived at eleven-ten on Wednesday before last saw him. We've also sent a copy of the poster down to Scotland Yard and asked them to get it put up at the London end. Plus, on the off-chance, we've sent it to all the Channel ports. He may only have arrived in England a day or two before he travelled to Bamford. I don't suppose anyone will remember him now. It's too long ago.'

'Did the ticket collector remember how he was dressed?'

Markby shook his head. 'Casual, that's all. All right, that could tie in with the zip you found, but not necessarily. Foreign clothing doesn't mean a foreign wearer. A lot of that fashion stuff is imported. Certainly lots of the haberdashery bits are, buttons, zips, trimming. The jacket from which the zip came could have been made up here and it could have been worn by a Scotsman in a kilt for all we know. It's not automatically to be linked with our man.' He dismissed the subject firmly. 'Are we going out for a drink? I'm not going to talk shop all evening. I've had enough of this case all day.'

More specifically he wanted to get out of Laura's house and the domestic intimacy it suggested. Time to put an end to a tête-à-tête threatening to lead him, at any rate, into deeper water. The images were escaping from the depths of his subconscious again, fluttering up like butterflies into the sun. 'Get a move on! Steve's waiting for us!' he said briskly.

Far safer to be somewhere where they'd be in the company of others and there would be no danger he'd unburden himself of any unwise declarations. This sensible resolve managed just to survive when she pulled a face, wrinkling up her nose and tossing back a wisp of brown hair.

It wasn't far to The Fox and Hounds, only a little outside of town and a stone's throw, Meredith realised, from the housing development. It was a cramped place, a former coaching inn, with tiny rooms which nowadays all ran into one another through open doorways from which the actual doors had been removed. Like all such inns it had a large former stable-yard and numerous outbuildings, one of which now seemed to house the kitchens. There was a strong smell of frying.

The tiny bar into which they squeezed was already crowded. Some of the people looked like locals and some like workmen from the building site. The accents of the voices which formed the background babble were many and varied. Alan touched her arm.

'Steve's here already!'

He was pointing towards a corner where a youngish man with curly hair and a crew-neck sweater sat with a pint before him and a folded newspaper propped against the table edge. He was doing the crossword even though concentrating against such a background had to be almost impossible. Markby pushed a way towards him and called his name.

The puzzler looked up, smiled, put away his paper and seeing Meredith, half rose to his feet, holding out his hand.

'You're Meredith! At last! He keeps you hidden away from us all!'

'Not his fault,' said Meredith. 'I live in London nowadays.'

There was a scuffle by her feet and a chair moved of its own accord. Meredith looked down startled and saw a small dog which was attached by its lead to a chairleg. It was tugging forward determined to greet the new-comers and taking the chair along with it.

'That's Patch,' said Steve Wetherall. 'Hang on, I'll unhitch him. The trouble is if I don't keep hold of him, he'll scurry off and get under people's feet. As he's a bit small-sized he tends to get trodden on.' He dragged his pet round to his side of the table and wrapped the end of the lead round his wrist. Meredith squeezed into the corner beside him and Patch put his paws on her knee and grinned happily up at her.

'I don't mind,' she assured Steve who was beginning to apologise for his pet's over-zealous friendliness. She patted the little dog's head. 'I hadn't expected to see so many people here tonight!'

'A good half of them come from the site.' As if to

underline this Steve nodded acknowledgement of a couple of greetings. 'They all know me,' he added unnecessarily.

Markby interrupted at this point to ask what they wanted to drink and having been informed, made his way to the bar.

'I visited your site the other day,' said Meredith. 'I suppose I shouldn't have done. I was snooping around. That is to say, I intended to snoop around and it was in a good cause, on Alan's behalf, but I didn't get much chance. The foreman threw me off.'

Steve grimaced. 'Jerry is the bane of my life. Between you and me he's a thoroughly unpleasant character. And his bite is as bad as his bark! I admit nothing's gone right on that site since the beginning. We had trouble with the underlying water table and then there was some problem with a load of bricks and well, frankly, we didn't need to find a body in the foundations!'

'No, that must have been a nasty shock. Alan said you were there when they found it.'

'When Daley dug it up. Yes, it was unpleasant. Daley's taken off into the blue since then and I can't say I blame him. I'd expected to see more men leave. Not one of them will go near that spot, you know. They won't even fill the trench in. Hersey doesn't help. But does he ever? If I'd thought of the idea, I might have knocked him on the head and put him down in some foundations!' Steve looked momentarily embarrassed. 'That's a joke in poor taste. But he keeps complaining that things go wrong and blames everyone but himself. If he did his job—' he broke off. 'Sorry, not your problem.'

'Are you the only architect working on that site?'

'My firm has the contract. Well, it's pretty much a one-man band so in a way, yes, I am. I put a hell of a lot of work into those designs and it's no secret I was hoping for some healthy commercial feed-back in the future. If you once get a good reputation for something in this business, it sticks. People come to you next time. By the same token, a bad aura round your name can finish you. That's what I mean about the body. It's nothing to do with me, the site, the developers, any of us. But it's like a bloody albatross round our necks, pardon my French!'

She sympathised and Steve sighed. Patch let out a small but impatient yelp. 'He wants his crisps,' said the dog's owner and picked up the packet which lay on the table. 'Excuse me. He always has a packet of crisps, bacon flavour.' He pulled the crisp packet open and began to feed them to his pet. 'This is the sort of pub where you can do this,' he confided. 'It's one reason why I come here. Too many of the other places round here have gone up-market and some don't like dogs at all.'

'Isn't that Alwyn Winthrop?' Meredith asked suddenly as the crowd parted by the entrance. 'Yes, you can't miss him, can you!'

'Alwyn?' Steve glanced casually across and nodded. 'Yes, he comes up here most evenings. It's his only chance to get off that farm, I suppose. Whenever I think my life is getting difficult I look at Alwyn and take heart. Poor devil. He's led a hell of a life, you know.' He crunched up the empty crisp packet into a ball and dropped it in the ashtray.

'I didn't, but I'm curious!' said Meredith frankly.

But Alwyn had seen them. He nodded a terse welcome and joined Markby who still waited impatiently by the bar to be served.

'Tell you some other time!' murmured Steve.

The barmaid had belatedly arrived from serving drinks in other areas of this rabbit-warren of a pub and greeted Alwyn with noisy cheerfulness. 'Evening, Alwyn, the usual? Mum and Dad keeping well?'

'Fine, thanks.' Alwyn was searching in the pocket of his tweed jacket and placed an assortment of coins on the bar. Steve pulled a wry face at Meredith. Most men went out for the evening with wallets. Alwyn had loose change in a pocket. That told its own story. Alwyn's reply to the barmaid had been spoken automatically yet Meredith fancied she could almost feel the underlying tension behind the words. At his age most men would be asked how the wife and kids were doing. Alwyn at forty-something was still at home, still unmarried, and people asked after his parents. No matter how old he was, Alwyn enjoyed, if that was the word, a permanent minority. It must be galling and perhaps it was more than that. There was something about Alwyn that spoke of a hidden, gnawing, very real despair.

He was now exchanging greetings with Markby, although on Alwyn's side the greeting was delivered in a slightly aggressive way and took the form of, 'I wish you'd bloody finish poking about on our land!'

'Sorry,' said Markby cheerfully. 'Case of need.'

'That damn fire was left by travellers, must have been! Dad's always let travellers camp on our land. He reckons if you treat them fair, they play fair by you. We've never had any problems with the travelling people.' Alwyn picked up his pint and nodded his thanks at the barmaid. 'Not like local kids. It might

have been them lit the fire. Young blighters muck
about doing all kinds of damage, break hedges down,
light fires, ride ruddy motorbikes around, worry the
sheep too. I've had to chase them off before now.'

'We'll see. We'll keep out of your way, Alwyn. We
won't disturb the sheep!' Markby grinned.

Alwyn wasn't amused. 'It's not the sheep and it's not
me. It's Jess! You know what she's like. All nerves.
This has upset her. She doesn't like strangers round the
place and coppers grubbing about in all the bushes and
leaving ruddy police vehicles parked all over the
place—' Alwyn seemed to recollect Markby's pro-
fession. 'No offence, Alan. But you know what I
mean.'

'Yes, I do. A lot of people feel that way about us.
Won't you join us?' Markby had picked up the tray
with the drinks he'd bought and indicated Meredith
and Steve.

Alwyn hesitated but detached himself from the bar
and followed Markby to the table. There wasn't much
room when they'd all squashed themselves round it.
Patch, who suffered more than most from the cramped
floorspace, solved his problem by taking a flying leap to
land on Alwyn's lap. Alwyn didn't seem surprised and
scratched the little dog's ears.

'Old friends,' said Meredith with a smile.

Alwyn gave her an unexpectedly shy grin and then
looked away.

'You don't bring your dog down here?' she asked.
She saw that look of mild surprise and before he could
answer, supplied the answer herself. 'I know, working
dog!'

'Whisky doesn't like crowds,' Alwyn said. 'Used to

being out in the fields. Like me,' he added unexpectedly.

'This place is crowded enough!' she observed.

'Used not to be, not before they started building at the site. I used to be the only person in the bar some nights.'

'Nothing round here is going to be the same again,' said Markby gloomily. 'Not since they started carpeting the place with bricks.'

'Will you tell him,' said Steve to Meredith and gesturing at Markby with his beer glass, 'that he is an antediluvian stick-in-the-mud and it's about time he got his ideas up to date!'

'Why me?'

'Because I've told him and he doesn't listen to me. He might listen to you!'

'Doubt it!' said Meredith.

'Look, the pair of you,' said Markby truculently. 'I can't see that ploughing up good farmland for more houses is a blessing, tearing out the hedgerows, destroying wild life, wild flowers, turning the ecology of the whole area on its head!' He turned to Alwyn. 'What do you say?'

'Me?' Alwyn shrugged. 'Land is as good as what it produces. Ours produces sod all. Haven't got time myself to go picking flowers.'

'You can't pick wild flowers,' said Meredith. 'It's against the law.'

'And why?' Markby asked triumphantly. 'Because there are so few areas left where any grow. Come on, Alwyn – and you, Steve! When we were kids we spent hours wandering about in the woods down by the river. I can remember when they were carpeted in bluebells in the spring and the primroses . . .'

'There are plenty of places left,' the architect said. 'Of course I was sorry to see Lonely Farm go. But it was derelict. Land is worth money. You can't just abandon it.'

Alwyn was watching Steve closely, listening, it seemed, to every syllable with a curious intentness. Now he looked away and down at the dog on his knees. He spoke quietly to the animal and Patch waggled his stumpy tail and nearly fell off his perch.

'Oh no!' exclaimed Steve suddenly with a groan. 'Not the wretched Hersey! Not on my night out! I refuse, I absolutely refuse, to buy him a drink!'

A loud, aggressive voice could be heard now above all the rest. The crowd moved with some alacrity and Jerry Hersey appeared making for the bar. He had smartened himself up slightly but not much. He still wore his cap and his eyes still had that maniacal glare behind the horn-rimmed spectacles.

'Good evening, Jerry!' said Steve resignedly.

Hersey paused by their table and glowered down at them. 'Oh, so you're all pally with the coppers, are you?' he said sourly. 'Telling tales out of school! What's she doin' there?'

'I'm having a drink if it's all the same to you!' said Meredith sharply. Being insulted by Hersey on the site was one thing. Here it was another. Here she had unarguably as much right to be as he did.

'Thought you might be taking up the floorboards!' said Hersey sarcastically. 'Lookin' for your bits of history! Hoping to find another body p'rhaps!' He turned his baleful stare on Alwyn. 'Alwyn! Evening!' he said almost politely.

Alwyn nodded. 'Evening, Jerry. How's it going?'

'From bad to worse! Ask him!' Hersey pointed a grimy finger at Steve. 'Or him!' The finger jabbed at Markby. 'Can't get a thing done!'

'You haven't heard from Daley, I suppose?' Markby asked him calmly.

'Course I haven't! Your lot frightened him off! It's a wonder we got anyone left working there!'

'Yes, it is!' snarled Steve with a meaningful glare at the foreman.

It bounced off Hersey. 'I'm goin' to get a beer and I'm goin' to drink it in another bar!'

'Thank God!' said Steve heartily as Hersey shambled away.

'He really is an unpleasant man!' said Meredith. 'I'm sorry you've got to work with him!'

'Jerry's all right,' said Alwyn, surprising them all considerably. They stared at him. Alwyn reddened. 'Well, he's not a fancy talker but he's all right in his way.'

'Blowed if I've ever been able to see it,' muttered Steve.

'You work in an office!' said Alwyn and this time it was Steve who reddened.

Markby broke in as peacemaker. 'You still play for the darts team at this pub, Alwyn?'

'No, had to chuck it in what with lambing and such. Couldn't get time to go to the away matches.'

'Here's someone else we know,' said Meredith suddenly. 'Here's your sister, Alwyn.'

Alwyn's mouth dropped open. He stared at her and then swung round on his seat, dislodging Patch unceremoniously.

Jessica had just come into the bar and behind her Meredith saw Michael Denton. There were still other customers between the new arrivals and the table, but Jessica had seen them and turned her head to speak to Michael who bent his head to catch her words. He nodded and the couple began to move their way. Before anyone else could say anything by way of comment or greeting or react in any way, however, Alwyn had leapt to his feet with a roar which made every head turn and all other conversation in the bar cease.

'What the hell are you doing here, Jess?'

In the silence, surrounded by a sea of watching, curious faces, Jessica spoke tolerably calmly. Meredith had to admire her. 'We've come for a drink, same as you. This is Mike, Alwyn, I told you about him, how I met him in town. We were at college together. Hullo, Meredith.'

'Hi,' said Meredith apprehensively. Beside her Alwyn was gathering up a head of steam like a volcano. Steve had prudently removed his pet from harm's way.

'Oh were you? Well, for your information,' Alwyn had turned his attention to Michael who had edged forward and was holding out his hand in greeting. Alwyn ignored it. 'I don't want my sister hanging round in pubs!'

He leaned forward threateningly, his huge fists clenched. His face had reddened and with his fiery crop of hair and jutting jaw he presented an awesome sight. Several bystanders were edging away. Quite irrelevantly, Meredith thought to herself that a hundred or so years ago Alwyn would have won his beer money in bareknuckle fights at county fairs. The barmaid disappeared precipitously into one of the other bars with the obvious intent of fetching the landlord. From the corner of her eye Meredith saw Markby slide his chair back from the table, leaving himself a free space so that he could jump up and intervene if it became necessary. She hoped it didn't, even with Steve at his side Alan would have his work cut out.

'Oh, don't be silly, Alwyn!' said Jessica, surprising Meredith by this unusual display of spirit. She didn't seem in the least dismayed by her brother's belligerent attitude. Alwyn looked taken aback too. He blinked, straightened up and unclenched his hands. 'There are lots of women here. Meredith's here!' Jessica went on.

'I don't care who's here. You're my sister and I don't want you here! You just go on back home!' he growled but he looked less certain and more sullen.

'It's quite all right,' said Michael, interrupting. 'I mean, it's quite a nice little pub, isn't it? I wouldn't take Jessica anywhere dodgy.'

'You won't take my sister anywhere and that's that!' Alwyn shouted, all his previous aggression returning. 'Who the hell are you, anyway, and what gives you the right to make so free and friendly?'

'It's up to me whether I go anywhere with Michael,' said Jessica stoutly, tossing back her long fair hair. She had made quite an effort with her appearance, Meredith noted, wearing make-up and two or three gold chain necklaces. Her cerise sweater suited her and its colour was reflected in her pale cheeks, flushed pink with emotion and something very like excitement. 'Or with anyone else, come to that! I'm not a baby and I don't need your permission. I think you're being very rude to Mike. I'm ashamed of you, Alwyn. I thought at least you had manners! Carrying on like a lunatic and in here, too, in front of all your friends!' She turned and took Denton's arm. 'Come on, Mike.'

'Wait a bit,' Denton said, digging in his heels. 'I don't like to leave it like this. Really, Alwyn, you've misunderstood—'

'Come on!' she insisted tugging him away. 'It's no use talking to him when he's in a mood like that!'

The two of them disappeared through the door. After a moment's uneasy silence, conversation began again in the bar with one or two glancing curiously at the group in the corner. The landlord, who had come quietly up, exchanged a glance with Markby, nodded, and went away again. Alwyn, still red-faced and seething, subsided on to his chair.

'She'll be all right,' said Markby soothingly. 'He looked like a nice lad.'

'Jess isn't like other girls,' Alwyn muttered. Meredith saw now that he was sweating. It was warm in here, but not that warm. 'She's been ill. He might be all right, that boy, or he might not, I don't know. But he won't understand how it is with Jess.' He looked both shame-faced and obstinate.

Meredith, because she sensed his emotional turmoil, tried to be helpful and put in, 'He's known her a long time if they were students together. I'm sure he'll understand. He must know about Jessica's troubles.'

She didn't know if Alwyn even heard her. He shifted awkwardly on his chair and then got laboriously to his feet. 'I'd best be getting on back.' He hesitated and muttered, 'Sorry about the fuss.' He pushed his way quickly out of the bar.

'He hasn't gone after them, has he?' Meredith asked, worried.

'Shouldn't think so. He's thought better of his outburst.' Markby picked up his drink. 'Alwyn's got the temper which goes with red hair. But he's devoted to Jess and I think she can handle him.'

'What Alwyn needs is to get off that farm!' Steve said vehemently. 'He's a bright chap. He could find something else.'

'He doesn't know anything except farming,' Markby said doubtfully. 'He's used to being out in the open air and his own boss.'

'Own boss?' Steve snorted. 'That's the last thing he is! He's tied to that ruddy place like some sort of medieval serf! You heard him, he can't even spare the time to play for the darts team! The farm always comes first and it's not like a business which shuts up shop at six in the evening. He works round the clock, day in and day out, weekends and holidays. In fact a holiday is something I don't suppose Alwyn has ever had! It's the fault of the old people, you know.'

'I suppose it's difficult for them,' Markby said. 'They've lost Jamie from the farm and it must worry them Alwyn will go too one day. Without him they'd be finished.'

'Don't feel sorry for them!' Steve argued. 'Oh, I know that old man Winthrop comes over as a rural character and his wife as a salt of the earth countrywoman . . . But I know they are bigoted, obstinate and tyrannical! No wonder that girl turned out as she did, a bundle of nerves! To stand up to the Winthrops you need a hide like a rhino! I hope that young fellow carries Jess off and marries her! Alwyn ought to know better than interfere. But he's changing as time goes by, getting more and more like the old man! He always had a quick temper but lately he's got surly. That was never Alwyn's way before.'

Markby sipped his pint and set it carefully on the table. 'Anything in particular upset him?'

Steve hunched his shoulders. 'Well, maybe I'm wrong, but I think it's something to do with the development. I don't mean he resents it the way you do! It's quite the opposite. Given half a chance, he'd sell Greyladies to developers, take the money and start a new life. But he knows he'll never be able to do it. He comes out to the site quite often. I suppose that's where he's got so friendly with Hersey. The site seems to fascinate Alwyn. To him it must be like watching ten pound notes grow. Makes a change from sheep. Sometimes it makes me feel quite odd, seeing him standing there in his gumboots with that dog of his, watching the bricks go up. Did you ever watch railway engines when you were a kid, Alan?'

Markby nodded.

'That's how Alwyn watches the brickies work, putting up walls. Can't take his eyes off them. Poor devil.' Steve raised his pint to his lips but then set it down again, exclaiming, 'Hullo, Dudley! We don't see much of you in The Fox and Hounds!'

A burly man who was edging his way towards the bar, stopped and gave them all an embarrassed smile. 'Hullo, Steve – Chief Inspector! No, I don't drink out in pubs much. But there was nothing on telly tonight and I said to my wife, why not just go out for a drink for once? Make a change.' He nodded to them and moved away, apparently unwilling to be drawn into further conversation.

'Dudley Newman, the contractor,' said Steve in

hoarse sotto voce. 'The wealthiest man in Bamford, if you ask me. You'll rarely catch him slumming with the rest of us!'

'Where's his wife?' asked Meredith, her curiosity aroused.

Steve peered into the throng and shrugged. 'Can't see her. Must be in one of the other rooms. Anyone care for another?'

'I must say,' she said as Steve set off for the bar, 'this pub is a very popular spot!'

'Darn sight too much so! I like a quiet drink myself. This place is like sitting in the middle of the market square!' said Markby, but he said it absently, drumming his fingers on the stained table-top and staring into middle distance.

Meredith regarded him thoughtfully.

'You know, Steve's right and it would be the best thing for Jessica if that young man carried her off!' said Meredith much later when she and Alan sat in Laura's kitchen over coffee.

'I was surprised to see him make so much fuss,' Markby confessed. 'Especially as he said to me not long ago that his sister ought to have more young friends and not spend half her time with Dolly Carmody.'

'Young friends in general isn't the same thing as one young man in particular!' said Meredith sapiently. 'He's a bit of an awkward blighter, Alwyn, isn't he? He didn't even like me examining the ruins of the meeting house. They don't seem to want anyone there on that farm except the immediate family. No wonder it's got such an introverted brooding air about it!'

'Glad you found that too, I was beginning to think it

was just my imagination. No, Steve is quite right, as you say, and not only about Jessica. Alwyn ought to get away. He's unhappy and it's souring him. As Steve says, he wasn't always like that. He was a cheerful sort of chap. Steve's probably right about the old people, even if he was a bit harsh. Winthrops have been at Greyladies for generations and naturally it's the centre of their world.'

He watched her pour out more coffee and added, 'It seems strange to see you sitting there in Laura's chair with Laura's coffee pot.'

'Wonder how they're getting on in France!' she said quickly.

'Under canvas with four kids? It must be a nightmare!'

'I admire Laura,' Meredith said honestly. 'To manage a career and children and a home, it takes some doing.'

'And you don't think you'd like to try it?' His eyes met hers over the coffee things.

There was a small, awkward pause. 'No, not really.' Meredith smiled wryly. 'Honestly, Alan. I must lack the domestic instinct.'

'It isn't just about keeping house!' She didn't reply and he leaned across the table and without warning kissed her on the mouth.

Damn! she thought. This was the moment she'd known would come eventually and she wasn't ready to deal with it, not just yet. 'It isn't enough, Alan,' she said, drawing back. 'I like you a lot. I'd even like to sleep with you. It would be very nice. But to make a whole life together there has to be something other to share than a bed.'

'I thought we did share other things.'

'Yes, but ultimately we don't see our individual lives in the same sort of setting. I'd be a rotten housewife.'

He drained his cup and picked up his keys from the table top. 'If I wanted someone just to keep house I'd have fixed myself up long ago. But perhaps you're right. I was a pretty lousy husband before, or so my ex-wife and her lawyer gave me to understand, and I dare say I'd be a lousy one again.' He stood up. 'Time for me to go. Case conference in the morning.'

'It's not your fault, Alan!' she protested vigorously. 'It's the way I am!'

'Sure, we're all the way we are. Good night.'

She listened dolefully to his car start up and go off down the street. She hated upsetting him but knew pretence was always worse in the end.

They were all at sixes and sevens, she reflected ruefully, she and Alan, Jessica and Alwyn, the obnoxious Hersey, poor Steve Wetherall who had his reputation now dogged by association with a murder mystery . . . Somehow those great yellow-painted diggers ripping up the countryside out there were just a symbol of the permanent disruption which affected all their lives.

Chapter Thirteen

Jerry Hersey, too, had quitted The Fox and Hounds that same evening in an unsettled mood. Not that he ever felt particularly at peace with the world. This didn't worry him. He was used to being at odds with everyone else. Though he would have denied it vigorously if anyone had accused him of it, the truth was that he took pleasure in his contrariness. It was his way of enjoying himself.

That evening, however, Jerry felt more than usually grouchy. Something had happened to upset him in addition to the usual grievances, something which really rankled. He strode along the unlit grass verge with the confidence of one who had walked this way by night a hundred times, hands in pockets and muttering to himself. The lights of Bamford and those of The Fox and Hounds were far behind him and there were no lights in the isolated cottage for which he made. The solitude didn't bother him but he disliked the chilly night breeze sweeping across the open fields on either hand. He wouldn't be sorry to get indoors. Rain was on the way. He could smell it on the wind. Garden needed it, mind you. Thought of a warm kitchen led him to quicken his pace. Betty would be long gone to bed, having left the back door on the latch for him. She didn't fear intruders, not out here.

'Although you can't trust no one these days, and that's the truth!' Jerry growled. 'Whole lot of 'em. All the ruddy same! And they acts so cheerful and butter-wouldn't-melt-in-their-mouths innocent! I knows better! Gawd, if'n I was to tell the half of what I knows, what I seen . . . There's a few folks round here should think themselves lucky!' He paused, his mind dredging up a long past snippet of Sunday School catechism. 'Whited sepulchres!' he announced virtuously to the open countryside around.

To his surprise a voice answered out of the darkness. 'Jerry Hersey? Is that you?'

'Bloody hell!' Hersey peered into the night. 'Who is it?'

The moon obligingly slid out from behind a cloud and briefly shone her silver light on the figure by the hedgerow.

Jerry grunted recognition but demanded, 'What are you doin' out here, this time o' night an' all?'

The other mumbled a reply.

'Well, I'm on me way home, beats me why you wants to hang about in the cold air!' Jerry began to walk on again but did not object as the other fell into step beside him. He was even moved to offer a grudging hospitality. 'I generally makes a cup of tea when I gets in. Betty, she don't hear nothing, sleeps sound. You can come and share it if'n you wants. I got one or two things I wants to say to you, anyway!'

'Oh?' The other stopped. 'Like what, then, Jerry?'

Jerry peered into the darkness, some instinct momentarily alerted perhaps by a slight change in the other's tone. But heavy cloud now obscured the friendly moon and he was damned if he could see. The long couch grass by the ditch rustled signifying the passage of some nocturnal animal and distantly, borne on the breeze, came the sound of the motorway which was never quiet. The sound led Jerry to think of the troubled building site and the discontent which had been simmering in him rose to the boil.

He thrust aside the hint of warning and began sourly, 'Well, fer starters . . .'

Meredith set out early the following morning for the vicarage to return Father Holland's book. Although it was not long after breakfast when she arrived there, no one answered her ring at the door. She was debating whether to put the book through the letterbox or whether in falling to the floor on the other side it might be damaged and she'd better take it home again, when she heard a roar of a motorcycle. She turned and saw a black-leathered rider on a Yamaha coasting towards her. He stopped and pulled off his crash helmet to reveal the bearded features of Father Holland.

'Good morning, Meredith!' he boomed.

'I brought the book back!' She held it up. 'But there was no one around and I was going to take it away again.'

'No one here, eh?' said the vicar dismounting from his metal steed and fishing his door key out of a pocket on his leather biker's jacket. 'Come in and have a cup of coffee. Barry ought to be here doing his gardening. Gardening!' The vicar snorted. 'If either Barry or the garden showed sign of improvement I'd be delighted. Success with one of them would be better than no success at all. Alas, they both continue the same. I told you he has to be supervised. He knew I was not at home because I passed him on my bike up in town. He was then supposed,' Father Holland underlined the verb heavily, 'supposed to be on his way here. The young blighter gave me a cheery wave. But clearly after he saw me he just abandoned duty and took himself off somewhere. He thought I wouldn't know if he turned up late. Well, I'm back before him so Barry has got a shock coming!'

They had progressed into the vicarage as Father Holland unburdened himself of this speech and found their way to the kitchen. It was extremely untidy and the morning post lay heaped up on the table.

'The woman comes in later,' said the vicar, rattling about amongst cups in a cupboard. 'Let's see, do you mind instant? It's quicker.'

'I don't mind. It's kind of you to offer coffee. I enjoyed the book by the way. I didn't have much luck with finding anything of interest at the old ruins.'

'Not surprised to hear it but I hope you'll press on with your investigations. I'm looking forward to reading your pamphlet in due course!' He stopped speaking to pour boiling water from the kettle into two mugs. 'Here we are!' They settled down at the table and Father Holland gave the unopened post a mistrustful glare. 'Deal with that later. As a matter of fact, I've just had a painful and unpleasant call to make. Lindsay's mother . . . you remember I told you about Lindsay? She overdosed on drugs.'

'Yes, I remember. What's happened to her mother?'

He heaved a sigh. 'She can't come to terms with it. Her husband doesn't know what to do. The doctor has given her tranquillisers. I got an SOS call from the poor man, the husband I mean, this morning and had to go over there. There really isn't anything anyone can do, that's the trouble. They've both got to live with it, I'm afraid. We all have.'

There was nothing to be said to that. After a short pause Father Holland began to talk again about Bamford in general and to ask Meredith about her work abroad. 'Pity you're not staying longer, you could have come and given a talk to the Youth Club.'

'I'll do it in the future some time, if you like.'

As Meredith was leaving a little later, Barry appeared, sauntering up the garden path.

'Morning, Vic!' he hailed them nonchalantly. 'Morning, ducks!'

'You young wretch!' roared Father Holland. 'Don't you "morning!" me! You should have been here an hour ago.'

'I met a mate up in town and just stopped fer a chat.'

'Don't add lies to your other sins! You saw me in town, assumed I'd be away half the morning, and nipped into the nearest pub for a quick one!'

'Thirsty work, gardening,' said Barry unabashed. 'Oh well, better get on wiv it then! Get the old mower fixed. You want to get a new one, Vic!'

He disappeared into a rickety shed and could be heard apparently throwing things around inside it.

'We are supposed to presume from that noise,' said Father Holland, 'that Barry is fixing the mower. Actually, you know, Barry can fix things, if he's a mind to do it.'

'Couldn't he learn to be a mechanic or something?' Meredith asked.

'He did work at a garage for a while but kept taking the cars to joyride. Barry is a problem.' Father Holland's eye rested on his motorcycle. 'If he touches that, I'll have his guts for garters.'

The shed door flew open and the mower roared out in a cloud of dust and grass clippings steered by Barry in the general direction of the flower beds.

Meredith left Father Holland yelling warnings and instructions above the noise. She did not feel that gardening and Barry were compatible somehow. On the other hand, in a curious sort of way, Father Holland and Barry were.

Alan Markby arrived at the station that morning to find Pearce standing in the doorway of his office, brandishing a slip of paper.

'Good morning, sir. A Mrs Chivers has just phoned.'

'Who is she, what does she want and has it anything to do with work in hand?' Markby demanded, making for his desk. 'If the answer to the last bit is no, then I don't want to know the answer to the first two bits. I've an appointment with Superintendent McVeigh to explain our lack of progress! Not even a name to our corpse! The traffic's solid at the roundabout. Why isn't someone down there sorting it out?'

'She's the married sister of Jerry Hersey the foreman at the building site,' said Pearce, unperturbed by news of traffic chaos. That was nothing to do with him. This was.

Markby paused in the act of lowering himself into his chair and froze with hands on the chair arms to glare at his sergeant.

'She's a widow,' said Pearce cheerfully now that he

had got his chief's attention. 'Hersey lodges with her. She's got a cottage about a mile and a half from The Fox and Hounds, going away from Bamford that is, along the road. It's in the middle of nowhere really.'

'And?'

'And Hersey didn't come home last night.'

Markby let himself fall back into the chair and scowled. 'I saw him myself last night in The Fox and Hounds. I spoke to him, dammit!'

'Yes – she said he left last night to walk to the pub, about half past seven or quarter to eight that was. She goes to bed early and she's a sound sleeper so she didn't worry that he hadn't come back by the time she retired or that she didn't hear him come in. But this morning she found he hadn't come back at all and that's unheard of. She's very worried.'

'Has she been in touch with the building site?'

'Yes, and he hasn't turned up there either. They're puzzled because, although he's not the best foreman in the world, he does turn up on time every day.'

'Damn,' said Markby softly. 'I don't like this. But I can't for the life of me see how it's got a bearing on our case, other than his happening to work at the site. Hersey? Perhaps he's . . .' He paused.

'A woman?' suggested Pearce half-heartedly.

'Only if she were blind, daft and desperate. No.'

'An accident?'

Markby sighed. 'We'll have to make it a priority. I've got a nasty feeling about this. Phone all the local hospitals. Include Chipping Norton. It's casting the net wide but it's best to be sure. If you draw a blank, go and see Mrs Chivers and go to the pub and try and find out what time Hersey left last night, and if he left alone. Oh, and find out to whom he was seen talking during the evening, other than to me and my party, that is. He went into another bar in the pub so I didn't see him after he left our group.'

'You don't think he's done like Daley and just taken off?'

'Why? Or if so, why so late in the day? He might just be lying drunk somewhere of course. Go on, get on to it! You won't find him hanging about here! I've got a case conference at eleven and I'm going to be late.'

Steve Wetherall learned of Hersey's disappearance when he arrived at the site at about ten that morning. The young man to whom Meredith had spoken was on the telephone to the contractor, Newman, and the girl in the blue suit was supplying tea and moral support.

The young man put the phone down, pulled a face and briefly informed Steve of the situation.

'Blasted Hersey!' said Steve morosely.

'So say we all. Mr Newman's not a happy man. He says to tell Jerry when he does turn up that he's fired.'

'They should have got rid of him weeks ago. I saw him last night. He seemed all right. His usual affable charming self! He's lead-swinging. Ten to one, he's sleeping it off somewhere!'

And with this Steve went about his work. At twelve he got into his car and drove to The Fox and Hounds to lunch on their steak pie and chips. As he walked in with Patch at his heels, he met Sergeant Pearce coming out.

'Found him?' Steve asked bluntly.

'No,' said Pearce. 'And it's no use me asking you if

he's turned up at the site, I take it. You saw him last night, didn't you, sir?'

'Yes, I was here with your boss and a couple of others. I didn't see him leave.'

'You're sure? The barmaid says she thinks he left between half past nine and ten. He'd certainly gone when the landlord called time. The girl thinks she sold him a beer just on half past nine but nothing later. They were very busy, unfortunately.'

Steve shook his head. 'No, I definitely didn't see him after he left our table. I didn't want to see him. He isn't my favourite person.'

'See him greet anyone, sir?'

'Other than the people I was sitting with, no. I can't help, I'm afraid.'

'Thanks, anyway,' said Pearce.

When Steve had eaten his lunch he stood outside The Fox and Hounds with his hands in his pockets and, despite a reluctance to do so, thought about Hersey. Hersey going AWOL was a nuisance. Without a foreman they'd have even more problems, and finding a replacement, getting things settled in with a new man, having to deal with Hersey when he did turn up . . . all these things cast a shadow over an already murky future. Steve was beginning to loathe this job. That he had originally had such high hopes of it made things worse. The whole development really did seemed jinxed.

Patch, at his feet, yelped impatiently.

'All right for you!' said his master, picking up a bit of stick and throwing it across the carpark. Patch ran to pick it up and set off with it. Steve followed him. This was their usual drill. They walked a little way along the grass verge so that Patch could explore the ditch and work off a little energy and Steve could work off the steak pie.

The stretch of road was quiet. Most traffic nowadays went on the new road. It was another nice spring day and Steve began to feel better. The Fox and Hounds was out of sight round the bend behind him and ahead there was nothing but a cottage in the far distance. Patch had dropped his stick, a boring item, was growling and worrying at something much more interesting in the ditch.

'Oy, leave it!' Steve called automatically.

Patch retreated a few steps, burrowed in a tussock of grass and emerged backwards carrying something in his mouth which he brought proudly towards his master.

Whatever it was, it glinted in the sunlight. 'What have you got there?' Steve stooped and held out his hand. Patch dropped his find, sat down and waggled his stumpy tail.

The find was a cracked pair of horn-rimmed spectacles.

'Oh, God,' Steve whispered. 'Those are Jerry's!' He picked them up hesitantly and stared around him. Jerry wore his spectacles all the time. He couldn't just have dropped them without knowing it. Steve's eye was drawn unwillingly to the ditch where Patch had been growling and foraging around. He swallowed and walked slowly towards the spot.

Patch bounced ahead, delighted that his master was going to see what he had found. He stood at the side of the shallow gully and barked shrilly. Steve caught at his collar and pulled him back. He knelt in the long grass and nettles, pushing them aside heedless of stung hands, and peered down into the ditch.

Jerry Hersey's sightless eyes, framed by a wreath of dark green dockleaves, stared back up at him. One calloused workman's hand lay across his breast covering his heart as if he took some kind of macabre oath in death. A trail of little ants ran busily across it.

Steve whirled aside and plunged away from the horrid sight. He stumbled along the grass verge, running back to The Fox and Hounds with the desperation of a man in a nightmare who cannot run fast enough to escape whatever it is pursues him. The blood pounded in his ears and he wanted to be sick. All round him the hedgerows burgeoned with new life but all he was aware of was the ending of life.

He staggered into the carpark and looked for Pearce's car but the sergeant had left. Steve wrenched open the door of his own vehicle and tried to contact Markby on his car phone but was told the chief inspector was in a meeting. So he told his tale incoherently to the desk sergeant and, as Pearce arrived back at the station in the middle of it, he told it again slightly more coherently to him. Then he got out of the car and picked up Patch who was worrying at his foot and put him inside, slamming the door on him. Nausea won at that point. Steve threw up the steak pie.

Then he walked miserably back to the ditch and sat shivering by Hersey's dead body, waiting for the police to arrive.

Chapter Fourteen

Traffic was moving by the time Markby reached the roundabout but crawling at a snail's pace. The cause, as it turned out, was roadworks which appeared to have sprouted to no visible purpose reducing everything to single line traffic. They were controlled by a yellow jacketed labourer with a Stop/Go lollipop who worked in lackadaisical tandem with a companion stationed at the other end of the short stretch to organise oncoming traffic. As Markby approached the lollipop swung round to Stop. He halted obediently, propped his elbow on the open car window and mulled over Pearce's news as he waited.

That Hersey had simply disappeared was unlikely. He wasn't like the rootless Daley, an itinerant labourer moving from site to site. Daley had moved on at the first sign of trouble, and whilst they were still looking for him, it wasn't surprising that he'd gone to ground.

Hersey, on the other hand, was a local man and lived with his sister not far from the site. Perhaps his local knowledge and permanent residence had got him the job as foreman. Otherwise it was hard to see why the contractors had hired him. Nevertheless, disagreeable and uncooperative as he was, Hersey probably knew all there was to know about building houses. Markby judged him forty or so years old and a man who had spent his working life entirely in the building trade. The purely local connections of such a man and his regular habits made him a most unlikely absconder – unless he had a pressing reason to take off. In which case, mused Markby, such a reason had arisen at some point late yesterday evening. Right up to and including the moment when Hersey had exchanged his cheerless greetings with them in the pub, the foreman had been his usual predictable, unsociable self, showing no sign of being about to bolt.

Markby turned his thoughts to his other and just now the more immediate problem of the unidentified corpse and the lack of progress in that case he had to report shortly to his superior. Nothing so far had come of his poster campaign. But who at the main ports had time to notice one face? There was always the London end, of course, where the man had boarded his train. So far he'd heard nothing from the Met. But there again, what was one more missing person to them? And one missing out in the sticks, moreover, far from their realm of interest?

He glanced impatiently at his watch. As if in response, the lollipop swung round to Go. Euphoria was short-lived. Despite having got past the obstacle, the traffic soon slowed to a crawl again. He had left himself plenty of time at the outset, but would still be late if this continued. He turned on his radio and was rewarded with a bulletin from the local station warning of holdups on this road and advising motorists to take an alternative route. There was, in fact, a turning off just a quarter of a mile down and if he took it and cut across country, normally a longer route, he'd avoid this and it might prove quicker in the end. The traffic inched forward again. He'd have to make his mind up. Markby decided on the detour and on reaching the turn, quit the jammed main road and thankfully set off between fields.

Surprisingly few motorists had followed his example. Perhaps they just didn't realise the detour existed. It not only offered open road, but sights such as that of a sparrowhawk which dropped like a stone to seize some small creature from the grass verge only yards ahead, of horses cantering playfully around their field and of a wonderful stretch of yellow daffodils being cultivated for Easter sales. The temptation to stop and watch all these was great but he resisted it.

His original decision and his resolve paid off. He arrived at his destination with three minutes to spare and the almost certain knowledge that had he remained in the queue he'd still be somewhere out there on the main road. He heard the clock strike eleven on a nearby church tower as he hurried into the building, his pleasure at having made it on time as yet unblemished by the first of a series of shocks that he was about to receive in the course of an increasingly eventful morning.

'Ah, sit down, Markby,' invited Superintendent McVeigh innocently. 'Traffic not too bad? You're on the dot.'

'As a matter of fact,' Markby said, 'it's stuck almost fast on the main road. I cut across country.'

'Those roadworks, I suppose,' said McVeigh. 'They were supposed to be finished by now. Not our worry, yours and mine, however.'

Markby didn't argue the obvious that yes, it was his worry if he had to negotiate that particular route to keep an appointment. He took the seat indicated and embarked without further preamble on the discussion he was here to pursue.

'It's just faintly possible there's been another development in the building site murder this morning, sir. I haven't added it to the file yet because it's just cropped up. It's probably completely unconnected with the case.' Briefly he described the circumstances of Hersey's disappearance. 'There's no reason as yet to suspect foul play. But Hersey is a creature of habit, it seems, and his sister is worried. Anything to do with that site is of interest, naturally. Hersey will turn up, no doubt. However, I'd like to know where he is and what he's doing.'

'It's certainly odd,' McVeigh said, moving awkwardly in his chair. He was a large man, not fat just solid, standing six feet four in his size twelve shoes. His frequent complaint was the chairs didn't seem to be made large enough, or at least the chairs supplied for his use weren't. 'Hersey . . . you've found him an awkward blighter, haven't you? Uncooperative.'

'Very, and so do others.'

'Mmn. Do you think, in the light of this apparent disappearance which we have no reason yet to suppose isn't entirely voluntary, that he might be concealing some evidence?'

'I'm almost certain Hersey knows more than he's saying. I couldn't offer you any proof for that. It's just a

220

gut feeling. I'm sure that if he does, he won't tell us just to spite us. But there again, I can't swear he has any pertinent information or if he has, whether he realises he has, if you take my meaning.'

'I take your meaning all right. Would you say he wasn't very bright?'

'On the contrary, within the limits of his world I'd say he was all about. Cunning rather than intelligent, perhaps, but certainly observant and possessed of a good memory. He is, however, as they say in the country, cussed.'

'How about honest?'

'Honest enough in his way, but his way mightn't be yours or mine. I don't see him in big-time crime. I think Jerry would act in his own interest. He might turn a blind eye to petty pilfering if it was worth his while. But since on the site he'd probably get the blame for it if it went on, I dare say he makes sure it doesn't. That's what I mean by honest in his own interest.'

McVeigh shifted his bulk again and muttered something uncomplimentary about the man who had designed the office furniture. 'And you spoke to him yourself last night?'

'Yes, but after that I didn't see him again. Pearce is out now trying to trace Hersey's tracks.'

'We'll leave it there for the moment, then.' McVeigh's massive hand strayed to a folder on the desk before him. 'It will all have to wait because there's something else. I have what you might call break-through news for you. But I don't know how you're going to take it!'

'Oh?' Markby eyed the folder suspiciously. A ray of sunshine came through the window and played on it tantalisingly. A breakthrough was definitely what was needed but McVeigh playing coy about it meant there were significant strings attached. Those he could do without.

'Take a look at this,' said McVeigh, opening it at last. He reached out over the desk and handed Markby a photograph.

Markby took it and studied it. 'Hey!' he exclaimed. 'This is the dead man! I mean, this is him alive!'

'Yes, it is. Looks a bit different, doesn't he?'

'I'll say!' Markby murmured softly. If he had not had experience before in this kind of thing he would probably not even have identified the man in the photo. The face was fuller, it looked good humoured, the mouth turning up in a smile and the corners of the eyes crinkling. A real living person not a death mask. If he'd had this photo to show around . . . Then suspicion struck.

He looked up. 'Where did you get this?'

'From France. Your hunch that he was a foreigner has paid off. He's, he was French.'

Two questions leapt into Markby's mind at the same time and in attempting to put them both at once, he became tied up. 'Why wasn't I – you mean he was a villain? I haven't received – when did you learn that?' he finished indignantly.

'Hold on and I'll explain!' McVeigh said placatingly, waving his shovel-like hand. 'Firstly, no, he wasn't a crook. He was a police officer.'

'What!' Markby half jumped out of his chair.

'And in reply to the other question I fancy you were trying to put: the reason the answer to your inquiry came first to me and not directly to you is that he was a drugs detection officer working under cover. Under cover means just that. No one knows.'

'We should have been told!' Markby said furiously. 'If we'd known we might have been able to protect him! He might still be alive! Or if not, we might at least have been able to tell the right people he was dead. Either way we'd have known who he was and not have wasted over a week running round in circles!'

'I admit,' McVeigh said reluctantly, 'there has been some lack of communication between departments, not to say confusion. There is some little carfuffle going on about it in high circles at the moment and the French, if it's any consolation to you, are extremely put out. They've lost one of their best men and accusations are flying thick and fast. However, to put it bluntly, that doesn't concern you. That's politics, if you like! What you have to do is find his killer.'

'Without any of the helpful information they're all sitting on!' snarled Markby resentfully.

There was a knock at the door. 'Ah, this could be the help you need.' McVeigh did not sound as if he particularly believed his own statement.

The man who marched in briskly radiating confidence wore a smartly tailored suit which served to underline the effect made by a pale, uncompromising face and a manner of sharp authority. Markby waited but he had an idea what was coming.

'This is Detective Chief Inspector Laxton from Scotland Yard, the drugs boys,' said McVeigh with the sort of determined heartiness a society hostess shows when a party threatens to disintegrate. 'He'll be also on the case from now on. You'll be working together with him.'

'Up to a point,' said Laxton, extending a hand which Markby took unenthusiastically.

'Quite!' said McVeigh irritably. 'Laxton here will be looking for the drugs which the Frenchman was presumably on the trail of, and you'll be handling the murder inquiry. It will overlap, naturally.'

Markby managed not to say that was all he needed. He wondered if McVeigh had ever heard the saying about too many cooks. But McVeigh wasn't to blame. A corpse in his area was Markby's pigeon but the drugs trail the Frenchman had been on was Laxton's. Yet it was likely that someone else would now take the combined glory if this case were cracked: but not the flak if it weren't. That would still be put down to incompetence on the part of the local police force. Successful, Laxton would go home boasting he'd saved their bacon. Unsuccessful, he'd return to base shaking his head ruefully and making jibes about rural coppers.

'So perhaps you can find Laxton a desk to work at and let him see your file on this.'

'Certainly,' said Markby grimly. 'And shall I see his file on it?'

'You can see all you need to know,' said Laxton.

'I've had them put this together for you!' said McVeigh hurriedly, handing over the slim folder on his desk.

As Markby left, Laxton preceding him out of the room, the superintendent managed to whisper, 'Sorry, Alan, but it's out of my hands!'

Bamford was a small station and it was evident from the first that the desk to be made available for Laxton's use would have to be squeezed into the corner of Markby's own none-too-roomy office.

'Let's see what you've got on this, then!' said Laxton cheerfully. He was evidently not a sensitive soul. In his pale face his close-set eyes darted about missing nothing. He had cropped hair and long pale hands. He reminded Markby of a croupier in one of the seedier gaming clubs. He handed over his file on the dead man and retired to his own desk to read the file McVeigh had handed him.

It didn't take long because there wasn't much in it. The photo. A brief run-down on the Frenchman's particulars. His name was Maurice Rochet. He was thirty-two at the time of his death, unmarried and came from the Pas de Calais. He had spoken fluent English and had worked outside France on similar assignments on several occasions. The shipment of heroin he was tracing was believed to have been landed from a private yacht along the south coast. It had been traced to London where, so it was believed, it had been divided up and repackaged. A raid on the warehouse had been fractionally too late. Consignments had already gone out in various directions and the one Rochet had been tracking was believed to have reached the south Midlands area. Rochet had followed in hot pursuit.

The Metropolitan drugs squad, no doubt smarting over the bungled warehouse raid, had been now further embarrassed by the loss of the French operative. No wonder they'd sent down Laxton to try either to recover the lost drugs or, failing that, to carry out some kind of damage limitation exercise. If necessary, thought Markby grimly, at the local men's expense, although that uncharitable thought could not be spoken and had to remain a grim suspicion. He was aware of his resentment at someone foisted on him and that he would have to watch out that he didn't let it bedevil his relations with his new colleague. Laxton himself, however, was not one of those people who inspired immediate sympathy and he didn't appear to be one who eased himself tactfully into a situation. Thick-skinned, thought Markby morosely, and sharp-witted. The worst possible combination. But from Scotland Yard's point of view, a good man to send. Markby, given the task, would probably himself have chosen to send Laxton.

'Did you know him, this chap Rochet?' he asked.

'Personally? No, I'd heard of him. Supposed to be a bright chap. He liked to work on his own. He'd infil-trated the outer edges of the gang but it seems they must have rumbled him after all.'

'But surely he reported back to someone? Wasn't he missed?'

'On that kind of job a man sometimes stays out of touch for quite long periods. Every report back is a risk. He may have known he was being watched. From what you have here,' Laxton tapped the file before him, 'he was probably the chap the old lady disturbed in her farmyard on the Thursday night. Have you searched that farm?'

'Witchett? We've had a look around. But that was because she called us in. Now we know what we're looking for, we'll search again more thoroughly. But this time I'll have to request a warrant.'

'They'll have moved the consignment out by now,' said Laxton reproachfully.

'If it was ever there!' Markby snapped. 'Anyway, with Rochet's body being discovered the heat is on and they may not have dared to try moving it.'

'Perhaps we ought to get a sniffer dog in,' said Laxton.

Pearce's voice was heard outside and Markby, bereft of an answer to the last remark, sighed with relief. 'Here's my sergeant. He's looking for a missing person. A chap called Jerry Hersey, you'll see his name in the file there.'

'Oh yes,' Laxton's long fingers flipped over the pages. 'Foreman on the building site where Rochet's body was unearthed. Any other connection?'

Pearce appeared in the doorway, flushed in the face and obviously the bearer of important news. When he saw Laxton he stopped short with his mouth open to speak.

'Detective Chief Inspector Laxton, Scotland Yard drugs division,' said Markby impassively. 'He's in on this now, so whatever it is, let's hear it.'

'Oh well,' said Pearce, nervously eyeing Laxton, 'they've – er – found Hersey.'

'Good!' said Markby, cheering up. 'That's one thing out of the way!'

'Not exactly,' said Pearce cautiously. 'I don't think you're much going to like this, sir.'

Chapter Fifteen

Markby stood on the grass verge with his hands in his pockets and the breeze whipping up his fair hair and watched as the usual routine was played through. The ambulance waited nearby just beyond a parked police car. The immediate area had been roped off and traffic cones put in the road to reduce it to single-line traffic. Down in the ditch Fuller could be seen, no doubt rejoicing in having another of the 'gumboot jobs' he found so interesting. Laxton in his city suit and shoes was standing looking bemusedly over a hedge at some sheep. He looked completely and utterly out of place. From his expression it was obvious he believed himself to have fallen into the direst backwater where life was lived at medieval level. One of the sheep he was contemplating stared back at him and then baa-ed noisily. Laxton searched in his pocket for a cigarette and wandered morosely away down the verge.

Fuller clambered out of the ditch and said cheerfully, 'From first examination I'd say a broken neck caused by a strong, well-aimed blow from someone who came up behind him. What's popularly called a rabbit punch!'

'Thanks,' said Markby flatly.

'All right if we take him away now? Your photographer's done his stuff. The sooner I can get him on the slab, the sooner I can let you know more specifically.'

'Certainly. Help yourself!' said Markby crossly.

He watched as Hersey's body was loaded into the waiting ambulance. Pearce sidled up conspiratorially and said in a low voice, 'Mr Wetherall is taking it very hard.'

Markby turned his head to glance in the other direction where the architect sat on the bank in a dejected huddle, his head in his hands.

'I'll talk to him. You stay here and, if Mr Laxton needs you, go with him. If the warrant comes through he'll want to search Witchett and I'd rather you went with him. Old Dolly knows you. I'll take care of this.'

He walked down the road towards Steve and stooped to touch his shoulder. 'All right?'

'No,' said Steve, looking up with haunted face. 'I'm not bloody all right. This is the second time this has happened to me in under two weeks! It's probably nothing to you, you're used to this sort of thing! But I'm not used to having dead bodies pop up under my feet!'

'I'm not that used to it either,' Markby said mildly. 'One never gets used to murder. Why don't we walk back to The Fox and Hounds and have a talk there?'

Wetherall got to his feet and slouched miserably off in the direction of the pub with Markby following behind. In the carpark Patch, who was incarcerated in his master's car out of the way, saw them coming and began to leap frantically about the back seat, loudly barking his objections at being left out of everything. Markby sat Steve down on a wooden bench and went to see if it was possible to get a whisky despite the pub having theoretically closed up for the afternoon.

'Here you are,' he said when he returned successful. 'That will help you.'

'I didn't like the man,' Wetherall said fiercely. 'But I didn't want him dead!' He took the glass and added gloomily, 'Cheers!'

'No, of course you didn't.'

'It was a hit and run driver, wasn't it?'

'What makes you say that?'

'It has to be!' Steve stuck out his jaw argumentatively. 'What else? It's an unlit stretch of road. It was late at night. Possibly the driver didn't even realise he'd hit someone.'

'No skid marks on the road or corresponding bruising on the body. Sorry, but I think we can rule out a car plus pedestrian accident. Someone seems to have very efficiently broken Hersey's neck.'

'All right, a mugger, then!' said Steve defiantly.

'Out here? On a country road? He'd wait all night and not get a victim. Nor was Hersey flashing money around last night according to the barmaid. Hersey was apparently parsimonious, never known to buy anyone a drink. Besides, a broken neck doesn't indicate muggers. Sorry, that's out too!'

'Then you're talking about another blasted murder!' Steve yelled. 'Who on earth would want to kill Jerry Hersey?'

'By all accounts, almost everyone who had anything to do with him!' retorted Markby dryly.

There was a long pregnant silence. 'All right,' said Steve evenly. 'I hated the sight of him. I even made a very bad tasteless joke last night to Meredith. I said, if

I'd thought of it first, I'd have hit Hersey over the head and buried him in concrete. But I didn't mean it. That is, I wouldn't have done it. And I didn't do this!'

'I'm not suggesting you did.'

Steve picked up the whisky and took a long drink of it. 'Look, Alan, I'm sure you've pulled out all the stops on this, but I wish you'd get this business cleared up. There will be hell to pay now at the site, once they learn of this. The whole workforce will just walk off. Newman will have a heart attack. I wish to God I'd never had anything to do with the entire project. It's accursed. I mean that. It's really as if some evil power had put a hex on it.'

He caught the glimpse of a smile on the other's face and burst out furiously, 'And it's not blasted funny! I'm not joking and I'm not being over-imaginative! You know there are stories about that spot where we're building, about an old burial ground thereabouts?'

'Yes, the Grey Folk's. But the exact location is doubtful. Meredith's very interested to find it.'

'I know. She went asking questions about it down there. Lucy – the sales rep – was there at the time and said Jerry nearly went up in smoke at the thought of more bodies, or bits of remains, turning up.'

'No one has found any, have they? Bones, I mean.'

'No – or no one has said if they have. Or they might have thought they'd found animal bones if they did because we all know there was a farmyard there.'

'Then it sounds to me as if you're not on the site of the burial ground. Listen, Steve, I'm not getting at you particularly, but it's very easy to let an old legend get on your mind and then quite ordinary mishaps start to look like jinxes or curses or what you will. All right, a murder is way out of the jinx category. But murders happen in the unlikeliest spots and one body in a trench doesn't mean haunted ground!'

Steve looked mildly abashed but still obstinate. 'It's just, well, it's been a peculiar sort of spot from the start. Several of the workmen have mentioned the atmosphere – and before the digger unearthed the dead bloke!'

Markby said soothingly, 'I doubt it will turn out to be the work of the supernatural. An all too human evil, I'm afraid.'

There was a pause. 'Who's that other bloke?' Steve asked. 'The one in the snappy suit?'

'A colleague from London come down to pursue a few inquiries of his own.'

Steve was distressed but not slow to realise the significance of this statement. 'It's turning out as important as that, is it?'

'May be,' Markby said noncommittally.

Another pause. 'What could Hersey have possibly been into?' Steve demanded irritably.

'Any suggestions?'

'No! Unless he'd sold off a few bricks or bags of cement on the side. You don't get killed for that!'

'Not usually, no.'

'I just wish,' the architect said moodily, 'that he'd got himself bumped off some other place and some other poor beggar had found him!'

'Yes, it was bad luck.'

'Bad luck?' Wetherall stared at Markby incredulously. 'Bad luck? Believe me, I'm getting paranoid over this! I'm beginning to feel someone is out to get me!'

'Oh yes,' said Markby slowly, 'I was wondering how to come round to that. It might be wise if you took a few simple precautions. Park your car in well lit places. Don't go walking with your dog over isolated fields. Keep windows shut and doors locked.' Steve was looking at him in horror. 'It's all right,' said Markby soothingly. 'I don't suppose you're in any danger. But we don't know quite what is in our killer's mind, do we? He may think, you see, that you know something, have seen something . . . Perhaps that's what he thought about Hersey and it got Hersey killed. So just be sensible.' He got to his feet. 'You can go on home now if you want. We know where to find you. Don't talk to anyone about this, will you? I'm just off to see Hersey's sister. She's been told about it. Ever meet her?'

Wetherall shook his head. 'Can't imagine Jerry having a sister. Can't imagine Jerry having a mother, poor devil.'

Mrs Chivers was a thin woman in her late fifties, with one of those very fine papery skins which, as the years advance, crumple up like old wash-leathers. Her greying bobbed hair was centrally parted and secured on either temple by a kirby-grip. Despite all this and the fact that her eyes were reddened with weeping, it was still possible to see that she had once been a pretty girl.

Twisting her workworn hands, she whispered in a barely audible husky croak, 'Jerry was a good man.'

Markby had not found Hersey so, nor had Steve nor Meredith nor almost anyone else who had dealt with the late foreman. Only Alwyn had ever been heard to say a good word for him. Nevertheless he said firmly, 'I'm sure he was, Mrs Chivers!'

She seemed to pluck up courage and strength and her voice became slightly louder. 'That's why I knew something had happened to him when I saw he hadn't come home. He never would have stayed out and worried me, he'd have said if he wasn't intending to come back.'

'Yes. Did Jerry have any problems, Mrs Chivers, that you know of?'

She looked perplexed. 'Problems?'

'Yes, personal troubles of any kind.'

'Oh no. They had some trouble at work.'

'What was that? Did he discuss it with you?'

She shook her head. 'They were the usual work troubles. Except when they found that dead body. Jerry was upset about that. They all were. The police asked questions.'

'I know. Did Jerry have any ideas about that? Who the dead man was or what he was doing around there?'

She shook her head. 'Jerry had a bit of trouble with kids, young hooligans! But that was a several weeks ago!' she volunteered suddenly.

'Tell me about that,' he suggested.

'They chased him on motorbikes! Young devils!' Her pale cheeks flushed and her voice grew louder. 'They chased him into the river and he had to come home and get dry clothes. Sopping wet he was! He could have caught his death!' The unfortunate choice of phrase struck her and she broke off with a muffled sob.

'But he didn't report this to the police?'

She looked vague. 'Oh, no . . . They were only kids. Had them helmets on, all smoky glass and you can't see their faces.'

It was a new train of thought and might be worth

235

investigating. But she clearly didn't know any more about it or she wouldn't be able to recall it at this moment. He changed tack. 'What did Jerry do in his spare time?'

'Only went to The Fox and Hounds of an evening. Weekends he did my garden.'

Markby was jolted. He hadn't liked Hersey and found him obstructive in every way. Yet apparently unbeknown to him, Hersey had been a fellow gardener. If he'd known, if he could have tried to approach Hersey in that light, won his confidence with a few words about controlling garden pests or new varieties of sweetpeas, anything, his whole fraught relationship with the man might have been different. Too late now to make use of the knowledge. But it made him uneasy. He'd been quick to judge Hersey. Perhaps Alwyn had been right.

'What about visitors?' he asked. She was looking perplexed again so he rephrased his question. 'Did anyone come to the cottage to see Jerry?'

She shook her head. Her eyes were beginning to fill with tears again. 'No. I don't know how I shall manage without Jerry! Since Fred died – my husband – Jerry did all the odd jobs round the place for me, all the painting and decorating, the garden, put in a new bath . . .'

'I'm sorry,' said Markby lamely but meant it. 'A woman police officer will call again later to have another talk with you. Have you got a friend who would come out here and sit with you for a while?'

'Elsie might,' she mumbled and added that she was quite all right, really, it was the shock.

'Elsie? Where does she live? Can we send a car over to fetch her?'

'Elsie Winthrop at the farm, at Greyladies. But she's probably too busy.'

'Mrs Winthrop!' Markby blinked and stared at her. 'She's a friend of yours?'

'Yes, we go to Women's Institute meetings together. She picks me up in the car.'

'So that's one reason Alwyn Winthrop was friendly with Jerry!' he mused aloud.

It wasn't a question but she took it as such. 'He knew Alwyn of course. But they weren't really friends. I'm out of town here. Greyladies Farm is about our nearest neighbour. Apart from The Fox and Hounds, of course, but I don't have anything to do with pubs.'

Markby tried to fit this tiny fragment of knowledge into the picture but finally added it to the jumble of bits and pieces he had in a kind of box of scraps in his mind. It didn't seem to help much but it illustrated what odd facts turned up if you just chatted to people. 'If you should think of anything, anything at all, which Jerry said or did which was unusual, not like his normal way, or which he noticed and thought was odd during the last two or three weeks, let me know. Just ring the station and ask for me, Detective Chief Inspector Markby or, if I'm not there, Sergeant Pearce.'

Outside the cottage he paused to look around him. The building itself was red-brick, dating from about the First World War. The garden was neat if uninspired. The vegetable beds showed tidy rows of spring planting and the forsythia bushes which a few weeks earlier had exploded in vivid yellow splashes against the red walls were going over and had already been carefully pruned out. All Jerry's work presumably. A life like a million others and suggesting no reason why anyone should want to kill him.

'It looks as if someone followed him from the pub,' said Pearce later. 'Unless he disturbed someone along that stretch of road as he walked home. But it's a quiet spot now the motorway's taken most traffic. He wouldn't expect to meet anyone between the pub and that cottage.'

'Unless someone was waiting for him knowing that was his way home.' Markby heaved a sigh. 'Damn, damn, damn. What is going on at that building site? Perhaps he quarrelled with one of the workmen, threatened to get someone the sack? No one liked him. A revenge motive? The other man, whoever he was, waited in the hedgerow knowing Jerry's drinking habits and under cover of dark, bam!'

'It's to do with the drugs shipment!' said Laxton in loud argumentative tones. 'You'll see. I'm going to chase up that warrant and get a search conducted at that farm, what's it called, Witchett?'

'Yes, you do that,' said Markby absently. 'I'm going to see Newman, the contractor. Pearce, you get back to the site and start questioning everyone again.'

'That'll make me popular!' said Pearce wryly. 'You'll find me in a trench full of concrete next.'

Markby scowled. 'Actually that's neither funny nor impossible. I'll give you the same warning I gave Wetherall. Watch yourself. Someone down there is a killer.'

Chapter Sixteen

Dudley Newman, when telephoned and informed there had been a significant but sinister development in the 'building site case' as Rochet's murder was now generally known, had suggested Markby drive out to his home.

The contractor lived outside Bamford on the edge of one of the surrounding villages. The house was a large one in its own grounds with an impressive wrought-iron gate set in high walls. The gate stood open, presumably to admit Markby, and it was difficult not to be over-awed, he thought, as he turned in. On the other hand, he couldn't help feeling that somehow, somewhere, someone was overdoing it a bit.

The chief inspector took the left-hand half of the pair of raked gravel semicircles which swept round to right and left of a central lawn and met up before the front door, a sort of private traffic system. As he drove up it he passed, discreetly tucked away behind a screen of bushes, a detached double garage. The house itself looked new, thought Markby, as he climbed out of his car and glanced up at it, well-built and luxurious. The sort of thing a successful, prosperous building contractor might well put up for himself. The front door was protected by a large, pseudo-Palladian porch, and floor-length windows in the rooms to either side could be seen to be hung with velvet drapes tied back with silk cords. Not the sort of thing one could afford on a policeman's salary.

He turned from the house to look around the garden. It was in stark contrast to the tiny scraps of land grudgingly given to the new houses at the site to form 'gardens'. Newman's house looked as if it might have been built in the middle of a field and the surplus ground landscaped professionally. There were banked conifers around the perimeter and other shrubs and trees. He walked to the corner of the house and peered curiously round it. In the distance was a white-washed wall pierced by another but narrower wrought-iron gate in an ornamental arch giving access to some sort of enclosure. The effect was vaguely Spanish and he felt reasonably sure that behind the wall was a private swimming pool. For him, this large and tidily kept acreage shrieked aloud that no one here had a gardener's heart. It was laid out for minimum maintenance with much lawn to be clipped by an efficient motor-mower and no flowerbeds to weed or design. To Markby, it was a sad waste of potential. He sighed and turned back to the classical door.

His ring was answered by the loud barking of a dog. It sounded like a large one of the guard type. Markby was not good with dogs, especially large dogs. Small ones like Steve's Patch he could manage but he had an alarming vision now of being confronted with a lean and muscular doberman or else some other vicious fanged face. Fortunately someone must have shut it away because the barking became suddenly muffled, to his great relief. The door was opened by a trim blonde in her early forties who wore a pink silk shirt and navy slacks. She smiled uncertainly at him as she ushered him in.

'Dudley's waiting for you. I hope it's not bad news. He's already very upset. I mean, he has been since they found that body in the footings. We – we've had to cancel our holiday. We were going on a Caribbean cruise and we were really sorry. We'd looked forward to it so much. But Dudley thought we ought to stay around until it was all sorted out, all the unpleasantness, I mean. Dudley has a tidy sort of mind, you know. He doesn't like loose ends.'

'Mrs Newman?' Markby returned politely.

'Yes – I'm sorry, I should have introduced myself.'

'We just missed meeting last night, I believe. I was at The Fox and Hounds with some friends and saw your husband. He was on his way to the bar to buy your drinks.'

She stared at him blankly then twitched her shoulders as if given a jolt and said, 'Oh yes, we don't go out often to pubs. Dudley thought it would be a nice change. He, Dudley, is in the lounge. Please come through.'

She turned and hurried, heels clicking, down the hall. As he followed her he realised that the dog was incarcerated behind a door at the far end. He could hear its claws scrabbling and heavy breathing as it pushed its nose to the crack of the door, sniffing out the intruder's scent. He hoped they wouldn't let it out until he was well off the premises.

She showed him into a large room looking out on to the garden to the rear of the building, more lawn and a

241

better view of the swimming-pool hacienda.

Newman appeared to have been pacing up and down on the colourful Indian carpet whilst awaiting his visitor. As Markby appeared, he advanced on him with that mixture of wariness and confidence which Markby recalled from their previous encounter.

'Chief Inspector!' He thrust out his hand. 'Good of you to take the time to drive all the way out here! Let me offer you a drink!' He indicated a large well-stocked cocktail cabinet. 'No? How about a cup of tea? Nancy will be happy to brew up for us.'

'Nothing for me, thank you,' Markby said, seating himself on a well-upholstered chair covered in bright birds-of-paradise patterned material. It sank beneath him and he subsided into a sort of feather depression out of which it was going to be very difficult to extricate himself elegantly. It left him sitting far nearer the floor than he'd anticipated with his knees stuck up in the air, and he had the choice either of wedging his elbows in by his sides or of lifting them out nearly at shoulder-height in order to rest them on the chair's arms.

Newman had taken the chair opposite but, more used to its characteristics, had managed to seat himself without collapsing ridiculously as Markby felt he had done.

'Enjoy your visit to The Fox and Hounds last night, Mr Newman?' Markby asked sociably.

'What? No, as a matter of fact, I – we – didn't!' Newman placed his hands purposefully on his knees, leaning forward. 'Look, Chief Inspector, I didn't want to meet you at the site because the men would be curious . . . and I didn't want to come in to the station because if word got round I'd been called in again, tongues might wag.'

'Oh?' inquired Markby. 'Whose?'

'You'd be surprised!' said Newman with feeling. 'Nancy would tell her mother and her mother would tell all her cronies. That woman's never liked me! My mother-in-law, I mean, not Nancy!'

'Yes, so I assumed. Well, I'm sorry to have to disturb you again, Mr Newman, and to be the bearer of bad news.'

'Have you found out the identity of the dead man?' asked Newman anxiously. 'I hope you're not going to say it's someone to do with the building trade?'

'The man in the trench? We do now think we know who he is. He was not in the building trade. We shan't be releasing his name just yet.'

'I see. Next of kin to be informed first, I suppose.'

Markby gave a non-committal grunt and nodded. 'There's been a second death, Mr Newman. That's what I've called about.'

It was interesting to see what kind of reaction blunt announcement of such news called up. Newman sat for a whole minute as if transfixed, sprawled in his feather-stuffed chair and gazing stupidly at Markby. Then his face turned scarlet and he whispered, 'At the site?'

'Not actually at the site—'

'Thank God!' Newman burst out then added quickly, 'I'm sorry if that sounds heartless but we've already so much trouble . . . and I was afraid you were about to say there had been an accident on site. The Health and Safety people arriving to put their oar in would just about be the last straw!'

'It was someone connected with the building site this time, I'm afraid,' Markby went on.

'The site manager phoned me earlier!' Newman sounded suspicious. 'All he said was someone had failed to turn up for work. Now you're saying someone's dead. Who?'

'Your foreman, Hersey.'

'He can't be!' Newman almost shouted, jumping in his chair. 'He can't be dead!'

'Afraid so. Of course this means added inquiries and added distress to you and your workforce, but I'm afraid it's unavoidable.'

His host's face worked alarmingly. 'You mean – not a natural death, not a heart attack or something? Jerry wasn't that young a man, well, forty. I know it's not old but, look here, are you quite sure he wasn't just ill and we didn't know?'

'I should have explained the manner of his death,' Markby said. 'He was the victim of a vicious and really quite efficient attack.'

Newman had begun to sweat profusely. He lurched out of the chair and towards the drinks cabinet. 'I'm going to have a whisky!' he muttered thickly. Markby watched as he poured it out, slopping it on to the glass surface of the cabinet. 'You sure?' Newman held up the bottle in query. 'Okay, say if you change your mind.' He splashed soda into his drink and came back to his chair.

'What you're saying, it's a hell of a shock and I don't mind telling you, it's knocked me for six!' he said after he'd drunk deeply of his whisky and soda. 'Jerry?' He frowned. 'Why the hell Jerry? How did it happen? Are you absolutely sure it couldn't possibly be an accident?'

A note of entreaty entered his voice.

'Definitely not an accident. Someone fully intended to kill him.' Markby saw the other wince at the verb and went on, 'He was also in the pub last night, by the way, did you happen to see him? I exchanged a few words with him myself.'

'I – don't think so,' Newman mumbled. 'It's a rabbit-warren of a place and it was packed out. If he saw me first, anyway, Hersey would probably have moved into a different room. Not for any specific reason, you understand, but Jerry wasn't sociable by nature, as I'm sure you've realised.'

'He wouldn't have greeted you in the hope, say, that you'd buy him a drink?'

Newman hesitated. 'He might, if I'd been alone. But Nancy was with me.' The contractor rubbed his hand over his sweating brow. 'My head is spinning! Tell me, tell me all the details. I have to know.'

Briefly Markby explained how Mrs Chivers had reported her brother missing and how Hersey's body had been discovered in the ditch not far from The Fox and Hounds. As he spoke he saw that Newman was regaining some of his self-possession and his mind was working feverishly, trying to sort the new information out. He was also, no doubt, trying to find an explanation which would absolve the building site from any involvement in Hersey's death.

When the chief inspector stopped talking, the contractor said aggressively, 'I don't understand it. Hersey wasn't a popular man. But kill him, who'd do that? It's nonsense to think any of the men would do such a thing! A clash of personalities on a site, that's common enough. It doesn't lead to murder! The men who work down there would do anything to avoid trouble.'

'Who hired Hersey to be foreman?' Markby asked.

'I did.' Newman put up a hand to forestall any question. 'Oh I know he's – he was – difficult and inclined to be surly and gripe but he knew the building trade inside out. He worked for me over a number of years so I didn't want to put him out of a job when he mightn't have got another that easily!' Newman's glare defied contradiction.

'I realise he complained,' Markby began tactfully. 'But did he complain about anything in particular?'

'Everything!' said Newman simply. 'All the time! Always did. Always been the same, Jerry. You just take no notice. Took no notice. Oh hell, all this past tense stuff . . .'

'Yes, it takes a bit of getting used to.'

'Jerry's sister,' Newman said suddenly. 'You say she reported him missing? She – knows, I suppose?' Markby nodded and Newman went on, 'I'll have to call round and see her. I did meet her once, a long time ago. Nice woman. I – I'll see if she needs anything.'

'Thank you,' said Markby, notching Newman up in his estimation. 'I realise this is going to make further difficulties for you with regard to your time-table at the site.'

Newman gave a resigned shrug. 'Can't do anything about it now. Whole damn project is jinxed.'

'Yes, I think Mr Wetherall the architect is inclined to feel that way about it. He found Hersey's body, incidentally, while he was walking his dog in the lunch-hour.'

'Steve did?' Newman looked startled. 'Poor chap. Good fellow, Steve. Nasty thing for him. He didn't like

Hersey but—' Newman broke off and looked aghast. 'Look here, Chief Inspector, I didn't mean by that – it just slipped out! I wasn't accusing Wetherall!'

'No, of course not. We realise Hersey was unpopular. Although he had his friends too. I've heard one of the local farmers speak up in his defence.'

'That wouldn't be the red-headed fellow?' Newman raised his eyebrows. 'I know he used to walk over to the site and chat with Jerry.' Newman set down his empty glass and leaned forward intently. 'Tell me, Chief Inspector, how do you find the local farming community? Do you have much to do with them? I find them, well, pretty uncooperative.'

'Really, in what way?'

Newman's manner became that of a man who is now going to talk on his own subject. His confidence gained and his distress evaporated as, almost with an air of relief, he launched into his story. 'The development company responsible for that site has wanted to build in the Bamford area for some time. It was a question of getting a suitable piece of ground and, of course, planning permission. Just by luck Lonely Farm came on the market, near-derelict. They snapped it up. The trouble was, they wanted a bit more land if they could have got it. They approached both landowners on either side.'

'Witchett and Greyladies Farms?'

'Yes!' Newman nodded. 'I went with the representative of the development company to both farms to discuss buying some land. The company thought, as I was a local man, it would be a good idea. I knew the local topography and my name's known about here. You understand how it is. Local people sometimes prefer to deal with a local firm. But we got blunt refusal from

both parties. In the case of Witchett Farm it seemed
ridiculous. The place isn't even working! But the old
lady there wouldn't budge. Wouldn't sell so much as a
few acres.'

Newman shook his head. 'A weird place, that.
Everything just left as it was when the last farm
labourer downed tools, oh, must be fifteen years ago
now or more. A bit like *Great Expectations* really, you
know, Miss Havisham! Everything frozen in a moment
of time.'

'Yes, I know!' Markby tried unsuccessfully to keep
the surprise out of his voice. Newman hadn't struck
him as a literary type.

'I'm a film buff,' said Newman. 'In case you're wondering. Love those old classic movies. You ever see
Great Expectations? The bit where the kid Pip stumbles
over the convict on the run! Marvellous!' He looked
slightly embarrassed. 'It's all right in films, isn't it?
Having your blood chilled. In real life, it's no fun. All
this, it's really got to me, I don't mind you knowing it.
But that's not what I was talking about. I was telling
you about our visits to the farms. As for the other
place, Greyladies!' Newman snorted. 'The old fellow
there, Winthrop, was abusive. No two ways about it.
He was damn rude!'

'How about his son?'

'Ah!' Newman winked knowingly. 'The red-headed
chap we mentioned just now. He didn't say much but
he listened to what we had to say which was more than
his father did! I reckon, if it had been up to him and not
the old man, we might have got somewhere! As a
matter of fact,' Newman lowered his voice as if they

had not been sitting in his own lounge without the slightest chance anyone would overhear them. 'Just between you and me – this is strictly off the record, Chief Inspector! – I had a word with him on his own one day, when I met him wandering around the site. I told him that if in the future the situation should change, say his father retired or changed his mind or – or anything else. Well, I meant kicked the bucket but I didn't say so. Anyway, I told young Winthrop, you just pick up the phone and give me a call. Even if it's long after this site is finished. I wouldn't mind putting in hand a small development on my own account. So you see, I wasn't altogether sorry that Mr Winthrop senior didn't want to sell now to the present developers. If, say, in three or four years' time I could get my hands on Greyladies Farm! Tidy bit of ground there and not far from the new motorway.'

Markby said suddenly, 'Also strictly between us and off the record, doesn't it ever concern you that you're changing the face of the entire area? That you're covering good agricultural land with bricks?'

'No room for sentimentality in business, Chief Inspector! Mind you, I'm not a philistine. Look at this place!' Newman proudly indicated his personal pile of bricks and mortar around them. 'I build quality homes, not rubbish. I'm proud of my firm and the work we do.'

'Quite,' said Markby in a depressed voice. 'Well, thank you for your time. We'll do our best to clear matters up as soon as we can. We shall have to go back to the site and talk to your employees again, I'm afraid. My sergeant, Pearce, is probably there now.'

Newman's gloom returned. 'Can't say that makes me

feel any better, Chief Inspector. But I understand you have your job to do. I just hope . . . well, I just hope no more bodies turn up!'

'Come to that, Mr Newman,' said Markby politely as he struggled up out of the feather-filled trap, 'so do I!'

He began to drive home to Bamford along the back roads, taking his time. He was, truth to tell, avoiding his own office space now occupied by Laxton. He needed to think and could do it better without his unwished colleague's ferrety face watching him.

As yet there was no proof that Hersey's murder was in any way linked with the first one. But Markby would have bet his last penny that it was. What had Hersey seen or discovered, and why the devil had the man been so cantankerous, refusing to confide his knowledge to the police? If he had done so, he might be alive now.

The sound of a car horn tooting impatiently startled him. Markby looked into his mirror and saw that the narrow road behind him, which had been empty, was now filled by an impressive dark blue BMW, anxious to pass.

Reproaching himself for his day-dreaming, Markby obligingly drew into the side of the road. The BMW swept past, mounting the grass verge on the other side, and pulled away in a cloud of grit. He only had time to notice that it had tinted windows and foreign plates.

Foreign plates? Markby became fully awake and pressed his foot on the accelerator. Bamford was not on the tourist trail. The only foreigner to come his way of late had been the dead Frenchman. Now a foreign car? A coincidence, probably. But a curious one and worth investigating.

Unfortunately it was not going to be easy to catch the BMW in his car, especially as driving on the narrow twisting roads called for some prudence, not that the other driver had shown much sign of that. Where would he be headed? Oxford was a likely destination for a foreign car like that but he was going in the wrong direction. To Bamford, then? If he was making that way, then Markby should catch sight of him eventually when the road straightened out. And after a few moments, he did.

The BMW was a dark speck on the road ahead travelling almost certainly now in the direction of Bamford. Markby increased his speed but the distance between them didn't lessen. If anything, it increased. Curiouser and curiouser. Did the BMW suspect he was being tailed? If so, why should it worry him?

Markby tried an experiment. He turned down a little known single-track shortcut which he knew linked up again with the original road a mile further on. When he re-emerged, the BMW was less than a quarter of a mile ahead. Its driver had slowed, believing he had shaken Markby off. Now abruptly the dark blue car accelerated away again. The driver had seen Markby in his rear-view mirror and was renewing his evasive action. To a policeman such an attitude is always suspicious. Some drivers of large powerful cars, of course, just disliked being tagged. But this chap, Markby felt it in his bones, was alarmed. He didn't know who Markby was, but for some reason he was conscious of pursuit and wanted to avoid it.

The road ahead made a left-hand curve and the BMW vanished from sight again. Twice more Markby was granted tantalising glimpses of it and then, when the road finally straightened out again, the vista was empty. The BMW had simply dematerialised.

Markby slowed. There were, as he recalled, no more turnings off until the outskirts of Bamford unless you counted a few tracks leading to farms and a quarry. He began to dawdle along, glancing from time to time in the mirror and at the same time keeping a sharp lookout to either side.

Even so, he almost missed it. It was pulled off the road behind a hedge, and parked in the entry to a muddy track running down the side of a coppice. Only the glitter of the sun on polished metal had drawn his attention to it and in the nick of time. Markby stopped his own car and got out.

As he walked back along the grass verge to the track entrance he noticed how quiet it was all round. There was no other traffic and no sign of habitation. The coppice trees rustled secretively. The only distinct noise was an occasional distant explosion. Someone was shooting pigeons in the woods. He approached the parked car warily. The hair on the nape of his neck bristled and he had that unpleasant feeling of lurking danger.

The BMW was empty. Markby walked round it, peering in its darkened windows. A man's lightweight raincoat lay on the back seat. He didn't try the doors, always risky. At best it might start a safety alarm and involve him in embarrassing explanations. At the very worst the car might be booby-trapped. Instead he called loudly, 'Hullo! Anyone about?' But there was no sign of the driver. A flutter of wings in the coppice alone responded to his words and then there was silence.

The most obvious explanation was that the driver of the car had stepped into the trees to answer a call of nature. Markby stared resentfully at the shiny car. Where had it come from? Where was it going? Whom did it belong to? Where, dammit, was he?

He found himself walking down the track by the coppice, ears strained. There were some old cardboard cartridge cases lying in the grass. Shooting around here must be commonplace. Perhaps that's what the BMW driver had come here to do, shoot pigeons. To go blundering into woods where there was a man with a gun who didn't know Markby was there wasn't advisable. There was little Markby could do but go back, abandon his quest and continue on his own drive to Bamford.

He made a slow, cautious retreat, hugging the treeline. Once he thought he heard a twig snap amongst the trees to his immediate right and halted to call out again, imagining that someone marked an unseen parallel course to his. But, as before, no one answered his query. Yet the driver couldn't be so far away. He must be able to hear Markby. He was hiding in there, lying doggo, and there was precious little the chief inspector could do about it.

Markby shrugged. No crime had been committed, after all. The driver of the BMW had been going a little fast but not beyond all reasonable limits out here on an open empty country road. If he had found him, Markby would have mentioned his speed with a mild warning, nothing more. As for his apparent attitude, if the driver was a foreigner he may well have taken fright at believing himself pursued out here on this lonely road. Highway robbery wasn't entirely unknown.

Markby reached the BMW and stopped. The sun shone down on it and on the back of his neck. It was quite hot in this sheltered lee of the woodland. Markby walked around the mystery car for the last time and noticed with some satisfaction that a large bird had decorated the gleaming roof surface. The plates weren't French, after all. They were Spanish. It deepened the mystery. He doubted that any other car with Spanish plates had been seen around here for a long time or would be in the future. Automatically, a trained policeman's instinct, Markby took his notebook from his pocket and began to jot down the licence number.

Only began, never finished. He was belatedly aware of a movement behind him and of another's presence. He started to turn, notebook and pen in hand and his mouth opening to explain what he was doing. Then stars exploded, he was briefly aware of a sharp pain at the side of his head and blackness engulfed him.

Chapter Seventeen

The back door of the cottage was open and Dudley Newman, standing with his hand half-raised to knock at it, could hear women's voices. After a moment's hesitation he rapped sharply and went in anyway.

They were sitting either side of the Formica-topped kitchen table with empty tea-cups before them, Betty Chivers and Elsie Winthrop. Betty had been crying and her eyes were reddened and swollen and her nose glowed from much scrubbing at it with the handkerchief clenched in her workworn hand. Even now he couldn't help thinking how impossible it seemed that a pretty lively girl could finish up like this, a worn-out drudge.

Mrs Winthrop looked up and when she saw who it was, asked belligerently, 'Oh, 'tis you, is it? What do you want?'

'I called to see Mrs Chivers,' he said stiffly. 'I employed Jerry. I just heard about – about it. The police came to see me.'

Mrs Chivers whispered, ''Tis all right, Elsie.'

Mrs Winthrop rose majestically to her feet. 'I'll just go on back home for a bit and organise Jess into getting the menfolk's tea. I'll be back later, Betty.'

When she had gone, Newman took her vacated chair and said gently, 'I'm very sorry, Betty.' She didn't reply and he went on a little awkwardly, 'If there's anything . . .'

'No!' She reached out and touched his sleeve briefly before jerking her hand back as if she'd taken some unheard of liberty. ''Tis all right, Dudley. Elsie's keeping an eye on me and – and I can manage.'

'All the same, if you change your mind you can leave a message for me at the site, you know. There's no need to go telephoning the house.'

She nodded. After a moment she looked up and said with a faint pathetic note of admiration in her voice, 'You done well for yourself, Dudley.'

'Pretty well.' His voice was flat.

'I want you to know I appreciate the way you did your best for Jerry, giving him a job all those years. I know well how he was with other folk. People didn't understand him and he didn't get along.'

'I couldn't do otherwise, could I?' he burst out resentfully, then sighed and raised his hands as if he would have physically pushed away some rebuke she might have made. 'I don't mean that the way it sounded, Betty. I was glad I could do something to help.' He glanced round the kitchen and burst out, unable to stop himself, 'Good God, Betty, I never thought you'd end up like this!'

'I'm not so badly off,' she said with a touch of defiance.

'I – I feel responsible . . .'

'Of course you're not, Dudley. Don't talk foolish. What you're referring to – well, we was only kids at the time. I wasn't sixteen and you were what – '

'Nineteen,' he said heavily. 'Betty, I want to pay for Jerry's funeral. He was my employee and I'd like to give him a decent send-off. Don't argue now. We'll talk about it later, when you're feeling up to it.'

He got up and went to the door. Glancing back and seeing her still sitting as he'd left her in that miserable kitchen, he fumbled for his wallet, took out two twenty-pound notes and stuck them behind a pottery hen on the dresser. 'To be going on with. I'll be back later, Betty, about the funeral.'

Hurrying back to his car he had reached it before he saw that Elsie Winthrop stood by it, implacably awaiting him.

'I was waiting for you to come out!' she said. 'I know what's brought you here well enough and it's no more than right you should do something for her! But you be careful, now! Though I dare say you will be because you wouldn't want folk knowing, would you?'

'You mind your own business!' he said angrily.

She gave him a look of malice. 'I mean to! That's why I'm telling you now to keep away from our Alwyn! I know you've been talking to him about selling Grey-ladies. Well, the farm isn't for sale and won't never be! You can leave Alwyn alone – leave all my family alone!'

'You stupid woman, don't you realise – ' he began, all his emotion channelled into his words.

She interrupted him. 'I realise well enough what your game is, my lad! I wasn't born yesterday! Now you leave my menfolk be. No telephoning the house, nei-ther! All your life, wherever you've gone, you've caused folk trouble and grief, Dudley Newman! So you mind me, good now! I won't let no one harm my family! You remember that!'

When Markby came round, he was lying on the grass where he'd fallen. The BMW had gone. He sat up, wincing, and gingerly touched his head. It was sore and throbbed abominably. Waves of pain washed over him and a swirling mist came and went before his eyes. He waited, struggling to gather his wits, for the last mist and stars to clear.

It seemed to take ages and once when he tried to stand up too soon in his impatience a searing pain again shot through not only his skull but his neck and upper spine and he was forced to fall back on the grass. It was a few years since he'd been slugged like this, so efficiently. From the recesses of his memory the phrase 'sustained a severe blow' floated up and he had a confused fuzzy image of a much younger self in a witness box giving evidence. He couldn't remember the case now, it was donkey's years back.

'Crass stupidity!' he muttered. 'At your age and with your experience! Letting it happen, someone creep up on you . . . it wasn't as if you didn't know he was hanging about in the woods over there.'

Embarrassment and humiliation hurt far more than the pain, dizziness or inconvenience. He spent too much time at a desk these days, that much was clear. He was forgetting what it was like to be at the sharp end. The rawest recruit would have known to summon assistance on his walkie-talkie as soon as he had taken a look at that suspicious BMW!

But physically he was feeling better. Markby looked at his watch. He'd been unconscious and sitting here altogether no more than twenty minutes although it felt much longer. The blow hadn't been that hard, just hard enough, and certainly delivered by a professional.

He saw ruefully that the knees of his trousers and elbows of his jacket were grass-stained. Trying to rub off the marks on the cloth, his eye fell on his pen lying nearby. He reached for it and remembered his notebook. It had gone.

Markby hunted around for a while but the driver of the BMW had definitely removed it. Nor, curse it, could he remember any of the licence number he'd started to write down. Training would normally have fixed it in his head, but the blow had successfully knocked it out again.

He got up and made his way back to his own car. It didn't take him more than a quick glance to see that someone had quickly and efficiently gone through that. But nothing had been taken or damaged. The BMW driver had just been checking. He had probably also – Markby's hand went to his inside breast pocket. Yes, his wallet had been removed and replaced. Everything was in it which should be in it, but jammed back untidily. The BMW driver had found and scrutinised his police ID card. What would he do now? Put as much distance as possible between himself and the locality, probably!

Markby contacted the station and reported what had happened, asking them to send out a message requesting a watch for a dark blue BMW with tinted windows and Spanish plates. Irritably refusing an offer of personal assistance, he drove slowly back to Bamford where he asked the fingerprint boys to check the doorhandle of his car and the surface of his wallet. But the BMW driver wouldn't have made the elementary mistake of leaving fingerprints. A professional at the job, definitely. But who?

He was relieved on regaining his office to find it empty. Pearce hadn't come back yet from the site and Laxton had stepped into town for half an hour, said Wpc Jones who arrived bearing expressions of sympathy from everyone in the building and hot coffee plus aspirin.

'Why don't you nip over to the cottage hospital, sir? Get them to take a look at your head?'

'I'm all right!' he snarled.

'You might be concussed,' she said knowledgeably.

He glared at her. 'I am not concussed!'

'It hasn't improved his temper!' said Wpc Jones, back downstairs.

Pearce arrived back at the station some time later to find his chief writing out a report of the incident. 'Stick this on Mr Laxton's desk!' Markby ordered, handing it over.

Pearce did as bid and expressed his concern at the attack. Markby grunted and waved his solicitude away. 'How did you get on?'

Pearce reported little success at the site where, he said, near mutiny reigned.

'They're all scared witless on hearing about Hersey. They think there's a maniac on the loose and he means to pick them off, one by one. Some are even asking if Daley really ran off or if he isn't also buried in a trench about the place.'

'For God's sake!' said Markby, startled. 'It's a thought. But we didn't think it. Perhaps we should have done.'

'Riordan, that's the fellow who shared a caravan with Daley when he worked there, he's been promoted to temporary foreman but there's precious little work being done.'

'People have murdered to gain themselves promotion before now,' Markby observed. 'Didn't you interrupt some kind of argument between Riordan and Hersey? What sort of chap is Riordan in your opinion?'

'Artful. Very clever at playing the simple workman but as canny as they come. The site manager more or less warned me to be on my guard. He's affable, mind. Just runs circles round you while offering you tea at the same time. He's a big feller and strong but whether he'd be violent . . . He was quite open about disliking Hersey. He even said someone would break Hersey's neck for him one day!'

'Did he, by Jove?'

'Yes, but surely since he said it, he wouldn't have done it? I think he only meant it as a figure of speech to indicate how unpopular Hersey was. None of them liked Hersey and they're honest enough about it, but that's as much as they'll admit. I couldn't get anything else out of them. None of them socialised with him and none of them can suggest anything regarding his private life. I left them all clustered together round a brazier discussing whether to walk off the site *en masse* or not. Riordan, incidentally, is for them staying. But then, if they go, it would leave him with no one to be foreman of!'

'Wonder if we'll find any of them still there tomorrow,' Markby said resignedly. 'I'm beginning to feel quite sorry for Newman.'

*

Later on, however, it was neither Hersey, Daley nor Newman's labour troubles which occupied Markby's mind. It wasn't even his own sore skull. It was DCI Laxton.

'He's asked us to go and have a drink with him at The Crossed Keys,' he said apologetically. 'It put me on a bit of a spot. I mean, I can't say he's my cup of tea but he is a colleague, he is away from home and he is staying at The Crossed Keys which isn't that jolly a spot to be on your own. So I thought perhaps we could just pop in there around eight and have a quick one with him.'

'All right,' said Meredith.

She hoped her relief at the ordinariness of this request didn't echo too obviously in her voice. She had been worried that he might be feeling rejected since her cool reception of his kiss after the visit to The Fox and Hounds. Or even that he might restart the vexed argument over the future course of their relationship. But either he was too busy to brood over it right now or he had made a conscious decision to shelve the whole matter for the time being. Either way, he sounded reassuringly matter-of-fact. That suited her, too.

'What's his name, your Met colleague?' she asked. 'Laxton?'

'That's right. Like the apple.'

'What's he doing down here anyway?'

'Oh, you know how it is,' Markby said vaguely. 'They sometimes send these bods around the country to see what we're doing.'

Laxton had changed out of his city suit when they met up with him in the lounge bar of The Crossed Keys. He wore slacks and a rather nifty Italian sweater. The lounge bar wasn't Bamford's most popular meeting place and they more or less had it to themselves apart from a couple of commercial travellers discussing business in one corner and a middle-aged man reading the paper and conversing at the same time with the barman.

'What'll you have?' Laxton asked cheerily.

Mindful of his head, Markby asked for tomato juice. Meredith, unaware of his experience, looked slightly startled but not to be outdone or wishing to let the side down, chimed in with a request for pineapple.

'Oh, pair of teetotallers, eh?' said Laxton. 'Or is that – ' he met Markby's eye and substituted ' – because of a diet?'

'No,' said Markby in sepulchral tones.

'Are you all right?' whispered Meredith as Laxton set off purposefully towards the bar.

'Yes, fine.' Markby tried to sound nonchalant. 'Just not in a drinking mood.'

'Quiet place, isn't it?' observed Laxton when he returned with a tray. He cast a disapproving glance around him. The armchairs in this lounge had seen better days and the carpet had faded. The one very bad print of the mail coach leaving a Dickensian scene in deepest snowdrifts did little to cheer the atmosphere.

'There are other pubs around, most of them much more lively,' Markby offered.

'I'm not a country-lover myself,' said Laxton. 'Gets on my nerves frankly. This town is as dead as a doornail. What on earth do you do for amusement?'

'We manage!' said Markby crossly. His head was beginning to ache again.

'I live in London,' Meredith said. 'I used to live down here, near Bamford. I liked it but it was the travel, commuting up and down to London every day. It was just too much. Otherwise I would have stayed down here.'

Markby glanced at her over his tomato juice. 'Would you?'

'Yes!' she said defiantly and reddened.

Laxton was oblivious to undertones and intent on pursuing his own argument. 'Haven't you ever tried to get yourself transferred somewhere else? I mean, careerwise this is backwater.'

'I like it here!' Markby was finding it difficult to control his irritation. 'Besides I'm a sort of local. My family has lived round here for generations and my sister and her family live in the town.'

'Born within the sound of Bow bells myself,' said Laxton serenely. 'You can keep all those sheep. There's a hell of a lot of them, isn't there, around here? Where we were earlier today the fields were full of the brutes.'

'It's market day tomorrow,' Markby informed him. 'Then you'll see plenty of sheep and other animals. The town will be busy all day, cattle transporters clogging up the streets, terrific racket and if the wind is blowing the right way, you'll smell it, too.'

Laxton looked suitably horrified.

'It's Maundy Thursday tomorrow!' Meredith remembered. 'Will they still hold the cattle market?'

'Oh yes. Life in the country goes on come what may.'

'Are you married, Mr Laxton?' Meredith inquired, feeling that this particular line of conversation had its pitfalls.

'Yes, two kids. My wife's a city girl but she likes to get out for the day, mind you. Teddington Lock, she likes it there. And we like to do one-day shopping trips across the Channel. The hypermarket outside Boulogne is a good place. You know it? You should go over there. It's a good day out. But she's like me, a Londoner at heart.'

'I hope you don't get detained down here among us too long, then,' said Markby mildly and winced as Meredith trod on his foot.

'He's all right,' she said later as they walked away from The Crossed Keys.

'You haven't got him sitting in the corner of your office.'

'No, true. But socially he's all right. He's a fish out of water down here but that isn't his fault. He's honest about it, that's all. Anyway, poor chap, the Easter break is coming up and I expect he'd like to be with his family and instead of that he's been sent down here.'

'Yes,' Markby mused. 'Laura will be arriving back next Tuesday.'

'And my stay will be over.'

'I wish you weren't going back to London!' he confessed.

'I somehow wish I wasn't going, either. Laxton finds it quiet but I find it peaceful. Even though unpleasant things seem to be happening like poor Hersey's death. I didn't like him but I wouldn't have wanted him dead.'

'Steve was saying much the same thing. As for your leaving Bamford—'

She met his eye and said firmly, 'It's best I do go, really.'

Markby's gaze fell on a garish display of chocolate Easter eggs wrapped in foil and surrounded by fluffy yellow chicks which filled a nearby shop window.

'Let's hope we're all able to spend a happy Easter!' he said sourly.

But to himself he was thinking: two unsolved murders, an untraced shipment of heroin, a gang, a killer on the loose, a mystery car driver who carried a cosh, Steve Wetherall on the verge of a nervous breakdown, as well as Laxton about to turn Witchett Farm upside-down in company with a sniffer dog! Some Easter break. He winced and unthinkingly put his hand to his head.

'You are sure you're all right, Alan?' she asked in concern.

'Absolutely. I just cracked my head getting out of the car earlier. Nothing much.'

There was no point in telling her about the BMW. He wished to foster the belief in her that he was good at his job, not the sort of incompetent idiot who got himself knocked cold. Besides, women fussed.

Chapter Eighteen

'Five!' sang out the man in the grubby jacket. 'Five, Five-fifty, five-fifty, six! Twenty-six bid! Six-fifty, six-fifty, twenty-seven bid!' There was a smart tap as a hard surface was struck. The man leaned from his rostrum. 'Next!'

A fresh gaggle of sheep was released from a nearby pen and driven towards the auctioneer. They milled around in confusion, pushed and pulled by the stockmen, a lean dog very like Alwyn's nibbling at their heels urging them to scamper in the required direction. Almost without a break in his expressionless voice the auctioneer began his litany again. 'Twenty-six bid, twenty-six-fifty, seven!'

Meredith sidled around the outside of the small crowd which attended the auction and tried to see round or over the solid phalanx of dark blue, green and khaki, colours beloved of countrymen and which gave to the market scene the appearance of an old sepia photograph, hand-touched with extra colour here and there. The warm smell of farmyard manure hung in the air. Muddy cattle in a nearby pen waited their turn and watched the auctioneer from afar as if interested to know how prices were going today.

Alwyn was standing at the back of the crowd with his
hands in his pockets and his cap pulled down over his
red hair. He was wearing a shabby waxed jacket today
and green boots, the little straps at the tops unfastened
untidily. His blue jeans were clean, however, he was
freshly shaved and managed in a haphazard sort of way
to give quite a gentlemanly appearance. Alwyn, Meredith thought wryly, was not without a certain style. His
face was expressionless. She didn't know whether he'd
seen her approach. He gave no sign, but neither did he
look particularly surprised when she touched his elbow
and bid him good morning.

'Hullo, there,' he said. 'How are you? Giving history
a miss this morning?'

'I'm fine. How are prices? Are you selling today?'

He shook his head and glancing down at her, took
his hands from his pockets. 'I didn't know you were
interested in sheep!' He had that ironic look in his eyes
again. Not exactly laughing at her, rather at something
else, some obscure joke of his own which she couldn't
share.

'It's interesting to see the market. After all, I live
in London, remember. I thought I ought not to leave
Bamford this time without taking a look. I've never
visited it before.'

'Not that much to see.' He moved back a little to let
someone pass. 'Lot of sheep and cows and I've seen
enough of them to last me my lifetime. 'Tis all right for
you, seems sort of cosy and old-world to you, I suppose. Farming's not like that. It's bloody hard work
and little reward. Hardly worth being in sheep. Price of
hay brought in at lambing time alone knocks the profit
out of it, three pound a bale these days. 'Tisn't as

though you could get a decent price for the fleeces. No one even wants to buy the things and you've got to pay the shearers. They don't work for nothing, you know. I'm the only fool does that!'

'Eight-fifty, nine, twenty-nine bid! Twenty-nine!' Tap. 'Next!'

'I'm not idealising it!' she said combatively. 'I know it's tough and uncertain and you're out in all weathers at all hours. I realise that for the hours you put in and the effort you expend the return is poor. But look, without making a direct comparison, still most jobs are hard graft with not as much reward as we'd like! Even the interesting ones aren't interesting all of the time. Even my job, which I normally enjoy, isn't much fun at the moment, stuck in London at a desk. I want to go abroad again but they won't send me. Everyone gets fed up with their job at some time. And we'd all like to be rich.'

Alwyn gave a grunt.

'Thanks for sending me to Dr Gretton, by the way,' Meredith continued. 'She's going to arrange for me to meet her father when he gets back. He's the one who conducted the dig ten years ago.'

'Funny old way to earn a living, that,' said Alwyn reminiscently. 'But probably makes better sense than farming. Who's Dr Gretton, then? Not the fellow who came out and dug up the paddock?'

'No, she's his daughter, a glamorous lady palaeontologist.'

'Bones,' said Alwyn dismissively. 'All bloody bones. You fancy a cup of coffee?'

'Please,' she said, surprised. That was Alwyn for you. One minute you felt he was hinting you were in the way and a complete idiot to boot, the next he was being hospitable.

'Some of the wives,' he explained, 'they run a sort of coffee stall over there.' He nodded towards the far corner of the market. 'They take turns to help out. Ma and Jess should have been doing it today but they had to cry off.'

'Oh, why?'

'Betty Chivers, that's Jerry's sister. She's still very shaken up and Ma's got her out at the farm today. Gives Betty a shoulder to cry on and get it out of her system.'

Meredith couldn't answer this at once because he was striding briskly ahead of her and talking over his shoulder. They fetched up at last in a corner under a corrugated tin roof where two sturdy ladies in quilted jackets were dispensing tea and coffee from an urn into polystyrene cups. Their red faces glowed in the crisp air and they greeted Alwyn with cheerful banter.

'Who's the young lady then, Alwyn?'

'Friend of a friend. Nothing to do with me!' said Alwyn a trifle ungallantly.

'You make him mind his manners!' one of them advised Meredith who smiled awkwardly, not quite knowing how or if to respond.

'Don't know if you take sugar?' Alwyn handed her a cup.

'No, not for me. Thanks. I need this, the wind's chill today.'

'Weather's changing. We've seen the last of the sun for a bit. You'll see, there's a gale brewing up.' Alwyn sipped at the dark brew in his polystyrene cup.

Meredith warmed her fingers on the little white tub

and said thoughtfully, 'It shocked me dreadfully to hear about Jerry Hersey. It's because I knew him, I suppose. Death coming to someone you know is always hard to accept even though I didn't like him much. In fact I didn't like him at all. He was extremely rude to me and I thought him thoroughly unpleasant. But that's not the same thing as wishing him dead.'

Alwyn said nothing.

'He was a sort of friend of yours, wasn't he?' she added. 'So I won't criticise him any more. Anyway, one oughtn't to speak ill of the dead.'

'A neighbour more like it. I didn't mind Jerry. We got along all right. You hadn't to take any notice of the way he talked. He was a good brother to Betty. Took care of her after her husband died.'

'So I understand. Poor woman. She'll miss him badly.' Meredith sorted out her next words carefully, seeing in his last words a possible angle from which to tackle Alwyn about something which she wanted to discuss. 'Alwyn, we all need someone to look after us when we're in a bad fix. Everyone needs someone. Why don't you like Michael Denton being friendly with Jessica? He seems a nice chap. They knew one another before.'

'She doesn't need him to look after her!' said Alwyn shortly. 'She's got us!'

'Of course she has! She knows that. But, well . . .' Oh bother it, Meredith thought, here goes for a bit of plain speaking. 'Perhaps Jessica doesn't want to spend the rest of her life on the farm. She's only in her early twenties, after all.'

Alwyn rolled the empty polystyrene cup between his hands. 'When Dad retires—' He paused and then added firmly, 'When Dad retires, I mean to sell up Greyladies. There will be money then. Jess can take her share and do whatever she wants with it. I've told her. All she has to do is wait a little while.'

'You said your father would never let you sell Greyladies, that's what you told Alan,' she argued.

'He's near seventy, is Dad,' Alwyn said calmly.

'Some people live till ninety.'

'I know it!' he retorted sourly. After a moment he added, 'I don't mean to wait till Dad dies. He's obstinate, the old man, but he's not a fool. In a few years' time he'll realise he can't go on and that it's up to me. I think he knows in his heart, though he wouldn't ever say so out loud, that I mean to sell. It's tough on the old boy.' There was a note of genuine regret in his voice as he spoke the last words. 'But I can't do anything else.' Now there was obstinacy.

'Yes,' Meredith said after a pause. 'It will be tough on your father. After so many generations at Greyladies, to think you will be the last Winthrop to farm there. It's sad.'

'Ma's more likely to put up a fight than Dad,' he went on unexpectedly. 'Ma's set her heart on keeping the farm going. She keeps talking about me getting married and raising a family there!' Alwyn gave a short derisive laugh. 'What woman in her right mind would come and live at Greyladies? The place is run down, the house – it looks all right but everything about it wants seeing to from the roof down. And never having any spare cash or be able to get away for a holiday. Modern women wouldn't put up with that kind of life and I don't blame them! But Ma, she sees it differently.'

'A lot of modern women wouldn't want that kind of life,' Meredith admitted. 'But there are still some who look for something other than having money to spare and a kitchen with all mod cons. You just haven't met the right one yet, Alwyn.'

'Nor ever likely to! Not around here, anyway!'

'Oh come on. Why shouldn't you?'

'All right,' said Alwyn in that disconcerting way he had, 'how about you? You look strong and healthy. You fancy coming to live at the farm? Plenty of fresh air. You won't need a wardrobe of fancy clothes. Got no central heating, of course, but I dare say you won't mind cleaning out the grate on a cold winter morning.'

'All right, you needn't be clever!' snapped Meredith. 'You like to make me look a fool, don't you?'

'You're not a fool. Sharp girl, you are. Alan's a lucky fellow!'

'Well!' she said after a moment's stunned silence. 'That's a compliment I didn't expect.'

His grey eyes rested on her face. 'But you wouldn't want to spend your life at Greyladies,' he said quietly. 'So why should any other bright girl, eh? Women have all got careers of their own these days.'

'What about your brother, is he married?' she asked after a pause.

Alwyn threw her a sharp look. 'Jamie? Who told you about him?'

'I think it was Steve or it may have been Alan. No, I think it was Steve Wetherall. He said your brother had left the farm and worked abroad somewhere.'

'He did the right thing, Jamie.' Alwyn tossed the empty cup into a refuse bin nearby. 'No, he's not the marrying kind. Always seems to have some girlfriend or other in tow, or so he says when he writes.'

'Where does he actually live? In which country? I've lived abroad a lot.'

'He moves around,' Alwyn said. 'In Spain, last I heard.'

'What does he do?' Meredith asked curiously.

'I don't know. Wheels and deals in the business line. He always had a good head for that. Now it's something to do with property, holiday flats. I haven't time to worry about what he does.' Alwyn moved away from the coffee stall. 'I've just spotted a fellow I fancy is looking for me. Give my regards to Alan when you see him.'

'Oh, yes, thanks for the coffee. I didn't mean to take up your time!' But he had gone, his tall figure striding through the crowd.

Had she followed him, Meredith would have seen, perhaps with surprise, that the person Alwyn had espied on the far side of the crowded market was Dudley Newman, obviously ill at ease in his surroundings and fastidiously keeping well clear of any mud or animals. He greeted Alwyn testily. 'I came here as you suggested, since I can't phone you now. If we could have met somewhere else, I'd have liked it better.'

'I wouldn't,' said Alwyn calmly. 'You'd like to meet me in an office, I suppose, where you fancy I'd be fiddling about scraping my boots on the doormat and doffing my cap to the secretaries. Well, this is my world and if you want to talk to me this is where you come. Dad hasn't come in today so it's all right.'

Newman's nose wrinkled as a waft of fresh manure struck it but he didn't argue any further, preferring to hurry their business along so that he could leave.

'Listen, Alwyn, I've told you I'm prepared to wait. But I can't wait indefinitely. In building developments you have to do things at the right time. I'd like to think I could make an offer for Greyladies within the next eighteen months or so. That would suit me.'

Alwyn scowled. 'It wouldn't suit me. Ma said she'd seen you over at Betty Chivers' place so I know you heard her view of it and the old man feels the same. They won't budge.'

'Now Alwyn,' Newman said in conciliatory tones, 'I know how you feel and how you're placed. I sympathise. I also know you're a reasonable fellow and you understand how I'm placed. Your mother's a good woman – but she doesn't understand business. Let's leave her out of this, eh? It's your father you need to tackle. Explain to him firmly that you're not prepared to carry on. He can't work the farm alone. He'll see he has to sell – and if he comes around to the idea, well, then, what your mother thinks about it is neither here nor there! She can be by-passed.'

Alwyn gave him an odd malicious look followed by a crooked grin. 'You don't know Ma!' he said.

Thursday morning never dawned but Dolly Carmody woke up thinking, ''Tis cattle market day!' and then she would remember that it wasn't, not for Witchett Farm any more.

Nowadays she didn't even go into Bamford shopping on a Thursday because the sight, sound and smell of the livestock which seeped into every corner of the town recalled too many memories. Her absence had lessened her links with many old farming friends whom she now rarely saw. She often thought of them, too, at this time so that, all in all, Thursday was a bad day at Witchett.

One habit she couldn't break was that of rising early. She came downstairs this morning and opened the back door for the cats, always her first act. They rushed in mewing loudly to be fed. They were supposed to have spent the night actively clearing the yard of mice but she knew well they spent it curled up in the shed where the hay was kept for the horses stabled at the farm. Nevertheless they put on a passable imitation of cats which had earned their keep and never failed to fall asleep again immediately after breakfast, just as though they really had been awake all night.

As the cats came in, the old spaniel went out sniffing around to see if anything had changed overnight outside. And Dolly put the kettle on and got out the bacon to cook her breakfast. But this morning, as she did this, she heard the old dog bark.

Curious she put down the frying pan and went to the door. A car engine could be heard, no, two cars at least, and coming nearer, coming to Witchett. Single motorists occasionally took a wrong turn and fetched up here, but not two together and it was too early for any of the horse owners to be arriving.

The cars swept into the yard. One was a van and a young fellow in uniform jumped out of it and let a labrador dog out of the back. Two men had got out of the first car and were coming towards her and a third vehicle had just driven in. Men were getting out of that and a uniformed woman, too. Suddenly the yard seemed full of people.

Dolly grabbed the spaniel and called, 'What's going on? This is my farm!'

'Good morning, madam!' said the leading man, a sharp-faced fellow with a town-dweller's voice and manner. 'Police. You'll be Mrs Dorothy Carmody? I have a warrant here to search the premises.'

'Search?' She gaped at him. 'Search Witchett? What for?'

'Well, we'll see about that, shall we, madam? Now then, we'll start with these outbuildings.' He turned as he spoke to give orders to the others. Dolly interrupted him.

'You can't!' He had thrust a piece of paper at her and she stared at it disbelievingly. 'I haven't got anything here to interest the police! How should I? It's a mistake, a terrible mistake!'

'Fraid not, madam. Perhaps you'd better go inside. The policewoman here will . . .'

'Look out, sir!' one of the other men exclaimed, darting forward. 'The old girl is going to keel over!'

Meredith had made her way out of the market, only narrowly avoiding being run down by a lorry turning into the congested entrance. From between slats on its high sides, eyes peered at her. More sheep. Poor brutes. But that's the way of it. Livestock. Dead stock.

Back in the High Street all was a-bustle. Meredith found herself going against the prevailing stream and had to dodge and wriggle her way through. At last she came up against a Guernsey sweater and a voice said in surprised tones, 'Oh, hullo! It's Jessica's friend, isn't it?'

'Michael!' Meredith stared at him, startled. 'I was just talking about – that is to say, I was just talking to Jess's brother, Alwyn.'

Michael's face darkened. 'Best of luck! You're more likely to get some sense out of talking to the sheep!'

'Oh dear,' said Meredith, pulling a face. 'I can guess. The Winthrops are being difficult.'

'Difficult?' His young face suffused with scarlet. 'They're impossible!' He sighed. 'Care for a pint?'

He wanted to unburden his troubled young soul. Fine. People did seem bent on offering her drinks this morning.

They obtained their pints in The Bunch of Grapes, a hostelry not unknown to Meredith from previous acquaintance. Her pint actually took the form of a pineapple juice. Michael was a devotee of 'real ale', she was not particularly surprised to discover.

'Are they all right?' he said argumentatively, when the two of them had found themselves a seat by the inglenook fireplace. 'The Winthrops, I mean. Are they all right in the head? Or are they all barmy except Jessica?'

'Strong-minded, I'd call it. Alwyn's got a funny sort of way with him but I think he's all right behind it. He's devoted to his sister.'

'You know the saying about with friends like that, you don't need enemies!' Michael Denton said with a ferocious scowl.

They sat for a while in silence while the bar slowly filled. Quite a few of the men in here looked as if they'd come from the market. Meredith hoped Alwyn didn't walk in and discover them. She felt she was very slowly winning Alwyn's confidence but the little progress made could easily be wiped out. Keeping one eye on the door, she waited for Michael to begin his tale of woe and after a few moments he did, setting down his glass with a deliberate motion.

'Do you know them well?'

'Not very, no. I've been out there to the farm. I wanted to do some historical research. Alwyn was helpful up to a point but I felt I wasn't wanted.'

'At least you got further than I did! I'm not allowed to set foot on that farm! I tried yesterday and the old man – have you seen him? He must be eighteen stone and most of it muscle! Except for the head, of course, which is bone! Well, I thought he was going to set the dog on me! He told me to leave forthwith, or in his own words, "bugger off!" Delightful old chap.'

'Ah, tricky.'

'I can't ring Jess up. She never gets to the phone first, the old lady does. Or Alwyn. You'd think, wouldn't you, that Alwyn would be more reasonable? It's like reasoning with a brick wall. What's wrong with me? I'm a primary schoolteacher not the captain of the local hell's angels! I don't go round breaking pub windows or emptying rubbish into people's front gardens! I don't have any notifiable diseases and apart from liking the odd pint I don't think I've got any particular vices! I've known Jessica for a long time. We've got a lot in common. I'd hoped to meet her in town this morning but you see, they've managed to stop her coming in!' he concluded gloomily.

Meredith said cautiously, 'I don't know if it's quite like that.' She explained about Mrs Chivers.

'It doesn't take both Jess and her mother to look after one distressed old lady!' said Michael obstinately. 'What's Jessica supposed to do? This Mrs Chivers is Ma Winthrop's friend, not Jessica's. No, they've made it an excuse to stop Jess meeting me.'

'I think they're genuinely worried about Jessica's health. She had a bad breakdown and now, well, two murders on the doorstep.'

'Yes,' he nodded. 'That last one is pretty grim. I mean, Jessica knew that man Hersey. Not well but he was a sort of neighbour. Which is another reason why she shouldn't be at the farm this morning listening to Mrs Chivers go on and on about it. If the Winthrops had any sense they would have sent Jessica into town with Alwyn, out of the way! Do you realise that in a manner of speaking they've virtually got Jess locked up out there at Greyladies?'

'That does seem to be the Winthrop way with daughters,' said Meredith, remembering Mary Anne.

'Well, I'll tell you something!' he said, thrusting out his jaw pugnaciously. 'They won't frighten me away! I'm blowed if I'm going to be sworn at and ordered off! Jessica wants to see me and I want to see Jessica and I'll find some way of doing it. Just give me time.'

Meredith had finished her pineapple juice. 'A hide like a rhino', Steve Wetherall had said was needed in dealing with the Winthrops. She wouldn't have described Michael as having that. He appeared a fairly sensitive young man in many ways. But in others she didn't doubt he had the requisite toughness to take the family on and he deserved a little help and encouragement. Commonsense told her that she ought not to meddle. No good would come of it. Alwyn would explode if he knew. But when she recalled Jessica's usually pale face and how pretty and enlivened she had appeared in contrast, entering The Fox and Hounds on Michael's arm, she knew without a doubt that meddle was exactly what she was going to do.

'I might be able to help you there,' she said cautiously. 'At least, I might have an idea.'

With her voice lowered because someone might overhear and report to Alwyn – there were far too many gumboots and crumpled waxed jackets drinking at the bar – she explained how Jessica rode over to Witchett Farm most days to help Dolly Carmody.

'So you see,' she finished conspiratorially, her head pressed against his over a couple of empty glasses for all the world as if they were planning the next Gunpowder Plot, 'you could meet Jessica at Witchett. The Winthrops wouldn't know, wouldn't even suspect.'

Michael was thinking it out and looking for objections. 'I don't know this old dear, Mrs Carmody. Anyway she's a lifelong friend of the Winthrops. She wouldn't go along with it.'

'She's very keen on Jess and very keen, incidentally, that Jess lead a normal life. Besides, I fancy she's a bit of a romantic at heart. She it was told me about the Grey Folk.'

Michael hadn't heard about the Grey Folk so there was a five-minute digression while she explained. Then they came back to the matter in hand. He was beginning to look hopeful, but doubtful at the same time, the two emotions alternating on his freckled face.

'How am I going to fix this up?'

'Leave it to me. I'll take you out to Witchett and introduce you to Dolly and we'll take it from there.'

Michael had overcome his doubts. 'Okay. When?'

'Now, if you like. I suppose Dolly will be there. The trip's not wasted even if she isn't. At least you can see where Witchett is. We'll walk back to the house I'm minding and collect my car. From there the drive to

Witchett will take fifteen minutes, even allowing for hold-ups with market-day traffic.'

'You're on!' he said enthusiastically.

Chapter Nineteen

Michael positively buzzed with anticipation beside her as she drove along the old B road looking for the turning to Witchett. Meredith was struck with a fear that this bright plan of hers might after all come to nothing and this nice boy would be disappointed. But nothing ventured, nothing gained.

The wind was whipping up and the sun had disappeared. The trees leaned out over the road balancing their branches and the hedgerows trembled. A few grey clouds had scudded up from somewhere and it looked as if before much longer they would get rain. Meredith cast an apprehensive eye at the sky. She should have known, given her previous mishap, to keep her eye on this twisty old road, quiet but by no means abandoned or hazardless.

'Watch out!' her passenger exclaimed suddenly and grabbed at the dashboard to steady himself.

Meredith swerved violently to the side and managed somehow to avoid plunging straight down into the deep ditch there. A large shiny BMW car had appeared without warning around the bend, hogging the middle of this narrow road and speeding along at around eighty. She had no time to see who was driving it but as they

regained their rightful course she said, 'Whew! Did you
get his number?'

'No, silly idiot! Just because it's a quiet road they
think they can use it like a racetrack. Wish I had got the
number. We could've reported him! Should do! He'll
cause an accident sooner or later.'

'Wonder who it was? Not many flash cars like that
around Bamford,' Meredith mused. 'I wonder where
he was making for, or coming from.'

'It was a funny sort of numberplate,' Michael said
after a moment. 'Foreign, I fancy! I wish I'd had
time—'

'Here!' she interrupted. 'Here's the turning to Witchett!' She drove down the narrow track and into the neat
yard of Witchett Farm. 'Dolly's car is here,' she said as
they got out. 'So she's at home.'

Meredith paused and looked about her. Somehow
Witchett looked different. Though still tidy by the standards of a working farm, yet it looked as though something had been through it like a whirlwind. The
tarpaulins had been pulled off the agricultural machinery parked under the open shed to their left and
deposited in an untidy heap. The door to the barn
where the fodder was kept swung open in the fresh
breeze and small bundles of hay blew about in the
opening and tumbled away across the yard. Tea-chests
brought down from the hayloft store stood in the yard
and crockery and newspaper wrapping protruded from
the open tops. 'Funny . . .' she said.

Michael, who hadn't seen Witchett any other way,
was entranced, however. 'God, this is a wonderful
place!' he said reverently. 'Look at that old horse-

drawn harrow! Just think what you could do with this place! I know what I'd do!'

'Oh?' Distracted, Meredith turned to him. 'And what would you do? Come here and farm?'

'No, not farm. I'm not a farmer and anyhow, farming's no money-spinner these days. I'd open a garden centre. A really big one and I'd have an agricultural museum here as an added attraction and perhaps keep a few old breeds of sheep and some heavy horses . . . You'd get people out here in droves! There would be something for all the family! Look at the land! Plenty of room to put up greenhouses and a shop to sell plants. Lots of land to have a plantation of young trees. You could grow Christmas trees! If I had the money, I'd buy a place like this and turn it into a real success in that way! But on a primary teacher's salary,' he added ruefully, 'there's not much hope of that!'

'But you'd really like to do it? You'd give up teaching?'

'If I had a place like this? Something to create, build up from the start? You bet, like a shot!'

As his enthusiastic voice faded, there came a creak and a footstep from the stable block to their right. A voice called out nervously, 'Who is it?'

'Dolly?' Meredith called back, starting forward. 'It's only me, Meredith, and I've brought a friend.'

A door opened and Mrs Carmody appeared. But the change in the old lady from the last time Meredith had seen her caused her to stop in dismay and then run forward.

'Dolly? What on earth's the matter? What's happened?'

Mrs Carmody steadied herself by putting a hand to the stable wall. Her untidy bun of hair had collapsed completely and her usually ruddy cheerful face was ashen and distressed. She seemed to have aged twenty years, and to have shrunken into a little old lady, a frightened and confused one.

'Let me help you indoors!' Meredith exclaimed, grasping her arm.

Mrs Carmody held her off. 'Who is he?' she asked, pointing at Michael. 'What does he want?' Her hand and voice shook.

'It's Michael Denton, a friend of mine and of Jessica's. Dolly, what on earth has happened?' Suddenly she remembered the speeding BMW and in a burst of suspicion added, 'Has someone been here? What's scared you, Dolly?'

'Yes, they came early, been gone now near on two hours. Breakfast time they arrived, just like that. I'd not eaten my bit of bacon . . .' Her rambling discourse trailed off into silence.

They? Meredith was getting confused. Not the BMW driver then. 'Who, Dolly?'

Michael had come up to them and was listening closely, his face concerned. 'We've got to get her into the house,' he whispered. 'She's going to collapse!'

Between them they half helped and half propelled Dolly Carmody into her own sitting room. The old spaniel which had been shut up in there heard them coming and began to yelp and scratch wildly at the door as they opened it. The dog ran around her mistress as Dolly was deposited on the sofa and licked her hand. It seemed to help Mrs Carmody pull herself together. She patted the dog's head and said in a way more like her usual forthright one, 'I'm all right, my dears. I've had a bit of a shock. It wasn't something I ever thought would happen out here at Witchett! Such a – a disgrace!'

'Listen!' said Michael, a practical young man. 'Is there any brandy over there in that cupboard? Because you need a drop, Mrs Carmody!'

'Yes, I do believe I will have just a small one . . .' She made an ineffectual attempt to tidy her hair. 'Oh dear, what a time for you two to come and find me all at sixes and sevens like this and everywhere so untidy! Will you have a drink of something yourselves?'

'Later!' said Meredith firmly. 'Now, Dolly, who's been here?'

'The police,' said Mrs Carmody simply. 'The police came.'

'Alan!' Meredith exclaimed incredulously. 'Alan came and upset you like this!'

'Oh goodness, no, dear! Alan wouldn't do a thing like that! No, it was another, a Londoner he was and with a warrant and a couple of other chaps. One of them had a dog. They took it round outside all over the place. It kept running about sniffing here and there. They turned everything upsidedown and kept asking questions. They didn't find whatever it was they wanted. Then they left.'

Meredith straightened up. Laxton! Of course. Just wait till she saw Alan! It might have been Laxton who'd done this, but Alan shouldn't have let it happen! At the same time she thought, I'll never be able to marry Alan and this is why. It's the police work. I couldn't accept it. I know they have to catch criminals but even so, there are things they do . . . But why here?

Michael held out a generous glass of brandy to Mrs

Carmody. 'Here we are. Where's the kitchen? I'll make some tea.'

'You're a good lad, you are!' said Mrs Carmody, nodding. She glanced up at him with a return of her old interest. 'Jessica's friend, did you say you were?'

'Yes, we want to talk to you about that . . .' Meredith hesitated. 'But in a minute. I'll show you where the kitchen is, Michael.'

Out in the kitchen they looked at each other. 'Sniffer dog,' whispered Michael. 'Drugs or explosives?'

'Here? Either of them? It's ludicrous!'

'Something must have brought them! They had a warrant. She said the chap in charge was a Londoner, not a local plod!'

'Yes, I think I've met him. I thought he was all right at the time but now I wouldn't know where to begin to express my opinion of the wretch!'

No wonder Alan was so reticent about what Laxton is doing here! she thought mutinously. He must be drugs squad or anti-terrorist . . . this was absolutely ridiculous! Dolly was no underworld gangleader! Then she thought, gangs. She'd mentioned that word to Alan when they'd talked about the body found in the footings. She'd asked him if he thought it was a gangland killing . . . Oh, the whole thing was getting worse and worse.

By the time they'd all had a cup of strong tea, Dolly Carmody had quite perked up and was worrying where the cats had fled to. 'They both just took off when they saw all the strangers and that funny sniffing dog they brought! I expect they'll come home tonight.'

'It's quite unspeakable!' said Meredith vehemently. 'And I'm going to have a word with Alan about it!'

'It's not his fault, dear. It wasn't his doing. But what did they want? They went up in that hayloft, you know, where I showed you and Alan the footprints. They pulled it all out, all the boxes, everything. They showed me a picture of a fellow, I think it was the same chap whose picture Alan showed me, only it was a different photo and much nicer. But I told them I didn't recognise him. They kept asking about the intruder I had on the Thursday. I couldn't tell them anything. And the disgrace of it! Police searching Witchett!' She was beginning to get agitated again. The spaniel, sensing it, whined and pushed her nose against her mistress's knee.

'Look, Dolly,' Meredith said. 'I think I ought to give your doctor a ring and ask him to call out here to see you.'

'I'm all right, dear, I am now, really. It's a blessing you two came, after all. I feel that much better now I've talked about it with you.'

'Yes, but tonight you may get a reaction. Your doctor ought to see you. What's his name?'

'It's Dr Pringle, dear. I've got his number somewhere.'

'I know Dr Pringle, I'll call at the medical centre when I go back,' she promised.

'Now then,' said Dolly suddenly sitting up straight. Her colour had returned and though still shaken she looked much her old self. 'What was it you two wanted?'

'This hardly seems the moment . . .' Michael began.

'Come along, spit it out!' she ordered, interrupting.

They explained Michael's dilemma. 'I know,' Meredith said, 'that it's asking you to deceive the Winthrops.

But Jessica's not a teenager, she's twenty-three. She does want to see Michael and they are being quite unreasonable.'

'They mean well,' said Mrs Carmody. 'It's a worrying thing when a babe is born late in a marriage. The parents want to know she'll be all right even when they're not around to look out for her. As for Alwyn, he means no harm. But he is obstinate. Now listen. I'll phone Greyladies now. You say Betty Chivers is there. Well, that means Elsie won't leave the place. I'll ask for Jessica. I'll say the police have been – the news will be all over the place soon enough – and I'd like Jess to come over and keep me company for a bit. Elsie will send Jess over, never fear.'

'It does seem a bit underhand,' Meredith admitted.

'Nonsense, I do need Jess. The horses haven't been mucked out and someone's got to give me a hand to tidy up the place.'

'I'll do that!' said Michael firmly. 'I've got all day. School is on Easter holiday. What I don't finish today, I'll come back and finish tomorrow. Don't worry about that. You and Jessica can't go lugging heavy weights about.'

'That's very kind, dear,' said Mrs Carmody. 'I'll drive you home later, I'll be quite all right by then. I'm feeling better already.'

Jessica clattered into the yard half an hour later on the roan pony. 'Michael!' she called out in astonishment and sliding from the saddle ran towards him. Then she saw the state of Witchett yard and alarm entered her eyes. 'What's wrong?'

They explained as best they could and the rest of the

afternoon was spent putting right the havoc wrought by the enthusiastic Laxton, his underlings and his sniffer dog. Meredith's opinion of the London man, already much lessened by the fact that he'd upset her elderly friend, rapidly became unprintable as she snagged her tights, tore her nails, hit her head on low beams and ricked her back in helping Michael return the tea-chests to the hayloft. The tarpaulins took all four of them to fix back over the farm machinery and peg down securely. As they worked the wind force increased, snatching the tarpaulin from their hands and blowing wisps of hay and dust into their faces.

Jessica had undertaken to clean out the loose-boxes, a job which had to be done regardless of all else and which Mrs Carmody had ineffectually begun when Meredith and Michael arrived. She informed them that Laxton's team had even searched the stalls and pulled all the straw about and the hay from the metal racks on the walls.

'Lucky none of them got kicked!' she said, her tone indicating that privately she would have liked one if not all of the horses to have kicked the unfortunate Laxton all over the yard.

Mrs Carmody kept them supplied with cheese and pickle sandwiches and fruit cake and gallons of tea. By four-thirty they all slumped down in the sitting room exhausted.

'Bless you, dears!' said Mrs Carmody, rattling the poker in the fire and sending flames roaring up the chimney. 'Oh, look, here's one of the cats. The other won't be far behind.'

A tabby appeared in the doorway and glowered at them all. Then it marched in a dignified way to the hearthrug and sat down with its back to them, whiskers quivering and all the fur on its spine stuck up in a ridge. Every so often it gave a twitch and its tail thumped on the carpet as it brooded on the intrusion of the sniffer dog.

'Been a real upset of a day,' said Mrs Carmody. But much of the distress had gone from her voice. The work and bustle had proved the best medicine. 'Now how about I make us pasties for supper?'

'I've got to go home,' said Meredith hastily. 'Alan's taking me out to dinner. Many thanks anyway. I'll call at the medical centre. Alan's not coming till seven so I've plenty of time.'

'Now don't you go blaming him for this!' Mrs Carmody said sternly.

'Hmn, well, I can't promise not to speak my mind. But he'll be cross too when he learns how Laxton left you!'

When she left the other three had moved to the kitchen. Mrs Carmody was rolling pastry, Michael chopping onions, Jessica peeling potatoes. Somehow the conversation had got round to Michael's idea of a garden centre cum farm museum.

'I think it's a great idea!' Jessica was saying. 'What you'd need is someone to look after the animal side of it while you look after the plant side.'

'Jessica knows about taking care of livestock!' said Mrs Carmody. 'There, I knew those old bits and pieces would come in useful one day. I'm glad now I didn't let them go to that dealer fellow!'

Some things seemed to be sorting themselves out, thought Meredith as she prepared to drive back towards Bamford. But a host of new questions had raised themselves. On impulse she turned the car down the stretch of new road which led towards the building site.

Work had stopped for the Easter break. The site was abandoned, windswept, isolated and sinister. Meredith parked the car and got out to walk along the strip of new road. The wind out here blew unimpeded and cut keenly right through her anorak and although she kept her hands in her pockets her fingers were already numb. She pulled up the hood of her coat to protect her ears but the wind snatched out her hair and sent it across her face and handfuls of grit battered her legs. The greyness of the sky was blackening fast. It wasn't late but the light was already poor.

Meredith turned aside from the strip of road, scrambled over a ditch and up on to as yet untouched pastureland. She picked her way cautiously across it. The ground was soft and uneven, dotted with tussocks of coarse grass and it would be all too easy to turn an ankle. There were patches of rabbit droppings to watch out for and without warning she disturbed a hare which sprang out and went leaping away before her making for the safety of distant hedgerows, a refuge which soon would be swept away.

She followed in the wake of the hare and when she reached the hedgerow became aware of a monotonous buzzing whine from the other side. Not the bulldozers which stood silent in the compound half a mile away. The noise rose and fell in volume as whatever machine caused it moved nearer and then away again. Meredith slid down into a ditch and climbed up the further side. She pushed her way through the tangled thicket of overgrown hawthorn and brambles.

Another area of former pasture lay beyond it but this had fallen victim already to the attention of the developers. No bricks and mortar yet rose here but more asphalt strips of road had been laid, scoring the churned turf in a crazy pattern, stopping at hillocks of mud, running out into flat grassland and leading nowhere as if a giant had started to lay out a maze in his garden but, losing interest, had abandoned it not nearly finished. Up and down this no-man's-land of pristine black tracks rode a pair of youthful motorcyclists on lightweight machines. Occasionally they left the strips of asphalt to attack the clay hillocks, practising their scrambling techniques, forcing their way up by scuffing their boots into the mud, the engines coughing. Then bouncing precariously down, they slithered into skids at the bottom and fetched up with a triumphant flourish.

The nearer rider spotted Meredith standing under the hedge and rode towards her, bumping his way over the tussocky terrain and coming to a stop directly before her. He settled back on the saddle and pushed up his visor like a knight of old turning aside from the joust to claim a favour of his lady.

''Ullo,' he greeted her.

She peered at the rectangle of face revealed. 'Barry, isn't it?'

''Sright. Seen you at the vic's. Goin' to buy a house, then?' This was evidently Barry's idea of a joke. He had pulled off the helmet and clasping it to his chest, jerked his flushed brow in the general direction of the distant buildings. He grinned broadly.

. . .

'No, thanks. Does the site management mind you riding round out here?'

Barry grinned. 'Yeah, the foreman comes running over here like a bat outa hell but he can't catch us. We have a bit of fun with him. We chased him right into the river once. He stood on the bank swearing at us and so we rode straight at him and he 'ad to jump. Fell right in. We didn't half laugh.'

'Sounds a bit dangerous,' she said doubtfully. She wondered if he had heard of the murder. Perhaps he didn't associate the name Hersey with his old adversary.

'Naw, he's a berk and a right bastard, too.'

Though inclined to agree with this assessment of the late Mr Hersey's character, Meredith felt impelled to say, 'You know he's dead, do you?'

'What – 'im?' Barry's eyes flickered with surprise and then caution. 'Nothin' to do with us.'

'I didn't say it was. Didn't you hear about the murder near The Fox and Hounds pub?'

'Oh, that one. Yeah. Was that him?' Barry thought about it. 'Well, I never,' he said surprisingly mildly. 'I'll tell my mate.'

'He could have taken your licence numbers and reported you, when you chased him,' she said.

Barry shrugged. 'It was just a laugh. He wouldn't have done that, anyway, go to the coppers. Not him.'

'Why not?'

Barry gave her the look of one who explains the way of the world to an innocent. 'He's the sort as doesn't like coppers. Didn't,' Barry corrected himself. 'Mind you, if he'd have caught us, he'd have killed us! But there's them as goes running to the p'lice and them as doesn't.'

True enough, Meredith thought. She doubted Alan would have disagreed with that.

'Do you and your friend come out here with your bikes a lot?'

'Yeah, if the weather's good.'

She picked her words carefully. Barry was accustomed to being one of the first accused when anything went wrong and his instinct for self-defence would easily be aroused. 'The weekend before they found the body in the foundations, were you out here then? I mean, if you were, you could have ridden right into the murderers and that could have been nasty.'

Barry breathed on his helmet and carefully rubbed off a smear of mud. 'We was out here that weekend but never saw nothing.' His voice held real regret. 'Wish we had. Bamford's a dump, nothing never happens, and when it does, we bleedin' miss it!'

'You didn't see any strange cars?' This jolted her memory. She asked on impulse, 'How about a BMW or any car with foreign plates?'

'Naw, only an old Land-Rover covered in mud. But I seen that before, lots of times. Belongs to the bloke what looks after them sheep. But we keep well clear of him, my mate and me.'

'You mean a tall, red-haired man?'

'Right, that one! He reckoned my mate and me we frightened his sheep. That was before they put down this bit of road and we used to ride anywhere in the fields. The old sheep used to peg it outa the way, didn't half run, but we never done them any harm. But that red-headed bloke, he threatened us with a shotgun one time! So after that, when we saw him coming, we'd hide behind the hedges till he'd gone.'

'Alwyn threatened you with a gun?' Meredith gasped. Alwyn had a temper, she'd seen that at The Fox and Hounds, and, brandishing a gun, must be a frightening sight. Farmers had the right to shoot dogs worrying sheep. Perhaps Barry and his friend were lucky Alwyn hadn't taken things a step further and peppered them.

'Yes, scared the shit outa my mate and me!' said Barry with deep feeling. 'I tell you, we don't mess about with him!'

There was a shout from Barry's companion, waiting impatiently some yards away.

'See you around,' said Barry, preparing to don his helmet. 'At the vic's perhaps.'

'Still gardening?'

'That's a doddle. The vic, he don't make no fuss. He's all right is the vic. You seen that Yamaha he's got? I wouldn't half like a go on that! Do a ton, no trouble.'

'I think it might mean a lot of trouble and it wouldn't be a good idea to go borrowing it, Barry!' Meredith said firmly. 'You'd lose a good friend in Father Holland.'

''S'all right, I won't touch it! Cheers!' He grinned, donned the helmet, waved and roared away.

Meredith turned back. At her feet the hedgerow plants struggled to survive amongst the churned clay and débris from the road construction; yellow celandine, wood anemone, nettles, dockleaves, clover, coarse grasses, all clung defiantly in patches to the blasted soil. There was something at once heroic and pathetic in Nature's tenacity. Soon enough the concrete would come and roll inexorably over them all, burying them for ever, burying them like the dead man.

Chapter Twenty

Inevitably she and Alan quarrelled bitterly about that Thursday's events. At first Meredith was so blinded by her anger and the memory of Dolly's frightened face and confusion that she wouldn't listen to what he had to say at all. When she did calm down enough to do so, it didn't make matters very much better.

Of course what had happened at Witchett that morning wasn't his fault. She had to concede that. Nor, as she could see for herself by the way he took her news, was he pleased to learn how upset Dolly Carmody had been. His mouth set tightly and she strongly suspected blunt words would be exchanged with the London man before long on the subject. But at the same time he dug in his heels and refused to condemn Laxton's actions to her. This closing of the ranks annoyed her more than anything.

'He was doing his job,' Markby said firmly. 'I admit I'd hoped to be able to arrange that Pearce went along with him, but either Laxton didn't realise that or he did but didn't want my spy along . . . either way, he wanted to run his own show and he was entitled to. That's what he came here to do.'

'Look for drugs? At Witchett? The Yard must be barmy.'

She saw Alan's face set obstinately. It was a police matter and he wasn't going to discuss it with her or even confirm what Laxton had been looking for. Nevertheless she pursued her point.

'A sniffer dog, it's obvious, isn't it? Let me tell you that your DCI Laxton is extremely fortunate Dolly didn't have a heart attack while he was there! She did have a sort of turn, a fainting spell, which put the wind up the police for a few minutes, as it should have done! But the wpc gave her a drop of brandy and she came out of it. Serve them right if it had been worse! What on earth did Laxton expect? A woman of her age, living all alone out there and eminently old-fashioned and traditional. Strangers arriving uninvited and unexpected at breakfast time like that, before she'd even had time to eat! A whole posse driving into her farmyard in a spray of dust like – like something out of a Western film! And then turning the place upsidedown and leaving it in a goddam awful mess which I and others had to clear up! As far as your pal Laxton was concerned, Dolly was left to clear it up herself! Couldn't he at least have had the basic decency to let her know he was coming?'

'Don't be daft,' Markby said wearily. 'What's the use of sending word ahead that you're on your way when you're looking for – for anything illegal?'

That was true enough. Meredith simmered in silence for a moment. 'It was a rotten thing to do,' she said at last. 'Correct or not.'

Alan leaned forward and she was surprised by the

ferociousness of his expression. 'We do a lot of what you'd term rotten things! Laxton does, I do, all policemen do! It's a rotten job! You didn't mind playing at detective, using the Grey Folk as cover to go prying around Greyladies and the building site. But real detective work is messier and there's far less pussy-footing around! We get down in the mud and stir things around and yes, we often emerge dirty! We cross-question parents whose children have disappeared and who are half mad with worry. We disturb the grief of the bereaved. We sit by the hospital beds of people who have been horrifically beaten and badger them to remember details of their assailant. All they want to do is blot all memory of the incident out and the likes of me won't let them! We don't like it, none of us, not me, not Pearce, not Laxton, but it has to be done!'

He sat back and added more mildly, 'It's better now than it was years ago. Now we have rape crisis centres and specially trained women police officers to deal with the victims generally, as well as a host of other people with special training. But when it comes down to it, at some point you have to put your own feelings on one side and ask the questions no one wants to hear or answer! Even the scandal . . . Have you any idea how many people have skeletons in the family cupboard? We drag all the dusty old bones out into the light of day, all the sad little secrets they've kept for years. Of course we assure them we won't use information that isn't in the end pertinent, but the mere fact that we know, that anyone knows, is enough to destroy some people.'

'I realise that!' Meredith interrupted sharply,

irritated by his self-righteous lecture. 'But if you couldn't warn Dolly, at least you could have got her out of the way!'

'Laxton wanted her there. He had his reasons. Perhaps I'd have handled it differently if I'd had the job, but I didn't. Perhaps, even if I had, I wouldn't have done any differently to Laxton!'

'It is the scandal,' Meredith said, glaring at him balefully. 'I think it's the shame of having a police search conducted at Witchett which has upset Dolly most of all. She even said to me at one point that it was a blessing her late husband hadn't lived to see this day. That's a dreadful thing for an old lady to be brought to say.'

'I'm sorry, of course!' he said stiffly. After a while he added in softer, reminiscent tones, 'I know what fear of shame can do. When I was a young chap, just starting out, I helped search a house in which a mummified body of a baby had been found. It turned out to have died over fifty years before. It had been born out of wedlock and as far as could be established it didn't survive more than minutes but the scandal, you see, in those days! So they bricked the body up in a fireplace and it wasn't found until the old lady who lived there died and the house was sold and torn apart for renovations. She'd lived there for over fifty years, not daring to move from the house in case the remains were found. Fifty years with the evidence of her girlhood folly the width of a brick away from her, always conscious of it, always terrified that some day, someone would find out. No one deserves to carry their guilt for a lifetime like that. Even the law doesn't punish anyone that severely these days.'

'But Dolly didn't do anything!' Meredith insisted, dragging him back to her complaint. 'And she's been punished for nothing!'

'Not for nothing,' he said quietly. 'For the wrong that someone else has done and of which she knows nothing, perhaps. An innocent person has suffered but that doesn't mean there has been no crime.' He fell silent and Meredith could think of little further to say although her sense of outrage was far from assuaged.

Neither of them now felt much like going out for the arranged dinner. Markby asked half-heartedly, 'Still want to go?'

'No, not really. Sorry. I know it's not your fault. But I'm upset still and sort of churned up inside about it. I couldn't sit and eat, certainly not in public.'

'There is a recognised police complaints procedure if Mrs Carmody feels she has been unjustly treated.'

'She wouldn't complain, she's not of that generation. Today's generation whinges. Hers just gets on with life.' Meredith looked up at him. 'I know what you've said is true, all of it. About having to do rotten things, I mean. But I don't think I could ever accept it.' She grasped the nettle determinedly. 'I mean, if we tried living together on any kind of permanent basis, it would drive us apart eventually. I truly think it would.'

'I can't stop being a policeman,' he said soberly.

'And I can't stop being me and feeling what I do.'

Markby went out of the room and could be heard pulling on his green weatherproof out in Laura's hall. He came back to say, 'I'll be going on home, then. Perhaps we can make dinner another night before you go back to London?'

'Yes, another night.'

It was by far the most damaging quarrel they'd ever had. They'd argued before often enough and had fierce but short-lived spats. This time it was colder, ran deeper. The wound of it would heal but the scars would remain. And Meredith couldn't help feeling that she and Alan were rapidly approaching an *impasse* in their relationship.

Markby had in fact learned earlier than Meredith of Laxton's visit to Witchett but not early enough to influence the style of it. When he had arrived at Bamford Station that Thursday morning, about the time Meredith was descending on Bamford Cattle Market, the search of Witchett Farm was already history.

'I know you meant me to go with him to Witchett,' Pearce said with an apprehensive look. 'But I didn't know anything about it until it was all over. He organised it himself.'

'All right, all right,' Markby sighed. 'Not your fault.' He glanced at the unoccupied temporary desk which had been set up for Laxton in the corner of the office. 'Where is he?'

'He came in early after the raid, was on the phone for ages and then went off again.' Pearce hesitated. 'He looked very put out.'

'He's put out! Dolly Carmody must be hopping wild.'

'He left a message that he can be contacted at The Crossed Keys.'

'Frightened we might look over his shoulder as he writes his report, is he?' muttered Markby unkindly. 'Or doesn't he want to give us the chance to crow over his failure? As if he was ever going to find drugs at

Witchett! What did he think Dolly was, a sort of Godmother?'

'Don't know about that,' said Pearce diplomatically.

As the day wore on and more information about the raid filtered back, Markby's feelings about the whole business became more aggressive. He had known that Laxton intended a search, of course, and he'd been prepared for Mrs Carmody to be angry. But not for her to have been reduced to a state of near-collapse. By the time he'd seen Meredith in the evening and had a first-hand account of Dolly's distress together with the unhappy row with Meredith herself about it, his mood was near-explosive.

Grist to the mill of his ill-humour had been added by the fact that he had been obliged to defend Laxton's actions to Meredith. Laxton was a fellow officer and they were theoretically working in tandem on, if on different aspects of, the same case. He also knew that if he'd been Laxton, he might very well have behaved in the same way. On the other hand, he might not. Not without reason had the Yard sent their own man who was free from local prejudice and uninfluenced by personal acquaintance and thus would make no bones about conducting a sensitive search. But neither did Laxton have to stay around here to face the inevitable long-term results of it.

On Friday morning when he went into work, it was perhaps as well that Laxton was still absent and to be contacted at The Crossed Keys. In that doleful hostelry, so Markby opined, Laxton was doubtless brewing up his next bit of mischief safe from inquisitive questions.

Markby stirred his canteen coffee and glowered into the middle distance. There was, despite anything McVeigh claimed, a faint hint of, well, not criticism. Sending Laxton had not been intended as overt or implied criticism of Markby's methods or ability. Laxton had been sent because he was a specialist and because this formed part of an investigation already begun on Laxton's patch. Nevertheless it was difficult not to feel some slight slur had been cast on the general efficiency of Bamford police force.

All right, they weren't specialists on the drugs scene but even in Bamford drugs weren't unknown. At this present moment, despite other matters on his plate, he was still concerned with the death of Lindsay Hurst and finding who had supplied the heroin which killed her. Without show and dash perhaps, but nevertheless slowly and methodically they were sifting through the little available evidence and doggedly following the faint trail that should lead them to Lindsay's immediate supplier and the men behind him.

They were a trained force, dammit, and one with an exceptionally good record of solving crime in all its various guises. What's more, they had a history of excellent relations with the general public. A relationship placed now in some jeopardy thanks to Laxton's heavy-handed techniques which might have passed without comment in the metropolis but out here would prove a talking point for months. Inevitably Bamford police would be blamed for what had happened at Witchett, unjust though this was. They had better brace themselves for some pretty hot accusations. Dolly was well known in and around Bamford and not only the farming community would be deeply affected.

Then there was Meredith's reaction last night, also predictable but nonetheless hard to bear. He wished now he'd never telephoned her to come down and house-sit for Laura. The idea had been to have an opportunity to take a little pleasure in one another's company. Not to have a row and exchange home truths. He'd probably made a fool of himself the other evening, rushed things. But it wasn't as simple as that. She couldn't accept the police work, that's what she said and she'd meant it. She'd never be able to accept it. Rachel, his former wife, hadn't been able to accept it either, but for an entirely different set of reasons.

Rachel had wanted a different kind of life to the one he had been able to offer her. It was the clipping of her social wings to which she had objected, not the nature of anything he was called upon to do in the course of police duty. Rachel had neither known much nor cared enough to inquire about police work. All she knew was that it meant he was called out unexpectedly, wreaking havoc with her arrangements and worked unsocial hours at the best of times. Add to that the inexplicable obsession, as she saw it, he had for plants and pottering about in his oldest clothes and it really had been more than she could take. To lead the life she had wanted she'd needed a different husband and being Rachel, once she'd realised this, she'd made no bones about it.

To be fair, the ending of his marriage had not appeared to him a disaster at the time but rather a release. He, too, had recognised it was a mistake. He, however, would have struggled on with it as a matter of principle. Rachel had had no such qualms. He didn't miss Rachel. But he did miss Meredith when she wasn't around. If he thought the day had now dawned which would see them parting for ever and she'd never be around again . . .

Markby felt a dull ache in his chest which he hadn't felt for a great many years, not since his early twenties probably. He wondered if he should telephone her, but she probably didn't want to hear from him this morning. He didn't blame her for anything she'd said. She was painfully honest and it was one of the traits he'd always admired in her. She had tried to be fair but nonetheless he felt he'd been lessened in her eyes. And all this, he thought with an upsurge of wrath, was down to Laxton! Laxton whom he had been so keen to defend, to stand by in a show of professional solidarity! Laxton who had so thoroughly messed up Markby's standing not only in the town but in the surrounding country, his relationship with an old acquaintance in the farming community and who, perhaps worst of all, had jeopardised his future friendship with Meredith.

Markby heartily wished DCI Laxton incarcerated for ever in the French hypermarket he so admired.

Chapter Twenty-One

There was little about Friday morning to raise Meredith's spirits. The weather was overcast and the wind chill. Early morning bulletins from the local radio station promised stormforce winds by afternoon. It was Good Friday, a day of sad thoughts. She had quarrelled with Alan. If the weather didn't buck up the Easter holiday would be washed out.

Laura's bouquet of spring flowers, as if in sympathy with the prevailing mood, was already showing signs of mortality. The irises had curled up and the yellow leaves of the daffodils were beginning to wither. Meredith changed the water and added an aspirin to it, trimmed off the stems and hoped for the best. The tulips were doing well and the freesia. She wished her problems could be cured with an aspirin.

Susie, in a lime-green jogging suit, called round to say, 'Gee, it's cold,' and announce that she and Ken were driving up to Scotland the next morning to spend Easter. She made it sound as if Scotland were just down the road.

Meredith mentioned that she might have left Bamford by the time they returned after Easter and Susie became emotional and said she must come round to dinner tonight and bring Alan. That didn't help. Meredith muttered that Alan was sometimes busy in the evenings. But she knew she was going to have to pass on the invitation which, in the current circumstances, was embarrassing.

Meredith put on her coat and walked into town. When she had been a child Good Friday had been a day when shops closed. Now most of them were open for business. Just one or two, mostly local firms, had shut their doors for the day. People were carrying overflowing bags of groceries. The approach of any public holiday seemed to affect shoppers this way. People stocked up for a siege. Meredith supposed she'd better buy a chicken or something for Sunday and then wondered whether Alan would be there to eat it with her, even supposing it was edible after her haphazard culinary treatment.

It was at that point she became aware that something was happening in the High Street. There was a policeman stopping traffic and clusters of shoppers stood by the kerb, necks craned. Peering over heads, she saw that a procession approached, walking at the side of the road but on the highway. It was led by two young men carrying a rough wooden cross. One was conventionally dressed but the other, she was surprised to see, was Barry in his motorcyclist's leathers. She supposed he had been press-ganged but if so, he looked remarkably cheerful about it. They were followed by Father Holland in cassock and surplice together with a fellow cleric, presumably non-conformist, in bands. Then came a choir, not singing at the moment but marching raggedly along clasping hymnsheets, and last of all a long crocodile of parishioners.

Father Holland spotted Meredith at the side of the road and waved an expansive hand. 'Join on!' he bellowed.

Meredith fell into step with the main body of the throng and someone pushed a hymnsheet into her hand. In due course they fetched up outside the doors of the church and Father Holland, assisted by the minister in bands, began to conduct an open-air service.

It was cold standing here on this windy morning. Meredith folded her arms tightly across her chest and shivered. The cross had been deposited in the church porch and Barry had perched himself on a nearby tomb looking, with his pinched urchin's face and gangling body, rather like some sort of sprite himself. Almost directly above and in front of him a medieval waterspout on the church tower terminated in a wickedly merry gargoyle with a thin face and a pixie hood cap. Between Barry and the gargoyle lay a thousand years of Christianity on this spot but they were uncannily alike, even unearthly so, as if the stone head had acquired a body and climbed down from its tower.

Meredith retreated a few steps to find shelter behind a gravestone and listen as Father Holland perorated, shouting out the words against the rising force of the gale which tugged at his surplice and those of the choir and blew his hair straight up in the air as if he'd had a fright. His broad face, surrounded by its bushy beard, was reddened by the cold and icy draught but he seemed impervious to it.

Above their heads rooks wheeled on the air currents around the church steeple and added their noisy cawing to the vicar's voice and the sound of traffic in the road outside. Barry in his black leathers, hunched on his perch like a scrawny raven, kicked his heavy boots against the side of the tomb and raising one hand, made it into a pistol shape and fired his imaginary gun up at the birds. Meredith saw his mouth form the sound 'Pow!' and that merrily wicked gargoyle grin flickered across his face.

Father Holland's voice forced itself into her consciousness.

'So let us look ahead to the coming Sunday when we celebrate the resurrection, when we think of rebirth and a new beginning. Let us all make our minds up to begin afresh!'

Father Holland fell silent and turned. The procession began to file into the church. Even Barry had climbed off his tomb and gone in, vanished by means natural or supernatural. Meredith reproved herself for her flippancy. That Barry was here represented a considerable achievement on Father Holland's part. The vicar seemed at last to be making progress with his unlikely acolyte. Perhaps there were never any lost causes. What one lost was the will to fight, the courage to struggle on with them. Meredith stuffed her hymnsheet into her pocket and set off resolutely for Laura's house. Begin afresh . . . right!

She walked straight in and telephoned Alan at the station. At first conversation was stilted as she told him about Susie's invitation and finally blurted, 'Look, I'm sorry about last night. It's not that I don't feel the same way this morning, but I know none of it was your fault and I'm sorry about the argument.'

'So am I!' He sounded relieved. 'I'm glad you rang. I was debating whether to ring you but I wasn't sure if you'd like that. I'm busy here right now but I'll collect you tonight and we'll go to Susie's. Will you have time today to drive over to Witchett and see how Dolly is? We're so overstretched here, what with two murders and still trying to trace the supplier in the Hurst case, I can't spare anyone or go myself.'

'Yes, of course I will. It was in my mind anyway.'

Meredith put down the phone. It wasn't such a grim day after all. She went next door and informed Susie that Alan wasn't busy, after all, and yes, they would be delighted to come to dinner. What time?

Susie said six-thirty, which rather startled Meredith who pointed out Alan might find the timing a bit tight. So then Susie suggested seven o'clock and did they mind meat loaf? Only it was the only thing she cooked which pretty nearly always turned out right. Meredith assured her, quite truthfully, that she liked meat loaf.

This all arranged to everyone's satisfaction, Meredith discovered it was nearly twelve, so she went back to Paul's kitchen and made an omelette. Shortly before two, she got the car out and set off for Witchett.

She might be feeling better but the weather was worse. Rainclouds had gathered overhead and the force of the wind now bent the heads of trees and gusts battered the car in a way which made driving along this exposed stretch of road an alarming experience.

She was glad to reach the safe haven of Witchett. The yard was deserted except for an old silver-painted Mini which she didn't recognise. In the drawing room of the farmhouse, Dolly Carmody and Michael Denton, to whom the Mini presumably belonged, were in close conversation before a fire which roared in the chimney as the wind dragged the flames upward. The cats and the spaniel huddled defensively together before it as the wind rattled the window glass.

'Hope I'm not disturbing you,' Meredith apologised. 'I came along to see how you were today, Dolly.' She shivered. 'It's a thoroughly miserable day out there and has got much worse since this morning. We're in for rain.'

'Oh, I'm much better, dear!' said Mrs Carmody in answer to Meredith's query. 'And you shouldn't have bothered yourself to come out in such dirty weather. You could do with a cup of tea, I'm sure!'

'Thanks, lovely. Alan asked me to call, but I would have done so anyway. Alan's very sorry . . . It wasn't anything to do with him, all that business yesterday,' she finished awkwardly.

'Don't worry, dear. And tell Alan not to worry. I really have quite got over it, thanks to young Michael here!'

Michael shuffled his feet, reddened and looked suitably embarrassed.

'We've been discussing his ideas for Witchett,' said Mrs Carmody. 'The garden centre. I must say, it seems first-rate to me.'

'It would take a lot of time and work to get it going,' said Michael quickly with a hunted glance at Meredith.

'There's no rush, the farm isn't going to disappear overnight,' said Mrs Carmody. 'You won't catch me selling out to those builders, never fear! Put houses on Witchett! Over my dead body! I told those two fellows who came so.'

'Two fellows?' Meredith asked.

'Yes, from the company developing Lonely Farm, or one of them was. The other was a local man, Dudley

Newman. I used to know his mother, years ago. I reminded him of that and told him I was surprised he'd even thought of coming to me and suggesting houses were built on Witchett! They went to Greyladies after they'd been here and I know George Winthrop sent them off with a flea in the ear. Elsie told me. It was several months ago.' She bustled out to put the kettle on.

'Your idea seems to have given her a new lease of life,' Meredith observed to Michael.

'I hope you don't think I've pushed her into it,' Michael said nervously. 'I really only mentioned it and she just seemed to jump at the idea.'

'She's been waiting for something like this,' Meredith told him. 'And it's the best way of taking her mind off what happened yesterday that anyone could devise! She longs to see Witchett working again. If it can't be a farm, and she's realistic about that, then what you propose is the next best. Anyway, you're still including the farm museum in your plans, are you? She'd love to think all her old bits and pieces would be polished up and put on show.'

'She's got some wonderful stuff,' Michael said. He paused. 'If I can persuade Jess to come in on it, it would be great.'

'She sounded keen when I left yesterday.'

'She was – is. But it's the family, the Winthrops. They'll try and put a spanner in the works, you'll see. They won't want her to do it and they can be pretty effective at getting in the way.'

'You know,' said Meredith after a pause, 'they really can't stop her if she wants to do it. I don't think Jess is incapable of standing up for herself if she's got motivation. Up till now that motivation has been lacking, but you've supplied it. Remember how she stood up to Alwyn in The Fox and Hounds?'

He sighed. 'Standing up to one person in a public place with lots of others around is one thing. Standing up to the combined Winthrops in private is something else. I'll be quite honest. I don't like Jess living there at Greyladies. I know it's her home but it's not the best place for her to be. We can't even get in touch with her today, Dolly and I. Dolly's telephoned three times but no one answers. The line's okay, the wind hasn't brought it down, but no one picks up the receiver.'

'They may all be out and about on the farm, busy.'

'Perhaps. But I would have thought Mrs Winthrop would have been around the house.'

'She may have gone to see Betty Chivers, Hersey's sister.'

He considered the suggestion. 'She may. But if so, she's taken Jess with her. If they haven't locked her in her room!'

'They wouldn't do that!' exclaimed Meredith, shocked. Then she thought of Mary Anne but sternly dismissed the idea: this wasn't the 1840s!

'Who knows what they'd do? I tell you, they're not like ordinary people. I don't like it. I'd go there myself and demand to see Jess if I thought I'd get past the farm gate. I might go there anyway and just barge my way in. Alwyn Winthrop can always knock me down, I suppose.'

'It is just possible he might!' said Meredith hastily. 'I don't recommend it. Look, why don't I drive over to Greyladies after I leave here? I've got the afternoon free and I'm half way to Greyladies already.'

'Would you?' His face brightened. 'I don't like to ask Dolly. She's still a bit shaky, no matter what she says and, anyway, I don't like involving her more than I have to. The Winthrops are her neighbours and she's had no quarrel with them before. I'd hate to think they fell out now over me. But I am worried about Jess. They may have found out about yesterday, that I was here when she rode over.'

'I promise,' said Meredith as Mrs Carmody was heard approaching with the tea-tray. She jumped up to help her elderly friend. 'They can't refuse to let me visit Jessica.'

It was all very well promising, thought Meredith when she left Witchett later, but the weather had really closed in now and what she'd really like to do was drive straight back to Bamford and shut the door against the storm. The rain had begun to pour from the sky in dull grey sheets which battered the car and washed across the windscreen as if someone had hurled a bucket of water at it. The windscreen wipers were next to useless. She leaned forward and strained her eyes into the murk. She couldn't even be sure of the location of the roadside. The treetops whipped against the darkened sky, the birds had all fled. No other motorist was out on the road and there wasn't a hint of human life anywhere. There were signs too that the road was going to flood. The drainage ditches on either side, now that the route was so little used, had not been cleaned out. Meredith drove unwarily through a large sheet of rainwater. It splashed up hissing on either side and she began to worry about the engine cutting out.

Greyladies might have been on the moon. Although

it was dark there were no lights showing in the house which stood etched against the angry sky. The barn was empty, the dog was out of sight and water ran from roofs in a torrent to splash down into deepening mire on the yard surface. A huge puddle had already formed in the middle which she carefully drove round before stopping in the lee of the barn.

Her eyes, automatically searching for the Land-Rover, fell unexpectedly on a newcomer to the scene. The BMW. The sight of that provided food for thought. It was the last thing she had expected to see. It had been parked under cover of a lean-to shed and a tarpaulin thrown across it. But the wind had caught at the corner of the heavy waterproof cloth and dragged it aside. Meredith peered from her car window at the numberplate which certainly looked foreign but which owing to rain and gloom she couldn't decipher. She wondered who the owner was, where he was, and whether the tarpaulin had been put over the expensive car to protect it or disguise its presence.

To find out this or anything else, she was going to have to get out, something she couldn't have felt less like doing.

She pulled the hood of her anorak over her head, opened the car door and made a dash for the house. Huddled under the inadequate porch, she knocked and rang but no one came. Where were they all? Perhaps some emergency had arisen with regard to the sheep? She stepped back into the pouring rain and quickly surveyed the windows of the house. They were so many unfriendly eyes and if human eyes watched from behind them, it was impossible to tell.

Meredith turned to run back to the car and her gaze

fell on the stable. There was no way Jessica would have taken the pony out in this deluge and it was just possible she was over there in the stable with the animal. Meredith made another dash, mud splattering her legs, water soaking her shoes, and reached the stable block.

The building was similar to the corresponding one at Witchett. The loose-boxes were about four in number but Jessica's pony the only beast in residence. It looked up, rolling the whites of its eyes and whinnying, as Meredith peered in. The storm had made it nervous. It stamped its hoofs and suddenly kicked out at the loose-box wall. Meredith made soothing noises and investigated further.

Beyond the loose-boxes was a kind of barn with a wooden stair leading to a hayloft which must run the whole length of the building above. Just as at Dolly's in fact. Meredith ducked into the barn, pushed back the hood of her anorak and looked about her.

It was tidy enough and in one corner stood an old pony-trap with shafts resting on the floor. Various odds and ends seemed to be stored in here but there was no sign of life. Meredith hesitated and then began to climb the wooden stair to the hayloft.

It was so gloomy up here that she could hardly make out anything except a small stack of sacks of animal feed. A stronger than ever gust of wind shook the building and made the wooden slats rattle. It felt as if the entire roof was about to lift off. From below her came another thump. The terrified pony was trying to kick its way out of its loose-box. She wished Jessica was here to deal with it. Meredith was inexperienced around horses and didn't fancy venturing into the loose-box with a frightened animal.

She shivered. There was no way she was going to try and drive back to Bamford until the storm abated a little. At least it was dry up here. She sat down on the stack of sacks and prepared to wait.

With nothing else to do, she also began to think. There was something more than odd about this farm, Michael was absolutely right in that. In fact there was something positively wrong about it. She did not blame Michael for wishing Jessica lived elsewhere. The Winthrops were a strange lot. Jessica was herself a Winthrop but by some chance of heredity not only looked different but was different. Perhaps Mary Anne had been like Jessica.

The wind howled through a gap in the rafters and Meredith pulled her anorak around her tightly. She heard the pony whinny and another crash as it kicked out again. If it got loose there was little she could do. She definitely wasn't going to try to catch it out there in the rain and gale.

The wind gave a high-pitched scream and she jumped. It wasn't difficult to think yourself back in the 1840s in these circumstances. Not difficult to imagine that, instead of the wind, it was the flames of the burning meeting house which roared outside as they'd done when they met Mary Anne's eyes as she ran to the window of her locked room.

There was the way they discouraged visitors to the farm, that was odd. After all, she had been admitted only because she had come on Alan's recommendation, she was sure of it. Michael had been unceremoniously thrown off. And why did they object to Michael so?

Then there was Alwyn's fascination with the building

site, bordering on an unhealthy obsession. Steve Wetherall had noticed it, seeing Alwyn standing day after day and watching the walls rise. And the footings dug.

Meredith sat up with a start. Alwyn must know everything there was to know about the day-to-day routine of the building site. How the footings were dug, the concrete poured, the walls built . . . Alwyn.

Barry and his friend had seen no strangers around the site during the weekend of the first murder, nor any strange car. But they had seen 'an old Land-Rover covered in mud' which they knew belonged to the red-headed farmer.

She was no longer conscious of the wind howling outside and rattling the wooden walls nor of the rain driving relentlessly against them. She began to think about the night of Hersey's death. Alwyn had left the table after the little scene involving Jessica and Michael Denton. He'd stormed out of the pub, but where had he gone? Hersey had left later . . . Had Alwyn still been roaming around outside?

Meredith shook her head. It didn't make sense. Hersey had been Alwyn's neighbour and friend. And what about the first murder victim? There was no motive. And would Alwyn kill? He might, she thought, he just might in the right circumstances. Alwyn was a powerful man and under a great deal of stress. He had threatened Barry and his friend with a shotgun. Who knew whether he had reached breaking point, or indeed, yet snapped?

But why? Meredith leaned back against a wooden pillar behind her and shook her head. Idly she began to trace with her finger the lettering on the sack which formed her seat.

'MILK POWDER. EEC PRODUCE. FEED TO CALVES ONLY.'

People took in their daily pint from the doorstep and never thought how it was produced. For a cow to be in milk she had to have calved. But if the calf drank much of the milk, the return to the dairy farmer was low, so the calf was taken from the cow and fed on dried milk powder which was in surplus in the EEC because too much milk was produced anyway. She supposed the system made sense somehow, although she wasn't particularly well versed in Common Market Agricultural Policy. Often it didn't seem to be logical.

And it especially made no sense here at Greyladies because there were no calves here. No call for powdered milk.

Meredith's head whirled and she forced herself to think logically, one step at a time. Alan said the Winthrops had previously kept cattle, beef cattle. Perhaps they'd bought calves for fattening and the milk dated from then. She wished she knew more about the system. But it was some time ago now that the failed experiment with beef production had taken place here. Sheep had been the mainstay of Greyladies for several years now, according to Alan. Would they keep unwanted milk powder stored?

She got to her feet and began feverishly to examine the other sacks. There were six of them, all containing milk powder. All were clean and dust-free and didn't look as if they'd been here very long. She hunted in her shoulder bag and managed to find a small nailfile.

It wasn't very sharp but it sufficed to cut a small hole in the sack. Powder spilled out. She tasted it cautiously. Milk powder all right. But she wasn't satisfied and after a moment's hesitation decided she might as well do the job properly. She ripped the sack along its entire length.

The powder rushed out on to the floor in a white cloud of dust and her first instinct was to be appalled at her own act of vandalism. But then she saw it, sticking out from the middle of the sack: a second package, plastic-wrapped.

Meredith tried to ease it out. Another white powder, carefully packaged up and hidden in this milk powder sack. She didn't hesitate this time, she ripped along the next sack down. More milk powder showered her in white dust. And again, in the middle of the sack was hidden a second smaller package, also containing white powder. But this other one, she was pretty well prepared to bet, wasn't milk. It was heroin.

It was at that moment that a door banged below and she heard men's voices.

Meredith froze and looked wildly about her. She had been so engrossed in what she was doing and the noise of the wind outside had been so wild, that she had failed to hear anyone approach. Wherever they had been, the Winthrops were back.

She looked down at her feet in horror. The evidence of her activities lay all around in a carpet of white dust. Nor could they be unaware that she was somewhere on the farm; they would have seen her car. She heard a dog yelp. They had that dratted dog with them and that probably meant at least one of the men was Alwyn. She heard the voices again and then silence as if one of the men had left the barn. There was the sound of someone moving about below and then a creak as the newcomer began to climb the wooden stair to the loft. Meredith looked wildly for a hiding place and considered crouching down behind the sacks, but they were too few to provide a truly adequate hiding place in a search. And that was what surely was being conducted. If the dog were brought up here, it would soon find her and in any case, she had no time. Alwyn's red hair appeared through the trap door and then the rest of him.

'Oh, there you are then,' he said. 'I saw as you'd come back. You shouldn't have done that.' His tone was equable, almost pleasant. She watched his gaze fall on the spilled milk powder and then travel to the ripped sacks and the protruding plastic packages. 'I thought you were bright,' he went on. 'Too bloody bright for your own good, you are.'

To say she wasn't frightened would be untrue. But now that she saw him, Meredith's panic turned into a cold determination born of facing the inevitable. Somehow all she felt was anger. Anger because this was such an evil business, because she could do nothing and because after all was said and done, she liked, or had liked, Alwyn.

She said loudly and firmly, 'How could you get involved in all this, Alwyn? It's despicable.' She pointed at one of the plastic packages protruding from the split milk powder sacks.

Alwyn's grey eyes narrowed. 'You mind your own business!'

'It is my business! It's anyone's who learns of a thing like this! Drugs, Alwyn! It's the foulest of trades! It destroys people, young people, and it destroys their families, the ones who love them . . . everything! How would you feel if a thing like that destroyed your family? How would you feel if it happened to Jessica! If she was murdered by this stuff? Because it does, murder! And that makes you a murderer!'

'Shut up!' he yelled at her and a great crack of thunder deafened them both almost at the same moment. She saw his mouth working and his face contorted in fury, shouting more words at her which she couldn't make out.

As the growl of the thunder rolled away she continued her furious barrage. 'Drug addiction isn't something which happens far away to people who aren't real, Alwyn! People who are somehow different and don't matter. It happens to people just like the ones you love! For goodness' sake, you must have heard about Lindsay? She was a local girl. She was Jess's age and pretty, with a family who loved her dearly. Now her poor mother lives in a permanent nightmare! A former choirgirl, Alwyn, good at school, just like Jessica. Perhaps Lindsay would have gone on to be a teacher too – if that – ' she flung out her hand again at the package, 'if that stuff hadn't intervened!'

Alwyn took a step forward with his huge fists clenched and she thought he was going to attack her. But he stopped and snarled, 'You don't know anything! I'm not what you said! I never – we never – we only—' His emotion choked him. He shook his red hair and ordered brusquely, 'You just get on down below!' He jerked his head towards the stair and stood back so that she could precede him down it.

The lightning flickered as she made her cautious descent. Try as she might she couldn't see any way out of this. Two men had already died. They wouldn't scruple to get rid of her. Then, as they reached ground level, an earlier thought came into her head: There are no lost causes, only the will. She mustn't give up now or lose her nerve.

'I'll let 'em know I've found you!' Alwyn muttered. 'You stay right there!' He walked to the barn door and cupped his hands round his mouth, preparing to yell the news out to the other searchers.

But something happened before he could. There was another crack of thunder and immediately after it, a tremendous crash and ripping of wood. The whole barn shuddered. Some large rectangular object flew out and landed with a smack in the middle of the puddle out in the yard, sending muddy spray up in a great fountain. It was as if there had been an explosion.

Alwyn gasped, 'What the devil is that?'

Chapter Twenty-Two

Alwyn might not know what had caused the tremendous crash, but Meredith did. The pony had finally kicked its way out of its stable and sent the lower half of the double door flying out into the yard.

Alwyn had rushed out of the barn, for a moment standing staring wildly into the night before being forced to make a desperate leap aside for safety as, with a shrill whinny and a thud of hoofs the pony suddenly emerged from the storm. Eyes rolling, ears laid back and tail high it galloped past the barn door.

Alwyn swore violently and, forgetting Meredith in the face of the new emergency, dashed in pursuit. The dog had been waiting at the barn door for its master, its long black and white coat soaked with rain and plastered to its body, its narrow wolf's muzzle even more accentuated. It appeared more than ever a beast of the forest and now its reflexes sprang into play. Here was an escaping animal, not a sheep, but nevertheless the dog knew its duty. It began to race around the muddy yard, crouched to the earth, wheeling and diving in and out in a vain attempt to round the pony up. The pony whirled and, head lowered, snapped viciously at its canine tormentor.

Alwyn had sprinted to the paddock gate at the side of the yard and dragged it open. Stationing himself there, he waved his arms trying to drive the pony away from the main exit from the yard and towards the paddock entrance. Above the storm Meredith could hear his whistled and shouted commands to the dog. In its efforts to obey it snapped at the pony's heels and then scurried back out of the danger of flying hoofs and formidable teeth. The lightning flickered again casting its own curious illumination on the scene, like a spotlight on some weird circus act.

In the ring formed by the yard the pony, ignoring the open paddock gate, careered round and round in a circle. Alwyn followed as clumsily as a clown, shouting and swearing, whistling shrilly at his dog and stumbling in ungainly and comic fashion through the mud. The dog grew ever more frantic in its attempts to corner the fleeing pony.

The pair of them would only be distracted for a brief time and Meredith knew this was her only chance. She ran out into the yard. The wind whipped at her hair and the rain beat into her face as she looked wildly first one way and then another, seeking a way out. She had also to watch out for the pony which in its own search for an escape, still plunged round the yard, Alwyn trying to drive it towards the paddock gate. He blundered past her without noticing her, slipping on the mud, his arms outstretched. Meredith saw with despair that he was nevertheless between her and her parked car. The car represented her one hope of escape from the yard and any minute now the other Winthrops, who could not be far away, would hear the commotion and appear.

Even as she thought this, she heard a distant voice

yelling, 'What the devil are you doing, Alwyn?'

Meredith's panic redoubled. She could neither run towards the car nor towards the farmyard gate. Any attempt to hide in the other out-buildings would be doomed. Suddenly, bizarrely, she was bathed in light. It was only for a fraction of a second and then it vanished. She thought at first it was the lightning playing across the yard again, but there was no following rumble of thunder. Then the light shone again, falling in a rectangle on to the muddy surface and illuminating her before vanishing as abruptly.

Meredith swung round and stared up at the façade of the farmhouse from which the beacon must have come. High up on the second floor someone stood at a window and gesticulated at her. Someone who again signalled by switching a light on and off. The figure was only a dark shape framed briefly in an orange electric glare and she couldn't tell who it was but she realised instinctively it must be a friend. Without hesitation Meredith plunged towards the house.

As she raced across the mud-filled yard towards it she prayed that the door was unlocked. The person who had signalled had done so because he or she could not or would not come down to the yard, why Meredith didn't know. She reached it and twisted the handle. It gave beneath her touch. She thrust it open, stumbled into the kitchen and shut it behind her, leaning back against the panel with her heart pounding and blood roaring in her ears.

The kitchen was warm and cosy, the heat emanating from an old-fashioned kitchen range although there was a modern gas cooker. That, presumably, was where all the cooking was done, the range just provided the heating for the room and very effectively. The table had been laid for a meal, plates and cutlery set out on a cheerful red-checked cloth and a huge round loaf of home-baked scone bread awaited the diners on a wooden board. A row of copper pots gleamed on the wall. It hardly seemed that she could be in danger here. But she was, even though somewhere in this house she had a friend. She had to find that friend or failing that, a place to hide.

In her mind, Meredith saw Alwyn descending the narrow stairs carrying the Bible box. He'd climbed more than one flight to fetch it. This old house must have attics and if she could hide up there, it might be possible to slip down late at night, let herself out and make her way back to Bamford on foot.

Meredith began to scramble up the narrow spiral stairs. She ignored the first landing because the rooms on that must be in use and offer no place to hide. Besides, this was not the floor from which her well-wisher had signalled. She continued up the next flight to the second-floor landing and here stopped to get her breath. Her heart beat like a drum and she had a painful stitch in her side. There were doors on either hand and the one to the left had a key in the lock. To her amazement, she suddenly heard an urgent tapping on its panels and a girl's voice cried, muffled, 'Meredith!'

'Jess?' Meredith dived forward and rattled at the door handle.

'It's locked!' Jessica called through the panels. 'They locked me in!'

So Michael was right! thought Meredith grimly. Nothing had changed here at Greyladies since Mary Anne's day! She turned the key in the lock and the door burst open. Jessica grabbed her unceremoniously and jerked her into the room, slamming the door on them both. Meredith stumbled across the carpet and collapsed exhausted into a wicker chair. Panting and unable to speak for the moment, she stared about her trying to take in her new surroundings.

This was clearly Jessica's bedroom. The wallpaper was pale pastel blue patterned with forget-me-nots and the quilt on the bed dark blue satin. A row of child's stuffed toys, much the worse for wear, perched on top of the chest of drawers and a motley collection of photographs was wedged in amongst their plush paws. Jess at college, Jess on the pony, a younger Alwyn smiling at the camera and looking relaxed and happy. Just the brief sight of that one photo would be enough to tell anyone how much Alwyn had changed and the strain he was under and had been under for years.

Jessica pushed back her long hair nervously and bent over her. She began to speak in a low, rapid voice. 'I saw you through the window when you drove into the yard!' Her tone sank to a hoarse whisper. 'I couldn't open the window and shout to you because Alwyn's wedged it! He hammered the wedges in and I couldn't get them out! I tried – ' She held out her hands towards Meredith. The fingernails were torn and bleeding. 'I wanted to warn you but there was no way! Why did you come?'

'Michael was worried about you. He's at Witchett with Dolly and I said I'd call by to see you. Why did they lock you in?' Meredith's sentences came out in a broken gasp.

'Because – because he's here . . . and they didn't want me to see him!' Jessica threw up her head, very

331

like a startled pony which has heard a new and sinister noise, and before Meredith could ask 'Who's here?' the girl added desperately, 'They're coming back!'

Voices drifted up from below and the stamp of feet on the wooden treads of the stairs. They had worked it out. They knew she hadn't been able to run out of the yard and wasn't hidden in the out-buildings. They knew she must be in the house.

Meredith looked frantically round the room. 'I could hide in the wardrobe!'

'Yes, yes!' Jessica began to push her towards the piece of furniture in question but then stopped and exclaimed in alarm, 'Oh, Meredith, the key!'

'Key?' For a moment Meredith didn't understand and then, with horror, realised that she was still holding in her hand the key to the bedroom. Her fingers must have been clasping it when she was pulled into the room by Jessica, still gripping it.

'He'll see, Alwyn will notice it's gone from the door!' Jess hissed. 'We've got to put it back!'

'Jess!' Meredith whispered back. 'Do you know what they've got out there in the hayloft?'

'No, I don't . . . I know it's something they don't want me to know about . . . Meredith, the key!'

'Oh, yes . . .' Meredith handed over the key and Jessica flew towards the door and pulled it open.

Alwyn, panting and mud-covered, stood outside on the tiny landing.

'You're a blasted nuisance, you are!' he said hoarsely as his gaze fell on Meredith. 'Jess, you get back in there and keep quiet. That damn animal of yours has just about wrecked the loose-box but I managed to drive him into the paddock and he can run himself out galloping round that! You, Meredith, downstairs!'

'I'm coming too,' Jessica said loudly.

'No, you're not, Jess. 'Tis nothing to do with you.'

'Heroin!' said Meredith clearly. 'It's heroin they've got out in the hayloft, Jess. Packets of it hidden inside those sacks of milk powder.'

Alwyn's flushed face drained of colour and for a moment she really saw murder in his eyes. He stepped towards her and she could not prevent herself automatically stepping back. Then a voice cut between them.

'You fool, Alwyn!' said Jessica loudly. All her alarm seemed to have vanished. 'You great stupid idiot! You let him talk you into this, didn't you?' Her voice rose in accusation. 'You always did let him talk you into anything! He'll get away with it, run off like he's always done and leave you to pick up the pieces! Can't you see it? He's not changed. He's still up to all his old tricks and you're still being taken in by them! I know he's here. I saw him drive up in that swish foreign car of his. Locking me in this room, do you think I don't know you're up to no good?'

Not for the first time, Meredith was startled and deeply impressed by the girl's apparent absence of fear in the face of her brother's anger. It was as though Jessica's courage lay dormant until things were at their worst and danger tripped the switch which summoned it up.

'All right,' Alwyn said sullenly. 'You come down, too. But I locked you in here so's you wouldn't be involved, Jess. What you didn't know couldn't do you no harm. Now you are involved, dragged into it with the rest of us and all because, because that stupid bitch told you!' He flung a hand out to indicate Meredith. 'And because now you're insisting. Think twice, Jess, for pity's sake! If you come down you'll learn it all and you'll be stuck with it like the rest of us!' He paused and added almost piteously, 'I wanted to keep you out of harm's way, Jess.'

'You great lummox,' she said with exasperation but also, Meredith realised, with deep affection. 'You never could think straight. Go on, Meredith, we'll go down and face them.'

They were all in the kitchen. They sat round the table for all the world as if about to start their meal, had there been any food on the plates. As Alwyn entered with the two women, they turned their faces towards them, staring. Elsie Winthrop glowered at Meredith, hatred in her eyes. Beside her, her husband just looked bewildered but obstinate too in the way of a simple man who knows things have gone wrong, can't see how and won't face up to the consequences.

There was another there, a stranger and Meredith couldn't guess at his identity. He rose to his feet as they came in and asked sharply, 'How the hell did she get up there? And who is she?'

He was as tall as Alwyn and as strongly built and his tanned features bore a resemblance to Alwyn's, but his hair was blond and his clothes looked foreign in their cut. There was something in his face which made Meredith's blood run cold. His eyes, grey like Alwyn's, were as hard as stones and behind them lay no pity, no weakness, no understanding of another's needs, only ruthless calculation. Beside him the others all looked hapless bumpkins. He looked – and she realised dully very likely was – capable of any crime.

'Why'd you bring Jess down?' demanded Mrs Winthrop. Her broad face reddened. 'We agreed she was to be kept out of it! 'Twill send her funny again, like she went before!'

'She knows what it is out there in the loft,' Alwyn said. 'This one told her!' He gave Meredith a little push, sending her stumbling forward.

His mother burst out, 'What did you want to come meddling for?' and to the hatred and anger in her face was added now despair.

The stranger treated Meredith to a long cool stare, assessing her potential as a problem. She did her best to meet the gaze with unconcern but she had a strong suspicion she wasn't doing very well. She saw his mouth twist in a cynical grimace, then he shrugged. 'We can take care of her.'

Meredith's knees turned to water and it was all she could do not to sink to the ground. There was no doubt in her mind what was meant by taking care of her. Where would they bury her, she wondered. On the farm? In another trench at the site? Weighted and thrown into the river? She wondered if she could gain time by telling them that Alan Markby knew she had come here and that if she didn't return, he'd come to Greyladies asking questions.

But in the first place this wasn't true. Alan believed her to be at Witchett and even if he did eventually trace her here, it wouldn't be for hours and all the Winthrops would need to say was that she had left. Alwyn could drive her car out into the countryside somewhere and park it in a lane. Her disappearance would be just another unsolved mystery.

She could still say it and hope to sound convincing, but this cold-eyed man would see through the pathetic pretence at once. What's more it might even have the opposite effect. The prospect of the police arriving soon might just make them hurry the deed. She hoped it would be painless, just a sharp blow on the back of the neck such as had dispatched Jerry Hersey.

'And me?' Jessica asked, interrupting Meredith's doleful train of thought. 'Am I to be taken care of too?' She raised her voice and tilted her chin as she spoke, staring straight at that stony gaze.

'You're family,' he said. 'You'll keep quiet.'

'No.' She shook her long fair hair. 'No, I won't, not this time.' Following on his, her voice sounded young and innocent but there was a touch of steel in it now. She was a Winthrop too.

As was this man, thought Meredith, realising only too well what his identity must be and that he knew she knew. Another nail in her coffin. How could he have done this to them? she found herself thinking. How could he have drawn them into his filthy business? Because he is incapable of caring, came the answer at once to her brain. He saw them only as being of use to him for a time. Did they realise it? Could they see him as he was? And did they realise what they'd done? Jessica clearly did and that was why they wanted to keep her away from him. Through her eyes they were forced to see both him and themselves clearly.

His attention had temporarily moved from her to Jessica. He leaned forward, resting tanned hands on the red-checked table-cloth. Those hands, thought Meredith, hadn't done hard physical work in years.

They were soft and manicured but morally they were black with dirt and he was indifferent to the prospect of soiling them again.

'You listen to me, girl,' he said to Jessica quietly but there wasn't a breath of sound in the room other than his voice. 'You know what's out there now, since she told you.' He nodded towards Meredith but didn't take his eyes from Jessica's face. 'No one, not the police nor any other, not even that boyfriend of yours Alwyn told me of, no one will believe you didn't know all along, that you weren't a part of it. You'd go to gaol like the rest of us!'

'Then I'll go to gaol,' Jessica said calmly. 'I should have gone to the police long ago. I knew something was wrong and they were hiding something. But you're right, I did think it was a family matter and I did keep quiet because of misplaced loyalty. But I didn't then know it was drugs. If I had, I would have told the police at once. But I didn't think even you had stooped that low. As it was, I didn't tell anyone about the man who was here on that Friday night.'

Alwyn uttered a muffled oath and old man Winthrop looked up and whispered, 'What do you know about that, girl?'

'I don't sleep well. You forgot. I looked out of my window and I saw you, Dad, and Alwyn carrying his body to the Land-Rover and driving off, about four in the morning it was. You killed him, didn't you?'

'No, they didn't!' her mother broke in harshly. 'You see, you know nothing about it, Jess! 'Twas me broke his skull. He was snooping out in the yard. I saw him. The dog woke me, yelping and rattling his chain. I thought at first 'twas him come . . .' She jerked her head towards the stranger who straightened up, taking his hands from the table top and folding his arms. 'I come downstairs and opened up the door and called out but he hadn't heard me and went on into the stable. So I reckoned it was someone up to no good. I picked up the old poker there from the range and went out. He was up in the loft and bending over the sacks. He started to turn when he heard me, but I hit him as hard as I could and then I hit him again. Then I fetched the menfolk and told them to get rid of his body.'

'He wasn't dead,' Meredith said shakily. 'Did you know he wasn't dead?'

Elsie Winthrop cast her a look of scorn. 'What did I care if he was dead or not? He looked dead enough to me! Anyway, we had to get rid of him! Couldn't leave him lying about the place!' She jabbed a stubby finger at Meredith. 'And you listen to me, Miss Hoity-Toity! Whatever I done, whatever we done here, we done it to save the farm! You remember that. Whatever we done, had to be. We done it all for the farm's sake!'

Alwyn spoke then, his voice strangled. 'Save the farm, this bloody farm? This place has swallowed up my life! Do you think I want it saved? Do you think I want to spend out the rest of my days here?'

'Now then, boy,' began old Winthrop in a hoarse growl. 'You'm talking nonsense! Course you'll stay here! 'Tis our farm!'

'I don't want it!' Alwyn shouted. 'Can't you get that through your thick heads? I don't want the blasted place!' His voice rang around the kitchen and made the copper pots hanging on the walls sing. More quietly he went on, 'I buried that fellow alive, as they say now, because of this damn farm! I killed Jerry because of this place! He knew, Jerry knew, we were up to something here! Jerry wasn't a fool.'

Alwyn turned to Meredith. She saw that all the fight and aggression had gone out of him. 'That night in the pub,' he said and his voice was weary, almost apologetic, 'Jerry took offence because I was sitting drinking with you and Alan and that architect fellow. Then Jess come in with the young chap. I knew if they got friendly he'd be coming out to the farm regularly and it wouldn't be long before he spotted something was wrong. I could see he was a bright sort of chap. I didn't know what to do. Anyhow, you know what happened, you saw it. Jess went off with the lad and I didn't want to sit there chatting with you as if there was nothing wrong! Everything was going wrong! After I left the place, I was still that upset because of Jess I went walking over the fields to calm down. On the way back, about an hour maybe an hour and a half later, I met up with Jerry on his way home. He started on at me about chatting to the police, all friendly. He said, Alan wouldn't be so friendly to me if he knew what we were up to here at Greyladies. He didn't know what it was we hid here, but he knew we hid something. "If I were to tell what I know", he said. I panicked. I just knew I had to shut him up, and I did. He was a fellow I'd never quarrelled with, Jerry, a good man and a good brother to Betty. Now he's dead and that poor woman left alone, and all because of this blasted farm!'

Alwyn sank down on a chair at the table, rested his elbows on the check cloth, put his head in his hands and began to sob quietly, his great shoulders shaking.

Jessica moved forward and put her hand on his red

curls and, looking across the table towards the stranger said, 'You'd best be off, hadn't you? You're finished here and you'll do no more harm to this family. God knows you've done enough. Don't you come back no more. You don't belong with us. We'll give you an hour to get clear and then we call the police.'

'Shut up!' he shouted. He lunged forward and shook Alwyn's shoulder fiercely. 'Pull yourself together, man! We can get out of this! All we have to do is shut her up! Jess won't talk, no matter what she says now! She wouldn't send the old people to prison!'

'Don't want the farm . . .' said old man Winthrop wonderingly as if he'd heard, or at least understood, the words for the first time. Nothing else in the proceedings meant anything to him. The arguments had swirled unheeded about his head. Now a chord had been struck deep in his very being. 'Don't want Greyladies? 'Tis ours, our farm. Always been Winthrops living here.'

'Dying here!' came in choked tones from Alwyn. 'And I'll die here if I don't get away! I don't want to die here, I don't want to give this cursed place my life!'

Old man Winthrop stared at him, the consternation on his red, weatherbeaten face slowly turning to resignation. 'Well then, 'tis no use us going on.' He turned his gaze towards the stranger. ''Tis finished, lad. All finished as you hear. Best put matters in order, then us'll be able to go peaceful.'

'You're all fools!' the stranger said furiously. 'And you can stay here and face the police if you like. I'm getting out!'

Alwyn raised his head and shouted, 'Yes, run! You

always did! You always ran away from here and came back when it suited you!'

The stranger didn't bother to reply. He turned and strode out of the door into the darkening yard and the storm, slamming the door behind him. Those within heard a yelp of pain. The dog, waiting patiently in the rain, must have run forward and been kicked aside.

Jess stooped over Alwyn who had begun quietly to weep again, the tears oozing out between his calloused fingers. Mrs Winthrop, perhaps from sheer force of habit or because she didn't know what else to do, got up and began to fill the kettle at the sink. The old man seemed to have lost all awareness of any of them being there. He sat staring at the wall opposite him and shaking his great round head. 'Don't want the farm!' he mumbled from time to time.

Outside, the BMW's engine roared as it raced out of the yard into the night and Meredith thought in despair, 'He's going to get away!'

Chapter Twenty-Three

As the storm battered at the windows of the police station, Markby wondered uneasily whether Meredith had driven out to Witchett. It was a pity he'd asked her to do so because it really wasn't the day for being out and about.

However, when she got to the farm she'd be all right. He was glad she'd phoned, very glad. And he'd see her tonight, after all. Until then she'd be all right out at Witchett. Dolly would stoke up the fire and have the kettle singing and there would be fruit cake and fresh scones. He imagined Meredith and Mrs Carmody sitting either side of the roaring hearth, tucking in and toasting their toes and quite envied them. Envied them a lot, to be truthful.

'All they had in the canteen,' said Pearce who had been sent to reconnoitre, 'are these biscuit things in foil and some cheese rolls. Or crisps but I remembered you don't like crisps. I didn't think you'd fancy a cheese roll either, anyway they looked a bit dry. I brought up a couple of the biscuits.'

'Thanks,' said Markby gloomily.

'I'd nip out to the shops only it's bucketing down.'

'Yes, oh well. Looks like it's going to be a wet Easter.'

'No chance of me having the holiday Monday, I suppose?' asked Pearce tentatively and without much hope.

Markby drew a deep breath but then thought, what the heck! Pearce wasn't one to wriggle out of dirty jobs or extra calls on his time and he deserved a break, so did his long-suffering family. They were overstretched now but they'd be the same next week, and the week after . . .

'I don't see why not,' he said, adding heavily, 'I've got DCI Laxton to help me.'

Surprised at his good fortune, Pearce said, 'Thank you, sir!' Then they both looked at the empty desk. 'He seems to like it at The Crossed Keys,' the sergeant added.

'Wants to keep out of our way and who can blame him? The rain's probably stopped him venturing out.'

There was a tap at the door and Wpc Jones put her head round. 'Are you free, sir?'

'No,' said Markby indistinctly. 'I've having my tea-break.'

'Only there a young chap here to see you. Poor lad looks a real drowned rat, he's had to come from the carpark through the rain. He's a bit distressed, too.'

'Oh, why, what's he done?'

'He went off when he'd been told to stay around. It's Daley, the digger operator from the site.'

'What?' chimed Markby and Pearce in unison.

'Shall I bring him up?' asked Jones. 'Or will you come down?'

'Bring him up here!' Markby ordered. He paused.

'Fetch another cup of tea, Pearce. I've a funny feeling that young Daley has quite a lot to tell us.'

Daley sat on the edge of his seat and clasped his hands nervously. Rain trickled down his face and his jacket was stained with dark wet patches. He looked both soaked and miserable, truly a drowned rat as Jones had described, and a most unhappy one. 'I know you said I shouldn't leave, sir, but it got to me. I'm sorry I took off like it, but I couldn't help it. I kept thinking about it, the dead feller and the way the old digger scooped him up. And there was the questions, they rattled me. So I went to my Auntie Bridie's, down at Reading.'

'And what brought you back?' Markby asked.

'She sent me. She did and Father Brady, between them. They said I ought to come back and tell what I knew. Only I've been too scared to do it. I don't want trouble. If a feller's a murderer, he doesn't feel too kindly about anyone fingering him. I mean, maybe he isn't a murderer, but it's a murder inquiry and if I say I saw him, then you'll be round there asking him questions, won't you, and he won't like it.'

'Daley,' said Markby patiently, 'you're not making a whole lot of sense. Why don't you start at the beginning and just tell me what you saw. Was it the victim before he died?'

It was by way of an inspired guess but Daley seized at it. 'It was, sir. Now I didn't tell you any lies. When I – when the digger scooped him out, I didn't recognise the poor bastard. He was covered in mud and dead as a herring . . . he looked different. I told you I didn't know him and I believed it. Then you came with the photograph. It still didn't look like anyone I knew but, on the other hand, there was something familiar about it.'

'Hold on!' said Markby. He hunted in the file on his desk and passed across the photograph of Rochet alive which McVeigh had given him. 'Does this help?'

'Yes!' Daley looked up in surprise. 'Now if you'd shown me this one, this picture of him, straight off, I'd have said I knew him. He looks different here.'

'He's alive there and we didn't have that photo until a few days ago. Where did you see him and when?'

But Daley wasn't to be hurried and could only tell his tale in his own way. 'I got to thinking. It worried me, that other photo you showed, the dead one. I kept thinking I'd seen him, or someone like that. Then one night I couldn't sleep. I dreamed about it, you know. I got so that I was afraid to close my eyes, I swear. I kept seeing it, popping up out of the earth like that, stark naked, like the Day of Judgement had come and all the dead was getting up out of their graves!'

'But you remembered?' Markby prompted before Daley gave way to hysteria as at their previous interview.

'I did. I was telling you. I woke up and there and then in the middle of the night I thought, I know you! I remember you! It was the Thursday before. That's when it was, I'm sure of it.'

Markby tried to hide his excitement and mounting irritation. If only Daley would get on with it! But Thursday was the day Dolly had disturbed her intruder. If Daley had seen Rochet on the same day then it seemed to make it almost certain the intruder had been Rochet.

'It was in the evening, up at the pub. The Fox and

346

Hounds it's called. It's on the—'

'I know it!' Markby interrupted.

'I didn't normally drink there. But that Thursday I went along with Joe Riordan. There's more than one bar in that place and the first one we sat in got crowded out so Joe and me, we went into the little place they've got at the back. There's only room for a couple of tables and a sort of a long seat in there. We got a table and that feller – ' Daley jabbed his finger at the photo of Rochet. 'He was sat at the next table. I'll swear to it. He was right next to me so I'm not making any mistake. He was talking in a funny sort of a way, through his nose a bit, so I remember him for that.'

'You mean he had a French accent?'

'Maybe that was it.' Daley looked doubtful.

'Talking,' Markby said. 'Talking to whom, Sean? Did you see the other one?'

'Oh, I saw him, all right. Knew him too. It was a big, red-headed feller as works on one of the farms around there. Always hanging about the site and watching us and friendly with Jerry, Jerry Hersey . . .'

'Get his statement typed up and signed and don't let him slip away again!' Markby ordered Pearce. 'Get him a hotel room and make sure he understands he's got to stay in Bamford! You'll have to tell him Hersey's dead and that will scare him stiff but it's better he learns it from us than from gossip. He's got to understand that we'll protect him and he's got nothing to fear.'

'What are you going to do?' Pearce asked as Markby reached for the phone.

'Get out there to Greyladies. Don't you see? Rochet got the wrong farm! He tracked down his man but he didn't know the lie of the land and he muddled up the farms. He was a foreigner, after all, and had a bit of an accent even though he spoke good English. He didn't want to ask too many questions in his French accent which would draw attention to himself. He made a guess. He guessed Alwyn came from Witchett and that's where he went first that Thursday night to search. That's where Dolly disturbed him. But he'd got the wrong farm and must have realised it straight off. The next night, Friday, he tried the right farm, he tried Greyladies . . . What's the number of The Crossed Keys? I hope to God Laxton is there. If he isn't I'll go on without him.'

'I'd better come too,' Pearce began.

'No, take care of Daley, he's like gold dust! We mustn't lose him again! Hullo? Crossed Keys? I want to talk to Mr Laxton. Yes, Laxton, will you fetch him to the phone please? It's urgent!'

Markby put his hand over the receiver. 'And because Rochet got the wrong farm, first time round, Laxton got the wrong farm yesterday! He searched Witchett when he should have searched Greyladies! Hullo, Laxton, is that you? I'm coming to pick you up. Straight away! Yes, a lead. You got the wrong bloody farm, Laxton! But now we're going to the right one!'

A little later Markby stood in the middle of Laxton's room at The Crossed Keys, his face heated with argument and awareness that he was getting nowhere. Laxton wouldn't move without a warrant.

'I've got egg on my face already, searching that other place, Witchett! I can't go from farm to farm like a ruddy paperchase! Give me some evidence that I can get a warrant on!'

'I told you, Daley saw Rochet with Alwyn Winthrop!'

'It's not enough!' Laxton said obstinately. 'They might just have been exchanging small talk, the way people do with strangers in pubs.'

'Then why did Alwyn deny to me ever having seen Rochet? I showed him a photo, admittedly of a corpse but recognisable enough, and only days after he'd been sitting next to the fellow all evening in a pub, talking to him. Yet he took a long look at it and said he'd never set eyes on him!

'The Winthrops have been acting oddly from the start. They don't want any visitors up at that place, they don't want the girl to have a boyfriend even though he's a perfectly respectable youth. They're hiding something! And I'll bet that Jerry Hersey was on to them and that Alwyn killed him because of it! His sister was Elsie Winthrop's friend and neighbour. She was one of the farm's few visitors! She's not a particularly perceptive woman but she may have said something to Jerry which he understood even if she didn't!'

Laxton's narrow face showed momentary indecision and Markby hastened to press home his argument. 'Look, from the very start of this the choice of burial site has bothered me. Whoever buried Rochet in that trench had to know about the building going on there. He had to know the way in which the trenches were dug for the footings and later filled with concrete and most of all he had to know that one such trench was standing dug and waiting over the weekend. It had to be someone with local knowledge of a precise type, if not someone who worked at the site, then someone who visited it often! Alwyn was always hanging around there, ask the architect, Wetherall! Steve told me that Alwyn was fascinated by the building process, like a kid watching train engines, Steve said. What's more,' concluded Markby stubbornly, 'if you won't go out there to Greyladies, I will. This is still my patch and I'm responsible for the villains on it – I'll get them with or without you, it's all the same to me!'

Laxton capitulated in part whilst maintaining a stubborn last-ditch defence. 'All right, all right, so we go up there, you and I, and we say we have reason to believe and all the rest of it . . . and then what? One of us stands guard on them all, holding 'em back with a pitchfork while the other searches the entire farm on his own?'

Markby snarled. It was a good point, though. 'Listen,' he tried to keep his voice calm, 'didn't you ever make a move without visible evidence? Didn't you ever get that gut feeling? Believe me, I know these people. I went to school with Alwyn. I'm not going to drag you all the way out there to Greyladies on a wild goose chase! I've got to live here after you've scarpered back to London! I know I'm right! Ask for a warrant and get your team together. But just hurry, for Pete's sake!'

Laxton pursed his thin lips. 'All right. We ask for an emergency warrant and back-up team – we'll need the dog.'

Of necessity it all took time, time Markby knew in his bones they could ill afford. It was little satisfaction to see that even Laxton now seemed infected with the same sense of urgency and unease.

At last, however, they were under way, their little procession speeding towards the farm. Markby led the way with Laxton sitting beside him. Behind came a police car with three men and finally a van with the dog handler and his educated beast. The weather was still foul, rain beating into them so that the windscreen wipers swished helplessly against a flood. Water rose up in great waves on either side and the gale battered the car. It was growing darker, the storm had obscured the sky and evening was drawing in also. To try and search Greyladies in these conditions, thought Markby dispiritedly, was going to be hell.

Laxton was obviously thinking the same, staring out of the window and muttering under his breath. 'They'll probably have the stuff under cover. I certainly hope so. I don't know how well the dog can work in bad weather. How much further?'

'We're here!' Markby snapped, turning with a flourish into the narrow track which led down to the farmyard.

'Hey, look out!' Laxton yelled.

Racing towards them were headlights, cleaving the gloom and rain. Markby braked and the car skidded towards the hedge before stopping a hair's breadth from the other vehicle. There was no room to pass. One or other of them would have to retreat.

'Why doesn't the idiot back up?' fumed Markby. 'He can see we've got others behind us!' The police car following and the van had both halted in the entry to the turn. The windscreen wipers swept aside the curtain of water for a moment and he added in a yell, 'It's that blighter who brained me! It's the BMW! There can't be two of them!'

'He's not waiting about to discuss it with you!' Laxton retorted. 'Come on, he's getting away!' He wrenched open the door and leapt out into the rain.

Markby didn't need urging. He had a personal score to settle with the owner of the BMW. The latter, sighting the police vehicles, had scrambled from his car and now plunged across the ditch at the side of the track. He was clawing his way up the bank towards the hedge bordering the field which ran alongside the road. Above the trees lashed to and fro and the hedge itself appeared as a dark billowing wave, shuddering and about to smash itself on the bank.

The fleeing man set the adrenaline flowing in the two police officers. Even if he hadn't been the driver of the mysterious BMW, their reaction in any case would have been as automatic as that of Alwyn's dog when it sighted the careering pony. Markby joined Laxton in the rain and shouted, 'Stop! Police!'

The fugitive took no heed. He forced his way heedless of scratched face and hands and torn clothing through the hedge, and began to run across the field. They raced after him, plunging through the gap he'd created. Dimly Markby could make out a series of odd humps and bumps in the middle of the pasture land across which they stumbled. Brief confusion was followed by realisation. They were in the paddock and those were the ruins of the old meeting house.

He hadn't time to reason out anything further. The lightning flashed straight down at them, illuminating the whole scene, fleeing man, ruins, trees and hedges. He smelled the burning and felt the heat on his face as he thrust Laxton to one side with a shout of warning and they both lurched forward on to their hands and knees. From behind them came an enormous crack. It was followed by one of the eeriest of sounds, one which long remained in Markby's memory. A long, deep-seated groan and creak as if some giant gave vent to the agony of a newly inflicted wound.

Indeed that was exactly what was happening. The lightning had struck the great oak which had hung so perilously out over the lane. Twisting on his knees where he'd fallen, Markby had just time to see that the mighty tree had split in half, right down the centre and the nearer half was toppling towards them, slowly down, down . . .

It wasn't slow at all of course. He knew that. It was all happening very fast, it just seemed slow to him as he lay on the ground helpless.

But it missed them. It missed them by a matter of feet and came crashing down to lie on the earth beside them, its topmost branches resting on the blackened stones of the ruined meeting house. And a second cry of agony went up, a human one.

'He's under it!' Laxton gasped.

The two of them scrambled up and stumbled towards the fallen monster. Laxton had pulled a torch from his pocket and flashed it over the branches. 'Where the hell is he?'

'Over there, I can see his foot!' Markby pointed. 'Help me lift this!' The constables from the police car had come running up. Between the five of them they struggled with the heavy branch but it was impossible to shift it sufficiently to allow anyone to crawl under it.

'We'll have to lever and wedge it up somehow and

radio back for an ambulance and lifting gear! He may have broken his back!' Markby panted.

'There's some stone blocks over there, sir!' one constable offered. 'If we could get a couple over here and lever up the branch and rest it on them . . .'

'Well, go on, then! See if you can move one or two, roll them over here and prop this branch up!'

'Can't budge them!' shouted the constable. 'They're buried in the earth! Hang on, there's a crowbar in the van and a spade!'

The tools were fetched and with great effort two of the stone blocks disinterred and manhandled towards the tree. Panting and cursing they somehow managed to wedge them under the branch which pinned the injured man to the ground so that it no longer pressed directly on to him, slowly crushing the life from him. While one of the constables radioed for help and an ambulance, Markby crawled into the narrow gap between fallen branches and sodden earth. Wet leaves stuck to his face and twigs scratched at his skin and tore his clothes. He had dragged off his raincoat before beginning and towed it along with him as he wriggled into the confined space.

As he reached the injured man, there was a groan. He was alive at least. Markby managed to put the raincoat over the victim. Laxton had gone round the other side of the tree, climbing cautiously through the branches, and now shone his torch down through a gap on to the injured man's face.

'Know him?' he shouted above the howl of the wind and the rustle of the leaves in the branches.

'Yes.' The yellow beam of the torch flickered oddly across on the stranger's features surrounded by a crown of twigs and imprisoned by branches. 'The Green Man!' thought Markby involuntarily and felt an atavistic shudder run through him. At the same time memory threw up a name. 'I haven't seen him in a few years but I know him! It's Jamie Winthrop!'

The injured man opened his eyes on hearing his own name and groaned. He focused on Markby's face bent over his and his lips parted. 'Alan . . . ?'

'That's right, Jamie,' Markby returned and his heart was suddenly heavy.

'You won't turn . . . me in . . .' The voice was faint against the storm but clear. 'We used to play . . . cops and robbers . . . in these fields . . .'

'I remember, Jamie,' Markby said sadly. 'But I grew up to be a real life copper and you're real life arrested, old son!'

It was some little while before they got down to the farm itself. Lifting gear had hauled up the tree and enabled the ambulance men to remove the injured James Winthrop, mercifully unconscious now. Markby and Laxton, both soaked to the skin and past caring how wet and cold they were, regained Markby's car. Jamie's BMW having been backed to the yard by one of the constables, they were all able to drive at last into the yard of Greyladies. Lights shone from the kitchen of the house but the yard was deserted.

'What's been going on?' Laxton pointed to the damaged loose-box and then strode over to the splintered door lying in the middle of the yard. He pushed at it with his foot. 'That's not storm damage, it's got a whacking great hole knocked in it!'

The constables had scrambled out of the other car.

The dog-handler opened the back of his van and his animal jumped down. It was the signal for bedlam to break out. At once and without any warning something flew out of the night and rain, something with red eyes and gleaming razor-sharp teeth and which gave voice to blood-curdling snarls. Laxton yelled, 'Cripes!'

The sheepdog had had a bad day. It was wet, cold and alone out here. It had failed to round up the pony and been forced to scuttle away from teeth and hooves, only later to be kicked aside by a bad-tempered human. But this was still its yard and this other dog was an intruder. Honour could be salvaged. The sniffer dog, an amiable labrador, was no match but no coward either and prepared to do its best. Battle ensued.

Markby left the others to separate the combatants and ran through the rain towards the house. He threw open the kitchen door and stopped, taken aback and quite bereft of speech for the moment.

They all sat round the table drinking tea. The stolid elder Winthrops, Alwyn looking gloomy and ill, Jessica pale but determined and beside her, Meredith. Meredith? He blinked and peered at her. She returned him a nervous smile.

'Hullo, Alan.'

The others all chorused a mumbled repeat of her greeting, like an early-morning congregation sleepily going through the responses. Mrs Winthrop rose to her feet and calmly fetched another mug.

'Alwyn,' said Markby knowing that he spoke but not altogether sure that the voice he heard was really coming from him. 'Can you call off your animal? It's trying to kill the police dog.'

'Oh, right,' said Alwyn, rousing himself from his

lethargy. He shambled out into the twilight. They heard him whistle.

'Did you catch him?' Jessica asked in a cold little voice.

'Yes. He's hurt but he's been taken to hospital.' Markby paused, seeing Mrs Winthrop from the corner of his eye. For the first time anxiety showed on her broad face. He found himself saying reassuringly, 'The ambulance men seemed to think it's not as bad as it looks.' Mrs Winthrop relaxed. 'Broken ribs most likely,' Markby concluded, adding in explanation, 'The old oak is down. It fell on him.'

'Meant to trim that tree,' said old Winthrop heavily. 'Never got round to it.'

'More of you fellows out in the yard, is there?' Mrs Winthrop broke her silence in her no-nonsense voice. 'Best make a fresh pot. Jess, put the kettle back on.'

'Yes, Ma.' The girl got up.

'Really,' Markby protested, 'we can't, we've come to search . . .'

''Tisn't necessary,' Mrs Winthrop said placidly. 'Us knows what you've come for.'

'It's in the hayloft,' Meredith broke in. 'It's hidden in bags of EEC milk powder.'

'Oh, is it?' he returned feebly.

'Yes, I've made a bit of a mess up there, I cut the milk bags open with my nailfile. Sorry about that.'

'Did you?' At this point his senses returned and he roared, 'What on earth do you think you're doing here? You were supposed to go to Witchett!'

Chapter Twenty-Four

'I suppose,' said Father Holland reflectively, 'that you would say mine was one of the caring professions. I like to think I do my best. But it always comes as a shock to discover just what is going on under one's nose, so to speak. Who would have thought of any kind of misdemeanour going on out at Greyladies Farm, let alone a serious crime like drug trafficking?'

'They didn't traffic in drugs,' said Meredith. 'Not the Winthrops at the farm. They just let Jamie store the stuff there.'

'James Winthrop,' said Markby fiercely, 'is about the lowest of the low in my book! A cheap and heartless little crook masquerading behind a flashy image, engaged in organising distribution of the goods but taking care never to handle the stuff himself. He used his own family, taking advantage of their weakness and general ignorance! He knew what a struggle they had to keep going! The couple of hundred he gave them every time he kept some of his foul business stock there, made all the difference to them! They didn't get any more out of it, you know. No cut of the profits. Jamie got all of that. He just passed over a bundle of twenty quid notes when he saw them. Still, it might count in their favour when it comes to court.'

'Thirty pieces of silver,' said Father Holland. 'Oh well, I dare say in due course I'll get a couple of sermons out of it. What's happening to the farm meantime, until the trial?'

'The Winthrop parents have been given bail under the circumstances, stock to care for and so on. Besides, the old folk aren't going to make a run for it. Where would they go? Alwyn's on remand, murder charges. It'll be a struggle without him but I gather young Denton is going over there every evening and weekend and a retired farmer living locally has turned out to help during the day. In the long term . . . who can say?'

'Poor Alwyn,' said Meredith with a sigh. 'I liked him.'

'So did I like him. But before you start feeling sorry for him, perhaps you'd cast a thought towards the man he buried alive!' Markby reminded her sharply.

'Bad . . .' said Father Holland. 'Think he realised the victim was alive?'

'Who knows?'

'I don't think he did!' Meredith stoutly defended him. 'He spoke as if he hadn't known. He was trying to hide the evidence which would convict his mother of being a murderess, after all. He thought Elsie had killed the man.'

'Did he?' Markby sounded sceptical. 'Oh, I know that's what he says now! Maybe he's even persuaded himself it was like that! But who knows what was in his mind at the time, whether he realised Rochet was dead or not? To put it mildly, Alwyn's state of mind was highly confused. In any event, he's hardly been thinking straight for years. A walking nervous breakdown, Alwyn! But on the other hand, who's to say at that moment he wasn't perfectly lucid? Read up M'Naghten's Rules. To my mind Alwyn knew perfectly well what he was doing. He certainly didn't make any attempt to find out for sure if Rochet was dead, or according to his own account he didn't. But did he? Suppose he did, suppose he realised that Rochet, though badly injured and probably dying, might just survive in hospital long enough to spill the beans about the true nature of the business being carried on at Greyladies Farm? You might say that Alwyn had a good reason for wanting to make sure of Rochet. Putting someone under four feet of concrete would do that. But this is off-the-record speculation on my part. I don't know, neither do you. A judge and a jury will decide all that! But if you want to feel sorry for someone, how about feeling sorry for the unfortunate Rochet? Or don't policemen count? Rochet probably had parents, brothers or sisters, maybe a girlfriend . . . How about a sigh or two on his account?'

'We prayed for his soul yesterday in church,' said Father Holland. 'Together with that of Jerry Hersey. At all the services. Put a bit of a blight on Easter. Easter Sunday service is usually a joyous affair with a theme of resurrection from the grave, not going down into it. I'm burying Hersey next Thursday, by the way.' He paused. 'Church was full of flowers for the Easter services. Nip in and take a look before you go back to London, Meredith, they're all still there. Elsie Winthrop had given a hand with arranging them, you know. She was on the regular flower rota. A dab hand with lilies, Elsie, so I'm told. Jerry Hersey's sister, Betty

Chivers, is insisting that Elsie do the flowers for Jerry's funeral because she always does them so nicely and anyway, Elsie is still her friend even if Alwyn broke Jerry's neck.'

'It's grotesque . . .' said Meredith after the ensuing silence.

'My dear Meredith, I am almost completely inured to the oddities of life. I've had some rum old cases to deal with in my time. As I said just now, the occasional thing can still give me a jolt, drugs at Greyladies for example. But as for Betty Chivers' desire to have Elsie Winthrop arrange her brother's funeral flowers? No, that doesn't surprise me in the least. It's going to be quite an elaborate funeral, even the choir's been hired. I understand the builder, Newman, is paying for it.' Father Holland broke off abruptly. 'More coffee?'

'No thanks, we must go soon,' Markby said hastily.

'Alwyn didn't mean to kill Jerry!' Meredith's mind was still running on Father Holland's last speech. 'I expect Mrs Chivers realises that. He panicked.'

'Did kill him, though, didn't he?' said Markby sternly. 'Strong chap, Alwyn. Being a farmer he knew how to dispatch a creature neatly. A quick chop and a broken neck. No problem.'

'Shut up!' she said vehemently. 'It's horrible!'

'Yes, it is, but you brought the subject up.'

'Yet it was all for nothing.' Meredith remembered Barry's words. 'Hersey wouldn't really have gone to the police with his suspicions, whatever he thought was going on at Greyladies. He wasn't the sort. If Alwyn hadn't been so upset about Jessica turning up at the pub in the company of young Mike, then his mind might have been working clearly enough to realise that

Jerry was only talking and grousing in his usual way and posed no real threat. I'm sure he did realise it later. He's very upset about Hersey, and Mrs Chivers being left all alone.'

'A sad case,' opined Father Holland, clattering coffee mugs together on a tray. 'Blind panic and guilty conscience combining in a big strong fellow like Alwyn were bound to produce violence.'

'It's a funny thing,' Meredith picked up the point, 'but mentioning Alwyn's strength like that reminds me that Dolly Carmody remarked to me how strong the women used to be on the farm. Well, working women generally had to be, manhandling the heavy irons and mangles and so on. What I mean is, I suppose Elsie must be pretty strong even if she is getting on in years.'

'Oh, as strong as many a man, certainly,' Markby agreed. 'When she hit Rochet with that poker, it was quite a blow. She knew she could kill and I believe she meant to.'

'And all for the farm . . .'

'Perversion of good intentions,' said Father Holland. 'And one crime leading to another. Once they'd agreed to let Jamie use the hayloft as a store, from there to murder wasn't such a long road, after all. Small wrongdoing leads to larger, as St Paul wisely warns us. Must press that point home on young Barry.'

'One thing puzzles me a bit still,' Meredith observed. 'I suppose it was clever of Alwyn to think of burying Rochet in that trench, but on the other hand, he had acres of farmland he could have used. It was their land and no one would have dug Rochet up.'

'He might well have been unearthed sometime in the future if Alwyn had finally managed to sell the land for development,' Markby pointed out. 'Don't forget the unwritten agreement he had with Dudley Newman. He didn't want to sell to Newman only to have the skeleton brought to the surface with the first lot of earth turned. He thought it safer to put it where cement would cover it. It was his bad luck that the trench had been dug too shallow and had to be deepened. And that, incidentally, was partly because Alwyn's friend, Jerry Hersey, had neglected to oversee the task properly! So in a weird sort of way, Jerry made the first move in a chain of events leading to his own murder. Or he didn't make it, rather. He neglected his job and from that little acorn did a mighty oak grow! Work that one into your sermon, padre!'

'For the want of a nail, the shoe was lost . . .' intoned Father Holland. 'Used to be able to recite all that poem. It ends up with a battle lost "and all for the want of a horseshoe nail".'

'Probably a couple of other things influenced the choice of burial site,' Markby went on. 'To begin with I fancy old man Winthrop didn't want Rochet buried on Greyladies land for superstitious reasons. He didn't fancy working alongside a man he'd helped put in the grave. And then don't forget that tradition put the old Grey Folk cemetery somewhere in the area of the building site. Perhaps there was a dim folk memory at work there, suggesting to both Alwyn and his father that it would be the best place to lay the dead man to rest, more fitting and respectable somehow, the nearest they could come to giving Rochet a decent burial.'

'The Grey Folk! Knew there was something else!' exclaimed Father Holland. He slapped his hands on his knees and went on briskly, 'Now, then, Meredith, before you leave, I've got something of interest here for you!'

'Oh yes?' Meredith's eye lit up. 'The Grey Folk?'

'Yes, indeed. I was talking about them with my old chum who runs *The Bamford Gazette* and he got interested and turned to his index. Lo and behold . . .' Father Holland got up and went to pick up a yellowed newspaper from his desk. 'Got to take great care of this and give it back, it's their file copy. An article, here . . . Nearly ten years ago, written by that chap Gretton who came out digging around the meeting house. He thought it might have local interest so he penned it and sent it to the editor of the *Gazette* who used it.'

Meredith took it and scanned it eagerly. 'Well, I'm . . . Good Lord. Alan, they all went to Australia!'

'What?'

'Here . . . And it was even reported in *The Bamford Gazette* of the day, 1845, Gretton has quoted from that original report in his article here. I didn't know the *Gazette* was that old!'

'Founded 1828,' said Father Holland.

Markby took the newspaper from her and scanned it. 'I suppose that after the meeting house burned down they decided to cut their losses. Gretton makes the point here that anyone with a trade or skill got free passage to Australia in those days so it made sense for them to all up and go. They were nearly all tradesmen or skilled artisans by the look of it. Their names are given here together with their occupations. And, Meredith . . . you should read this last bit!'

Meredith regained the newspaper and eagerly ran her finger down the list Matthew Gretton had unearthed. 'Five Phillipses. That must have been the entire family which Mary Anne ran to warn on the night of the fire. No wonder she went there, they were sect members!'

'Read on,' said Markby with a smile. 'Last name on the list!'

'Mary Anne Winthrop, dairymaid,' said Meredith wonderingly. 'So that's how it was! Mary Anne got to know some of the sect because the meeting house was so close to the farm, this Phillips family most likely, and she became a convert. The Winthrops probably tried to prevent her and when they couldn't they burned the meeting house down! If you ask me, the Winthrops have always been a dangerous lot! Given to drastic action, at any rate! I begin to think Mike Denton may have had a narrow escape!'

'She got away in the end, though,' said Markby. 'Sailed away to a new life with them.'

'Perhaps she married one of the Phillipses . . .' said Meredith, 'there are three male ones here without wives attached.'

'Speculation, Miss Mitchell.'

'Bet she did. Tell you another thing, there was no mention of it in the family Bible. They recorded the roof blowing off in a gale but not a member of the family leaving for Australia. Poor Mary Anne was cut off, never mentioned again when she stuck to her guns and her new religion. Unforgiving lot, the Winthrops.'

'Not a proud moment in Bamford's history, the persecution of the Grey Folk,' said Father Holland. 'I'll preach about that one day. Good subject.'

'We have got to go!' said Markby firmly. 'We promised that Meredith would call at Greyladies and say goodbye to Jessica before she goes back to London tomorrow.'

'Look forward to seeing you again soon,' said Father Holland enclosing Meredith's hand in his massive paw. 'And to reading the pamphlet!'

'I'll have to write it, you know,' Meredith said as they walked back down the vicarage drive.

'Laura will put you up if you need to come back and pursue your researches.'

'Won't impose. I'll give you a call and you can book me in at The Crossed Keys.'

'I've got a house . . .' he said mildly.

'Hum, well, we'll think about that. Haven't you got reputation or something in this town?'

'Even policemen have a private life.'

'Bet it wouldn't be private for long in Bamford!' There was a long silence. 'On the other hand,' she said, 'if you fancy a break in the Big City, there's always Toby's flat in Islington.'

They walked on for a few minutes in silence. 'Reputations . . .' said Markby unexpectedly. 'Times change but in some respects attitudes don't. At least, not amongst the elderly. I fancy the good father nearly put his foot in it back there.'

'He did stop suddenly after mentioning Newman, didn't he? I noticed that. What's the connection? Surely—' Meredith paused before asking incredulously, 'Surely not?'

'Why ever not? Years ago illegitimate births were hushed up but the local vicar at the time would have known that Jerry was in fact Betty Chivers' son. There may be some note in parish records referring to the baptismal register of the day. Even now, even with

Jerry dead, Newman can't come forward openly. There's Betty's reputation, you see, and his own. His wife wouldn't like it much and I gather his mother-in-law already disapproves of him.'

'Does she? Perhaps she knows more than she's telling, then!'

'People,' said Markby, 'always do. It's one of the things that always makes police work so difficult. Respectability, you see, is often seen as more desirable than justice! Jerry may rest in peace. But Newman and Betty Chivers have got to carry their secret to the grave.'

Jessica and Michael Denton were sitting on the stone remains of the meeting house walls in the paddock, their heads close together, when Meredith and Alan Markby found them. Nearby the pony grazed peacefully. The evening was warm, sunny, and a soft breeze caressed the leaves on the branches of the fallen oak which still sprawled across the pasture land. The hole in the hedge had been unpicturesquely blocked up with a sheet of corrugated iron.

'Hullo, there!' Meredith hailed them and they broke apart guiltily and turned.

'Oh, hi, Meredith!' said Jessica with a smile.

The newcomers found themselves seats on the sun-warmed stone blocks. 'Where's the dog?' Meredith looked around. 'It's usually first on the scene when visitors come to Greyladies. I didn't see it in the yard.'

'Mr Jennet's got him, that's the old retired fellow who comes over to help now. He's used to a working dog and it's best he goes to someone who's used to handling a sheepdog and knows how to feed him and treat him. I mean, Whisky's not a pet and Dad wouldn't have him put down because he's a good working dog. Mr Jennet still has a smallholding and sometimes he does a bit of extra work shepherding if anyone needs another pair of hands, so Whisky will be useful to him.'

'How do you think you'll manage, Jess?' Markby asked her.

She shrugged. 'Well, we'll make out until the trials . . . which won't be for some months, or so we gather. But we have to face the fact that both Dad and Ma may get prison sentences. Even if they don't we can't go on now. Dad's will's broken and even Ma doesn't seem to care any more. It's – it's losing Alwyn.' She looked down abruptly and Michael Denton reached out and took her hand to give it a reassuring squeeze.

'I'm okay, Mike!' she said, but didn't release his hand. Looking up, she went on more briskly, 'Dudley Newman has been to see us.'

'Well, I'm blowed!' said Markby angrily. 'He might have had the decency to wait until the trials were over! Ruddy ghoul!'

'He did apologise for bothering us now but he explained that he wouldn't want to wait and then miss the chance of buying Greyladies if it came on the market. He wants to put houses all over it, of course, and he says he can get planning permission. He's offering a lot of money.'

'Is he?' asked Markby grimly. 'Even so, Jessica, I'd get an independent valuation of the land as a potential development site for housing. Mr Newman is a businessman and I dare say he'd like to make a bargain.'

'Don't worry,' said Denton. 'I'm keeping an eye on things. Jess and I mean to get married, by the way . . . when it's all settled of course. That won't be for a year or two.'

Congratulations were offered and then Meredith asked, 'Will you go ahead with the garden centre and farm museum at Witchett?'

'All being well. Dolly's still keen and if a good price is got for Greyladies, Jess's father would be interested in putting some of it into the garden centre. Not that he cares about potted plants and shrubs for borders. He can't understand anyone growing anything you can't eat! But he's been Dolly's neighbour all his life and he'd like to think that Witchett at least will escape the developers, even if Greyladies won't.'

They all fell silent. Markby's eye fell on the fallen oak. 'Fair old bit of wood there. Going to leave it where it lies?'

'No, someone's coming next week with a chainsaw to cut it up.' Jessica glowered at the oak. 'I used to keep on to Dad about that tree. I was always afraid it would come down in a high wind and fall on Nelson.'

The pony looked up from his energetic scrunching of the grass and whinnied.

'I believe Jamie's making good progress in hospital,' Markby said after a while and was immediately sorry he'd spoken.

'I couldn't care less!' Jessica burst out passionately. 'Yes, I could, I wish he'd been killed!'

'Come on, Jess, you don't mean that!' Michael murmured.

'Why not? I know he's my brother but he brought nothing but unhappiness to us! Alwyn was always influenced by him. Jamie knew how to impress Alwyn, talking big about business deals and owning property abroad. Alwyn's always been a straightforward sort of person. He's never understood that someone could be devious like Jamie!'

'It will all come out in Alwyn's defence,' Markby said soothingly.

'It won't make that much difference, though, will it?' she asked bitterly. 'He killed Jerry and can't blame it on anyone. He'll probably get life or at the very least a long sentence.'

'I can't comment on that, I'm afraid,' Markby said.

Jessica pushed her hair back from her face. 'I thought he'd killed the other one too, I didn't know it was Ma . . . I – I took flowers over to the building site and put them on the spot where the body was found. It sounds silly but I wanted to say I was sorry, somehow, for what we'd done.'

'You, was it?' Markby asked. 'My sergeant saw a bunch of primroses and couldn't think who'd placed it. It confused us for a while.'

'Did it?' Jessica looked miserable. 'I didn't mean it to.'

'Of course you didn't!' said Michael Denton belligerently.

'It wasn't serious!' Markby put in hastily. 'We just wondered.'

'I didn't help, though, did I?' she interrupted him.

'We were all to blame in one way or another! The others all let Jamie manipulate them the way he knew how to do. He never managed it with me so much and they kept me away from him because of that. They knew I'd argue. Even when I was a little kid I could see how he was and they knew I'd say they shouldn't do it and start telling them things about Jamie they didn't want to hear. But I did know they were up to something and I did see them carrying that poor man. No, let me speak, Mike, it's got to be said! I could have saved Jerry, couldn't I, if I'd gone to the police at once about the first man? Will I be charged, Mr Markby? Withholding evidence or something like that? Or am I an accessory?'

'I understand it's unlikely you'll be charged, Jessica. The prosecution has enough on its plate with the charges to be brought against the other members of your family! You didn't know about the heroin. They kept you out of it even to the extent of imprisoning you at one stage! You tried to help Meredith and when through her you found out the truth, you made it clear you would go to the police. Besides,' added Markby awkwardly, 'forgive me mentioning this, but you've only recently recovered from a serious breakdown.'

Michael gave him what could only be described as a dirty look but Jessica pulled a rueful face.

'You can talk about it. I don't mind! And if I don't mind, Mike, you don't need to! I don't need protecting – I was always telling poor Alwyn that. He wouldn't listen. It's what he was trying to do, you know, really – look after me.'

There was another awkward silence and she tossed back her hair.

'They let Ma go and see Jamie in hospital. She still refers to him as "our Jamie" and I can't make her see how wrong it all was.'

Jessica kicked her heels against the blackened stones of the ruins. 'She still thinks of him as being rather smart in the business sense. "Our Jamie always had a good head on his shoulders!" she said quite proudly when she came back from the hospital: "When he's got this behind him, he'll soon get back on his feet." I replied, because I was so angry and frustrated not because I wanted to hurt her, "They'll lock him away for years and years, Ma, and quite right too!" She just said, "Oh, our Jamie's got himself a clever lawyer fellow." I asked her if our Jamie was going to pay the clever lawyer to act for her and Dad and Alwyn, too. But she just said it didn't matter about her and Dad. "I don't know about our Alwyn," she said. "But I dare say they'll understand he meant no harm!" Honestly, I just can't get through to her.'

'Don't keep on about it, Jess,' Michael urged. 'Try and put it out of your mind!' He looked up and gave Meredith and Markby a defiant glare. 'She doesn't need to be reminded of it every flipping second!'

'Oh, right, well we'll be off,' Markby said, reproved.

'I'll be back in a few weeks' time, probably,' Meredith said. 'I hope – well, I hope all goes as well as it can.'

'Thanks. Sorry you had a fright, Meredith.'

'Oh me, I'm tough!' she said.

'Are you?' Markby asked as they walked back to the car. 'Tough?'

'Resilient, anyway.'

'Hope Elsie Winthrop proves to be that. She may not accept the gravity of what's happened now, as Jess was lamenting. But there's going to come a moment when she'll have to face up to it, probably when the gaol sentences are handed down. I've seen people like Elsie go quite berserk when they've finally had to face facts. Their brains aren't used to assimilating new ideas and situations and they sort of blow a mental fuse. There's a bit of the bully in Elsie too, and she's not used to having to take her directions from others. I reckon it just hasn't all quite dawned on her yet. I'll never forget walking into that farmhouse kitchen and all she did was tell Jess to put the kettle on for more tea!'

'Poor sad Winthrops. All those generations shut away on that farm just utterly absorbed with their own affairs. Elsie's always been a Winthrop, did you know? Father Holland dug that fact out. She was a cousin of sorts and her name was Winthrop before she married.'

'Raises interesting possibilities of in-breeding. They probably married each other over generations. Come to think of it, they probably didn't trust anyone who wasn't called Winthrop. The whole thing's depressing. Can we talk about something else?'

'Yes, but there is just one last word I must say. You see, Alan, I've been thinking. You remember Steve Wetherall saying that whenever he got fed up with his life, he thought about Alwyn's life and that made him feel better? Well, all this has made me more realistic about the FO and this desk job I've been saddled with in London. It isn't what I'd choose, but it could be much worse and there's always a hope of change. So I won't grumble or hand in my resignation. I'll just soldier on and hope for an overseas posting one day.'

'Thought you might, somehow,' he said in a depressed voice.

Meredith put her arm through his. 'I honestly don't think that whatever happened, we'd ever find ourselves going and visiting show houses, Alan.'

'Maybe not.'

She squeezed his arm. 'You haven't forgotten that we are expected at seven sharp at Ken and Susie's to partake of meat loaf? Better not be late, seeing as we didn't make it on the previous occasion and the meat loaf baked into a solid brick. Susie's all agog to hear a first-hand account of my adventures! I haven't had time to sit and tell her yet. They cancelled the Scottish trip by the way and are going later when they'll have more time. They've been looking at the map and reading the guide-books and have decided they need at least a fortnight, so they're going in the summer. Susie's full of the lochs and the braes, the bens and glens and things. Ken has Scottish roots and they're going in search of them hoping to find the laird of Mac-whatever. But our coming to dinner with such interesting table talk will compensate for the delayed trip north. She says it beats anything they've discussed at Neighbourhood Watch meetings!'

'Well, just stick to telling her what happened to you and don't draw me into it.'

They drove into the outskirts of Bamford. 'It all worked out in a funny way, didn't it?' Meredith mused. 'Thinking of what Father Holland told us and what happened at the meeting house all those years ago and what happened last Friday. When I saw young Mike and Jessica sitting on those ruins in the afternoon sunshine holding hands and the pony grazing and everything so peaceful, I couldn't help wondering if the Grey Folk know that they've been avenged.'

'I would have thought that wherever their spiritual bodies are now, they were beyond thoughts of vengeance.'

'It's just that when I first went there to draw out a ground plan, it was eerie. I felt as if someone watched me. It wasn't a happy place. Now, despite Jamie's accident, there's a kind of calm about it. It's like the end of *Wuthering Heights*. You know, "I listened to the soft wind breathing through the grass; and wondered how anyone could ever imagine unquiet slumbers for the sleepers in that quiet earth".'

'You're getting fanciful, my girl,' said Markby.